Praise for

Give My R...

"Richard Engling knows Chicago's famously chaotic and glorious storefront theater scene like the back of his hand. It's the perfect setting for absurd comic hi-jinx."
– Chris Jones, *Chicago Tribune*, author of *Rise Up!* and *Bigger, Brighter, Louder*

"Richard Engling is undoubtedly a writer's writer. It's hard not to read him without marveling at the skill of construction. But the technical virtuosity of *Give My Regards to Nowhere* is performed like prestidigitation: it's a magic trick performed in plain view. The novel is comic, wise, and riveting. It gives us the theatrical world, but also the world of anyone whose ever struggled against the odds. But Engling is also a reader's writer, those who read him without fretting about how these marvels are executed will turn each page with a thrill of discovery and immersion in this richly entertaining novel."
– Liam Heneghan, author of *Beasts at Bedtime*

"A scrappy, big-hearted backstage comedy layered with mordant wit and full of a deep, abiding love for its characters, which is wholly appropriate for a story set in the scrappy, big-hearted world of Chicago theater."
– Adam Langer, author of *Cyclorama*

"Without a doubt, the best examination of the theatre trade I've ever read. Insightful, satirical, painful, but joyous. Richard Engling brings a wonderful cast of characters together in a way theatre kids and non-theatre kids can thoroughly enjoy."
– Darren Callahan, dramatist for the BBC, SyFy, author of *City of Human Remains* and *The Audrey Green Chronicles*

"A meager bank account, a tiny Chicago storefront theater with metal seats flecked with rust, and an enormous dream of a Broadway hit that *no one will never forget*. That's the stuff of Richard Engling's engaging new novel. A longtime denizen of Chicago's famed storefront theater scene, Engling vividly captures the disparity between grand artistic ambition and what reality has to offer in this very funny, briskly written, and often touching book. Fans and inhabitants of Chicago's (or any city's) theater scene will feel right at home, but so will any reader who has held tight to a chimerical dream they firmly believe must be within reach."
– Mark Larson, author of *Ensemble: An Oral History of Chicago Theater*

"Hilarious, witty, touching, intelligent, and spot-on. Engling's novel about the many joys and incessant headaches of running a storefront Chicago theater is truth that could only be told as believably as it is, as fiction. The characters pulse with life, conflict, tons of drama, and humanity. Entire chapters are laugh-out-loud funny, and issues of marriage, friendship, loyalty, and the nature of theater and art flow through every sentence. A one-sit read, I promise!"
– Nadeem Zaman, author of *The Inheritors* and *Up in the Main House and Other Stories*

"The rollicking ride through the underbelly of the acting world and the determination of a man who sees his world fall apart and come back together in a new way as the show goes on will attract anyone interested in drama, theater, Chicago backdrops, or a drive to succeed against all odds. However stacked against him they may be."
– D. Donovan, Senior Reviewer, *Midwest Book Review*

ALSO BY RICHARD ENGLING

Body Mortgage

Antigone and Macbeth: Adaptations for a War-Torn Time

Visions of Anna

Give My Regards to Nowhere

A Director's Tale

Richard Engling

Polarity Ensemble Books

Polarity Ensemble Books
www.polarityensemblebooks.com
Cover design by Laura Boyle

Also available in audio and ebook editions.

ISBN 978-0-9776610-7-7

Printed in the United States of America

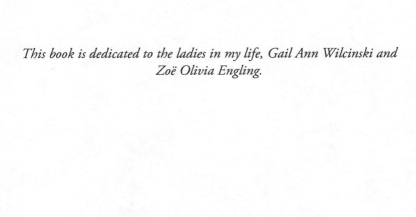

This book is dedicated to the ladies in my life, Gail Ann Wilcinski and Zoë Olivia Engling.

Special thanks to Gail Wilcinski, Martin Uthe, Jeanne Fredricksen, Bob Fiddler, Cathleen Ann, Cate Anderson, Ann Keen, Rory Leahy, John Wolforth, Darren Callahan, Rachel Proulx, Alex Ireys, Chuck Palia, Amy Gray, Nadeem Zaman, RJ Coleman, Mark Larson, Darci Stratton, Liam Heneghan, Anthony Williams, Allan Nowakowski, and Jeff Jacobs, as well as to Nicky Lovick, and Zoë Engling for suggestions concerning this book, and to all the brilliant actors and other theatre professionals in Chicago, especially those who worked with me and/or with the late, great Polarity Ensemble Theatre.

1

Friday, October 7, 2003

Dwayne Finnegan was aware, as he took a breath, that this was the moment that could make or break him. He found that prospect deeply exciting. "What makes sex better?" he said, an intimation of pleasure in his voice. "What makes food better? What propels dancers irresistibly across the floor in one another's arms?" He raised his dark eyebrows and grinned his lopsided grin. "The same thing that will put this production over the top," he whispered. Brad Cunningham, the man who could transform his life, leaned toward him and began to grin back. It was working! Dwayne wound into the final details of his pitch. All his talent as an actor, as a director, as a student of Shakespeare flowed into this. He would triumph!

"What would take *Titus Andronicus*," he said pointedly, "Shakespeare's most violent, least favorite play, and turn it into an event that no one in the city of Chicago will be able to resist?" He let the question hang in the air, then stood up and raised his arms. "Listen! Imagine if we could resurrect Jimi Hendrix and put him on a platform at the top of the set overlooking the action, playing his iconic electric acid blues to drive the choreographed swordplay, to propel the throat-cutting, to punctuate the beheading, and to agitate and exacerbate the sexual violence that fills this play. We would have a *Titus Andronicus* like no one has ever imagined. Electrifying. Visceral. Tribal drums. Hendrix guitars. Propulsive music. Kick-ass performances. A production that no one will ever forget." Dwayne's heart raced with the excitement. "And it's driven by music originated by greatest guitarist the world has ever known." He clapped his hand on the tabletop and slid back into the booth next to Tom, his choreographer and co-conspirator.

What did Brad think? Brad also leaned back across from them, and dropped into deep thought, looking like a sphinx, as he so often did. Dwayne waited. The silence carried on until Dwayne forgot to breathe. So much depended on this! Dwayne's life depended on this!

Be cool. Just be cool.

"I like it," Brad said at last, sitting up again in the window booth at the Elephant & Castle Pub. A train rattled by on the elevated tracks out in front of the restaurant. An automobile honked and a police siren sang in the distance. "I like the whole concept."

"And Foxx?" Dwayne asked. That was the most important question. What about Foxx?

"This is something I could take to Foxx."

Brad's words surged into Dwayne's soul. He had to control his urge to shout out a halleluiah. Tom vibrated with joy next to him.

Brad, of course, still looked cool. He brushed a piece of lint from his suit jacket and adjusted the collar of his black silk shirt, gazing out at the corner of Wabash and Lake. Cars and pedestrians flowed past on the other side of the glass.

"Excellent," Dwayne said, covering a gasp for breath with a little laugh. He had to remember to keep breathing! He leaned back with what he hoped was a casual elegance. If Brad recommended him, it could redeem his reckless life choices. No more groveling for pennies. He could even get health insurance. And hire his friends. But more important, he could graduate into productions that operated under Actors Equity union rules, which meant he'd be working during the daytime, and he and Angela could have their evenings together like a normal couple, and she wouldn't want to divorce him. How he would love to be a union man! Actors Equity Association. The Stage Directors and Choreographers Society. He could be a *real boy.*

Be cool. Just be cool.

"Oh my god!" Tom gushed. "That would be so amazing!" He clapped his hands and took a sip of his Grasshopper. Of course Tom was not going to be cool. Tom had all the cool of a love-crazed golden retriever puppy.

"You know what Foxx's Emerging Directors Program did for me," Brad said.

Yes, Dwayne knew, and that's what he wanted for himself. Brad had gone from a nobody to a high-profile director. Of course Dwayne also knew how much of Brad's success came from sucking up other people's ideas and talent.

"From The Public Theater to Broadway to a Tony nomination," Tom interjected, practically singing. "I knew you were going to be a star ever since Dwayne and I were kids in your summer camp!"

Brad gave a dry chuckle, then frowned and cleared his throat. "See, here's the thing: This would be the first time I recommend someone to Foxx. So it's important that it go well. Otherwise, my stock with him falls. And that costs me."

Dwayne felt his stomach clench. "What do you mean?" His pitch had gone so well. He'd really sold him. But now what?

A hostess led a couple past their booth toward at table at the back. The man looked annoyed. Tears welled up in the woman's eyes, and she choked back a sob. "Why do you have to do this?" the man grumbled under his breath.

Was everyone having a bad time?

"You know how it works," Brad said. "The Tony nomination put a feather in my cap. When I didn't win, it took it back out."

"But you're a *Tony-nominated director*," Tom sputtered. "No one can take that away from you."

"The day *before* the Tony ceremony, everyone wanted to kiss my ring," Brad said. "The day *after*, they all looked at me with pity and moved away. *That's* the reality of New York."

"Gee," Tom said.

"So if you shine," Brad said, leaning in towards Dwayne, "it reflects well on me. But if you don't, the next time I suggest something to Foxx, it's tainted. I'd like to help you, but what happens if your little show sucks? If you do badly, maybe later Foxx will turn me down for something *I* want. Then *I'm* screwed because *you* failed."

It was always about Brad.

"You've known me since I was sixteen," Dwayne pleaded, struggling to keep his voice reasonable and confident. "You know how hard I work." And that was true. Dwayne had fallen in love with the theatre guided by Brad. He'd been a mediocre high school student, uninspired in the classroom, uninterested in anything other than swim team. He tried out for the school plays his sophomore year, but he wasn't cast. Then Tom, whom he didn't know well at the time, convinced him to enroll in Brad's summer theatre camp at Evanston's Ridgeville Park District. Brad was leading it as an independent study project for his junior year at Northwestern. That changed everything. Dwayne worked hard and sucked up everything Brad taught. And Brad was good. The next year Dwayne started getting lead roles in the high school plays and even his grades improved. When he graduated, Dwayne chose to go on to Northwestern University because Brad was continuing on to graduate school there. He invested every bit of his soul in what Brad taught.

Brad knew exactly how hard he worked.

"I do," Brad agreed sincerely, if only for a moment. "Still, if you fail to impress Foxx, it costs me."

"How much?" Tom demanded, his voice sharp.

Brad leaned back, eyes wide. "What?

Tom slapped his hand on the table. "How much does it cost you?"

"You mean in dollars?" Brad asked.

"At Northwestern Dwayne was brilliant in your *Marat/Sade*—and in your *Desire Under the Elms*—and that helped you get your MFA. So if you can't trust him based on that, then, yeah, dollars. How many dollars does Dwayne have to risk?"

Wait! Money? Why is he talking about my money?

"I'm not looking for a bribe," Brad demurred.

"I'm not suggesting a *bribe*, Brad," Tom snapped. "I'm saying if you think you are risking your clout with Foxx, maybe Dwayne could risk some money. If Gregor Foxx sees Dwayne's *Titus Andronicus* and accepts him in the Emerging Directors' Program, Dwayne gets his money back. If Foxx doesn't like the show to the point that Dwayne embarrasses you, you get the money to make up for it."

"Wait…" Dwayne said. *What the hell is all this talk about money?*

"Maybe there *is* some merit in that," Brad mused.

"So how much?" Tom demanded. "Five grand?"

"Five grand!" Dwayne sputtered. He didn't have five grand.

"I doubt Dwayne *has* five grand," Brad said.

Dwayne blushed deeply red.

"Then what?" Tom said.

"Two grand sounds about right."

"Done!" Tom said. "I'll hold Dwayne's money in a special account. After Gregor Foxx makes his decision, one of you gets it. Good?"

Brad nodded. "Good!"

"Wait!" Dwayne said. Had Brad really said *two thousand dollars*?

"You don't want to risk it?" Brad said. "It's okay if you don't. I don't *need* to make a recommendation. But if you do, I'll call him." Brad raised his eyebrows and smiled sweetly.

How often had Dwayne seen that face on Brad, his *this is what you want, isn't it?* face? Brad Cunningham was a prime manipulator. He'd been that way from the start.

But Brad had opened a world that excited Dwayne like nothing else. To create on one's feet, to collaborate with other artists on the stage, to make the words come alive, he loved it! He loved the experience of losing himself in a role. To perfect a performance. To live the story on stage as something new every single time.

Brad had been his ideal. He studied Brad. He watched how he moved with economy and grace. He had a slender, intelligent face with a pointy nose and active bright-blue eyes. He gestured with long, thin fingers that reminded Dwayne of Nosferatu. Working with Brad was both exhilarating and daunting. He inspired his young actors, but he also manipulated emotions in cruel ways. More than once Dwayne had comforted a fellow actor in tears after one of Brad's workshops.

Nevertheless, Dwayne had done some of his finest work with him. He and Tom had both gone to Northwestern because of Brad. (Would they ever pay off their pricey student loans?) If Brad could get him into Foxx's program, Dwayne might finally have a paying career. This could transform his life.

"You'd call Foxx right now?" Dwayne said.

"Right now."

"But I have to gamble two thousand dollars?"

"I think that's fair." Brad pulled out his cell phone and waved it in the air. "If he likes you and your show, you don't lose a thing. But if he asks why in God's name I sent him to your horrible production, I collect the damages."

"This is so exciting," Tom said. He scrunched up his shoulders.

Sure, Tom was excited. It wasn't his two grand. Dwayne had known Tom since they were freshmen in high school. When they first met, Dwayne had been put off by his over-sized personality. Tom's hair was dyed in four different colors repeated in small clumps all over his head. He wore multitudes of beads, pendants, and jewels around his neck, and his clothing was thickly festooned with sew-on patches ranging from Smokey the Bear to Girl Scout merit badges to rainbows and unicorns to Peterbilt semi-trailer trucks. They became real friends later when Dwayne saw how talented and graceful Tom was—and how loyal.

Tom was his creative partner for the staging of *Titus*. He would choreograph and design the violence and play one of the roles. Tom and he had already been at work on the concept well before Dwayne knew there was a possibility of getting into the Emerging Directors program at the Public.

But two thousand dollars!

While Dwayne thought it over, the hostess led a family of four to a table toward the back. A little boy about six years old brought up the rear of the group. He stopped at their table and stared at Dwayne. Dwayne looked back at him, puzzled by the boy's interest.

"You're ugly," the boy said. He turned and followed his family back to their table.

Dwayne looked at Tom. Tom patted his wrist. "You're not, really," he said.

One never knew what was going to happen. If Brad recommended him and the show went as well as he imagined, he could be directing shows at the Public the following season and continue building his career from there. *The Public Theater* in New York City, for the love of God. The holy temple that Joe Papp built. But *Titus* had to be more than good. It had to be brilliant!

And now Brad wanted him to wager two thousand dollars.

Should he risk it?

Dwayne had two thousand dollars in a special vacation account. It was the only savings he had. His wife Angela taught fifth grade in the Chicago Public Schools, and they lived almost exclusively on her salary, and she was sick of it. She was sick of Dwayne rehearsing at night because everyone had day jobs. She wanted to travel. She wanted the things that a two-income couple could afford. But Dwayne's low income and their hefty debts held them back. He made pennies as a non-union actor and director. Sure, he did other work, but he was ashamed of how little he made laboring on-and-off as a bartender and as an office temp.

He wanted to surprise Angela with at least one thing she wanted. He'd been secretly stashing away bits of cash for four years in an account with six percent interest. He bought all his clothes used at resale shops and banked the difference. He was super careful in buying their groceries and stashed away the money he saved. He cancelled his health insurance and put what would have been his monthly premiums into the savings. He planned to surprise her with a trip to Italy. He couldn't wait to see the look on her face. She deserved a vacation in the land of her ancestors, and he was determined to take her there. He was so close to having enough.

But, *Holy Mary and the Flaming Rockettes*, this was his chance! Gregor Foxx! The Public Theater of New York City! This could catapult him to a real career. Hardly anybody made a living directing theatre in Chicago. You were always working on a shoestring for a joke of a stipend. To make a living you had to work in New York. You had to get union jobs. And if he could do that, maybe they could take regular trips to Europe. And get out of debt. And he could work in the daytime and be home in the evenings. They could have a full life. All the things they wanted together!

"Tick Tock," Brad said, waving his phone.

Fucking Brad Cunningham. Idea stealer. Manipulator. After all they'd been through, Brad should give his recommendation for free. Putting up money was one more humiliation. Why the hell had Tom suggested it? He could wring his friend's lanky neck.

"Come on!" Tom encouraged. "*Titus Andronicus* is going to be brilliant. Electric guitars. Stylized violence. You've got a great choreographer." He smiled brightly and raised both hands. "Taa-daa!"

Dwayne did think it was going to be brilliant. Fuck! He wanted this so badly. If he lost the two grand and couldn't take Angela to Italy, it would break his heart. How long would she put up with his starving artist bullshit? He was thirty years old, for god's sake.

But the Public Theater had launched Brad. It also had launched *Hair*, *A Chorus Line*, *Sticks and Bones*, and had meant so much to so many careers: Coleen Dewhurst, Gregor Scott, Kevin Kline, Ntozake Shange, Marvin Hamlisch, Jose Rivera, Suzan-Lori Parks. This type of opportunity did not come twice.

Holy Cajetan, patron saint of gamblers, help me!

He had to take the chance.

"Call him," Dwayne said.

Brad smiled and nodded. He flipped open his phone, selected a number, and put it to his ear. He grinned at the two friends as he heard someone answer.

"Hello, Gregor?" he said. "I have got a candidate for you…"

♦ ♦ ♦

Brad completed the call while they listened. Gregor Foxx would come to the opening night of Dwayne's *Titus Andronicus*. The production would be Dwayne's audition, followed by an interview. Then he'd be in or out.

"Have Tom put the money into an account within two weeks and send me a copy of the statement," Brad said. "Otherwise, I tell Gregor you aren't available, after all." Brad smiled coldly, gave them a quick salute, and swept out the revolving doors to pick up his bags at the Palmer House and fly back to New York.

Dwayne felt his stomach twist. He opened his mouth and let out a painful burp. Why had he agreed to put up two thousand dollars? If he didn't get in, he'd be doubly humiliated. He'd never be able to keep it a secret from Angela. Sure, he'd been able to keep it a secret while it was going to be a delightful surprise for her, but if he lost the money? He'd be morose, she'd see it, and she'd make him confess. It'd be all over.

Be cool. Be cool.

Tom gave him a brilliant smile. "I can tell you're apprehensive, but I totally believe in you. My god, I could have two personal friends directing on Broadway! To audition for you two! What a dream!" Tom sprang his lanky self out of his seat and turned a quick and impressive pirouette in the restaurant aisle. Two women at an adjacent table laughed and applauded. He bowed. At six foot six, his gracefulness was especially impressive. He was as tall as Tommy Tune.

Dwayne slapped the table top. "Why in god's name would you say five thousand dollars?"

Tom slid back into the booth. "That's how much confidence I have."

"Confidence risking *my* money!"

Tom closed his eyes and took a deep, cleansing breath. "We can pull this off," he said. "We've got Bobby. We've got Coco. Our concept is brilliant. Hendrix guitars! Dancing with severed heads! We are going to be great!"

Sure. In theory it was going to be great. But in live theatre, there was so much that could go wrong. You had to depend on the talents and dedication of so many different people. You never knew what might happen.

"Don't worry!" Tom insisted. "It's in the bag."

Dwayne rested his forehead on the tabletop in front of him. If only he could believe it.

2

"**D**wayne!" A stunning baritone cut through the chatter of the restaurant. Bobby had burst through the revolving doors on the Wabash Avenue side of the building. He winked at the hostess in passing. For Bobby, flirting was a way of life. He joined them at the window booth.

Bobby was supposed to have arrived an hour earlier to take part in the pitch. He was producing *Titus* as well as acting in it, but punctuality was not one of his strong suits. No matter. Dwayne had done very well without him.

The three men took turns embracing. Bobby smelled pleasantly of coconut oil. Sunlight from the large plate-glass window shone off the dark flesh of his shapely skull. He was a tall, handsome man and a riveting actor. Even more handsome and riveting than Dwayne himself, he'd have to admit. Bobby's Hamlet had been wildly acclaimed. Dwayne got nice reviews as Horatio, but nothing like the enthusiasm for Bobby. The show had been extended and could have been extended again if the theatre space had been available. However, there had been actual complaints in some of the reviews about having a black Hamlet in a largely white cast. It was 2003, for the love of Jesus Christ of the Latter Day Bloggerati! Happily, the controversy had helped sell tickets.

What Dwayne loved about Bobby, however, was how alive he was on stage. Every moment with him was something new. When you delivered your lines to Bobby, he was listening as though it were the first time he ever heard you say those words. He reacted to what you said exactly the way you said it that day. He might understand your words in an entirely different way than he had in yesterday's performance. Having Bobby as a scene partner was truly exciting.

Dwayne always tried to be just as alive and in the moment on stage, but when you were acting with someone who said their lines the same way every night and didn't actually look at you when you spoke, it could be difficult. Dwayne loved being on stage with Bobby, and he was really looking forward to directing him.

"Where's Brad?" Bobby asked.

"He just left," Tom said.

"I drag my ass to Elephant & Castle, and he's already gone?" He looked around the room as if expecting to see Brad chatting in one of the English-style booths with the office people and tourists. Waitresses bustled from group to group. A long bar with a multitude of beer taps ran down the center of the room with a bartender in white shirt and suspenders behind it. But no Brad anywhere. "Fake-ass British pub nonsense," he muttered. "Why'd he want to meet here anyway?"

"They've got three hand pumps of English ales at the bar," Dwayne said derisively. "Apparently, he *fell in love* with hand-pumped English beer when he was directing in London." How pleasant it was to make gentle fun of someone so much more successful than he.

"Directing in London," Bobby said. "Goody for him. Does he speak with an English accent now?" Bobby's lip curled with distaste. "I wanted to catch him in person. The only Broadway director I know, and he never returns my calls."

"That's Brad," Tom said.

"You *are* an hour late," Dwayne added.

"An hour?" Bobby looked briskly at his watch, raised his eyebrows, and immediately changed topics. "What're you having?" He looked at Dwayne's glass. "An ale, hand-pumped I presume, and something *green* for Tom," he observed. "I'm off the beer. Too fattening." He raised his hand for the waitress. "I've switched to White Russians."

"Isn't that made with half and half?" Dwayne asked.

"Heavy cream," Bobby said. "With Kahlua to give a little flavor and vodka to take the edge off." He ordered his drink and gave the waitress a friendly wink.

No need to tell Bobby that a White Russian was far more fattening than beer. Bobby worked out daily. Women of all races, ages, and creeds swooned when he took off his shirt.

"This is a Grasshopper," Tom said solemnly, raising his glass to his lips.

"There is progress to report," Dwayne said happily, feeling proud. Why shouldn't he feel confident? Confidence bred confidence. He'd really nailed it with his pitch to Brad. If Brad loved the concept, Dwayne had to believe it was going to succeed. Right?

"Gregor Foxx will be attending opening night!" Dwayne said. "Someone far more powerful than Brad will see you in the show."

This could mean great things for Bobby, too. It could mean great things for them all.

"So it worked out." Bobby sounded oddly regretful.

"Yes." Dwayne looked at Bobby quizzically. He recharged his enthusiasm. "And I've got a terrific costumer lined up. Peaches Brown. Tom will do the fights and the choreography, of course. And he's solved the problem of how to cut off someone's hand onstage!"

"Yeah. I was looking forward to that." Bobby shook his head and sighed. He looked out the window as another train squealed around the corner of the elevated tracks, then back at Tom. "Just out of curiosity, how *were* we going to do that?"

"Hold on," Dwayne said, trying to suppress his rising panic. "What do you mean *were*?"

"Yeah, sorry. I should have said something before. I've decided to fold up the tent."

"Fold up what tent?" Dwayne felt a wave of rising horror.

"No show. The party's over." Bobby shrugged as Dwayne's mouth fell open. He opened the menu as though he were looking for something to order.

"What do you mean?" Dwayne said. "Are you saying we're not doing *Titus Andronicus*?" His voice rose in volume with every sentence. "That's ludicrous. We *are* doing *Titus Andronicus*. You are the one who asked me to direct *Titus Andronicus*. Gregor Foxx is coming to see *Titus Andronicus*."

"Yeah. No," Bobby said. "Sorry. We're not doing it, after all. I've already committed the money elsewhere."

"What? But why?" Dwayne sunk back out of breath. What was

this fresh hell? He was gambling $2,000 that Foxx would like this show. This could be a break-through for them all. Why would Bobby *do* this?

"I have some really soul-shattering choreography planned for you as Aaron," Tom objected, sounding deep sad.

"I'm sure you do." Bobby laid a hand on Tom's. "I'm sorry. I really did want to play that villain. *Coal-black is better than another hue that will betray with blushing the close enacts and counsels of thy heart!* What great lines. He's so race-proud and ruthless. I know you and Dwayne would have created a kick-ass production."

"So why are you doing this?" Dwayne demanded. "This could lead to a role on Broadway!"

Bobby gave a winsome smile. He shrugged. The waitress brought his drink. "Thanks, sweetheart," he said. He looked around, trying to avoid the subject. "This actually isn't a bad place, Elephant & Castle. We used to drink here when I was doing *Henry the Fifth* down the street at The Storefront with The Hypocrites."

"Fuck Elephant & Castle and fuck The Hypocrites," Dwayne said. He leaned in toward Bobby and spoke in an intense whisper. "You can't pull out now. I mean, this show will be huge. And we have a whole future planned beyond that. We're going to do *Othello* again. You are going to play Iago this time, just like you wanted. Everyone in the cast is going to be black and Othello the only white actor. That is going to blow people's heads off."

"Yeah. I love playing those bad guys. I was really jonesing to do Iago. I'd started to think maybe *you* should be Othello instead of directing. You were so great as Horatio."

"If you liked me as your Horatio, you're going to love it when I'm directing you in *Titus*," Dwayne insisted.

"Well…" Bobby said vaguely. He grimaced and deflected his gaze out the window.

"We've been planning to do these Shakespeare & Friends shows for years," Dwayne moaned. He felt as angry and as heartbroken as when the beautiful Heather Gracely, his high school sweetheart, had dumped him because Trudy Farrington, captain of the cheerleaders, had told Heather that Dwayne was not in her league. But he *was* in her league! He was cast as Sky Masterson in *Guys and Dolls* his junior year. His junior year! That was Marlon Brando's role. Could he have been cast in Brando's role his junior year of high school if he wasn't in Heather Gracely's league? He'd been crazy about her. And now this from Bobby. A little push and there'd be tears rolling down his cheeks. Even greater than his desire to have a paying career was his desire to work with really talented people like Bobby and Coco and Tom, and, yes, even Brad. It was every bit as intense as being in love with the ridiculously pretty Heather Gracely. There was nothing like the thrill in the rehearsal room when people were coming up with new ideas and finding their way through a script, discovering ways to play it so it sang, so that it knocked the audience *out*. Truth be told, Dwayne would do that even if he were being paid nothing at all. (Which, in fact, was pretty close to what he was usually paid).

"Yeah." Bobby pushed out the words. "This is the way it's got to be."

"But why?" Dwayne pleaded. "We're building a great company."

"I know," Bobby said, not meeting anyone's eye. He took a sip of his White Russian and looked back out the window at the traffic. A cute young woman in a short skirt walked by the window and glanced in their direction. Bobby gave her a wry smile and a little finger wave.

Dwayne felt a surge of outrage. He *needed* this show. "You've got to have a reason! You asked me to direct what has to be Shakespeare's worst play," Dwayne insisted. "I thought what the fuck? *Titus Andronicus*? Every five minutes somebody else gets butchered. Your role, Aaron, is a totally racist invention—but with you playing it that's transformed to Black Power. And then Tom and I began imagining all the violence choreographed to Hendrix guitars. How amazing that would be. And now you're pulling the plug?"

"Yeah, I know," Bobby said.

"But why? What happened to the money from *Hamlet*?"

"Look, I just suddenly took the long view. Yeah, I can play Hamlet and Othello and Iago if it's my own company in a little storefront space and everyone's getting paid twenty-five cents. But the only roles I get offered from the big companies are slaves and thugs. I've been talking to the really established Chicago dudes—and I'm talking about the white ones, too. Have you ever been to Don Gleason's crib? That dude hustles all the time. Commercials. Day player TV roles. Character parts at the Goodman. Leads at Northlight. He's in both the unions, SAG and Equity, but he lives on ramen noodles in a tiny Uptown efficiency. He's fifty years old, and he's got nothing for retirement. And he auditions *all the time*."

"You're a better actor than Don Gleason," Tom said.

"Maybe," Bobby said. "I don't know. But will I have a more lucrative career? Not in Chicago."

"What are you going to do?" Dwayne asked.

"I'm using the *Hamlet* cash to buy a used motorcycle and a few months of rent money. I've already put down a deposit on an apartment in L.A., so I'm sorry, but too much of the money is already gone. Did you know they want a deposit and the first and last month's rent up front? Crazy! So it's too late to change my mind. Frankly, if I'd known the Foxx thing was going to work out, I would have waited. But I've never seen Brad do anything for anybody, and I didn't think he'd do it this time, either. So there it is. I'm going to L.A., and I'm going to give it at least five years."

"Wait a minute," Dwayne said, his face getting hot. "I helped raise that money. Can you legally do that with the *Hamlet* money?"

"I can do what I want. Shakespeare and Friends was not a nonprofit."

A train on the elevated tracks shrieked around the corner. They all turned to look. It seemed to rock precariously as it rounded the curve.

"An El train once derailed at this corner," Tom said. "I saw the pictures. The cars were hanging down in a row, still connected to one another."

"So you'll take the money and to hell with everyone." Dwayne leaned in, eyes squinted, neck muscles clenched. "Fuck the company."

"Hey, I still care about everybody," Bobby said. "As for Shakespeare and Friends, you can have it if you want. But you'll have to raise new funds. I'll write a press release that I'm naming you the new artistic director."

"But no money?"

"Not unless you got a motorcycle to sell."

3

Dwayne plopped butter into the Dutch oven and poured some of the good olive oil around it. Inside he was still seething. He moved the butter around in the oil with a wooden spoon as it began to bubble, and then stirred in a pile of sliced garlic. He blended the ingredients like an alchemist in his laboratory. Cooking usually soothed him. Beautiful aromas rose to his nose. He tried to focus on the smells and on his cooking to keep from screaming aloud.

"So just like that, he cancels the whole thing?" Angela said. "That doesn't seem like Bobby." She pulled the kitchen step stool up next to the stove and sat on it. Down the long hallway of their Rogers Park apartment the October sunset streamed into their living room. It had been a weirdly hot day for October and Angela was sweating. She grabbed the front of her flimsy cotton blouse and puffed it back and forth to cool herself. Sadly, they'd already put away the little window air conditioner from the bedroom for the winter. "I hope it's cooler tomorrow." Her fifth-grade classroom was not air conditioned. "I don't want to deal with a bunch of overheated ten year olds all day." She pulled a hair tie out of the pocket of her shorts and gathered her thick, wavy black hair into a pony tail to get it off her shoulders. Dwayne noticed, of course, how sexy his overheated wife looked in her moist and flimsy top, but he was too annoyed to feel aroused.

"Yeah. Just like that. Cancelled." His throat tightened until he felt like he could choke. He stirred the garlic in the sizzling butter and oil and ground some black pepper and sea salt into it. He kept the heat low. He didn't want the garlic to brown. It had to soften to a light translucence to release its most delicate flavor. "If I don't have a production, I lose my bid to the Public. Brad thinks if the production is as good as I promised, the slot in the Emerging Directors program would be mine."

"If you get another production, can you show him something else?"

"Sure, but I need to show in February. How would I get something new that fast? Anyway, Foxx is expecting to see *Titus*." He picked up a plate of sliced mushrooms from the worn linoleum countertop and slid them into the butter and oil. He put the empty plate into the old porcelain sink. A blur of rust stain ran down from the base of the faucet where a slow leak seeped water. If Dwayne were making real money, like Brad did, they could afford to live in a nicer place. "I was really getting excited about this production of *Titus*." He'd pictured it all so clearly. A wave of grief hit him, and his eyes blurred with tears. It was like he'd lost a friend. He sniffed hard and shook his head. He went to the refrigerator for the bowl of mussels so Angela wouldn't see.

"Yeah. I was pretty curious to see this myself. Being married to *you*, I've seen a lot of Shakespeare," she said with a hint of extreme burden in her voice, teasing him. "But I'd never even heard of *Titus Andronicus*. What's it about?"

He sighed and cleared his throat to settle his emotions. "Titus is a Roman general just back from defeating the Goths," he said, feeling the weight of defeat himself. He poured a cup of chicken broth into the pot followed by a dash of white wine and stirred. "The old emperor died and his two sons are fighting over the throne." Dwayne picked up the bowl of shiny black mussels, freshly scrubbed, resting on a bed of ice. He scooped the mussels off the ice and dropped them into the Dutch oven onto the bubbling liquid like soldiers to the slaughter. "Titus throws his influence behind the emperor's older son and wins him the throne. The new emperor promises to make Titus's daughter his queen, but she's already engaged to the emperor's younger brother. So instead the emperor marries the sexy Queen of the Goths, whom Titus brought back as a prisoner. The new queen hates Titus. The queen's henchman, Aaron, helps her plot all kinds of horrible revenge."

"That's who Coco and Bobby were going to play?"

"Yeah. We were doing the play because Bobby wanted to play

Aaron, and he wanted Coco for the queen." Dwayne threw a handful of chopped cilantro onto the mussels as they slowly opened and stirred them into the bubbling liquid, bathing them in the garlicky sauce. The aroma blossomed around him. He put the lid on the pot to let them steam. "So Aaron encourages the queen's sons to rape Titus's daughter. They also kill the emperor's brother and frame Titus's sons for the murder. Aaron tricks Titus into believing that if he cuts off his own hand, the emperor will free his sons. Titus cuts off his hand, but the emperor had already beheaded his sons."

"And so the zaniness ensues," Angela said.

"Exactly." Dwayne carried a salad out to the dining room table and returned for a loaf of French bread from the oven.

"Wait, you were using the oven in this heat?"

"Just a low heat," Dwayne said. "I know you like it crispy." He put the bread on the table and returned.

"I'd like you crispy," she muttered in mock threat.

Dwayne put his hands on her shoulders. "And I like you salty sweaty." He quickly licked her cheek. "Delicious."

"Ugh! Don't be a cocker spaniel, Dwayne!"

He rotated the mussels with the spoon to further bathe them in garlic sauce. "Yes." At least the food would be good. "Dinner is served." He carried the pot to the table and rested it on a trivet. He had to admit, the dish was a thing of beauty. It looked wonderful, smelled wonderful, and it would taste wonderful.

"So you were going to have all this violence performed to acid rock guitars, and Tom was going to have everyone doing Bob Fosse dance moves?"

"Something like that." Dwayne spooned mussels into large shallow dinner bowls. "Tom found this amazing device. It's about the size of a can of Sterno. It has a button on the side and when you press it these blood-red scarves come flying out and flutter in the breeze of the fan. Titus would be hiding one of these and eject the scarves at the sword blow when he chops off his hand to signify gushing blood. With the dance, the music, the lights, it would have been a spectacular show to watch." He breathed a mournful sigh. If only Bobby hadn't pulled the plug.

"Too bad." She ate some mussels and bread thoughtfully. Dwayne poured wine and passed her a plate of salad. He tasted another mouthful. The seafood attempted to redeem his soul.

"You know, you should do it anyway," Angela said. "If you let this slip by, who knows if you'll ever get a chance like this again?"

"You think so? The thing is, directing is already a lot of responsibility. I've never produced a show. Producing is a whole lot more."

"Didn't Bobby produce, direct, and play Hamlet in *Hamlet*?"

"Actually, yes, he did," Dwayne admitted. She had a point. Maybe this could work. But then he remembered. "After that he swore he'd never direct again."

"Yeah, but you won't be acting. So: two out of three. But he did all three, and *Hamlet* was a big hit. You even extended. Do you really think Bobby knows so much more than you?"

Dwayne grimaced. "It's not that he know more than I do. Bobby is just…" What? How do you define Bobby? Incredible charisma. Incredible cool. "He's more relaxed somehow. He expects things to work out, and they do."

"So you need to work on your inner Zen? Is that what you are saying? Because with the planning you've done, it seems like you've got a lot in place for this to be a great show."

Dwayne looked up at the ceiling. That was also a point. He looked back at her. "I've got Tom. I've got Coco. I've good designers lined up. Bobby would have been brilliant, but we can find another actor. He said I could keep the company name. Our *Othello* and *Hamlet* got really good reviews. Especially *Hamlet*."

"You were the sexiest Horatio." Angela reached over and ran her hand up his shoulder to his neck. It was nice she was being so supportive about this. Sometimes she got impatient with the long, late hours and nonexistent money of storefront theatre. But they both knew this could be a step to a real paying career. "The sexiest."

Dwayne cocked an eyebrow at her and smiled. His wife was a beautiful woman. More beautiful in fact than the ridiculously pretty Heather Gracely of his high school memories. He knew he was a good-looking man. He was not *out of his league* looks-wise, Trudy

Farrington be damned. Even Bobby complimented Dwayne. His mouth curved upward at the corners and the arch of his eyebrows gave him a clever, mischievous look, like he was constantly ready with a quip. Dwayne looked like someone eager for fun, and it made men want to be his friend and women (and some men) want to sleep with him. That's what Bobby said, anyway.

"So what do you need to make this *Titus* happen?"

"Money." Dwayne sighed. "Bobby gave me copies of his past budgets. I'd need at least ten grand."

"Ten grand is not a fortune. Though, obviously, *we* can't take on any more debt."

"Obviously." Dwayne felt his stomach twist. If he *were* able to raise the money somehow, he'd still have to risk two thousand dollars or Brad would pull the plug with Foxx. Should he tell Angela about that part?

He looked up at his wife, enjoying her dinner. She smiled at him.

No. No way. The Italy trip was to be a surprise. She didn't even know about the money he'd squirreled away. If she did, she would never agree to risk it.

But if he lost it, he knew she'd find out. He wouldn't be able to hide it. She'd find out, and he'd never live it down.

"So. Money," she said simply.

"Yeah. That's the thing. I don't know how Bobby found the money."

"Your brother has money. Why don't you ask Jonathan?"

Dwayne felt his throat involuntarily tighten. His brother Jonathan was six years older. They'd never been close. "That'd be a useless exercise in humiliation. Jonathan already thinks I'm a failure. *Pouring good money after bad.* Yeah. No thanks."

"Well, you don't want to end up like your dad, always regretting what you didn't do."

Dwayne's father had a long and undistinguished career as a journalist at second-level publications like *The Evanston Review*. He'd never gone beyond community college, never won an award, and never finished the novel he'd worked on his entire adult life. He didn't feel good about himself. Nor did he think seeking a career in theatre was a good idea for Dwayne, since he envisioned as disappointing a life for his son as his had been for him. His oldest son, Jonathan, on the other hand, was highly motivated. He'd put himself through medical school on a combination of grants, loans, and jobs, and now was a practicing pediatrician on the north shore. Unlike Dwayne, his student loans were paid off, he had plenty of money in the bank, and a vacation home in Wisconsin.

"Jonathan thinks Dad's a loser, too. I can't go to Dad for the money, either."

"So skip the relatives," Angela said. "It's not like you don't know anyone else with money."

4

Monday, October 20, 2003

"So you want us each to kick in six grand, and then we don't even get it back after the show?" Chaz said, fixing Dwayne with a doubtful stare.

"Well, you absolutely *could...*" Dwayne said, flashing his signature smile and speaking in what Chaz called his *weasel* voice. Dwayne raised a finger for the bartender. He needed to gather his thoughts. "Another Hennessy, Dewar's and Jameson, please," he told her. Behind them, traffic flashed by on Devon Avenue outside the storefront windows. Dwayne was making the pitch to his two oldest friends, sitting at the corner of the bar in Cunneen's, a quiet little tavern in Chicago's Rogers Park neighborhood. Chaz and Dwayne had been friends since freshman year at Evanston Township High School when they joined the swim team. They learned fortitude together, arriving at swim practice at 6:30 a.m. and diving into that cold water in midwinter while their classmates were still warm in bed.

Aleister and he had been friends even longer, since Dwayne was expelled from Pope John XXIII School in the fifth grade. In the fourth grade Dwayne had a pretty young nun who encouraged him to express himself. The old nun who taught fifth grade had different ideas. When their conflict came to loggerheads, the school principal, a scary priest, invited Dwayne and his family to find another school. Aleister had taken mercy and befriended the awkward new kid when he arrived mid-semester at the public school. They'd been buddies ever since.

Unlike Dwayne, his two friends were highly successful in lucrative professions—very impressive for men who'd just turned thirty that year. Dwayne felt like an adolescent in comparison. However, perhaps their successes could now feed his own. After some gentle prodding from Angela, he'd come up with a plan. If he could get a loan from Chaz and Aleister, he could produce the show himself and then pay them back from ticket sales. Or maybe even get them to invest long term.

"Absolutely! After the show I could pay you back your money, plus a split of any profits, and that'd be that. But another option is to keep the seed money in. Totally an option. You'd get a percentage of the profits of the show and the seed money would carry over to allow us to produce our next show. Instead of getting back the loan immediately, you'd get a share of the profits from every show we do!"

"*If* there are profits," Aleister said. He finished his cognac and slid the snifter forward.

"Well, yes, *if*," Dwayne agreed.

Aleister had always been the most subdued of the three (and the most intelligent, and came from the wealthiest family), but he'd become nearly dour since his wife died three years ago. Aleister seemed much older than his thirty years.

The barmaid brought their new round of drinks.

"If we lose money, and we don't have sufficient funds for another production, I'd refund what's left to you, and that'd be it. So, yes, you could take a hit. But look at the figures from the past two Shakespeare and Friends productions. Both of them turned a profit. Enough of a profit, in fact, that Bobby is able to use it to start a new life in L.A." He tried very hard to make that sound like a positive outcome.

Chaz had the proposal open in front of him on the bar. He reviewed it and frowned. Aleister was looking at Dwayne.

Dwayne hopped up and turned the pages of the proposal. "The figures are on page seven," he said, putting his finger on a column of numbers. He sat back down and took a sip of his fresh Jameson.

"Yeah," Chaz said, "but, Dwayne, you didn't direct either of those shows. You were among the actors. The common denominator was Bobby. He produced and starred in each, and he's gone."

"True. My directing credits have been with other companies. But using the Shakespeare and Friends name will bring us some reflected glory. We're putting out a press release that Bobby is naming me the new artistic director."

"Shakespeare and Friends is a stupid name," Chaz said.

"Really?" Dwayne squirmed. "I thought it was an asset."

"You're planning an edgy, sexy, kinetic *Titus Andronicus*. Acid rock guitars, colored lights, theatrical dance. Shakespeare and Friends sounds like a children's theatre."

"Huh," Dwayne said. He ran his hand along the smooth dark wood of the bar. The name felt like the only asset he had. He was loath to give it up. "You agree?" he asked Aleister.

"Shakespeare and Friends?" Aleister said. "It does sound…tame."

"Bobby picked it because he wanted to focus on Shakespeare, but he didn't want to be limited to Shakespeare," Dwayne explained.

"Basing a name on your programming is backward thinking," Chaz said, shifting to his annoying professional voice and swirling his glass of scotch. He was truly full of himself. "A name is your most essential branding. It ought to make your audience feel something."

"Huh." Dwayne felt his pulse begin to race. "So we just throw away the only name recognition we have?"

"Shakespeare and Friends did two shows. It ain't Steppenwolf," Chaz said.

Dwayne felt his face turn hot.

"Look, we can still do the new artistic director press release," Chaz continued. "Announce the name change at the same time. Get Bobby in on an interview with you before he leaves town. New! Exciting! All keyed to your upcoming production."

"Sounds like you might get some PR help from someone you could not possibly afford to hire," Aleister said, lifting his snifter of cognac in a toast. Chaz had recently been hired into a management position in public relations for the McDonald's Corporation. He'd jumped into a generous six-figure salary. It more than made up for the daily commute from Evanston to Oak Brook.

Chaz's new salary was part of why Dwayne felt bold enough to ask them for money. He knew Aleister did well as a North Shore psychiatrist—and Aleister had never touched Lisa's wrongful-death money, though Dwayne would never mention that.

"Maybe Dwayne was looking for us to be silent partners," Chaz said to Aleister. He flipped to the budget page of the proposal. "But looking at these figures," he said to Dwayne, "you don't have much devoted to marketing and PR. I don't know how Bobby managed to sell seats based on this."

"Word of mouth and good reviews," Dwayne said.

"Word of mouth? Jesus, man," Chaz said. "This isn't going to be another Glacier National Park, is it?"

"*Bloody fingers of Saint Thomas!*" Dwayne said. "Don't bring *that* up again!"

Four years earlier Dwayne had come up with the bright idea of the three friends and their wives taking a vacation together. They rented a camper that was large enough for them all to travel in, but not large enough to sleep them all. They took along a pup tent in which each of the couples would take turns sleeping while the other two had the camper. The men had also worked out a scheme for how they could take turns having the privacy of the camper for making love with their respective wives. In practice, however, the wives recognized that the other couples would know when they were doing it, and so they all refused. No one had any sex for the duration of the vacation, for which Chaz and Aleister both blamed Dwayne. It also rained half the days of their trip and the pup tent leaked, so they all crowded into the camper and some had to sleep sitting up, for which *everyone* blamed Dwayne. And that was the last time they'd attempted to vacation together.

"That would have been a great vacation if it hadn't rained!" Dwayne said.

"Maybe," Chaz said airily.

"*Bloody fingers of Saint Thomas?*" Aleister said.

"Chaz doubted me. Doubting Thomas," Dwayne replied, as though the connection were perfectly obvious. "*Put your fingers into my wounds*, sayeth the risen Lord unto Thomas."

"All right, all right," Chaz said, picking up the proposal again, "But let's work on these numbers. I'll help you with the marketing and PR. That's like adding thousands to the budget, pro-bono."

"Does that mean you're in?" Dwayne said, his voice rising to a girlish pitch.

Maybe this could work out, after all.

"I've got to do something with my McDonald's signing bonus," Chaz said with a grin. "Bonnie makes way too much money dissolving people's marriages to think my bonus is something special."

"I can't believe it! That's fantastic!" Dwayne got up and gave Chaz a huge hug, lifting him off his bar stool.

"All right! All right!" Chaz protested.

"What about you, Aleister?" Dwayne said. "Are you willing to take a risk?"

He swiveled on his stool toward Dwayne. "This will keep you on track with your application to the Public Theater?"

"It's the only thing that can."

"So we're each putting six thousand dollars at risk," Aleister said. "And let's face it, there's a good chance we could lose it." He looked Dwayne in the eye. For a moment, Dwayne felt like protesting, but these were his best friends. He had to be honest.

"Yeah," he admitted. "You absolutely could."

"So what are you risking, Dwayne?" Chaz asked. "I don't see any investment from you."

Dwayne hesitated. Should he tell them about the two thousand dollars he could lose?

No! Loose lips sink ships! He absolutely did not want Angela hearing about the money. Besides, he felt embarrassed that he had to risk two grand to someone who had every reason to believe in him. If Dwayne had to put up two thousand dollars for Brad Cunningham to recommend him, how good could he really be?

"We can't take on any more debt." Dwayne took a deep sigh and then looked them each in the eye. "I'm putting in my time. I'll be working at this eighty hours a week, and I'm not getting a large stipend." Chaz looked at him with a cold eye. Aleister didn't look convinced either. "I won't even take the stipend if the show loses money," he said in a sudden burst of inspiration.

"So the line items for directing, producing, wherever else there might be a stipend coming to you, you'd defer that and only take it if there's a profit?" Chaz said.

"Right," Dwayne said. He felt a sudden knot in his stomach. Angela would not like the sound of that. Not take money when everyone else was getting paid? Why did he suggest that? He took a gulp of his Jameson.

Did he absolutely have to tell her?

"Well, that's easily six grand worth of your time, even though you are budgeted to receive far less than that," Chaz said. "What do you think, Aleister?"

"Well, if a cheap bastard like Chaz is in, I guess I have to be."

"Hey!" Chaz complained.

"All right!" Dwayne shouted.

"And if you can get PR help from a pro like this guy, you'd better take it," Aleister said.

Dwayne felt a surge of joy and relief. He had the money. He could make it happen.

"Okay then, how would you use Aleister?" Chaz asked. "It'd be nice if he could meet some pretty actresses."

"Yeah, never mind," Aleister said. In the past two years, Chaz had set Aleister up on a series of blind dates. He remembered none of them fondly.

Dwayne started running the figures again in his head. They'd agreed to kick in six grand each. Was twelve grand really enough? Maybe he should have asked for more...

"Come on, Aleister," Chaz said. "You can't spend all your spare time writing books no one has seen."

"I like writing," Aleister said.

Bobby's productions had been very bare bones. Dwayne wanted to do more technically—which would take more cash. And Chaz had made a good point about needing marketing money.

"I've known three people who've published nonfiction," Chaz said. "None of them wrote more than a chapter and an outline to sell it. You haven't sold the first book and you're already writing a second? I think you're using these books to hide from the world."

Still Dwayne would have Chaz to help him with publicity. That was like money in the bank.

"I have an agent now." Aleister gave him a pleased grin.

"Very nice!"

While Dwayne was agonizing over money, they'd gone on to a

whole new topic. What would it be like to commit six thousand dollars to a risky venture and think nothing of it? They could lose that money, and it'd be little more than an inconvenience. Six thousand more in debt would put him in the ground.

"Your new agent was amazed you had a completed manuscript, right?" Chaz said.

"Well…" Aleister looked up at the ceiling and laughed. "Actually, she *was* pretty surprised."

"You got an agent?" Dwayne said. "That's great! Who is it?"

"Her name is Binky…"

"Binky!" Chaz interrupted. "That's an adult person? Binky?"

"She's one of the leading agents in New York," Aleister said. "She represents Toni Morrison and Donna Tartt and a lot of other famous writers."

"Wow," Chaz said. "Binky. Who would have guessed?"

"Apparently, anyone who knows New York publishing," Dwayne suggested, pulling Chaz's chain. He suddenly felt very happy. This was going to work!

A patron with a long salt-and-pepper pony tail and a Cubs hat came in the front door, followed by a swirl of autumn leaves and a momentary surge in traffic noise. They looked out the big store front window at the cars whizzing by. The new patron sat at the bar a few stools down and asked the barmaid for a PBR. Dwayne felt a wave of love for the City of Chicago. Where else could you sit down with two old friends in a venerable storefront bar and raise twelve thousand dollars to put up a show that just might lead to a Broadway career? It was a true blessing. And beyond that, in what other city would twelve thousand dollars possibly *be enough* to find really great actors and put up a show that could be taken seriously?

Nowhere.

He looked at his two friends. He loved them both. And, Angela, his beautiful wife who'd prompted him into action. He loved her most of all.

"I still think we need to get our friend Aleister out into the world," Chaz said. "Even if it's to write an article on the psychological underpinnings of *Titus Andronicus* as revealed in the Dwayne

Finnegan production. I can get it into print to help sell tickets. And if he happens to meet a pretty actress in the process…"

"You are a moron," Aleister suggested.

Dwayne laughed excessively.

"Moron? Is that a psychological condition?" Chaz asked. "Maybe you could prescribe something." He drained his scotch.

"There is no cure for what you've got," Aleister said.

"And yet Chaz knows a fantastic investment when he sees one!" Dwayne interjected gleefully. "Let me buy another round. We need to celebrate the launch of this production—and Aleister's new agent."

"I hope this isn't an example of how you're going to be spending our money," Aleister said.

"Listen," Chaz said, pointing upward. A Jimi Hendrix song had come on the Cunneen's sound system. "Watchtower."

"Hendrix's version is so much better than Dylan's," Dwayne said.

"Psychedelic rock," Aleister said. "That's what you plan for *Titus*, right?"

"It'll be a psychedelic dream," Dwayne said.

"Psychedelic Dream," Chaz repeated. "Now that's an evocative phrase. Much better than Shakespeare and Friends."

The three men looked at each other for a moment. Dwayne's eyebrows arched mischievously and a clever smile lit up his face. "You mean like the Psychedelic Dream Theatre?" He dropped into a deep movie-trailer-announcer voice: "*Bringing to theatre what Hendrix brought to guitar.*" They all three smiled widely. "*Holy hot ticket Jesus*, the fucking Psychedelic Dream Theatre," Dwayne shouted exuberantly.

"I like it," Aleister said.

"Make it so, Number One," Chaz added.

5

Thursday, October 23, 2003

Dwayne held the phone to his ear as it rang and rang at the other end. His stomach churned. This was the twelfth time in three days he'd tried calling the Vox Populi Theater where they'd been set to perform *Titus Andronicus*. No one ever answered. Did he still have a space? Bobby had reserved the same theatre they'd used for *Othello* and *Hamlet*, but he admitted to Dwayne he'd withdrawn the deposit. Dwayne needed to know if someone else had claimed their slot. If so, he was in serious trouble. It would be very late to find a new theatre to rent for February. Probably too late.

Angela swept by in a flash, giving him a kiss goodbye before she left for school.

"Wait," he said. "Let me drive you."

"Why?" she said suspiciously.

"I need to drive down to the Vox Populi, and then I have a temp gig in the afternoon. I'll never make it on public transportation."

"Then how am I supposed to get home?" she said, walking out the door. "Don't keep following me."

"But I must," Dwayne said, following her. "I'll come and pick you up."

"I'm late, Dwayne." She hurried down the stairs with him still following. "I can't mess with you this morning." She pushed through the heavy entry door and headed toward their car, parked on the street below the elevated train tracks.

"No mess. Let me be your chauffeur."

"My school day ends at 3:30. When does your temp job end? Five p.m.?"

"You know you never leave school at 3:30. When have you ever left before 5:30?" He slipped swiftly around her, unlocked the door and hopped behind the wheel.

"You are a blister on a boar's behind," she groused, getting into the passenger seat.

"I love you, too, darling," he said, turning the key and bringing the car to rattling life. He pulled into the street. He attempted to entertain her with stories of movie director John Huston's exploits, whose biography he was reading, but she sulked the entire way.

After Dwayne dropped Angela at school, he headed west. He parked the battered ten-year-old Toyota Corolla in front of the Vox Populi Theater. This was one of the oldest venues in town for low-budget theatre companies. The building had been a Catholic school, like the one he'd attended, before attendance dwindled and it had been converted to theatre spaces, artist studios, and offices for small nonprofits. Dwayne's stomach tightened as he recalled childhood experiences with the nuns. He climbed the wide limestone stairs and went inside the lobby and around the corner to the office. It felt like walking to the principal's office.

Would the Vox Populi still be holding the reservation for *Titus Andronicus*?

"Fuck no!" Ron Pricker said.

Dwayne's heart sank. Pricker was a spectacularly unpleasant human being. Dwayne had found him sitting at his wildly messy desk in the office behind the box office window. A large lighting instrument spilled its innards onto the desk in front of him. He had a pair of needle-nose pliers in one hand and a soldering iron in the other. The room smelled like molten solder and burnt transformers. It reminded Dwayne of the distant aroma of burning tires. Pricker was wearing protective goggles, which he did not take off.

His office was a large room with huge posters of events that had taken place in the huge auditorium at the Vox Populi. Big name comedians. The occasional touring musical. Famous folk singers and mid-level rock concerts. Pricker tended to lavish his attention on the big acts in the large space and let the little companies in the two under-one hundred seat theatre venues fend for themselves.

"Well, can I get it back reserved again?" Dwayne asked. "Bobby said he reserved the same space we used for *Hamlet* and *Othello*. We're planning to load in Sunday, January 25ᵗʰ and run through February."

"Not at the Vox Populi you're not," Pricker said. He leaned over, set down his smoking soldering iron, partially pinched his nose with his fingers and blew snot into a waste basket. Dwayne felt his stomach roll.

"Come on," Dwayne said. "We've been good tenants. Our shows did well." He tried one of his dazzling smiles.

Pricker wiped his nose with his sleeve and looked at him in mock amazement. "Good tenants?" he said. "Are you fucking kidding me? After both of those shows you left so much trash next to the building, I had to pay for a special pickup." Pricker's fat, pock-marked face arranged itself into a nasty mask of disgust. "You can't just bust up your set when you're done and leave it in a pile outside. Bobby still owed me money, so I took it out of his deposit when he cancelled your February slot. He cursed me out. Called me a thief."

Dwayne remembered the *Hamlet* strike. They had nowhere to store anything for the next show, so they had no choice but to throw it away. They'd filled the dumpster and then the show's technical director was amazed when Bobby told them they could pile the rest of the trash on the ground next to it. "Absolutely," Bobby'd said. "Totally fine."

Apparently not.

"You guys poured paint into the slop sink and left it there to dry," Pricker continued. "All you had to do was rinse it down. It takes one minute of running the water. Instead it hardened, and I had to spend hours replacing the trap. You didn't paint the stage floor back to black. You didn't stack the lighting instruments in the seats. I wouldn't even *want* you back." He got up from his chair and took an ancient ellipsoidal that was missing its lens from a row of lights against the wall and put it on his desk. He began taking parts from it to repair the one he'd been soldering.

"Look, we aren't the same company. Bobby left town. We've got new investors. New staff. We need that slot Bobby reserved. This would be a whole new relationship with a new team looking for a mutually beneficial long-term relationship." He tried the dazzling smile once again.

Pricker glanced up from the back of the ellipsoidal. "And yet I see before me someone who was part of the same old team of arrogant assholes."

Arrogant assholes?

Arrogant asshole was what people called Rod Pricker. The mother of the actress playing Ophelia had proudly confided to Pricker at the box office that her daughter was in the show. "Is that right?" Pricker had said, his voice dripping with sarcasm, tossing her tickets at her. "Well, good for fucking you."

She'd been so shocked and insulted, she'd burst into tears.

Pricker went back to his repairs. The wiring inside the lighting instrument looked like it had been set on fire.

Say something!

"Look, I was just an actor with Shakespeare & Friends," Dwayne insisted. "This is a new company. New management. And I'm going to make sure we do everything by the book." Dwayne grinned like a lunatic.

All right. He could feel in his face he'd pushed it too far.

Pricker looked up from the damaged light. He straightened up slowly, like he was struggling with an achy back. He stared deep into Dwayne's eyes.

"Fuck you," he said.

Many people wondered how a nasty human being like Rod Pricker could be in a position to deal with the public. The fact was, the job fell into his lap. Rod had been an assistant to the last guy who ran the performance spaces. When that guy got sent to jail for embezzling funds, the management put Rod in charge of the facilities. It was a sad day for Chicago theatre.

"Come on," Dwayne said. "Bobby is gone. I need that February run."

"The February run is out of the question," Pricker said flatly. "Both studio spaces are booked for February. And there's no way you could afford or fill the auditorium," he scoffed. "Even if I wanted to rent to you—which I really don't—the first slot I have open is three weeks in April. And then I've got a four and a five-week slot in July and August. You want to get on your knees and beg for one of those?"

"I've got to have February," Dwayne said. "It's February or nothing."

"Then it's nothing," Pricker said. He turned his attention back to the burnt wires in the ellipsoidal. "Don't let the door hit your ass on the way out."

◆ ◆ ◆

Dwayne sat in his car outside the Vox Populi. What was he going to do? This was October. How would he find a venue for a February run? Affordable theatre spaces booked up a year in advance.

He drove east on Belmont until he passed Schubas Tavern on Southport. Schubas was a gorgeous vintage two-story building with a Schlitz beer globe inlay near the roof. He'd seen some great bands play there. He was tempted to pull in for a quick beer to regroup from his disappointing meeting, but he had a temp gig with an insurance company to get to in Old Town. It started this afternoon and ran for two days after that.

Within a couple blocks on Belmont the Bailiwick Theatre and The Theatre Building appeared on his right. Both venues had multiple stages and offered rentals to smaller companies. He should pull over right now and see if either place had a February opening. But if he did, he'd be late for work.

He felt horribly conflicted, but continued on. When he got to Lake Shore Drive, instead of veering right onto the entrance ramp toward his job, he kept going straight under the viaduct, around the bottom of Belmont Harbor and parked by the Chicago Yacht Club. He had to take a moment to think.

He got out of the car and walked toward the water. A brilliant October sun shimmered down on the harbor and the lake. It was a beautiful, mild fall day. A breeze off the lake clattered the rigging of dozens of sailboats in the harbor, releasing sounds like a symphony of wind chimes. A young boy was flying a kite on the grassy hillside by the water. (Why wasn't he in school?) Dwayne walked out to the harbor entry and looked south toward the Loop. The lake stretched as far as the eye could see. The autumn air was clear and cool, and the skyscrapers stood up in the light: Lake Point Towers by the water, the John Hancock and the Sears Tower with their huge dual antennas, and all the rest. Seagulls flew and swirled and cried over the water. He loved the city. He loved this view. He loved the lake. It renewed his spirit.

Was he going to spend the next two and a half days of his life earning temp job pay or was he going to get out and find a venue for a show that just might transform his life?

Daniel Burnham said: *Make no little plans. They have no magic to stir men's blood.* Without Burnham, this gorgeous lakefront park stretching the length of the city might not exist.

But it did exist, and it did stir Dwayne's blood.

He had no time to waste.

He flipped open his phone and called his dispatcher at the temp agency to tell her he could not make the afternoon booking. There was a long silence. He watched as the boy on the hillside jogged backwards a few steps to keep his kite afloat.

"Dwayne, you already confirmed," she said coldly.

"I know," he said. "I feel really bad, but something came up."

"Our clients depend on us to fulfill our obligations. That's the whole point of a temp agency. You're scheduled to be there in less than an hour. I can't find a replacement for you in that time."

"I know. I'm so sorry."

"What is this? A last-minute audition?" She sounded disgusted. The agency used a lot of actors and musicians. That could sometimes be a burden.

"No, no…" Dwayne said. But then he had no idea what to say. *I lost my venue?* What sense would that make to her? "I, ah…" Oh, what to say? His mother died? No! In the hospital? "I, ah, I had to take our dog to the vet," he said in a rush. "He's really sick."

"You have a dog?" she said slowly.

Fuck! Did she know Dwayne was allergic to dogs? Had he mentioned that?

"Yes," he lied.

The boy jogged backwards to the sidewalk along the water as the breeze died and his kite plummeted toward the ground.

She didn't say anything. The phone felt slippery from nervous sweat.

"A pomegranate," he invented desperately.

"What?" she said.

Pomegranate? That wasn't a dog breed. "A Pekinese," he corrected quickly.

"Your Pekinese is sick," she said, her voice laced with disgust.

"That's right," Dwayne said. He considered inventing a disease, but decided it was best to keep quiet. Suddenly he could hear Humphrey Bogart's voice in his mind: *Get up off the floor, Angel. You look like a Pekinese.* What movie was that?

Suddenly the boy was jogging backward across the sidewalk, straight toward the edge over the water.

"Stop! Stop!" Dwayne screamed, running toward him. The boy stopped short, just before going over the edge into the waves.

"What? What's happening?"

"Good Lord, a boy almost fell backwards into the lake."

The boy watched his kite crash down. He shrugged his shoulders, looked back at the water, and waved at Dwayne.

"The lake?" the dispatcher said. "You said you were at the vet."

"Yes, I am!" Dwayne said. "Um. The dog is in with the doctor right now, and I'm just taking a walk while I wait. The office is right by the lakefront."

There was another long silence.

"Those are the stupidest lies I've ever heard," she said. "Forget about the next two days, too." She hung up on him.

Maybe he should have let the kid fall into the lake.

Well, it was done. It didn't feel great, but *he could make no little plans!*

He dashed to the car and drove back to The Theatre Building. Unfortunately, they were fully booked for February and so was the neighboring Bailiwick. Not good, but he had a computer back at the apartment and a phone in his pocket. He drove back to Lake Shore Drive and turned north toward Rogers Park. The light shimmered on the water all the way out to the horizon, but it didn't buoy him up as much as before. He felt guilty now. The money. He'd turned down two and a half days of paying work. He'd offered to pass up his stipend for the show. He was being financially irresponsible.

What would Angela think? She was supportive, but she was also convinced he could be bringing home more money. He hated when she was disappointed with him. She had that passionate Italianate blood. And when she was pissed, she wouldn't have sex with him. At times like this, sex was the only thing that could calm his blood enough to sleep at night. Besides, he craved making love with his wife. She was so beautiful. She was wonderfully affectionate, she had a terrific body, and she was great in bed. If he couldn't have sex with her, on top of everything else, his head might explode.

He drove back to the apartment and began looking up and calling venues. He called and called and called. And nobody answered.

At four-thirty he stood up from the desk and shouted at the top of his lungs: "DO ANY OF YOU MOTHER-FUCKING VENUE OPERATORS EVER ANSWER YOUR MOTHER-FUCKING PHONES???"

No one answered his scream, either. It was time to go pick up Angela from school, and he hadn't made any plans for what to make for dinner.

And he still had no clue where they could perform *Titus Andronicus*.

6

Saturday, October 25, 2003

A piece of dishware hit the kitchen floor and burst into a million pieces. Out in his living room, Bobby pretended as though he hadn't heard. "I don't know what to tell you, Brother," he said, reclining comfortably on his black leather and chrome sofa. "I thought Pricker would hold the space for you. But I had to get the money out. I had to put a deposit on an apartment in LA. Did you know they want the first *and* the final month's rent as a deposit out there? It's crazy! And rents are way higher than here!"

Another dish hit the floor and exploded. Dwayne looked toward the kitchen door. He tried sitting up like a serious human being in the bean bag chair, but it resisted his efforts. "Should I be here?" he asked. Bobby had introduced him to a very beautiful but very sulky-looking young woman when he'd entered the apartment. She had a large afro like Angela Davis and dimples that made her face both sexy and adorable even through her anger. Dwayne said hello, but she disappeared into the kitchen without a word.

"She just needs to work some things out. It's good you're here. Give her a little time to cool off."

"Really?" Dwayne said. He looked doubtfully toward the kitchen door. "Because this feels…awkward."

"She didn't know I was leaving town," Bobby confided. "She just found out a few minutes ago."

Something glass smashed against the wall.

Bobby shrugged, a long-suffering smile on his face. "You can't take dishes on a motorcycle, anyway," he said. "But I was hoping to sell those for a few bucks. Say, you interested in this couch? Or that bean bag?" Bobby's apartment was small, but his furnishings were largely tasteful, aside from the bean bag. Near the kitchen door he had a wrought-iron rolling bar cart with rocks glasses and a couple decent bourbons atop. The walls were adorned with African-themed prints.

"You've been in my apartment," Dwayne said. "You know I don't need any furniture." Another dish smashed in the kitchen. It sounded like a plate. "Apparently she thought she deserved to hear your plans earlier," he whispered. Bobby nodded to the right and then the left, as if considering the thought from both sides. Then he leaned back in his seat and his shirt fell open revealing a sculpted chest and stomach. Dwayne felt even more like he was invading the couple's privacy, but now he also felt a weird stirring of envy. Bobby had an incredible face and body. That sort of thing was an asset for an actor, and Dwayne loved to act almost as much as he loved to direct.

"I do like her. She is super hot." Bobby spoke low so his words would not carry to the kitchen. "We been keeping company for six months. That's pretty long for me. I been dating white women for a while before that, so meeting her was like coming home. *This* girl, she takes you *back*." He let out a deep sigh. "I'm going to miss her." He leaned in closer. "What do you think my chances are for goodbye sex? I was really looking forward to something special. You know?"

Another plate smashed in the kitchen.

"She seems annoyed," Dwayne said. He needed to get out of there. "But look, I've got to ask you. I've called all these places." He struggled forward mightily in the shifting chair and put a legal pad in front of Bobby. On it was a list of theatre venues and phone numbers written in pencil. "The ones crossed out are already booked for February. I'm still trying to reach the others, but that's only a handful. Can you think of any more? I've got to put this show up in February, or there goes my chance with Gregor Foxx."

"Yeah, that's a bitch." Something large shattered. "And so, maybe, is that," he said, cocking his head meaningfully toward the kitchen. He immediately shook his head. "Naw. That ain't fair. She's just offended I didn't tell her."

"A lot of that going around," Dwayne said darkly.

"Oh, I suppose you're mad at me, too."

"How could you cancel our space at the Vox Populi without

telling me? You left me high and dry."

"I needed that money."

"But if you'd said something, I could have replaced the deposit, and you'd have had your money, and I'd have the space."

"I hate when people are mad at me," Bobby said. "That's why I didn't tell you sooner. *Oh, Bobby, don't go, blah, blah, blah.* I can't handle that shit."

Another dish met its doom.

"But when the truth finally comes out, it's even worse," Dwayne said, pointing toward the angry noise. "And what about my thing with Foxx? Why would you do that to me?"

Bobby looked embarrassed for a moment. He shook his head. "Honestly, man, I never believed Brad would actually recommend you. When has he ever done anything for anyone but himself? I thought he was just stringing you along, making a last ditch to get into the pretty, straight boy's pants."

Dwayne collapsed back in the bean bag. "Fuck," he breathed. He tried to sit up again, but he felt trapped, as though he'd sat in quicksand.

He knew what Bobby was talking about. Over the years, Brad had patted his ass way too many times. One drunken night at a college party he'd clutched Dwayne's crotch in his hand. "Come home with me," he'd begged, his breath stinking of scotch. Dwayne shoved him away. Brad leaned against the wall to steady himself. "It'll be however you want it. Nothing you don't want to do. I'll make sure you love it." He reached out to grab Dwayne's shoulders, but Dwayne sidestepped and Brad collapsed, hitting the wood floor hard. "Fuck!" he'd said dully. Brad wouldn't feel the pain until the morning, but Dwayne still felt the disgust.

It wasn't the only time he'd had to dodge Brad's advances.

"I'm sorry, man. I truly am," Bobby said. "Here, let me take a look." He picked up the legal pad and ran down the list with his finger. Bobby pointed to one of the venues on the list and laughed. "You can probably get into the Chicago Repertory Arts Playhouse. Although I can't say that you *want* to get into the Chicago Repertory Arts Playhouse."

"Why not?" Dwayne rolled awkwardly off the side of the bean bag chair to his hands and knees, got up, and sat on the leather sofa next to Bobby.

"Nobody *wants* to be in the Chicago Repertory Arts Playhouse."

"I've seen shows there," Dwayne said. "I've seen *good* shows there."

"It's fine if you're in the audience. Producing there is another matter. But if you do decide to try there, go in person. Raymond Green never picks up his phone."

"Everywhere else I've called is booked up."

"Then I guess you going to be at Chicago Repertory Arts Playhouse. You poor bastard." He grinned and cackled, cocked his head to the side, and slapped Dwayne on the knee. He laughed some more. Dwayne felt all the blood rush into his head. *Motherfucker.* He got up quietly and walked into the kitchen. Bobby's angry girlfriend looked at him in surprise. "Pardon me," he said. He picked up a large soup tureen in both hands and smashed it to the floor.

7

Sunday, October 26, 2003

D wayne went straight from Bobby's place to the Chicago Repertory Arts Playhouse, but Raymond Green was not there. Then Dwayne spent the rest of the day calling and visiting other venues. They all said the same thing: if you wanted a space, you needed to reserve it a year in advance—unless you were willing to work at the Chicago Repertory Arts Playhouse—and they'd laugh.

On Sunday he returned and was directed up to the larger performance space on the second floor of the building. Raymond Green was kneeling on the stage over a fog machine with its back panel removed. He had a bald spot with dandruff gathered around its circumference, like snow at the edge of a clearing in the prairie grass. He had a bulbous nose with enormous pores and tracings of visible veins. His tee shirt rode up on his hairy back and the top of his ass crack was exposed above his belt and jeans.

"Raymond Green?"

Green straightened up and looked around slowly. "Right," he said. "What can I do you for?"

"Ah…" Dwayne gave a little laugh.

Is this who I am now? Pretending to laugh at 'what can I do you for?' *How desperate are you, Finnegan?*

"Yes," Dwayne said. "I'm looking for a performance space for February."

"Great," Green said. "I can let you have this one."

Dwayne felt an immediate mix of relief and dismay. He looked around. This space was much bigger than what he'd been seeking. The stage floor was surrounded on three sides by rows of seating risers, and there were probably a hundred old-fashioned theatre seats in each section. That would be a lot of tickets to sell. Many of the seats had upholstery tears repaired with duct tape. A couple had the fold-down seat cushion missing. In fact, a lot of things seemed in strangely bad repair. Many of the lighting instruments hanging on the grid overhead were hollow: No lenses or lamps in them. Why would they be hanging if they couldn't be used? And bare wires hung down from the grid. The heavy black curtains that masked off the backstage had weird stains and a few paint splatters.

The stage itself was large and covered with used lumber, old platforms, and flats with twisted frames, much of it unsalvageable junk. It was a "black box" theatre with the walls, floor and ceiling painted black. This ensured nothing would catch the light except the action on stage, helping keep the audience's attention focused, but the paint hadn't been refreshed in a long time, and large sections of it looked streaky and battered. The seating risers were well-worn and the edges of the stairs going up the rows of seats were splintered.

However, it was a space and it was available.

Dwayne had seen a number of shows in this building. He knew the Playhouse had two spaces of less than one hundred seats and then this large main stage space on the second floor and another one just below it. "I don't think I have the budget for a room this big. I was thinking of one of the smaller spaces."

"No can do, partner," Green said. "Both of the studios are booked for February. *A Christmas Carol* opens in here a week before Thanksgiving. Everybody's got to do the fucking *Christmas Carol!* And then this space is empty after the first week of January until the second week of March."

"What's the rent in here?" Dwayne said.

"Three thousand a week."

"Jesus." He couldn't do three thousand a week with the money Chaz and Aleister were putting up.

"Three grand includes box office, lights, sound, and a smoke machine if you need it." Green tapped the rusty piece of equipment he'd been working on with his toe. "I'll have it good as new by the time you're here."

"I can't afford that." Dwayne sat down in one of the seats in the front row and felt something tap the back of his head. He looked back. It was one of the wires hanging from the overhead grid. He pushed it away from him.

"If you fill these seats, you can make plenty of money," Green said. "The profit margin is way higher than for filling either of the studios."

"And if I don't fill them, I stand to lose a lot more money." He felt a weird tingling sensation in the back of his neck. It was the wire. He brushed it away again.

"We send out an e-blast every week," Green told him. "We really push the shows on the main stages. Our e-blast reaches over 15,000 addresses."

Dwayne felt the tingling again. It was like a muscle at the base of his hair follicles was twitching. He reached back to push away the wire again. He felt it touch the palm of his hand, and suddenly his hand grasped around the wire involuntarily and his entire body began shaking uncontrollably. *Sweet Boner of the risen Lord, what was happening!?!?* All his muscles clenched furiously. He tried to scream, but only a garbled snarl would come out of his mouth.

Green looked at him curiously, then raised his eyebrows as he saw what was happening. "Sorry," he said.

Dwayne felt his brains boiling out his ears.

Green grabbed a piece of wood from the rubbish on the stage and used it to yank the bare wire out of Dwayne's furious grip. With the wire removed, Dwayne collapsed to the floor, his muscles quivering. His teeth had clenched so tightly, he felt pulverized enamel between them. He blew air out of his lungs, making an extended Z sound, and then gasped air back in.

"Hesus Chreet un um blasstickle," he said into the floor.

"Yeah, sorry," Green said. "I guess that was a live wire."

Dwayne dragged himself to a seated position on the floor, took a deep breath, and shook out his arms. His body shivered and felt hot at the same time. His eyeballs hurt from his eye socket muscles scrunching.

"Boy, I hate when that happens," Green said. "The last company did some fucked-up shit with the electrics. I've really got to supervise people better. You think they're professionals, but they're not."

"What was zzz zzat?" Dwayne gasped.

Green walked over to the hanging wire, grabbed it by the plastic insulation and looked up where it met the grid overhead. Then he touched the bare end of the wire with the back of his index finger. It jerked toward his palm and broke contact with the wire. "I think that might have been 220 volts," he said, sounding impressed. He let the wire swing away from him, then looked up again. "Naw," he said. "Naw. What am I thinking? That's 110. We only use 220 for the welder. They couldn't have tapped into that. Unless they got into the HVAC feed."

What the living fuck? "Non. Na. Why?" Dwayne said, still finding it hard to control his mouth. "Why…that…was…there?"

"Oh! Ha, ha," Green laughed, understanding Dwayne's question. "They had a very strange lighting plot. Some of the instruments were under the audience seating. It was not a good idea. I still haven't removed all their weird wiring. They were supposed to do that, but they didn't. Obviously. From now on, I've got to approve everyone's lighting plot before the show loads in. So keep that in mind."

Dwayne dragged himself up off the floor. What kind of a fucking nuthouse was this?

He looked carefully at the seat in front of him. No wires. He lowered himself into it. He felt so tired all of the sudden. All his muscles ached.

"Yeah, just rest a minute. You'll bounce back. I had a professor at Columbia College. Well, I don't know if he was actually a *professor*. He might have been an adjunct. It seems like most of the teachers were adjuncts, paid next to nothing. It's no way to run an army!" Green laughed.

What the hell was he talking about?

"Anyway, I've never met anyone who knew more about electricity, and he said it was good for your heart to take a little shock every now and then."

Dwayne glared at him. "Unless, of course, it kills you."

"There is that," Green agreed. "But look at the bright side:

You're not dead." Green considered that for a moment. "I should forget about renting to a theatre company and set this up as an electric shock health spa."

"I'm sure that'd be a wild success," Dwayne said acidly, trying to roll the tension out of his neck.

"Yeah," Green said, detecting his sarcasm. "Maybe not. How many tickets does your company typically sell?"

"We used to be called Shakespeare & Friends." Dwayne stood up and stretched, finally starting to feel normal. "We did pretty well in a seventy seat space at the Vox Populi. But we only sold it out totally a couple times."

"Yeah. Our studios are sixty seats. That's probably the size you want." Green pulled a hammer from the loop on the side of his overalls and slapped the handle against his palm, thinking it over. "You know, I've been wanting more resident companies. Repeat customers make my job easier." He slapped the hammer handle into his palm some more, thinking. "Look. If you sign on to be a resident company, I'll give you this space for the price of a studio your first time out. One grand a week."

Resident company? Dwayne doubted the Psychedelic Dream Theatre would do another show after *Titus Andronicus*. But Green didn't know that.

A grand a week would fit his budget. And Dwayne loved the large thrust stage in this space. It would offer him a lot of flexibility as a director.

"For me, it's probably too late to find someone for the February slot anymore. I'd rather get a grand a week than have it empty. You commit to doing your future shows in this building; I'll give you the deal."

"A grand a week sounds great!" Dwayne said. "But these are a lot of seats for us."

"Yeah," Green said. "Sixty people in a seventy seat house looks sold out, but sixty people in a 300 seat house looks like a loser. We can mask off some of the rows of seats to make the space smaller." He got up and led Dwayne over to the seating riser on stage right. "See the pipe up there?" he said, pointing to a pipe above the back of the second row of seats. "We can hang flats from that. It looks like the space ends here. The other two rows disappear. We do that on both sides. One hundred seats gone. Poof! And I've got a curtain that can mask off the back row of seats in the center section. That brings you down to 175 seats. You get one hundred people in here; they got space to drop their coats on the seat next to them. The place looks full and everyone's comfy."

"That sounds fantastic," Dwayne said. He leaned his hands onto the back of the metal theatre seat in front of him and got a terrific jolt. His hands clenched tightly onto the chair back, and his whole body started vibrating uncontrollably.

Holy Judas!

He tried to scream, but his throat clutched up. The seat began to rattle as Dwayne's body shook uncontrollably.

"Oh fuck," Green said. He used the claw of his hammer to pull Dwayne's hands off the back of the theatre seat. Dwayne stood and staggered down the row like a cinematic zombie, his eyes rolled back in his head. He stumbled down the two stairs, and fell into a pile of splintered lumber.

"Ah, argh, ooah, aftfft," he said.

"Sorry about that," Green said.

"Yoag aggge oum faging idiant," Dwayne said angrily. His tongue felt like someone had tried to pull it out with a pair of tongs. A sharp piece of wood poked up into the side of his scalp.

"Don't try to get up too fast," Green said.

"Wire zee farg donut yee helg mig gatt oop?" he demanded, his eyes shooting daggers of hate.

"Yeah, here, let me help you up," Green offered. He took Dwayne by the still-quivering arm and pulled him into a sitting position. "Just take a deep breath when you can. No need to rush it." He reached into the pile and pulled out a bottle of water. He blew the dust off it. "Looks like this was never opened." He twisted the cap off. "Yep. That was still sealed. Here." He handed the bottle to Dwayne. "It's best to hydrate after a shock."

Dwayne used his left hand to force his right hand open enough to take the bottle, but he gripped it too hard and half the water shot out the top and landed square in his lap.

"Oh, I'm sorry," Green said. "Now that looks like you pissed your pants. Which does happen sometimes with shocks. You'd be surprised."

You'd be surprised if I shoved this bottle up your ass, Dwayne thought vehemently. He lay down onto his back and breathed shallowly until his muscles slowly returned to normal.

Once he could control his movements again, Green led him backstage where there was laundry equipment for costumes. He found a toga for Dwayne to wear while his pants and underwear took a spin in the dryer. Then they headed for Green's office. They passed by people in the hallway. This being a theatre, no one gave Dwayne's toga a second look.

Green marked out the weeks on his production calendar. "You can load in Sunday January 25 and strike on Sunday March 1. Usually you load in on Monday, but I can give you an extra day this time. That's five weeks. Five grand. What's the name of your company?"

"The Psychedelic Dream Theatre."

"Huh," Green said. "Seems appropriate."

8

Wednesday, October 29, 2003

"Rosencrantz!" Coco Nesbit cried as she swept into the barroom of the John Barleycorn Memorial Pub. She stopped inside the door and threw her arms open. Everyone in the room turned and looked. And looked some more. Coco Nesbit glowed with beauty and raw animal magnetism. Her skin shone with a deep coco glow, her eyes large and playful, her cheekbones high and pronounced above fleshy red-rouged lips that made her admirers long to kiss them. She wore a tiger stripe short jacket, open, with a fur collar teasing around her neck, a skin-tight spandex top beneath. Her long legs were hugged all the way down to her high heeled sandals in gleaming black yoga leggings. She was stunning.

Tom jumped from his chair where he'd been sitting with Dwayne and Chaz. "My lady!" he exclaimed. "My queen." He sashayed into her arms.

"No, no, my dear," she said in a deep thrilling register as she hugged him to her breast. "*You* are *my* queen!"

Tom gave a high trilling laugh. "So true," he cried. "So true!"

Coco had played Queen Gertrude in Bobby's *Hamlet*, and was just as responsible for the show's success as Bobby. She appeared a little young to be Bobby's mother, but her Gertrude was a phenomenon. She played a conniving queen who looked certain to have plotted her husband's murder with the brother-in-law she subsequently married. Her affection for her son, Hamlet, was so cloying as to seem incestuous. She was intriguing and disturbing and fascinating to watch. Dwayne imagined she might be even more amazing as the cunning and ruthless Tamora in *Titus Andronicus*, and he needed to make sure she was still committed to the production. Bobby's defection had shaken him.

"I have missed you *so* much!" she said. She kissed Tom hard on the mouth. His eyes rolled twice around their sockets.

"And I you," he squealed. He kissed her on both cheeks.

She turned abruptly toward the table where Dwayne and Chaz stood waiting. "*There are more things in Heaven and Earth, Horatio, than are dreamt of in your philosophy.*"

"Your majesty." Dwayne took a deep bow, then approached and hugged her tightly. "And, may I say, you look gorgeous."

"Of course," she said, sighing with the burden of her beauty. "And you, Dwayne, as pretty as ever. And looking so clever! I'm sure you have something brilliant planned for us all! All right, all right, sit, sit, sit," she commanded, waving them back to the table. She settled herself regally once they'd taken their seats. The three young men sat at a high top table of heavy, dark wood adjacent to a bar of even heavier, dark wood that wrapped around the center of the room in a giant horseshoe. Rotating slides of classic artworks projected onto screens high on the walls around the great barn of a room. Classical music played from the sound system. Models of sailing ships adorned the walls. The room was visually elegant, but to the nose, the John Barleycorn Memorial Pub had the stale-beer-spilled-on-the-floor-for-decades aroma of your typical neighborhood dive. It was located in Lincoln Park near a couple off-Loop theatres where they all had worked, so they knew the place well.

Chaz stretched out a hand. "Chaz Ackersley," he said.

Coco took his hand and shook it, giving him the most intense of smiles. "Coco Nesbit." She turned toward the bar as the bartender came near. "Vodka martini, Barry," she called to him. "Nice and dirty."

Barry nodded.

"I admired your Queen Gertrude very much," Chaz said, "Although you are much too young and beautiful to have been Bobby's mother."

"Yes, thank you, but you might not know, black women don't age so swiftly as white women, wrinkling up as they do like abandoned apricots. Black women retain their succulence for decades. However, you're correct. I would've had to have given birth to Bobby at two years old." She turned her gaze back on Dwayne. "What's this nonsense that Bobby won't play Aaron?"

"He decided to go to L.A. He believes he'll never be able to earn a living here."

"That punk," Coco said. "You build a *reputation* here, then you *parlay* that into money in L.A. He don't know nothing."

"You are so right," Chaz said. "People, *critics*, were insane for his Hamlet. And his Hamlet could not have shown like it did without the cast that surrounded him. Your Gertrude. Dwayne's Horatio." He noticed Tom looking at him expectantly. "And Tom's…Rosencrantz, of course."

"There are no small parts," Tom insisted.

"Vodka martini, extra dirt," Barry called from the bar. Tom hopped up to fetch it. They all clicked glasses and drank. Coco turned back to Dwayne. "But what Mr. Ackersley said goes both ways. Working with Bobby burnished our reputations, as well. My Gertrude, your Horatio, we got a lot of good notices. Would that have happened without Bobby in the lead? He talked about doing a whole series of shows with the best actors from *Hamlet*. I never read *Titus Andronicus*, but the way he described our roles! Tamora and Aaron: Queen of the Goths and her lover and chief co-conspirator, both of them incredibly ruthless. And then a reverse-race *Othello*? I was going to be Desdemona. Who has ever seen a black Desdemona? He was so excited about this. I got excited, as well."

"Me, too," Dwayne said.

She looked sadly up at one of the art slides flashing on the screen, then back at Dwayne. "I'm not sure I want to do this without Bobby."

"Wait." Dwayne lowered his voice to an insinuating whisper. "Wait until you hear the way we intend to stage this."

"I don't know, Dwayne," she said. "This is a weird-ass play. Even Bobby said it usually comes off super racist. I trusted Bobby in that role. Bobby and me together. And you directing, of course. But if we can't get someone with Bobby's fire and talent, what's this gonna be? I don't want to be in some racist bullshit."

"It's not going to be like that," Tom said with deep offense.

"Tom has some amazing plans for choreography and violence," Dwayne assured her. "We'll have live music. We'll find the best actors."

"But what if you don't?"

Dwayne *could not* lose Coco. She was too good. Too talented. Too absolutely arresting. "Look." He lowered his voice and leaned in toward her. "I don't want all the actors to know this. It'd make some of them too nervous. But I want *you* to know that Gregor Foxx is coming in from the Public Theater in New York City to see this production. I'm up for a slot in their Emerging Directors Program. But that also means Gregor Foxx will see your Tamora."

"Gregor Foxx? Oh my god! I played Beatitude Blessing in *Black People Rising* at eta Creative Arts. I loved that show. He wrote that."

"Exactly," Dwayne said. "Imagine him seeing your Queen Tamora and thinking: I need to bring Coco Nesbit to the Public Theater in New York City."

"Yes!" she said, rocking her shoulders back and forth and smiling brilliantly. Then she fixed Dwayne with a look that was all business. "So that ain't going to happen unless we got us a kick-ass Aaron and a Titus of real stature." She looked down at the table and squinted her eyes for a moment, then sat up and looked at Dwayne sharply. "I want to sit in on auditions and have approval over the casting of Aaron. I want approval of any photography of me that will be used in promoting the show. And I want double the stipend you proposed."

"Done!" Chaz said.

Dwayne looked at him in shock. Why the hell was Chaz opening his big trap?

Coco looked at Chaz quizzically, amusement curling at the corners of her eyes. "And just who are *you*, Mr. Ackersley?"

"I, Ms. Nesbit, am *the money*," he said, putting a layer of sex in his voice.

"Ah," she breathed, responding to his gambit. "The *money*. It's so nice to meet *the money*."

"We are going to make sure you get everything you want," Chaz said, leaning in, dripping with horn dog intensity. Coco seemed to enjoy it.

"Well, yes," Dwayne said nervously, "I mean, within reason." He tried to kick Chaz's ankle but hit the chair leg instead.

"In addition to being one of the producers, I am going to be in charge of the marketing and P.R. As of this moment, I am quite sure your image must be a central feature. A lot more people are going to be aware and in awe of *Ms. Coco Nesbit.*"

"Well, I like the sound of that," she breathed. She turned to Dwayne. "Under these conditions, I think we can do business." She turned and leaned forward and ran her fingertip under Chaz's chin and then touched it to his lips. She stood up, drained the rest of her martini, shook Dwayne's hand, kissed Tom's cheek, gave Chaz a wink, and swept out the door.

"She is…remarkable," Chaz said, voice hoarse with desire. He glanced back at the door, as if hoping she would reappear. "Wow. I think that went rather well."

"Are you out of your mind?" Dwayne said. "*We are going to make sure you get everything you want?* Coco Nesbit brought the *Hamlet* costumer to tears."

"But her Queen Gertrude looked great," Chaz said.

"And that costumer swore never to work with us again."

Tom slurped at his cocktail and shook his head at Chaz. "You know not what you have done."

"You have released the Kraken," Dwayne said.

Chaz's phone rang. He answered and blushed deeply red. "Oh hi, honey." It was his wife, Bonnie, the red-haired, passionate, love-of-his-life who made her living as a divorce attorney.

9

Friday, October 31, 2003

Dwayne and Angela plodded out of the downstairs studio into the shabby lobby of the Chicago Repertory Arts Playhouse with the rest of the audience. Angela leaned toward his ear. "Well, that was absolute garbage," she muttered. She frowned and stepped aside, pulling her foot abruptly up from something sticky on the carpet.

"At least the show was mercifully short," Dwayne said.

They hadn't actually wanted to see the play, but he was desperate to meet with the production's stage manager. He hated watching a bad show. You felt your life passing by, the grave getting incrementally closer as you sat, a prisoner of an excruciating boredom, longing to sneak out the door. But as much as you wanted to escape, you couldn't do that to the actors on stage. Being an actor was hard enough. You couldn't humiliate one another.

Dwayne knew how that felt. The very first show he'd done in Chicago had embarrassed him nightly. He'd landed a dream role: Jack Worthing in *The Importance of Being Earnest*, the romantic lead with a new company called Kumquats in Retrograde. Dwayne loved the script. It should have been wonderful. Dwayne had spent his four years at Northwestern pushing his body and brain to become the ultimate actor. In addition to various courses in acting and directing, he took classes in jazz and modern dance, fencing, hand-to-hand combat, quarterstaff, mime, and circus arts. He learned to move gracefully and magnetically on the stage. He was lithe and handsome. And he had wonderful comedic timing.

The first time he'd met the actress playing Gwendolyn, his love interest in the show, his heart raced. She was gorgeous. He felt immediately smitten. She shook his hand and looked him up and down like he was a race horse that had just lost her money. "You are a very pretty young man," she said finally. "But if you think we are going to fuck just because we are playing Jack and Gwen, you are wrong." And she turned and walked away.

Sadly, that moment predicted the tone of the production. The cast delivered what are some of the wittiest lines in the English-speaking theatre as though they hated one another—and the director found that hilarious. Even at the end of the play, as the two lead couples went off to supposedly happy marriages, the actors sneered at one another and the director laughed with delight.

The audiences, however, did not share his pleasure. Dwayne could hear audible groans as the cast cut into one another. He tried to play his role light and loving, but in the context of the rest of the performances, he looked like an idiot. Night after night, at least half the audience disappeared at intermission. Some got up and left during the first act.

He had called Brad Cunningham for advice. "Everybody gets stuck in a shit show now and then," Brad told him. "See it through, leave on good terms, and never work with them again."

"There's no way I can quit? No acceptable excuse?"

"No. But next time you see a listing for a company with a name like Kumquats in Retrograde, don't audition."

The show Dwayne and Angela had seen tonight had not been as bad as *The Importance of Being Earnest*, but it was close. They attended because Dwayne needed to talk with the show's stage manager, Joan Dunam. She had worked *Othello* and *Hamlet*, and Bobby had asked her to stage manage *Titus Andronicus*, as well. Dwayne had been trying to confirm, but she hadn't returned any of his calls or emails. Like performance venues, good stage managers were booked a year in advance. A stage manager could make or break a show.

"Hi, you!" Tom said, coming out of the thinning crowd, dressed and made up as David Bowie in his *Aladdin Sane* persona. "I didn't know you were coming to this. My friend Barb is in the cast."

"Give her my condolences," Angela said. "You look charming."

"It *is* Halloween. And you look *tres fabuleuse*."

"Thank you." Angela was wearing a low-cut dress that accentuated her resemblance to a young Claudia Cardinale.

"Oh, Joan," Dwayne called out, seeing the stage manager hurry though the lobby with a basket full of props. She was short and stocky, dressed in a black shirt and slacks. Her hair was done in a blunt, humorless page boy. She leaned forward as she walked with a relentless force.

Dwayne moved swiftly to block her path in the most polite manner he could manage.

"Dwayne," she said, breathing as though slightly exasperated. She looked at the other two. "Tom," she acknowledged with a nod. She frowned a moment, then remembered: "Angela."

"Yes," Angela said. "Hello."

"I wanted to make sure you've got us on your calendar for *Titus Andronicus*," Dwayne said. "I've been trying to get in touch with you."

"I don't take actor calls before a production begins. There are none of your questions I can answer until I have a rehearsal schedule."

Smile. Be accepting. Give the facts.

"I'm not acting. I'm directing *Titus*," Dwayne said.

She suddenly took in the oddity of Tom's appearance and looked him up and down.

"David Bowie. Aladdin Sane. Today's Halloween!" Tom chirped.

She turned back to Dwayne without comment. "You were an actor in *Hamlet*," she said, looking past his left ear.

"Yes. But I'm directing *Titus*."

"Huh," she said. "Directing." She looked as though she wasn't sure if she approved of this. She continued to look past his left ear. "Are you sure you won't be acting?"

"I won't," Dwayne said. *Smile. Be cool. Give the facts.* "I'm directing."

Angela looked at Joan as if she were some strange form of sea life.

"Huh," Joan said. "You have experience at that?"

"I've directed more shows than I've acted."

"Huh," she said. "Well, good luck with that." She started to head away with her basket of props.

"Hang on. We've got a production meeting scheduled for

Wednesday the twelfth. Do you have that on your calendar?"

She stopped and turned abruptly toward him. "I hadn't heard anything from Bobby in a while. I thought maybe *Titus* was cancelled. Dry Moppets wants me to do their show in February."

Dwayne felt his heart start racing. *Be cool.* Joan was a truly competent stage manager, which was a hard thing to find. Sure, she was also a strangely cold fish, but that wasn't bad in a stage manager. You wanted someone who didn't get caught up in backstage dramas. Besides, finding anyone even halfway decent would be near impossible at this late date. "Did you tell them you would?"

"Not yet." She rolled her eyes. In addition to Dry Moppets being almost as stupid a name as Kumquats in Retrograde, the company did not have a great reputation. She knew it, and Dwayne knew it.

"Good. We really need you," Dwayne said. *Lay it on.* "This is going to be a great show. At least it will be if we've got you. If not, I don't know."

Joan made no discernible reaction to the compliment. "And you are directing?" she repeated to the middle of his chest, looking straight forward from her short roundness. For some reason, this fact seemed to amaze her.

"Yes," he said. *Be cool. Give the facts.* "I'm directing and producing."

"But you're not acting?" she asked straight at the shirt button above his diaphragm.

"No. Not acting. Directing and producing."

"Because Bobby played Hamlet and directed *Hamlet,* and that made my job a lot harder."

"I know it did," Dwayne agreed. He glanced at Angela. She made an *Oh, wow* expression and turned away to pretend to look through the show postcards in the rack on the wall with Tom.

"If he'd had an assistant director, it might have been easier, but he didn't."

"Right," Dwayne said.

She took a deep breath and looked up at the ceiling and talked rapidly. "Because the stage picture is very important, and it shouldn't be the stage manager's job to make sure the stage picture is good. I've got a lot of other duties." She stopped for a moment, but continued gazing up unwaveringly at a spot on the ceiling. From the postcard rack, Angela craned her neck to see what Joan was looking at, but Dwayne secretly waved her off.

Joan took a deep breath and continued: "Bobby was always asking me: Did that look right? Is the composition good? Is anyone upstaged? Sometimes after rehearsal we were in the rehearsal space for an extra hour reconstructing the blocking so he could imagine how it had looked. He didn't have time to think that through during rehearsal while he also had to think about playing Hamlet. I don't want to deal with that again."

"No, you won't have to," Dwayne said.

"You promise," Joan said, her eyes still focused steadfastly on a spot on the ceiling.

"Yes, absolutely. Gregor Foxx is coming to see this. If he likes it, I'm going to get to work in an Emerging Directors program at the Public. That means the world to me. I'll be totally focused on my directing. You know, Foxx is the artistic director of the Public Theater in New York."

"I know who Gregor Foxx is," Joan said, looking Dwayne almost in the eye. She was actually looking at his mouth. "Why would you think I don't know who Gregor Foxx is?"

"Sorry. I don't like to assume."

"Theatre is everything to me," Joan said to Dwayne's chin. "Actors think tech people are stupid or something. But actors regularly get their own schedules mixed up."

"They do," Dwayne agreed. He felt confused. Joan's voice sounded so emotionless, but her words indicated that he'd really offended her. "They absolutely do. Yes. Sorry!"

Be cool.

"You've got a copy of the rehearsal schedule?"

"I do," Dwayne said. He pulled it out of the book bag on his shoulder. He never went anywhere without his show portfolio. Sometime he'd get an idea, and he'd have to sit down and write it out immediately. He refused to risk forgetting an idea. He gave her his copy of the schedule. He could print another.

She scanned it and nodded.

"Okay," she said abruptly. "I'll see you Wednesday the twelfth. At the Vox Populi?"

"No," Dwayne said. "We're going to be doing the show here at the Playhouse."

Now Joan looked him directly in the eye for the first time. "Here?" she said abruptly. There was something resembling actual emotion in her voice.

"Ye...yes," Dwayne said.

"Which space?" she said.

"The upstairs mainstage."

Joan turned her eyes down to the floor and shook her head for the longest time. She stared up again at the spot on the ceiling. "Can you at least get the downstairs mainstage?"

"That's the only space open," Dwayne said. "Not only here but in the entire city of Chicago, as far as I could find."

She continued shaking her head. "We aren't rehearsing here," she said at last.

Dwayne hesitated. Had that been a question? "I don't have rehearsal space reserved yet."

"Don't reserve it here," she said to a spot on the floor. Then she plodded away backstage with her basket of props. Tom and Angela rejoined Dwayne.

"Well, she's a charmer," Angela said. "Definitely on the spectrum."

"The spectrum?" Tom asked.

"Don't say it," Dwayne said.

"The autism spectrum," Angela said. "When you teach in the public schools, you see all these things. She's toward the mild side. Maybe she's got Asperger's."

"You shouldn't be saying that," Dwayne objected again. "Isn't that confidential?"

"For my students it is," Angela said. "But she doesn't look like a fifth grader to me. We're just talking. You two don't have to blab it around."

Dwayne looked doubtfully at Tom.

"What?" Tom said. "I don't blab."

"You live for gossip."

"I live for parties," Tom corrected. "And I'm going to a Halloween party right now. Want to come?"

"We're headed down to Wicker Park to the Double Door," Dwayne said. "The lead guitarist in one of the bands is also an actor, and I think they might be good for *Titus*."

Angela pulled a flier out of her purse. "These guys."

Tom looked at the flier. "Giant Rat of Sumatra?"

"Just the kind of band name theatre people would concoct," Angela said dryly.

"The guitarist is hot!" Tom said, looking at the photo.

"Ry Joodey. He leads the group," Dwayne said. "If they perform as well as their EP sounds, I might be asking Ry to music-direct the show."

Tom looked wounded. "You should have invited me! I'm the choreographer. I should have a voice in this hire!"

"Don't *you* start to make me crazy," Dwayne warned.

"I need to talk to Chaz," he sniffed.

"Nope," Dwayne said. "But you *are* welcome to come to the Double Door and give your opinion. I'll buy you a drink."

"Sold!" Tom turned to Angela. "I find guitarists incredibly sexy."

"I hope he's gay, and horny, and into very tall dancers," she said.

Tom looked deeply touched. "You are *so* sweet! I love you."

10

Saturday, November 1, 2003

Bobby had begun the process of producing *Titus Andronicus*, and then scattered the pieces to the wind. Pulling it back together made Dwayne's life feel as chaotic as the world at large. It had been two years since the Twin Towers had been destroyed on 9/11. America was fighting two wars simultaneously with an Alfred E. Neuman impersonator as President and Dick Cheney pulling the levers of power. California was on fire and the Terminator sat in the Governor's mansion. Chicago celebrated thirty-seven years of having a Daley as mayor by reelecting Richie Daley. And Dwayne had put two thousand dollars into an escrow account overseen by Tom. It was nuts.

Dwayne needed to touch base with set designer Ingrid Baardsen. They'd talked on the phone, and she was still on board to design. He needed to make sure she was progressing toward a set that would work for his vision of the show. Right now Ingrid was in a production meeting at the Playhouse for the same Dry Moppets show that had wanted Joan to stage manage. It would be going up around the same time as *Titus*, but as long as they didn't have the same tech week, it wouldn't be a conflict for Ingrid to design both. Ingrid had designed, built, and tech directed *Othello* and *Hamlet* for Bobby.

Dwayne was riding the Red Line south to meet her at the Playhouse. He looked out through the dirty window of the El train at the wide expanse of monuments in Graceland Cemetery. Autumn leaves swirled among the century-old graves, statues, and family mausoleums. All those decades of concentrated death made him think of the bodies coming back from George W. Bush's wars in Afghanistan and Iraq. All the lies and waste and people dying for nothing offended him to his soul.

Who was the George W. in *Titus Andronicus*? The emperor? Tamora tricks him into attacking Titus's family just like George W. had been tricked into invading Iraq by Dick Cheney. Cheney and friends claimed Iraq was developing weapons of mass destruction. They said Iraq had supported al-Qaeda's 9/11 attack. Both those claims proved to be false, while our soldiers continued to die.

Could Dwayne make a parallel between the emperor and George W. in the production? But then who was Titus in today's reality?

The train rolled on past Wrigley Field. It had been just two weeks since the Florida Marlins beat the Cubs right here in Game 7 of the National League Championship. No pennant. No World Series. Another heartbreak.

Who would Cubs losing pitcher Kerry Wood be in *Titus Andronicus*? He hit a two-run homer in the second (the pitcher!) and still his team lost.

No, no, no. That was ridiculous. There was no Cubs parallel to *Titus Andronicus*. It didn't line up for the Bush administration, either. He would not dress up the Emperor as George W. He would direct the show as planned and let the audiences draw their own meanings.

Dwayne arrived at the Playhouse at 4 p.m., the time Ingrid said her Dry Moppets meeting would end. He looked around the shabby lobby. A wave of disappointment flowed through him as he recognized this was the first thing Gregor Foxx would see the opening night of *Titus*. The view out the huge plate-glass window onto Lincoln Avenue was nice enough: a busy Chicago street with music clubs and restaurants and bars. But inside, the carpeting was decades old with huge, vomit-colored stains. The box office space next to the entry was slapped together from plywood and had not been repainted in years. On the other side was a tattered black curtain with a tear at the bottom masking off the entrance door to the main floor studio theatre. The short hallway that led to the main stage entrance had hunks of plaster hanging from the lath. Directly in front of him, three two-by-tens lay atop two ramshackle sawhorses that served as a concessions stand. Raymond Green skirted the fact that he had no liquor license by giving away free soda, beer, and wine for a "suggested donation." An ancient, horrifically battered refrigerator that had been scavenged from an alley stood behind the ad hoc concessions stand. It suddenly rumbled loudly to life, startling Dwayne.

The place was a mess.

Maybe Foxx would see it as Chicago storefront chic. Then Dwayne noticed that the bottom of his shoe was glued by some unidentifiable substance to the carpet. Chic? Not likely.

Be cool! Be positive!

On the plus side, some things were falling into place. Joan would stage manage. Ry Joodey and *Giant Rat of Sumatra* had sounded great last night at the *Double Door*. (Angela loved them, too, though her wish for Tom did not come true. Judging from the way Ry looked Angela up and down, he was neither gay nor into male dancers.)

Ry was excited about *Titus* in his own laid-back, ultra-cool, unflappable way. So Dwayne had his music director and his band.

"Dwayne Finnegan!" His name boomed down the stairs as though echoing from Valhalla. Ingrid Baardsen, her chin-length straight ice-blond hair swinging behind her above her large, Viking warrior body, clomped down the stairs in a pair of black leather combat boots. A huge canvass bag was slung over her ample shoulder. "There you are!" She strode directly to him and locked him in a robust embrace. "How the hell are you, Horatio?" she said, squeezing the air out of him.

"Good, terrific," he gasped. "Good to see you."

She waved him over to the alley-salvaged furniture by the plate-glass window and plopped herself into the love seat. Dwayne sat in the easy chair. His usual physical grace was impaired by the suspicion that the furniture might harbor fleas. She pulled a huge sketch book out of her bag and put it on the battered wooden cable spool that served as a table.

"*Titus Andronicus*," she said enthusiastically. She opened her book to some sketches.

"You've already begun!" Dwayne felt both relieved and worried. She was definitely on the project, but she was already developing ideas when they'd only had a vague discussion of what he wanted. What if she were barking up the wrong tree?

"As soon as I heard the show was going to be here, upstairs, I reworked my design."

"How did you hear the show was going to be upstairs?" Dwayne asked.

"I hear everything. I know everything."

"I don't even have a contract signed yet."

"Oh, ha!" She shook her head. "You're never going to get a contract from Raymond Green. Putting up a show in this place is like putting up a show in an abandoned warehouse. But it's cool. You just have to be ready for that."

"Well," Dwayne said, taken aback, "I mean he's supplying us with a lighting system, sound system, fog machine, box office…"

"Ha, ha, ha, yeah!" She threw back her big shoulders. "Ha, ha, *maybe*…if any of that is actually *working*." The smile lit up her pale broad face and rosy cheeks.

"You are scaring the shit out of me," Dwayne said.

"That's good. You know why? I also scare the shit out of Raymond Green. And that's the only way to get the smallest amount of cooperation out of that son of a bitch. I mean, I love the guy. He's a sharp guy. But the only deadline he recognizes is opening night. And then maybe it's too late, and oops, he doesn't have the right parts to fix whatever's not working. No, you need a Viking woman to put the fear of the Valkyries into that slippery bastard." She flexed her biceps, which Dwayne had to admit was impressive. "I mean, he does know his stuff," she continued, "but he's really slow to *use* any of that vast knowledge he's got."

"We'll need a really good tech director then," Dwayne said.

"I'll TD the show. That's the only sensible choice. I have a lot of experience with Green."

"You've tech directed here before?"

"Oh yeah. I'll be TD'ing the Dry Moppets show in the upstairs studio, too. So I can make sure each show gets what it needs from the upstairs inventory. The Moppets show is just a dumb, lights-up, lights-down, nothing-tech show. I can make sure *Titus* gets all the best stuff."

"Well…" Dwayne felt some sense of relief. "That sounds good."

"Yeah," she said enthusiastically. "I wouldn't do anything less. A managing director has to take care of her company."

What? Dwayne stopped. "Managing director?"

"Bobby asked me to be managing director of Shakespeare & Friends going forward, after we closed *Hamlet.*"

"Oh." Dwayne felt further confused. "But Shakespeare & Friends is no more. This is the Psychedelic Dream Theatre Company."

"Potato, potahto. I saw the press release that Bobby had named you artistic director, and you changed the name. Congratulations!"

"Listen. We aren't even thinking of looking for a managing director right now. We just want to get through this first show."

"Yeah," Ingrid agreed. "Why would we search for a managing director when we've already got one?" She smiled at him brightly, looked at her wrist watch, and closed her sketch book abruptly. "Jesus, I've got another production meeting up on Ravenswood with Remy Bumppo. Great company, but did you know it's named after a cat and a dog?" She shook her head. "The company names in this town. Crazy. I've got to get out of here. I'll see you on the twelfth with the rest of the team." She slid her sketch book back into the enormous bag and swept toward the door, her combat boots clomping.

"Wait!" Dwayne called.

"Don't you worry! It's going to be great!" she exclaimed.

And she was gone.

Dwayne hadn't gotten more than a glance at the sketch. He had an impression of platform elevations. That was something he wanted. But did he really want Ingrid Baardsen as his managing director? She was a bulldozer. She was deft at schmoozing, and often gave a person the feeling that she was totally on their side. However he'd also seen her leave people in tears. And this meeting had started and ended and he hadn't achieved any of the things he wanted—except to make sure she was working on the design.

Anyway, he hadn't promised her anything. The press release made it sound like this was a continuation of Shakespeare & Friends, but it was really a whole new company. Ingrid needed to realize that. Dwayne hadn't named her managing director. He just needed to make sure things were clear.

11

Monday, November 3, 2003

D
wayne felt a drop of nervous sweat roll down his side from his armpit. He lifted the spreadsheet he was supposed to be working on to reveal a phone list hidden beneath. He dialed the next number on it and ducked his head out of the cubicle to see if anyone was coming.

"Ebenezer Baptist Church," a happy woman's voice said at the other end of the line.

"Hi, this is Dwayne Finnegan." He was a little out of breath from nerves. "I'm calling to see if community hall room B would be available for the week before Christmas and then most of January. I'd like to rent it as a rehearsal space."

"Hello?" the happy woman said. "Could you speak louder?"

Saint Anthony's tongue!

Dwayne felt guilty doing this when he was being paid to do something else. But what was his alternative? He leaned out of his cubicle again to see if anyone was listening. He was shocked to discover Ron Buster standing just outside.

Mother of dog!

"Mr. Mulligan," Buster said brightly, with an unmistakable threat in his voice. (Did he think Dwayne's name was Mulligan?) He stood about five feet five inches tall and, like many short men, took his authority very seriously. His curly salt and pepper hair was brushed straight up, about an inch long. It reminded Dwayne of an overused wire brush. The top ends of the hairs looked as sharp as needles. Buster glared at him through his large black-framed glasses. He wore a severe black suit and white shirt with the neck open and a tuft of chest hair showing.

"I'll have to call you back," Dwayne said into the phone. He hung up.

"Not from here you won't." Buster stepped forward to block the entrance to the tiny cubicle. Dwayne felt immediately claustrophobic. His stomach turned over. He hated sneaking. He hated being caught even more.

"I noticed your phone extension lighting up. I don't believe the task I gave you required *any* telephoning."

This was Dwayne's second week working a temp assignment at Wrigley Neighbors Realty. It was a small office out of which fifteen real estate agents worked, but they were seldom around. They were usually out at showings or at the real estate attorneys or whatever. They annotated their progress on various properties on paper, and Dwayne transcribed their notes into a spreadsheet on the computer.

At least that was what he did when he wasn't on the phone trying to find a rehearsal space. It seemed most spaces were already taken. And the people in charge of the rentals were only available during office hours.

"So I have to ask: Are you doing what I pay you to do?"

"Just a quick call, Mr. Buster." Dwayne smiled brightly in full actor mode. "I'm right back at the spreadsheets. Don't worry about a thing." Dwayne looked down at the realtors' notes on his desk and up at his computer screen. The monitor had gone to the screen saver of the Wrigley Neighbors Realty logo bouncing around like a Pong ball. He nudged his mouse to bring back the spreadsheet screen and began typing in the next cell, hoping Buster would walk away.

"That won't be necessary, Mr. Mulligan."

"No worries, sir," Dwayne said brightly. "I'm on it. And my name is...."

Buster snatched the papers from in front of Dwayne. "That won't be necessary," he insisted, compressing the anger in his voice. "I'm calling your agency for a replacement. I want someone who works for his pay."

"Mr. Buster..."

"We are done here." Buster flipped through the sheets in his hand and found Dwayne's phone list of rehearsal spaces on the bottom. He crumbled it up and tossed it into the waste paper basket under Dwayne's desk.

Dwayne got up slowly, feeling much like he'd felt as a child, sent by the angry nun who taught his third grade class down to the scary priest who was the school principal. He grabbed his book bag that held his lunch and pulled his crumpled phone sheet out of the garbage. He looked at Buster. "Are you sure…"

"Absolutely sure, Mr. Mulligan. You are neither stately nor plumb, nor are you an honest worker."

"What's that?"

"Illiterate as well, it would seem. Goodbye, Mr. Mulligan."

"Finnegan," Dwayne said. He edged past Buster, got his jacket from the break room, and walked out onto the sidewalk in front of the building, feeling very low indeed. He needed that temp job. Angela's salary wasn't terrible, but it wasn't enough. They both had student loans, and they had payments on the car and the rent. And all of Dwayne's health insurance and a portion of Angela's (although Dwayne had been diverting his premiums into the vacation fund). It seemed like they'd never get out of debt. The only way they could live on her salary alone and make their payments was if they seldom went out and lived on a diet of brown rice and beer nuts.

She'd be so annoyed that he'd lost his job. She would fix him with that severe look that she no doubt trained on her errant fifth graders. It made him squirm. But what was he supposed to do? He was trying his best to make everything work.

His mobile phone rang. It was Ingrid Baardsen.

"Hey, Dwayne. Do you mind if we rehearse at a different location on Thursday nights? I've got a place that might work, but it's not available Thursdays. I might be able to find someplace else for Thursdays."

Dwayne felt instantly annoyed. "What are you talking about?" An ambulance blew by, its siren wailing. "Hang on." Dwayne turned up the volume on this phone and stepped back into the alley to distance himself from the street noise.

"What were you saying?"

"Rehearsal space. I'm trying to find something that will work within the budget. I know it's best to rehearse all in the same place. Whenever you have more than one location, you risk the actors showing up at the wrong place. Ha!" she barked. "Actors! Am I right?"

What in the sweet carbuncles on the neck of the Risen Christ was she talking about?

"You're trying to find rehearsal space?"

"Yeah," she said simply.

"You don't even know when we're rehearsing."

"Sure I do. I got the rehearsal schedule from Joan."

"How do you know the budget?"

"I went over it with Chaz. He gave me a check so I can make a deposit to hold the space. I told him the managing director handles the finances, not the artistic director, so he gave me a checkbook. He created an account with his and Aleister's investment. I love Chaz! I guess you guys go way back?"

Sweet Jesus fucking cactus in the desert! Dwayne had to hold the phone away from his head for a moment so that he wouldn't scream at her.

"Why didn't you tell *me* you were looking for rehearsal space?" he said, losing the battle to keep his voice at a conversational level. "I just now lost my goddamned temp job because I was looking for rehearsal space while I was supposed to be working."

"Well." She took a deep breath. "That wasn't bright, Dwayne. Why would you look for rehearsal space when I'm looking for rehearsal space?"

"How in hell would I know you're looking for rehearsal space?" he shouted.

"Listen, Dwayne, there's no point in getting your knickers in a knot," she said impatiently. "Everybody knew I was looking for rehearsal space. Don't you talk to anybody? You've got to keep the communications open to run a theatre company. As managing director, I'm always talking to everyone."

"You are not the managing director!" Dwayne shouted. *"And you didn't talk to ME!"*

"If we are going to be partners, I don't intend to put up with shouting." She hung up.

Dwayne looked into the face of his phone in disbelief. The blood pressure surged into his head and his ears began to ring. He cocked his arm back to smash his phone against the wall with all his strength. "GODDAMN IT ALL TO HELL!" he shouted at the top of his lungs.

A rat ran out from beneath the dumpster next to him and scurried down the alley, looking back at Dwayne in alarm. Dwayne held back his arm with difficulty and then forced his phone back into his pocket.

Chaz gave Ingrid a checkbook?!? Chaz hadn't given Dwayne a checkbook. Dwayne didn't even know Chaz had opened an account! What the living fuck?

He headed back out onto the street toward the CTA station, past a pawn shop and a storefront bar, breathing deeply but still raggedly, hoping to lower the tension he felt all through his body. He stopped and wrapped his arms around a street pole and hugged it a moment, a few frustrated sobs escaping his throat. He stood there, hugging the post until his breathing settled down. Then he noticed a parked taxi driver looking at him with a derisive expression, and he broke off his light pole embrace and continued on down the street, looking in any direction other than the taxi.

He stopped and leaned against the brick wall of a pizza joint and breathed deeply until he calmed down.

Sure, she should've told him, but the truth was he didn't want to spend another minute searching for rehearsal space. Maybe it made sense for him to leave it to Ingrid and concentrate on getting ready to direct. That was most important.

He felt a wave of misery wash over him. Why had Bobby left him? Fucking Bobby! Why had Dwayne had to beg money from his friends? Why had he lost his job? He sat down on a bench at the bus stop. He felt a sob coming up in his throat.

Get hold of yourself, Finnegan!

He stood up, and hopped up and down, and began reciting affirmations to regain his composure: He was talented! He was good-looking! He was smart! He was young and strong! He had a fleet and agile body!

Chin up, mother-fucker!

A bus pulled up at the stop and the driver looked down at him expectantly. Dwayne waved him off and strode swiftly up the street and turned the corner to head east toward the El station.

Yes, let Ingrid find the rehearsal space. Just let her do it! He would focus on directing. He would sit down with the script and the ground plan of the set. He would do the pre-blocking as he usually did, taking the tokens from the Monopoly and Clue boxes to represent the actors and moving them around the ground plan, plotting out the entrances and exits and stage movement in advance. He would discover arresting stage pictures for the most dramatic moments of the play. That's what he loved! Not the chores of producing. Let Ingrid do the drudge work. And he'd go to the temp office right now and apologize. Maybe they'd keep him on the roster. Maybe they'd give him a new assignment tomorrow. Maybe he wouldn't have to explain anything to Angela.

12

Wednesday, November 12, 2003

I t was 7:40 p.m. and most of his creative team had already arrived. Dwayne opened the door of his second-floor apartment to Ingrid Baardsen. He needed her production design. He'd fantasized planning the blocking of the show, but then realized he didn't have a ground plan from her yet.

He led Ingrid into to his living room. His apartment was a handy place to meet. The rents in Rogers Park were lower than anywhere else on the northside lakeshore, perhaps because it was the farthest north neighborhood in Chicago. He and Angela had a large two-bedroom apartment with a big formal dining room, a cockroach-plagued kitchen, and a living room with a large, semicircular bay of windows overlooking the CTA El tracks. They did have to pause conversations occasionally as a train rumbled by, but there was plenty of space for everyone.

The room was outfitted for gatherings. Well-worn sofas, love seats, and easy chairs butted side by side all the way around the semicircular room. He had found pretty much all of the furniture free. It looked like a used furniture showroom. Dwayne loved that about the apartment. There was plenty of room for a big group to sit and have lively discussions. He loved being a host. He loved everyone talking and drinking and enjoying themselves in his home. He loved it even more when they were talking theatre and planning a production.

Angela was in the back bedroom grading papers at the battered wooden dining room table she and Dwayne shared as a desk. She didn't love having a crowd in the place, but she tolerated it. To her mind, a lot of these theatre people were a little too weird.

Stage manager Joan Dunam sat in a chair with her back to the windows, her gaze centered up on a spot on the ceiling. Tom was chatting up the good-looking guitarist Ry Joodey on the love seat along the north wall. The costumer, Peaches Brown, sat across from them on the sofa on the south wall, her large sketchbook on the scruffy coffee table in front of her. Her hair was dyed in wide streaks of pastel and teased into a surreal pompadour. She wore a masculine black tuxedo jacket and trousers with a white button-down shirt open to offer a generous view of her cleavage tattoos. Betty Boop posed on the side of her left breast and a kitten wearing a fedora at a rakish angle adorned her right. Dwayne noticed her stiffen when she saw Ingrid. Was Peaches uncomfortable around Ingrid? He'd have to make sure that didn't create problems. He wanted his staff to enjoy their work.

Ingrid stopped at the head of the room. "Did y'all hear about this suicide bombing? Twenty-three people killed at an Italian police base in Iraq? Why are the Italian police in Iraq?"

Nobody knew. And nobody wanted to dive into a political conversation.

Dwayne clapped his hands and rubbed them together to stir up enthusiasm. "Okay, we're all here except our lighting designer," he said. He took a seat on the sofa with Peaches. "But we've got a lot to accomplish today, so I think we should get started, and I can fill him in on anything he misses."

Ingrid dropped her huge canvas bag on the floor with a clump and sat in one of the chairs opposite Dwayne. "He's not coming." Her tone inferred that Dwayne should already know that.

"Why not?" Dwayne said.

She stretched out her combat-booted feet in front of her. "He's not with the project anymore. I'm doing the lighting design."

"What do you mean he's not with the project? How did that happen? He was hot for this production. He's a terrific designer. He had to completely rearrange his schedule to make it work."

"Yeah." Ingrid shook her head and sighed. "That was too bad. He was really pissed at you."

"Why was he pissed at me?"

"I looked at his preliminary designs, but they didn't fit your concept. I told him I had to let him go. He'd turned down other jobs to do *Titus*, and now it was too late to get those back. He couldn't believe how inconsiderate all this was. He was really mad at you."

"You took it upon yourself to fire him? And that made him mad at me?" A vein began throbbing in the side of Dwayne's head. He'd talked much longer about his concept with the lighting designer than he had with Ingrid. It had been a big score to get him to sign on to *Titus*. He'd won two Jeff awards for his lighting designs last year, and he was becoming super popular.

"I had to protect your concept, Dwayne," she said reasonably. "You have a vision. I've got to make sure it gets realized."

"What the fuck, Ingrid? You and I talked once, briefly, about my concept! How have *you* become the final arbiter of my concept?"

"Bobby told me all about it months ago," Ingrid said. "And Tom really elaborated it for me in the past couple weeks."

Dwayne looked at Tom who smiled uncomfortably.

"And Ry and I had a long conversation yesterday," she continued. She pulled a folder from her bag, took out a sheet, and handed it down to Ry. "Speaking of which, I listened to your CD and EP and the stuff on the live tapes, Ry."

"Wait a minute! Wait a minute! Wait a minute!" Dwayne shouted. "You can't go firing people I hired. That is not your place!"

"Well, Dwayne, I can, and it is, and I did," she said evenly. "His design included a lot of rental equipment that frankly we don't need and can't afford. Chaz insisted I keep this show under budget. He and Aleister are not going to kick in a penny more, and, according to Chaz, you are not in a position to pony up, either."

Dwayne stopped cold. He couldn't argue with the money part.

"These are the songs that I think would really work for the show," she said breezily, turning to Ry.

"Wait a minute," Dwayne insisted. "That still doesn't give you the right to fire someone I hired."

"Dwayne, it's done," she said simply. "We are moving on." She handed a duplicate song sheet to Tom. "Look these over and see what you think about choreographing movement or dance to these. I notated act, scene and line numbers where I thought the songs might fit."

Ry looked over the list. "Yeah," he said. "I'll have to compare it to the script, but I was thinking about these numbers, too."

"Thanks," Ingrid said brightly. She leaned back in her chair.

Dwayne stared at her for a long moment. He looked at Ry, and Tom, and back at Ingrid. Were they really all just going to ignore him? And what was this about the music?

"Is there a reason I don't have a copy of all the recordings?" Dwayne said to Ry.

"You didn't ask," Ry said. "Tom and Ingrid asked for them. I figured they were sharing with you."

"No." Dwayne smiled uncomfortably. "I have the EP, but I need the others." He looked at Ingrid. "And could I have a copy of that sheet?"

"Oh!" Ingrid said. "I didn't think of making a copy for you! I should have had one for Joan, too. But the people who needed to see it first have got it," she said brightly, nodding at Ry and Tom.

Dwayne stood up, struggling to keep his voice calm. "Look, everybody, we have to kick this thing off together to make sure we are heading toward the same vision. I need to oversee that vision with each of you and collaborate with you directly." Tom nodded, looking vaguely guilty. Ry looked relaxed and disinterested. Slightly stoned? Peaches was looking down at the cover of her sketchbook. She seemed troubled. And Ingrid, damn her, was paging through some papers in her bag.

"Do you hear what I'm saying, Ingrid?"

"Absolutely," she said, now looking at her calendar book. "This is a collaborative art form. It takes constant communication." She fixed her eyes on him suddenly and pointedly. "That's what I've been trying to tell you all along, Dwayne," she said loudly, with an edge of harshness in her voice. "This takes communication!"

Dwayne felt a surge of outrage. *She* was taking *him* to task?? She held his gaze a moment longer, looked down at the date planner, and shook her head. "Damn it," she said. "I can't stay a moment longer. I've got another meeting." She threw her planner back into her huge canvass bag, got up abruptly, and shook Dwayne's hand. "All right. Good meeting. See you soon." She strode toward the door.

"Hang on!" Dwayne darted in front of her so she couldn't get out the door. "I need a floor plan today. And we need to talk about this managing director business."

She put her hands on his shoulders and smiled radiantly. "Thank you so much, Dwayne," she said, her face overcome with gratitude. "I have absolutely taken on *way* more than I should. And I appreciate you recognizing it. But I *can* handle it. I *will* handle it. It'll totally be worth it. Your vision is a monster! It's going to kill!" She gave him a body-crushing hug and slapped her hands to the sides of his shoulders. "Just *communicate* more!" She pulled two large design sheets from her bag and tossed them on the coffee table. "Ground plan! Front rendering! Boom! I'll have the 3D model next time," she shouted. She waved to them all. "Bye, everybody," she shouted again and swept past him out the door.

Dwayne stood there, astounded. Suddenly Peaches was brushing past him, too, clutching her sketchbook. "Gotta go," she breathed. And she was out the door.

Was she crying? What in the blood-red tears of the Magdalene was going on here?

13

Saturday, November 29, 2003

Actors auditioning for the bloody, violent *Titus Andronicus* looked a little odd performing on the set of *A Christmas Carol*. For some reason, its designer had decided the set should be painted in bright pink and blue pastels. Still, Dwayne was grateful to be able to hold auditions in the same space where his production would be. He and Tom sat in the front row of the center section of audience, a long table set up in front of them. Dwayne wrote his notes on the actors' headshots. A long 2x12 spanned the top of the armrests of the seats behind them. Atop it were five stacks of the headshots of actors they'd seen so far. The stack to the farthest left was the *Yes Yes Yes* pile of actors who excited them the most. Then came the *Yes Yes*, the *Yes*, the *Maybe*, and the fifth stack furthest right was the *Sorry, But No* stack. The stack positions were very important. Dwayne would use them to decide which actors to call back for what roles in the final auditions.

Chaz, Ingrid, and Angela were observing from the back row of the theatre. Everyone was tired. It'd been a long night. Dwayne was worried about finding a good replacement for Bobby. He was glad he still had Coco. Losing her would've been a disaster.

Joan stuck her head in the door. "Orlando Gunn," she said, and disappeared back to the waiting area. A tall, muscular, black actor strode into the center of the performance space.

"Hello, Orlando." Dwayne summoned a big smile. "Thanks so much for coming in today." He wanted every actor to feel relaxed and welcome.

"Yes, yes, hello," Tom said a bit too flirty. Orlando was extremely good-looking, and his skin-tight shirt revealed tremendous muscle definition.

Orlando extended his headshot toward them, and Dwayne reached for it. "You are the director?" he said, putting it into Dwayne's hand.

"Yes, Dwayne Finnegan. And this is Tom Collins, our fight and movement choreographer."

"Don't mind us," Angela called from the back row. "We're nobody important."

Orlando chuckled and nodded, stepping back into the center of the performance space, looking very self-assured.

"What are you doing for us today, Orlando?" Dwayne asked.

"I'd like to do the St. Crispin's Day piece from *Henry V.*"

Dwayne nodded encouragingly, belying the fact that he'd heard the St. Crispin's Day speech murdered seven times today already.

Orlando took a deep breath and fixed Dwayne with an imperious stare. "This day is called the feast of Crispin," he began. Dwayne looked down to write a note about Orlando's assurance in taking the stage, but Orlando shocked him by dropping to his knees directly in front of Dwayne to capture his eyes again. "He that outlives this day, and comes home safe, will stand a tip-toe when this day is named," he continued, smoothly rising to his feet and striding the stage, holding Dwayne's gaze always in a lock. Dwayne felt curiously trapped. He wanted to write a note about the quality of Orlando's voice. He looked down, but suddenly Orlando's forearm was thrust between Dwayne's eye and the sheet on which he wrote. "...And rouse himself at the name of Crispin and will say, these wounds," he said, pointing to a scar on his own forearm, "I had on Crispin's day." He swirled back from Dwayne, still holding his gaze.

Does he not realize I need to make notes??

Orlando continued, and when Dwayne was tempted to write a note, Orlando slapped a fist to his chest, shockingly loud. "...We shall be remembered—we few, we band of brothers; for he today that sheds his blood with me shall be my brother..." And on he went, holding Dwayne's eyes until the end.

When he finished, he took a beat, smiled, and said thank you.

"Thank you." Dwayne smiled back. Orlando saluted sharply and exited.

"My god!" Tom exclaimed, leaning into Dwayne.

"Wait, wait, wait," Dwayne said desperately, trying to remember his notes and get them down.

"Wow," Angela said from the back row. "He was super sexy."

"I'm telling you," Tom agreed.

"He was pushy. He might be trouble," Ingrid said. "I'd call his past directors and find out if he's a nightmare."

Dwayne put his headshot into the *Yes Yes Yes* pile. Not every actor realized they shouldn't play directly to the director. Orlando was the only one they'd seen who looked like he might approach Bobby's magnetism.

Joan shuffled into the space, followed by Peaches. "Orlando Gunn was our final actor of the night."

"Could I talk with you about something?" Peaches asked timidly. "In private?"

"Sure." Dwayne followed her out into the empty second-floor lobby. The lights were out, but an orangish glow from the streetlights outside illuminated the room through the tall windows along the wall.

Peaches stepped from foot to foot, twirling someone's headshot in her fingers. She squinted her eyes and shook her head. "Look." Her voice came out high and squeaky. She cleared her throat and tried again. "Look, I know it's not my place at all to comment. I know the director casts and it has to be based on what the actors do in the room. I absolutely know all that."

Where was this going?

"It's okay," Dwayne said.

"I just want you to know that I know that. And so anything I say…" She looked up at the ceiling and didn't seem to know how to finish that sentence. She suddenly thrust the headshot at him.

Dwayne looked at the headshot. "Melinda Raphael." The photo showed a pretty, smiling girl in her early twenties. Long, wavy chestnut hair framed a face with large, soft eyes, and a kissable mouth. She had auditioned earlier in the night. "Sure. What about her?"

"I convinced her she should audition. I really wanted her to work on this show. I know she'd be fantastic. She's so right. But I know she had a lot of nerves. You know. We all have a past. I'm just asking you to give her a chance, despite whatever she did in her first audition."

"Actually, she did very well." Dwayne handed her back the headshot. "I'm planning to call her back to read for Lavinia."

"Really?" Peaches looked flabbergasted. "She seemed so..." She strained her face, looking for the right word.

"She was nervous?"

"She was..." Her eyebrows popped up. Her face tilted back. Now Peaches seemed on a roll of inability to finish sentences.

"You and Melinda are friends?"

Peaches eyes widened. "Oh..." She had to think about that one. "We are..." Her voice trailed off and she shook her head, her face going through contortions, completely stymied to explain what exactly she and Melinda were.

"Anyway, I'll keep in mind your confidence in her," Dwayne said. "It's always good to know what the creative team is thinking." He smiled at her and headed back into the theatre.

What was that about?

When he got back down to the performance space, Chaz and Ingrid had picked up his carefully arranged stacks of headshots and were rearranging them into their own stacks on the table. He felt angry blood rush into his head. "Goddamn it to hell, what are you doing?"

"What's the matter?" Chaz said.

"I arranged those stacks in the order of my preference. Those piles meant something."

"That's what we're doing," Ingrid said. She pointed at the first pile. "These are my favorites. The other stack is Chaz's favorites. The middle stack has the ones we both love. And down there are the discards." She tossed Orlando's headshot onto the discard stack.

"Goddamn it!" Dwayne shouted.

"You really need an attitude upgrade, Dwayne. I'd like to see a little gratitude. It's not like I have nothing else to do." She swept out of the room.

His stacks! Some of those headshots had no notes on them. Everything depended on which stack he'd put them in.

Chaz picked up the stack of his favorites. "Some of these actors don't even look like their headshots. Did you notice that?" Dwayne glanced at Chaz's stack. Every one of them was a pretty actress. Some of them he remembered as being firmly in his "Sorry, But No" pile.

"Yes," Dwayne said loudly. "That's part of why my stacks were so important. Where's Tom?" Maybe Tom could help him fix his stacks.

"He took off. He was hoping he could catch up with Orlando for something."

"Great." Dwayne hoped Tom wouldn't scare Orlando off. Angela came down and joined them. "Well, that was amusing," she said. "You ready to go home?"

"I've got to see if I can reestablish my stacks while it's still fresh in my mind. However, after seeing one hundred twenty actors over five hours, I'll be lucky if I can remember my own name." His muscles still trembled in annoyance.

"You can stay here if you want," she said. "I'm going home. And I'm taking the car."

"Okay." He felt annoyed and oddly sad. He wished at least Tom were here to help him reconstruct what he'd seen.

Angela handed him two granola bars from her purse and then took him in her arms. "Don't be sad, Dwayne," she whispered in his ear. "Remember: You are living the dream."

14

Sunday, November 30, 2003

Late the next night, after the second round of auditions, Dwayne crept quietly into the kitchen. On top of everything else, he didn't want to wake his wife. She, at least, should have a good night. The time on the microwave said 11:15. Angela went to bed at ten on Sundays. She had school Monday morning. He found her note on the kitchen island: *Pizza in the oven. Salad in the fridge.*

God bless his saintly wife! He was so hungry.

Dwayne had seen actors from noon until 6 p.m. It was exhausting. And everything went to hell after that. He felt the frustration welling up in him again.

No! He wasn't going to think about that. He was going to have some delicious pizza that his beloved wife had saved for him. And a beer. First a beer. Yes! He pulled a Miller High Life from their aged fridge and snapped the cap off the bottle. The Champagne of Bottled Beer. See? Life could be good.

He opened the oven. No pizza. Of course, it'd be in the other side. Their huge old stove had twin ovens. The one on the left had a warming setting of 170^0, but the lowest setting on the right-hand oven was 275^0.

Their kitchen had a number of unusual features. The freezer had to be defrosted quarterly or a glacier would encroach on the top shelf of the fridge. The kitchen island had been built as the bar for Harry Hope's Saloon in a production of *The Iceman Cometh*. It had been headed for the trash when the show closed. Instead Dwayne and a friend cut it in half with a circular saw. Half went to the friend's place and half to Dwayne and Angela's. The security bars on the window overlooking the back porch and stairs had been scavenged from a downstate prison by Dwayne's shady landlord, giving it a less-than-cheerful aspect.

Dwayne opened the oven door. The handle slipped out of his beer-bottle-moistened fingers and the door slammed shut with a tremendous bang. He cringed, thinking of Angela sleeping in bed. He hoped he hadn't woken her. The spring in the oven door might have been repurposed from a heavy duty pickup truck. It was ridiculously tight, and he always forgot. That thing had slammed on him a million times.

He carefully opened the door again, pushing it all the way down, and took the pizza box out of the oven, setting it on Harry Hope's kitchen island.

"You're back." Angela stood in the kitchen doorway in her bathrobe, her curly black hair mussed from the pillow.

"I'm sorry." Dwayne's heart broke with the pain of having awakened her. "The oven door..."

"I heard. It's all right. I wanted to hear about your auditions. I knew I wouldn't see you in the morning. We've got one of those stupid seven-thirty confabs." Her principal thought nothing of wasting his teachers' time in extra meetings.

"I'm sorry," Dwayne said.

"So how was it?"

"We saw a lot of really good people," Dwayne said positively.

"And several crazy people, right?" She settled herself onto a barstool at Harry Hope's kitchen island with a grin. "I love watching the nutcases. I truly do."

"We had one guy throw himself on the floor doing a Macbeth despair soliloquy, but he was off-balance, and his forehead hit with a whack. When he got up, he had this huge red welt, and he seemed a little unsure of the rest of his lines."

"My god."

"I don't think he planned that. Everyone gasped when he hit."

"So the whole party was watching again? Ingrid and Chaz and Tom?"

Dwayne took a deep breath. Angela took in the pain on his face. "They messed with your stuff again?"

Dwayne put his hands on the bar and closed his eyes.

"Ingrid drove you crazy, right?" She took a sip of Dwayne's Miller High Life, then got up and got him a new one. "What about the throw-self-on-the-floor guy? I guess you're not calling him back."

"Actually, I am." Dwayne pulled himself back from the emotional abyss. "He was fully committed."

"Sounds like he ought to *be* committed."

"Ha!" Dwayne opened the pizza box. "I'm sorry. I'm so hungry." He picked up a slice and took a bite. It was hard and dry. He chewed it, but it was so dry, he had to take some beer in his mouth at the same time to soften it. He chewed and chewed, and then swallowed, and had to take another gulp of beer to get it down his gullet.

"I guess it was in the oven too long, huh?" Angela said. "I thought you would have been back earlier."

He looked at the slice in his hand. So dry. So unappealing. He'd been so happy she'd saved pizza for him. It lifted his heart when he'd seen her note. And now it was inedible. It was so disappointing. So disappointing at the end of such a disappointing day. His arm dropped to his side, and he shook his head.

"Hey, Dwayne, come on. It's not so bad."

But he couldn't shake it off. It was that one last thing, late at night after a long and difficult day. He bent over and put his head down on the bar.

"What did they do to you, Dwayne?" Angela got up and took the slice out of his hand and wrapped her arms around him. She rubbed his back while she hugged him. "It's all right. Just watch this."

She got a saucepan out and put it on the stove, poured half a jar of pasta sauce into it and lit the fire. Then she got a bag of shredded mozzarella out of the refrigerator and dropped a good fistful atop the sauce. Dwayne wondered what she was up to.

"Just watch." She took out the chef's knife and cut the squares of hard pizza into half their width. "The Guiseppellis know how to resurrect pizza. This is a trick I learned from my Grandpa Guiseppelli. Sit down."

Dwayne sat at one of the barstools, his misery abating, and Angela brought the pan of bubbling, cheese-topped sauce to the table.

"You just take one of these." She picked up one of the narrow thin crust pizza slices, dipped it into the hot red sauce and scooped up some of the cheese atop. She held it over the pan to cool and then popped it in her mouth and chewed and swallowed. "Delicious."

Dwayne tried it. The sauce moistened the dry crust and the extra melty cheese made it tasty. "This *is* good," he declared.

"See? Even after a hard day, the foods of Italy can resurrect your spirit."

"Your grandfather used red sauce out of a jar?"

"He'd sooner walk barefoot over broken glass. No, the sauce would be from a deep kettle of homemade red sauce. And he made his own mozzarella and grated it himself. But it's the same principle."

"Thank you, Angela."

"Okay, Dwayne, tell me something funny that happened today."

Dwayne took a deep breath. "Okay. We had this one actor, very fetching young thing, who seemed to be taking pains to make sure we could see down her blouse, bending forward and bowing, addressing *Your Majesty* in her monologue, and then I heard this tremendous clang from behind me and turned to see Chaz banging his head into one of the light instruments overhead as he stood up to get a better view. Then he lost his balance and tumbled into the row of seats in front of him."

"Ha!" Angela snorted. "That's fantastic. I love Chaz, but he is a terrible horn dog."

"You don't know the half of it."

"Why? What happened?"

"I needed to decide who to call back so we can schedule them for Tuesday. I thought Chaz and Ingrid would give me their lists of who they liked and go away, and Tom and I could go over our notes and make the decisions. But those two insisted on sticking around for the whole thing. I couldn't convince them to get out of there." He shook his head and stuffed another sauce-dipped slice of pizza into his mouth.

"Did you straighten her out on the managing director business?"

"I tried! She kept saying: *That's not the issue right now. We have to focus on casting.* And then she'd say: *Don't worry about me overextending myself. I want to do this.* As if *that* were my concern."

"Did you get through with selecting the actors to call back?"

"Ingrid wanted to skip over call-backs with seven of the actors. *I'm ready to cast these roles right now,* she says. And she puts down a list of names assigned to roles. *I've got their phone numbers written down, so I can get on the phone and offer the roles tonight. We can get through call-backs in half the time,* she says. And she's looking very proud, like she's come up with this terrific idea."

"What did you do?"

"I told her: *You are not to call any actors ever for anything.* She looked very offended. And I repeated: *Never...for...anything! You do not have actor contact. Out of bounds.* She says: *A managing director offers the talent their roles and oversees their contracts.* But then Joan stands up, God bless her, and she says: *A managing director draws up the contracts. But roles are offered by a casting director or the artistic director. All other cast communications go through the stage manager.* And she looks Ingrid in the eye and says: *I will not have confusing communications going to the cast.*"

"I've never seen her look anyone in the eye."

"Me neither," said Dwayne. "But she protected her turf."

"That's good."

"But I still couldn't get rid of the two of them. Chaz kept insisting I cast all the prettiest girls. *Look at television,* he says. *It's all beautiful people. That's what the audience wants.*"

"Horn dog," Angela muttered.

"And Ingrid wanted to discuss her favorites at length, trying to insist I commit to casting before we even had call-backs. It took hours to get rid of them, and then after that, it was hard to remember what we'd seen and liked. Those two scrambled my thoughts."

"I'm sorry, Dwayne."

"I want this show to be fantastic, but they make my job harder. I wish I could lock them out of callbacks."

"I've got an idea," Angela said with a delightfully evil grin.

15

Monday, December 1, 2003

D wayne stood at the antique porcelain urinal, emptying his bladder thoughtfully. Classical music wafted through air that also carried the stale scents embedded in the grout of the floor tiles at the John Barleycorn Memorial Pub. Dwayne mused on the interplay of sound and scent as he zipped up his fly. The stale aroma created a curious synergy with the musical musings of Ludwig Van Beethoven and the visual array of the graciously yellowing porcelain beneath his hands as he washed them at the sink.

Interplay is all.

Dwayne was the arbiter of interplay. His job was to convince a group of wildly eccentric individuals that their deepest desires would be fulfilled if they designed and performed in harmony with what Dwayne wanted—not because it was what Dwayne wanted—he had to keep them believing they were doing what *they* wanted. And in the end, it *would be* what they wanted, for they, above all things, wanted their work to shine in a highly successful production.

Right?

Dwayne emerged from the Men's Room and saw Aleister had arrived and was seated at the bar. He approached and laid his hand gently on Aleister's shoulder. His dear old friend. He needed to bring him into the interplay.

Dwayne signaled the bartender who was walking past behind the bar. "Hey, Barry. Could you get my friend, Aleister, a Remy VSOP? And a PBR for me." The bartender nodded, and Dwayne slid onto the seat next to Aleister.

How to broach this?

"I'm kind of concerned about your investment in the show."

Aleister leaned back and looked at him suspiciously. "Really? About my investment? How's that?"

"It's about the casting," Dwayne said. "So much of the success of a show depends on getting the right cast."

"Sure…"

"Good casting is essential. I *really* don't want you or Chaz to lose your money."

"That'd be my preference, as well." The bartender brought their drinks. The men clicked beer bottle to brandy snifter and enjoyed a first sip.

"However, Chaz and Ingrid are making casting difficult."

"Ah. You want me to get them out of your hair," Aleister said flatly. "I wasn't planning to attend auditions. I figured I wrote you my check, and I'll see you opening night."

"Which would have been great!" Dwayne said. "But I was thinking if you and Chaz and Ingrid had an *investors' meeting* after we'd seen all the actors, the three of you could go off to that. And Tom and I would be able to cast the show in peace." Dwayne looked at Aleister hopefully. This had been Angela's idea, and he loved it.

Aleister appeared oddly sad.

"The audition process is fascinating!" Dwayne encouraged. He pulled his barstool in closer to his friend.

Aleister raised his eyebrows. "Actually, it sounds like casting is one of those sausage situations. The end result might be delicious, but you don't want to watch it being made."

Dwayne slumped against the bar. "You're right! But I really need to get those two out of my hair. They don't just give opinions, they insist on them, *ad nauseam*, until I can't even remember what my own opinions were."

"Why would Chaz think he knows anything about casting?"

"Chaz just wants to cast all the prettiest girls. Even in the male roles."

"Sounds like Chaz." Aleister gazed into his cognac with a forlorn expression.

"I could deal with Chaz, but Ingrid Baardsen is like a Viking marauder, decapitated heads rolling at her feet. And my production is on a boat drifting out to sea while she shoots flaming arrows into its sail."

"You're the director. Throw them out."

"I must've asked them thirty times to leave last night so that Tom and I could finish the callback list, but they kept wrangling with me for three hours."

"How am I supposed to help with that?"

"I'll tell Chaz you need to meet to go over the budget and discuss plans for marketing. It's your money at stake, so you have a vested interest. Budget and marketing is totally a managing director concern, so Ingrid would have to attend."

"I thought you didn't want her as managing director."

"I don't!" Dwayne's face creased with frustration. "But Chaz gave her the company checkbook and nothing I say seems to affect her. Once this show is over, I'll never use her for anything again. But for now..."

"Yes, I see."

"I need help, Aleister." He took a deep breath. "Remember in fifth grade, when I came in mid-year? I was the new kid and the other boys were tormenting me, and you became my friend."

"You are the only person I've ever heard of getting thrown out of a Catholic school. Even your little sister made it through high school."

"She told all the adults she planned to be a nun to cover her drinking and indiscriminate sex. But when I got kicked out, it was you came to my aid. I need your help again."

Aleister turned to face the bar, and looked down at the wood surface in front of him. "I read the script yesterday afternoon."

"Yeah?"

"The amount of violence is really overwhelming." He spoke so quietly, Dwayne could barely hear him. Classical music played discreetly in the background.

"It is violent."

"When I got to that point where they raped Titus's daughter and cut out her tongue so she couldn't report them, I just kept thinking of Lisa." He still didn't look at Dwayne.

"I'm so sorry." Dwayne put his hand on his friend's shoulder. It had been three years since Aleister's wife Lisa had been killed. The pain was still fresh.

"When that junkie shot her," Aleister said, "she fell down on the floor." Dwayne leaned closer to hear. "I asked the clerk later, did she have any last words, but he told me she couldn't speak. She was trying to get a breath, but her throat was choked with blood. She died, gagging on the dirty floor of that convenience store. It was like her tongue was cut out of her." He started to sob.

"Oh, come on, come here." Dwayne got up and gathered his friend in his arms. They stood and hugged by the bar as Aleister sobbed. The bartender came by with a quizzical look.

"His wife died," Dwayne whispered.

Barry nodded. "Sorry for your loss." He brought back glasses, the bottle of Rémy Martin, and poured out two shots. "On the house."

"Thanks, Barry."

"This world is just as violent and cruel as Shakespeare's," Aleister said.

"Yeah." Dwayne was getting emotional himself. He'd loved Lisa, too. Where Aleister was slow-talking and intellectual, Lisa had been bright and energetic. Petite, blond, and pretty, she was always a breath of life. They'd spent a lot of time together. Dwayne, Aleister, and Chaz had been friends since they were kids. As they dated and married, Angela, Lisa, and Bonnie became part of that circle. In fact, Dwayne had introduced Aleister to Lisa.

"I'm so sorry. And forget I asked about tomorrow. I'll figure out something else."

"No, it's fine. I'll do it."

"Really?" Dwayne said.

"Yeah. But I'm not sitting through the auditions. Just tell me what time you think it'll be ending, and I'll show up. I can bring them over here for the meeting."

"Oh my god, thank you," Dwayne said. "You don't know this means to me."

16

Tuesday, December 2, 2003

The sound of Chaz whispering distracted Dwayne once again. He wasn't paying much attention to the callbacks. Every possible moment, he was huddling with Coco Nesbit, who was already cast as Queen Tamora. She was there to read in scenes that involved her character. She also wanted a voice in who would play Aaron, Bobby's former role. She seemed to be enjoying Chaz's attentions, which worried Dwayne. What would Bonnie think of the way her husband was carrying on?

Joan came into the space and announced the next scene. "Orlando Gunn, the soliloquy with Tamora."

"Hey, everybody." Orlando strode into the space with the cocky assurance of Samuel L. Jackson in *Pulp Fiction*. Coco hopped down onstage to join him. The pastel-painted set of *A Christmas Carol* looked especially absurd behind the two of them, but there was plenty of empty stage in front of it for them to work.

"Great," Dwayne said. "In Shakespeare's original, you'd be alone on stage for this soliloquy, but we'll be doing it as a dance. Tamora will circle you, dancing, with the music low, as you begin the soliloquy, and then you'll come together at the end and the band will get louder. Tom will provide choreography in rehearsal." Tom waved. "But for now, just play with it." He wasn't expecting much from this improvised movement. It was an experiment to look for the chemistry between the two actors and how well Orlando could think on his feet.

"Great," Orlando said. "Love to."

"And don't address it to me." Dwayne remembered Orlando's first audition. "Address it to your scene partner and to the people in the top back row. Be large!"

Orlando nodded. He and Coco looked at one another for a moment, smiled, and then he started in. "Now climbeth Tamora Olympus' top," he declaimed, his voice thrilling, gesturing to the gorgeous Coco, "Safe out of fortune's shot; and sits aloft…" She closed her eyes for a moment and then began to glide across the stage in a slow dance step. "Secure of thunder's crack or lightning flash; advanced above pale envy's threatening reach. As when the golden sun salutes the morn," he reached his hand up into the sky and it was as though they could see the sun burst over the horizon. "And, having gilt the ocean with his beams, gallops the zodiac in his glistering coach, and overlooks the highest-peering hills." He swept gracefully to her side as she danced and effortlessly picked her up by the hips and carried her smoothly aloft, as though she weighed nothing. Dwayne was amazed. The two of them were gorgeous together: Their sculpted faces and dark, smooth complexions. Breathtaking.

"So, Tamora." He swept her downward and then aloft again, Coco's trajectory through the air seeming to follow the direction of her gaze. Orlando's face exuded charm and mischievous evil. Dwayne loved it.

"Then, Aaron, arm thy heart, and fit thy thoughts, to mount aloft with thy imperial mistress." He brought her down into his arms, face to face. "And mount her pitch," he said, the two of them gazing into one another's eyes like passionate lovers, "whom thou in triumph long hast prisoner held, fettered in amorous chains." They stepped together in a dance, something like a tango, and yet more modern and somehow also timeless and very sexy, and he spun her, increasing the tempo of the dance, giving his lines more loudly, more forcefully: "Away with slavish garments and servile thoughts! I will be bright, and shine in pearl and gold." The pleasure of evil showed in his face once again. He spun her back to him, and away again across the large stage. "To wait upon this new-made empress." He bowed down, paused, and gave the audience a gleaming, calculated smile. "To wait, said I? to wanton with this queen!" He pulled her tight and ground his hips into hers, and she moaned with pleasure. "This goddess, this nymph, this siren, that will charm Rome's Saturnine, and see his shipwreck." Then he dipped her and, tucking both arms below her, lifted her into the sky like an exquisite offering before flipping her smoothly back to her feet. They faced each other, smiling in their mastery, turned to the audience, and bowed.

"Wow," Tom shouted. "Bravo!"

Everyone in the room applauded. Coco turned to Orlando and gave him a kiss on the mouth. She sidled past Tom and Dwayne at the table in the front row of the center section of seats. "I guess you got your Aaron," she murmured, sotto voce.

Dwayne didn't reply, but inside he had to agree. Orlando was absolutely electric. And the two of them showed tremendous chemistry. He'd felt positively aroused—and a little frightened—watching them.

He made a couple notes on Orlando's sheet. When he looked up, both Chaz and Joan stood in front of him.

"Are you ready for the next?" Joan said.

"I'm not so sure about Orlando," Chaz said, very quietly. "I'm not sure he's right for Aaron."

"Orlando is gay," Joan said dully.

"Oh," Chaz said. He thought about it for a moment. "Actually, I thought he looked pretty good."

"Jesus," Joan said under her breath. "I'll bring in the next actor." She went back out into the hall.

"Have you checked in with Bonnie tonight, Chaz?" Dwayne said pointedly. "I know you drove straight here from Oak Brook."

Chaz pretended to be confused. "Yeah, don't worry." He returned to his seat.

The callbacks took longer than needed. They were seeing some actors Dwayne would have ruled out if Ingrid and Chaz hadn't messed with his headshot stacks. It was a shame to waste their time (and his). But it all worked out.

He was tremendously pleased with Wallace Proctor, a barrel-chested veteran actor in his mid-fifties, with a grizzled face and salt and pepper hair. Wallace looked and acted every inch the Roman general: tough, determined, and no-nonsense. But when he played the scene in which he discovered his daughter's rape and disfigurement, he was heart-breaking. And when his emotions shifted from emotionally crushed to vengeful, he was terrifying.

Dwayne loved him.

When Ingrid was about to leave for the producers' meeting with Chaz and Aleister, she set a cast list in front of Dwayne with every role assigned to a specific actor. "I think we can agree that you will use at least half of my suggestions," she said.

Dwayne did not respond.

"Coming?" Chaz called to her. She frowned, but followed him and Aleister out of the performance space.

Dwayne set her list aside. He might look at it after he and Tom had made their choices. Or not. He had great actors to choose from. He felt very good indeed.

17

Wednesday, December 10, 2003

"Well, all right." Wallace's deep baritone came over the phone line. "Time to strap on the harness once again."

Dwayne held his headshot in his hand, picturing the actor at the other end of the line looking gruff but pleased. "Then you accept the role?"

"Absolutely, old man. It's a shame you don't pay more, but I could have guessed. Typical non-Equity pittance. But I love the role. Is Coco Nesbit in this?"

"She plays Tamora."

"Wonderful," Wallace said. "I've seen her work. Formidable."

"Joan will be in touch with all details."

"I look forward to it. Excellent!"

Dwayne loved calling actors to offer them a role. It was one of his favorite things about directing. So many of them were so happy to be cast. Most accepted the role on the spot. In a few cases an actor turned down a role, and Dwayne had to call his second choice, but those actors were also very good. By the end of the week, he had his full cast confirmed.

However, a few days later when he was back at the Playhouse for a design meeting, he wondered why his production staff couldn't behave as happily. Chaz was sitting at the head of the table, and Coco was sitting in his lap, running her fingers through his curly hair. Upstage, the pastel set of *A Christmas Carol* completed the scene.

"You see this, Peaches," Coco said to the costume designer, allowing some Caribbean lilt to play into her voice, "the amount of kink he got in his hair, this Chazzly-boy, he might well have some African ancestors."

Peaches opened her mouth, then closed it. She appeared vastly uncomfortable. Ingrid was looking through a stack of drawings and ignoring everyone else entirely.

"Really?" Chaz said. "How would that be?"

"Over the years, lots of light-skinned blacks decided to pass, and they filtered into white society and never came back, never told their children their true history, thinking it would be better for them. So you got some people who believe they are totally white, but they got some great great African grandmammy that was brought over on the slave boats."

Chaz tilted his head. "Huh."

"But you see, a deep, dark skin woman like me, my ancestor women didn't have no truck with the master's pecker. We didn't get the white man blended into our genes."

Dwayne felt stymied. On the one hand, a beautiful actress was sitting on his married friend's lap. Shouldn't he say something about that? On the other hand, the actress was also a black woman who was, however casually and playfully, talking about slavery. And Dwayne never felt like he should say anything when black people were talking about slavery.

"All right," Ingrid said loudly. "I've got another meeting in an hour up in Rogers Park, so let's get started." She pulled a laptop with a large screen out of her big canvas bag, and started it up on the table in the center of the stage. The team crowded around to see. "Now, Chaz, Aleister, and I had the preliminary marketing meeting last week while Dwayne and Tom were working on casting. We got some great stuff started." She brought up a browser and logged onto their newly created website. The header read Psychedelic Dream Theatre across the top in a font like that on the cover of Jimi Hendrix's first album. Below that was a sultry photo of Coco lounging in a revealing costume. And below her was the headline *Titus Andronicus*, with details about the production below that.

"We got some exceptional publicity photos," Chaz said. "And God bless Peaches for constructing costumes so quickly."

"All this happened in the past eight days?" Dwayne asked. This was far more than he expected. "Costumes, photo shoot, website?" He noticed Peaches looked even more uncomfortable than before.

"We did a photo shoot in here." Ingrid gestured to the stage space around them. "I knew just how to set up under the lights to get those terrific shots."

"Click through to the photo page," Chaz said.

Ingrid clicked on a link to a slide show page showing photo after photo of Coco in a variety of sexy costumes. Dwayne wondered how she could have that many costume changes in the show.

"See, I kept the light off the set, so the background is just black behind her. You can't even see this pastel monstrosity upstage." She flipped her hand toward the *Christmas Carol* set. "Very dramatic."

"I love how I look," Coco purred, leaning on Chaz's shoulder as they viewed the slideshow.

"I told them it seemed…odd to be constructing costumes before the director had seen the designs," Peaches said nervously. "Sorry, Dwayne, but Chaz said…"

"Absolutely," Chaz interrupted. "This is all on me. Peaches was fantastic. I'm giving her a bonus. We needed publicity photos ASAP. She showed us her preliminary sketches. We tweaked them a little bit together, and voilà!" He gestured to the screen.

"These costumes are *based* on my preliminary sketches." Peaches' voice trembled. "But what they look like *now*…" She shook her head and appeared to be holding back tears.

"She was a really good sport," Chaz said heartily.

Dwayne watched as shot after shot of a luminescent Coco flashed on the screen. "No photos of Wallace, Orlando or Melinda?"

"Yes!" Peaches said, surprisingly forcefully. "Why aren't we getting any photos of Melinda? I mean, she is really beautiful." She looked around at all the design team members, trembling. She avoided looking at Coco, who looked insulted by her outburst.

What was this about?

Chaz broke the awkward silence. "We had to move quickly," he said. "Dwayne and Tom were still finalizing the cast. And I think it's undeniable that these photos of Coco are going to sell more tickets than anything we could have done with Wallace or the rest."

"You are so sweet," Coco purred, running her finger up the back of Chaz's ear.

"Marketing, darling," Chaz said. "It's basic marketing."

"If we attract an audience expecting something sexy," Dwayne said, "won't they be disappointed with a show that's full of violence and revenge?"

"Sex and violence!" Chaz said brightly. "They go together like soup and sandwich!"

"Are the costumes all right, Dwayne?" Peaches asked, her lower lip trembling. "I thought I should call you, but Chaz and Ingrid said no."

"They're a bit more risqué than I was expecting."

Coco blew a raspberry.

"Tamora trades on sex," Chaz insisted. "Look at how she goes from prisoner to Queen of Rome! That's all about her magnetic sexuality."

"That's true." Dwayne admitted reluctantly. He looked over Peaches' preliminary drawings and the alterations. He didn't want to make her any more uncomfortable. He knew how Ingrid and Chaz could be bulldozers. "Well, we'll see how these costumes work with the rest of the design as we proceed."

"Oh, nah." Coco stood imperiously. "*These* are the costumes I'm wearing. Ain't no doubt about that."

"Well, we'll see," Dwayne said quietly but firmly.

"The full costume design must work together…in harmony." Peaches sounded nervous but forceful. "Costume designs are…" Peaches looked uncertainly from Dwayne to Chaz to Coco and back to Dwayne again, and then looked down at the table. "…the *director* must approve all the designs."

"Uh huh," Coco said lightly. "Well, well, well…"

"Let's look at more of the website," Ingrid interrupted.

"Peaches is absolutely right about the designs," Dwayne said. "We also need to see more of the cast."

"We can get action shots once we are in rehearsals," Ingrid said brightly. She clicked the link to the Who's Who page. There was Dwayne's headshot as artistic director on the left. On the right was a short bio that Ingrid had picked up from the *Hamlet* program. She had not asked him to supply an updated one. Next was Ingrid's headshot and a much longer bio for her as managing director.

Dwayne felt his gorge rising.

"Ingrid said she wasn't sure she could continue as managing director beyond the run of this show," Chaz said. "But I told her to list herself as managing director anyway. We want to give the appearance of a full, robust organization."

"It really is taking on a lot," Ingrid said. "Producing, designing set, designing lights, tech directing, overseeing marketing, creating the web site, finding rehearsal space…"

Dwayne didn't know whether to agree or throw up his hands and scream. She had taken on half of those tasks without consulting him. He didn't want to be in charge of everything, but his was the eye that had to make sure everything worked together. He'd lost his temp job needlessly looking for rehearsal space while she was doing it without telling him. Which reminded him: "Where *are* we rehearsing, anyway? I keep trying to find that out from you."

"Here, silly. I told you that."

"No. You didn't tell me anything, Ingrid. And what do you mean by *here*? Here on this stage?"

"No, no, no. *A Christmas Carol* will be running in here. We're rehearsing in the rehearsal room."

"Rehearsal room?" Dwayne said. "There's no rehearsal room in this building."

"Oh, Dwayne." She chuckled as though he were pulling her leg somehow. She looked at her oversized wrist watch and jumped out of her seat. "I've got to run. Another production meeting!"

"Wait! We've got to discuss some adjustments to the set so I can finish pre-blocking." With audience on three sides of the action, how he arranged the actors on the stage was more important than usual.

"Don't worry," she said, grabbing her laptop off the table. "It's going to be great." She snatched up her shoulder bag, and shot out the door.

18

Sunday, December 14, 2003

The day before the first rehearsal, Dwayne got a call from Joan. "You've got to get over here." No *Hello*. No *This is Joan*.

"Where is here?" Dwayne said.

"Playhouse." Her tone suggested Playhouse was one of the seven circles of hell. She hung up. Dwayne had been going over his notes for the first rehearsal, but now he was worried. Angela was deep in grading fifth-grade essays, so he took the car to the Chicago Repertory Arts Playhouse, his stomach churning.

As he drove down Lake Shore Drive, gusts of wind whipped up white caps on the lake all the way out to the horizon. It blew in from the east across the water with nothing to stop it. He felt the car rock as he drove. The temperatures were in the upper twenties, but the wind made it feel sub-zero. Personally, he felt buffeted by both the airstream and his sensations of bedlam and anarchy.

Bobby had been totally comfortable with other people in charge of their areas. He didn't even *want* to know what they were doing. He just focused on his own jobs, and it turned out wonderfully for his *Othello* and *Hamlet*. But Dwayne was preparing for Gregor Foxx. He needed to know that things were proceeding toward a unified vision.

He turned on the radio. George W. Bush was announcing the capture of Saddam Hussein. So that would make W. a big hero now, Dwayne supposed. He turned the radio off. He toyed again with the idea of modeling the emperor on Bush.

Nah.

He exited the Drive at Fullerton and circled around to come up Lincoln from the south. It was Sunday, so Dwayne could park for free in front of the theatre.

That would be the highpoint of his day.

"Sorry," Raymond Green said to him as he walked into the lobby, "I totally intended to have everything out of there." Green had a typically vague expression on his face and a box full of electrical connectors in his arms.

"What out of where?" Dwayne said.

"Your rehearsal space. I would have had it cleared by tomorrow in time for your rehearsal, but your stage manager wants it cleared today. Which is fine, but I'm tied up at the moment. So you're on your own." He disappeared behind a curtain into the main floor main stage theatre.

Dwayne went up to the rehearsal room and found Joan angrily sorting boxes and stacks of stuff into three piles. She did not look at Dwayne as he entered the room. "Ten pounds of shit in a five-pound bag," she muttered. She continued to sort as Dwayne took off his jacket and hung it on a coat tree by the door.

The room had a colossal amount of crap: Styrofoam heads for styling wigs, cheap plastic and wooden swords, puppets, boxes of scrap wood, boxes of posters and programs, rolls of fabric, spools of wire and cable, model airplanes with parts of their wings broken off, a small stove, an ancient refrigerator, a wild array of living room, dining room, kitchen and desk chairs, a small kitchen table, side tables, a coffee table, a giant papier-mâché man-eating plant, two machetes, a box of rubber noses, stacks of old scripts, costumes hung up on rolling racks and costumes folded and stacked on the kitchen table and costumes thrown into a heap on the floor.

There was no room for people to stand, much less for actors to rehearse a play.

"Where is all this supposed to go?"

"Basement," Joan said. "And garbage. Fortunately no shows are closing this weekend, so we've got plenty of space in the dumpsters."

"Did Green tell you what's trash and what's to be saved?"

Joan looked up into the ceiling directly above his head. "Have you ever *met* Raymond Green?"

"I guess that means no," Dwayne said.

Joan grunted. She pointed at the stack of boxes and materials closest to the door. "I got started on sorting. Let's take this stuff first." She put one box atop another and picked them up. Dwayne followed her with a large, heavy spool of cable in his arms down the hallway, down the stairs, across the lobby, into the door of the studio theatre. They carried the materials across its stage through the door at the back into its tiny dressing room, through that dressing room into the larger dressing room for the main floor main stage, onto that stage and up the aisle to the back of the theatre. They continued into a treacherously organized back stage to a dangerously steep stairway down into an ancient basement space with a moldering brick foundation. A slow stream of water trickled across the basement floor. The air felt massively humid and imbued with mold spores.

It was a tiny basement space given the size of the building above it. Apparently, one hundred years ago, or whenever this building was built, its architects decided to dig only a partial basement. The space that was available was divided into flimsy lockers made of slat wood. There was plenty of space between the slats to see what was in each locker, and none had padlocks on the doors.

The locker on the farthest left was empty and had wood pallets across the floor. "We're going to put all the electrical, lighting equipment, tools, and usable lumber and hardware in that one," Joan said. "I found those wood pallets in the alley. Everything that was in this locker had been ruined by sitting in water, so I already put all that in the dumpster. The pallets will keep this stuff dry." She pointed at the next locker. "This one will be for costumes, wigs, prosthetics, and hand props." She pointed at the next. "Furniture, practical lights, large stage props, and weaponry in here." She pointed at the final locker that was already fairly full. "Scripts and any other paper goods that look worth saving in here, on top of the other stuff. Got it? You'll be in charge down here."

"Got it," Dwayne said. "You have helpers coming?"

"Peaches. Ingrid was too busy," she said bitterly. "Peaches didn't sound like she'd come until she heard there were costumes and wig holders, and I told her she could take home whatever she wanted."

"Can we really do whatever we want with this stuff?" Dwayne said.

"Obviously Green doesn't give a shit or he would have already dealt with this. My plan was to save the costumes that are folded or on hangers and throw away the rest. Peaches will do something more nuanced." Joan's voice simmered with suppressed rage. At no moment while she was speaking did she look at Dwayne. She hadn't looked at him since he'd arrived.

"Okay." Dwayne got on the phone and discovered Tom and Chaz were willing to join them.

With the four of them to stack stuff into the lockers or dump it into the dumpsters while Joan decided what should go where, they were able to clear the rehearsal room in two and a half hours. Dwayne was amazed, given the mess it had been at the beginning. He had moments of trepidation, such as in throwing out boxes of typed play scripts (whose archive was this?) and when they used two machetes to chop a giant man-eating papier-mâché plant into disposable pieces for the dumpster. Surely someone would do *Little Shop of Horrors* again sometime, but Joan assured him that this particular man-eating Audrey was in such poor condition, it would have to be rebuilt anyway. Chaz and Tom enjoyed chopping it to bits.

Once the rehearsal room was cleared, swept, and damp mopped, Joan shoed them away so she could tape out the set and prepare for tomorrow. Dwayne took the other three for beer and pizza in thanks. He sent a large Italian beef sandwich, fries and a soda up to Joan.

Taping out the set was a basic necessity. Stage managers took the ground plan of the set and used multiple colors of gaff tape to mark out the locations of walls, doors, entryways, stairways, platforms, and other features on the rehearsal room floor so that actors could orient themselves to a set that had not yet been built. Some stage managers liked help and camaraderie while they taped out the set. Others preferred to work alone. Joan fell into this latter camp.

♦ ♦ ♦

When Dwayne arrived at the rehearsal space for the first read-through the next day, Joan seemed extra annoyed.

Then he saw it.

The room was not big enough to contain their entire set. Joan had centered the set in the space that was available, but rather than stop taping where the space ran out, she continued to tape out the rest of the set going up the walls. If they could have folded down the walls, the entire set would playable.

In one sense, taping the rest of the set up the walls of the room did allow the actors to see how much more set remained. On the other hand, the tape up the walls looked like the angry work of an insane person. The actors giggled at it as they arrived.

Having worked with Joan before, he expected her to call the group to order when six p.m. arrived. She, however, just sat in her chair staring at the tape on the wall. The cast chatted together, seated around the double table, their scripts in front of them.

"All right, everybody," Dwayne said. "We're going to get started. We'll go around the table and..."

"Before you do anything," Joan interrupted, looking around at everyone except Dwayne. "Take a look at the contact sheets I put at your seats. Make sure all your contact information is correct."

"Yes, please do that." Dwayne waited a moment, but Joan seemed to have drifted back into her own world. "Okay. I'd like to start with..."

"Also look at the rehearsal calendar," Joan interrupted again. "I need to know right away if there are any changes in your conflicts. If you don't have a conflict listed on a date, you are assumed to be available to rehearse."

She looked down at her notebook.

Dwayne waited. "Anything else, Joan?" She didn't look at him. She didn't respond. He waited a few moments. "All right! I'd like to start with..."

"Ingrid will be handing out your contracts and photo relea forms at the end of the evening," Joan interrupted again. "So ma sure you review and sign those before you leave." A few of the act laughed, then looked away.

What the hell was she doing? A director depended on his manager. She kept order. She kept things moving. She recorde blocking so that when everyone else forgot, she could tell then was supposed to be where and who moved when, and when precisely a light change should take place or a sound cue happen. On opening night, command of everything shifted from the director to the stage manager. His relationship with her was essential.

"Okay, thank you, Joan." Dwayne forced himself to sound cheerful. "Why don't you introduce yourself, and we'll go around the table clockwise?"

"I'm Joan Dunam," she said flatly. "I'm your stage manager. You have a problem with anyone or anything, you bring it to me." She looked down at her notebook.

"Oh!" Peaches said in surprise, sitting to Joan's left. "You're done?" she asked Joan. Joan nodded almost imperceptivity. "Yes. I'm Peaches Brown. Ha ha! I never wear brown. Not even my hair," she said, pushing her fingers through her multi-pastel hairdo, "though it used to be brown." She looked down and thought that over for a moment, then looked up making an effort at lightness. "I'm your costumer! Ha, ha!" She looked around with something like panic in her eyes, even though the cast smiled and applauded her. "I'm not an actor. I don't like attention. I don't even like to introduce myself. So please be kind! Ha, ha!" Her gaze darted from person to person, as though she feared someone might attack. "I'm bipolar and genderqueer," she blurted. "But you don't need to know that," she added regretfully. "But Melinda already knew that, so I thought it was ly fair…" She gave Melinda a shy, vulnerable smile.

Melinda, however, looked back at her coldly. "We are not what hink we are," she said.

wave of absolute panic crossed Peaches' face. Dwayne feared d burst into tears. She made a choking sound in her throat, tand up, sat back down, closed her eyes and took a deep ryone looked either mystified or embarrassed except looked annoyed. Peaches took another deep breath and which were shimmering with tears on the surface.

is under control! Ha, ha! I love actors. And I'm t to make sure you look great!"

u are," Coco said. She leaned back and winked at g to be gruffly friendly, but Peaches looked at

Coco with yet another type of a stricken expression, as though Coco were making a threat.

"All right!" Ingrid dove in, mercifully. "I'm your set and lighting designer, and the managing director of Psychedelic Dream Theatre, which, I do believe, is at least a somewhat better name than Kumquats in Retrograde..."

Dwayne looked at her in shock, but the introductions continued on around the table, while Peaches regained her composure.

When it came time for design presentations, Peaches was able to say the character's names as she held up each of her costume renderings, but all other words failed her. She could have told the actors about how character attributes had inspired her designs. She'd researched each fully and the depth of her thought would have given them a boost in appreciating what Shakespeare had created and may even have helped inform their acting choices. However, she felt the roles belonged to them, the actors who had to live them on stage. Even though her art supported theirs, she felt almost like an interloper to give her opinions of the essences of their characters. Besides, she was feeling too emotional to say much. Later she'd regret all that she'd left unsaid.

"Okay!" Ingrid burst in loudly when it came to her turn. She unveiled a three-dimensional model of the set. As she spoke, Ry was plugging in his guitar into a small rehearsal amp. "Here is what you'll be acting on." The set sported a bare stage space with three large platforms behind, each spiraling to the next one higher. On the highest platform, figures of musicians stood to the rear with some performance space in front of them. On the second highest platform a coffin was stationed at its back against the curtains.

"You'll have all of these areas for action." Ingrid pointed to the bare floor, the open parts of the platforms, etc. "You'll have entrances and exits out the downstage voms, and these three points at the back." She indicated spots at the back of the stage.

"I'm sorry," Melinda asked. "What's a *vom*?" Peaches flinched when Melinda spoke, but Melinda was now ignoring the costumer entirely, behavior which seemed incongruous with her looks. Melinda was a pretty young actress with wavy chestnut hair and large soulful eyes that suggested someone too soft-hearted to treat Peaches the way she had. Dwayne had found her emotional responsiveness in the auditions to be extraordinary. He'd cast her as Titus's daughter, Lavinia. He expected the audience to find her absolutely heartbreaking as she was brutalized over the course of the play.

"Short for *vomitory*," Joan interjected, speaking to the center of the table, "from the Latin *vomitorium*. The wide aisles up which a theatre pukes its audience out into the street, essentially."

"Oh!" Melinda's eyes flared at this graphic description. Some of the actors chuckled. Joan showed no amusement.

"The band will be onstage," Ingrid continued. "At the top of the show, lights will come up on this coffin, and they'll begin to play."

This was the first Dwayne had heard about the coffin.

She nodded at Ry, who wound into a mournful Hendrix-sounding acid rock solo, working the strings of his guitar and an effects pedal. He played a couple bars and brought the volume down to below speaking volume. "At that point, the house lights will be down, the light on the coffin will be brilliant, and a waterfall of blood will flow out from under the lid. The coffin will be sitting on a rolling truck with a basin that catches the blood and pumps it back up to continuously flow from under the coffin lid," she said. "Then the lights will flash bright into the faces of the audience, blinding them for a moment, and when they can see again, the cast is in place at the Tomb of the Andronici!"

Well, the opening scene *was* at a tomb, Dwayne considered, though a coffin suggested a wake rather than a tomb. He found himself really annoyed to be hearing about such a bold visual element with the rest of the company, rather than having discussed it in session with his set designer—and more importantly, having *approved* it—in advance. Clearly she'd discussed it in advance with Ry, who had already worked up a musical idea for the introduction.

Bobby had enjoyed being surprised by new inventions from his staff and actors when he was directing. The sound and the visual seemed like an arresting way to begin the show, but Ingrid's habit of leaving him out of the design process irritated the hell of out of Dwayne. However, he wasn't going to call her on it in front of everyone. He'd talk with her in private.

"You can compare the model to the tape Joan has laid out to get a feel of the space. Joan taped out the parts of the set that do not quite fit in the room going up the walls." Ingrid laughed. "This room is smaller than the stage, but you'll adjust," she said blithely.

Joan looked like she could chew nails.

Next the actors read through the script. After that they discussed the movements of the plot and the motivations of many of the characters and the style of action. Dwayne answered lots of questions. They looked excited to be working of the project.

Wallace Proctor, who played Titus, approached Dwayne as the others were filing out at the end. In his middle fifties, Wallace was the oldest member of the cast. "Say, Dwayne," he said with a somewhat cockeyed grin. "That coffin at the top of the show is a bold move. But don't you think people will be shouting *plagiarism*?"

"How's that?"

"Well, you must know that bleeding-coffin-at-the-top-of-the-show bit comes from Reg Camper's famous *Hamlet* at Wisdom Bridge. It's a great bit. Did you see it?"

"No," Dwayne said.

"Terrific show. One of the great moments in Chicago theatre. You would have been what? Ten years old? It's almost twenty years now. Aidan Quinn as Hamlet? I mean, if our show is supposed to be an homage to Reg Camper or something, then sure. But if not? I can't think what the critics will say about stealing something so distinctive. And that white-out effect where the audience is blinded by lights as the scene changes? That's stolen from *Warp!* by the Organic Theatre."

"Huh," Dwayne said.

Well, he was going to have to do something about that. Sooner or later, he was headed toward a show-down with Ingrid.

19

Thursday, December 18, 2003

Melinda trembled on stage in such a state of apparent trauma, Dwayne felt frightened. Then he was impressed. She looked exactly as traumatized as Lavinia would actually be, having been raped by two men, having her tongue cut out, and her hands chopped off. He didn't expect to see that level of acting this early in rehearsal. He'd been stopped in his tracks while circling the stage to see the action from every angle.

"Come, come, Lavinia; look, thy foes are bound," Wallace (playing Titus Andronicus) said. He led Melinda downstage to where Tamora's sons, Chiron and Demetrius, were tied with ropes, a dagger in Titus' one good hand, a basin carried on the stumps of Lavinia's wrists. Tears ran down Melinda's cheeks. Dwayne felt disturbed once again. This was a blocking rehearsal. Many of the actors were just going through the motions as Dwayne told them where he wanted them to move on the stage. How was Melinda in this emotional state at this stage of the game?

He couldn't ponder it long. Dwayne scurried back and forth to the each side of the stage to make sure his blocking looked good for all three sections of audience. Since the room was not wide enough to accommodate the full set, Dwayne had to step onto the acting area, which was distracting for the actors. He hated to do it, but if the blocking didn't work, he needed to fix it now. As he returned to his seat, he saw Joan holding the sides of her skull as though it were in danger of exploding. He forced himself to ignore her.

Wallace was also amazing as Titus. "O villains, Chiron and Demetrius!" he cried to the bound sons of Tamora. He circled his daughter Lavinia (Melinda) with reverence and mourning. "You killed her husband, and for your vile fault two of her brothers were condemned to death." He choked back a sob, settled himself, and raised his arm that ended in a stump. "My hand cut off and made a merry jest; both her sweet hands, her tongue, and her spotless chastity." He raised his hand with the gleaming dagger. "This one hand yet is left to cut your throats. I will grind your bones to dust and make two meat pies of your shameful heads." He approached them with the dagger held aloft.

"Great! Great!" Dwayne moved in close with them. "Okay, this is the point you cut their throats, Titus. We'll have the blood machines spouting fabric blood. And once again, people," Dwayne said, raising his voice and making sure he had the attention of everyone, "make sure you have all your blocking marked in your scripts. We are off until January 4th for the holidays. I want you all to come back with your lines memorized so we can work these scenes with the movement and the choreography, so please be ready!"

Dwayne sat back down and watched his actors with pride. Wallace enveloped Melinda in his arms as they left the stage. She gave him a weak smile. Melinda had been good, certainly, when she auditioned, and she had one of those soft, pretty faces that immediately pulls sympathy. But Dwayne was shocked now at how emotional she could be.

He watched as the actors got into place for blocking the final scenes of the play. They'd worked hard this first week. He'd been like a jack-in-the-box, jumping to his feet to move them around. Tonight they'd finish blocking the final scenes before they went away for two weeks.

As they worked, he glanced over at Joan's prompt book. She was still treating him coldly, but he loved how she kept the blocking. She put notations in the script as well as diagrams of the actors' movements drawn on floor plans of the set. Despite her personal oddness and inexplicable resentfulness, he found her acutely professional.

Titus' son Lucius had the final lines of the show. He walked over to where the beautiful Coco Nesbit lay dead on the floor. "As for that heinous tiger, Tamora. No funeral rite, no mournful bell shall ring her burial; but throw her body forth to beasts and birds of prey. See justice done on Aaron, that damned Moor, by whom our heavy haps had their beginning." He paused a long moment in solid seriousness, then took a comic bow. Everyone cheered. Dwayne was delighted. He leaned over and looked at Joan's clock.

"Okay, ten minutes until the official end of rehearsal. I will email you notes. If you have questions for me, I will hang out as long as you like. And Tom and Ingrid, don't leave until I talk with you." He stepped back with a feeling of accomplishment as Joan gave her notes and handed out the rehearsal schedules for after the holiday break.

His cast displayed that wonderful blend of seriousness and playfulness that defined a good rehearsal process. Some of them were way into research; others relied on intuition and emotion. Some were clearly working harder than others, but they were all progressing, and at this moment, he loved them all dearly.

Joan raised her voice. "Okay, that's the end of my notes. If you have questions, you can hang in. Otherwise you are free to go, five minutes early."

Cast members cheered and began to disperse. Chaz, who had been there to watch a number of rehearsals, left with his arm around Coco, which Dwayne found painfully disturbing.

Tom and Ingrid sidled up to Dwayne. "What's up, boss?" Tom said.

"There's a problem with the bleeding coffin prop," Dwayne said to Ingrid. "It turns out that prop was used in a famous production of *Hamlet* directed by Reginald Camper at the Wisdom Bridge Theatre in 1985."

"A coffin is a pretty generic prop," Ingrid said.

"It was at the top of the show, all alone on stage, eerie music behind it, and suddenly nonstop blood comes flowing out from under the lid."

"Wow." Tom looked at Ingrid. "That's exactly what you described. Did you see that show?"

"In 1985? I was eight years old living in the Quad Cities."

"If we use that bit," Dwayne said, "people will think we are making some homage to Camper's *Hamlet*. Or ripping it off."

"I can't believe this." Ingrid looked uncharacteristically distraught. "I totally thought I'd invented that bit. I swear."

"Maybe you'd heard about it a long time ago and forgot," Dwayne suggested.

"I guess that's possible. I thought it was such a cool idea for your concept! I'm embarrassed."

"Listen," Dwayne said. "I like your idea. I want to start the show with an arresting image like that." Ingrid still looked uncharacteristically abashed. "What if we used your idea, but instead of a coffin, it's a large pie, tilted toward the audience so they can clearly see the top? And Titus comes in and makes a slice, and the blood starts to flow out of it. He stands facing the audience, knife in hand, blood flowing behind him. Ry and the band are playing something disturbing and portentous, and then the surge of lights temporarily blinds the audience, and, bang!, the pie is gone we are into the scene at the Tomb of the Andronici."

"So we foreshadow the final scene…" Ingrid said.

"And we give a tip of the hat to Reg Camper's *Hamlet* without plagiarizing it…" Tom said.

"And we introduce the music and the stylized movement of *this* production by including Titus and the knife. You'd choreograph that, Tom," Dwayne said.

"I like it," Tom said.

"I can't believe I *stole* that idea," Ingrid said.

"George Harrison didn't realize he'd written 'My Sweet Lord' to the tune of 'He's So Fine', either," Dwayne said.

"I have no idea what you are talking about," Ingrid said.

"It doesn't matter. The point is, with this alteration, *your* idea works for *our* production, and it's something new," Dwayne said. He was hoping this would assuage her embarrassment and lead to a more collaborative working relationship.

"I like it," she said. She plunged a hand forward and shook Dwayne's. "Excellent!"

Dwayne felt a surge of pride. He *was* going to make this better between them.

A familiar woman's voice sounded from behind them:

"Everyone's gone?"

Dwayne turned to see Bonnie standing at the door of the rehearsal room, looking very annoyed. He felt immediately guilty for what he'd witnessed from her husband.

"I thought this was supposed to run until ten p.m." Bonnie looked darkly at Dwayne, her curly red hair threatening to engulf her face.

"We finished a few minutes early." Dwayne turned to the others. "Ingrid, Joan, this is Bonnie, Chaz's wife. You know Tom, I think," he said to Bonnie. She nodded and pushed her hair back.

"I wouldn't have guessed Chaz was *married*," Joan said in her weird deadpan, gazing forward into space. Tom and Ingrid both looked more embarrassed now that Joan had spoken. Everyone had seen Chaz and Coco flirting shamelessly.

"I need to take off," Ingrid said.

"I can lock up," Dwayne said to Joan. "You're all free to go."

"Why does Chaz need to be at every rehearsal?" Bonnie asked as the others fled the room.

"He hasn't…" Dwayne started; then he realized Chaz had been at every rehearsal that Coco attended. Perhaps he'd been with Coco on her off-nights, too. "He hasn't absolutely *needed* to be at every rehearsal," Dwayne amended. "I mean, I never *told* him he needed to be here every night," he said, grinning nonsensically. "You know. I'm not even sure *what* he's doing, because I'm focused on directing, ha ha ha." She turned her head slightly, quizzically, like a dog who's trying to understand what a human might be saying.

Dwayne stopped himself. Why was he laughing? What the fuck was he talking about?

"I *think*," Dwayne said, inventing furiously, "he's been observing rehearsals to get ideas for the marketing. And he's been taking photos. Lots of photos. You know. The action photos of the rehearsal. And…and he's actually been very helpful on the production side. You know, protecting your investment," he said, grinning haplessly again.

"Yeah?" she said, her expression unforgiving. Dwayne could imagine her using that look to devastating effect in the courtroom. Her face looked pale, flattening the color of her myriad freckles.

Bonnie made very good money as a divorce attorney. She could probably not care less about the cash Chaz invested. "You'd better not be lying to me, Dwayne Finnegan." She looked him up and down with something resembling disgust, and then walked back out of the rehearsal room.

Jesus Christ and the prevaricating bridegrooms.

20

Tuesday, December 23, 2003

"**D**o you know how to mix a Boulevardier?" a well-dressed gentleman at the bar asked. He spoke just loudly enough to be heard over the piano on the sound system.

"Of course, sir," Dwayne replied. He was also well dressed, behind the bar, wearing a vest and a bright-red tie, with his dark button-down shirt rolled up slightly at the wrists. "Excellent choice. Do you have a bourbon or rye preference?"

"Knob Creek would be fine." The gentleman turned slightly toward the attractive young woman beside him. "And a Patrón margarita for my friend."

"Very good, sir," Dwayne said. The young woman gave him a meaningful smile, and Dwayne turned to grab glasses and mix their drinks.

With two weeks off rehearsals, Dwayne was able to land a substitute bartender gig at the boutique Whitehall Hotel in the Gold Coast neighborhood. Dwayne was an experienced bartender, and the holidays were a great time to work. In the spirit of the season, people tipped generously.

He mixed the two drinks with a theatrical flourish and swept them into place in front of his customers. The young lady gave him a modest round of applause.

Bartending was one of those occupations in which a good-looking man like Dwayne could expect a number of flirtatious offers from women of various ages over the course of an evening. However, Dwayne would never mess around on Angela. His wife was beautiful, passionate, a great lover—and if he cheated she'd probably kill him in a spectacularly painful way—or have it done by someone from the shadier branch of the Guiseppelli family.

Nevertheless, he did enjoy the attention.

As he returned the bottles to their places, he heard a familiar voice behind him. "Well, well, well, this is a surprise!"

He turned to see Chaz taking an open seat at the bar and Coco settling herself beside him. Dwayne opened his mouth to speak, then closed it again, at a complete loss. He hadn't had a chance to inform Chaz of Bonnie's visit to rehearsal.

"What are you doing here?" Chaz asked. "I thought you'd switched to office temp work to keep your evenings open."

"I did. But I got caught making *Titus*-related phone calls on my last assignment, and I got fired."

"Too bad," Chaz said. "So, back to bartending!"

Coco leaned toward Dwayne and cocked a finger at him to approach her. He did so, and she whispered in his ear. "If we order here, can we take our drinks up to our room?"

Dwayne backed away, his face reddening. "Ah. Well. Yes. Yes, hotel guests are allowed that…flexibility."

She smirked at his discomfort. "You may mix me a pink lady." She got back up off her bar stool and leaned in toward Chaz, brushing her lips across his cheek. "I'll be back." She headed off with sultry slowness toward the Ladies Room.

Dwayne held up a finger to Chaz, quickly filled the drink orders for an impatient party of four and shot back to him. "What the fuck are you doing? Are you insane?"

"I've never experienced anything like this." Chaz spoke low so as not to be overheard. "She is the sexiest, more gorgeous creature I've ever encountered."

"What about Bonnie? Your beautiful red-haired wife is a knock-out! Have you decided your marriage is over?"

"No, no, no," Chaz said. "I love Bonnie. I would never give her up. This is just a fling. I'm not fooling myself. Coco will get bored and toss me to the side. But it's unbelievable while it lasts." He leaned in closer over the bar and lowered his voice more. "I mean that face. That body…" He moaned with pleasure at the memory. "…it's like she can grip my dick with her pussy…"

"Don't tell me that shit!" Dwayne whispered back. He saw the door to the bar open and Angela came through, a flash of brilliant curly red hair behind her. "Oh fuck. Don't look. Don't turn. Flee!"

All the blood drained from Chaz's face. He swiveled on his bar stool, slipped neatly to his feet, and walked away in the opposite direction of the entrance toward the Men's Room.

"Hi, honey!" Angela said, leading her friend to the bar. "Bonnie says Chaz has been ignoring her as completely as you've been ignoring me, so I suggested we surprise you and have you mix us fancy drinks."

"What a pleasant idea." Dwayne turned his best bartender smile on them.

Angela looked at him with bemused suspicion. "*What a pleasant idea?* What is that? Your Whitehall Hotel Bar persona?"

Dwayne managed a more genuine smile. "Yeah. How do you like it?"

"If you're going to be leaving me to my own devices while I'm on Christmas break, you'd better be to be pulling in major tips. You need a little more pizzazz."

"Well, it's spectacular to see you both," he said, edging up the pizzazz. "What can I get you?"

Angela screwed up her face in thought while Bonnie took off her coat and sat next to her. Bonnie looked annoyed. Almost as annoyed as she'd looked when she came to rehearsal and didn't find Chaz. Dwayne shot a glance to the tables at the back of the bar, wondering if he'd see the back of Chaz's head. Nope. He must be hiding out in the Men's Room.

"I'll have a Brandy Alexander," Angela said. "Made with vanilla ice cream. Can you do that here?"

"Absolutely. And you, Bonnie?"

"How about an Absent Husband?" she said pointedly. "Can you make me one of those?"

"Um, ha, ha." Dwayne was not sure how to respond, especially under the circumstances. "Actually, I've never heard of a cocktail called the Absent Husband."

"Well, that's what I want." Bonnie lifted her freckled brow in challenge. Her hair seemed to glow redder in annoyance. "If it doesn't exist, why don't you invent one? You're a creative guy." She said it as though that were a damning insult.

"Hey, great idea," Angela said. "Make it a good one, Dwayne. It might catch on. You could become famous for inventing it. The Absent Husband created by Dwayne Finnegan, Whitehall Hotel. That sounds kind of...legendary."

"Okay." Dwayne thought furiously. "An Absent Husband...belongs in a martini glass." He put a martini glass on the bar and dropped ice into a cocktail shaker. He turned to look at the bottles behind him and plucked Tanqueray from the array. "We start with gin, for chagrin." He poured a healthy shot onto the ice.

"Gin for chagrin," Angela echoed. "That's a nice start."

He replaced the Tanqueray bottle and plucked out two more bottles. With his left hand he poured in a scant shot of Martini Riserva Speciale Rubino. With his right hand he poured an equal amount of Campari. "And, because we must take the sweet with the bitter, we add sweet vermouth and bitter Campari." He put the lid on the cocktail shaker and shook it violently. "We shake it like we would shake the recalcitrant husband..." At this Bonnie finally cracked a smile, and Angela laughed aloud. "We strain it..." He poured the mixture into the martini glass. "...and top it off with Champagne..." He uncorked a champagne bottle from the cooler and gently filled the martini glass to the top. "...to restore the effervescence of life..." Then he took a strip of lemon peel, lit his lighter and held it over the glass. "...and to reignite the flame of passion..." He pinched the peel so that little spritzes burst into tiny flames over the drink, and dropped the peel into the glass. "...we add the finishing touch."

The two friends applauded. "That was brilliant, Dwayne!" Angela said. "I loved the fireworks from the lemon peel! How does it taste?"

Bonnie took a sip and grinned at her. "It's good!"

"Inventing cocktails?" Coco asked, suddenly standing next to Bonnie.

"It's called the Absent Husband. Coco, I don't believe you've met Bonnie, Chaz's wife," he said pointedly. "And this is my wife, Angela."

"Where *is* Chaz?" Coco asked in clear irritation.

"He's, ah..." Dwayne started.

"He's in Oak Brook, Illinois," Bonnie said, also sounding irritated. "Instead of being with his wife in this yuletide season, he's planning some McDonald's PR campaign."

"Is that so?" Coco said doubtfully.

"When he's not in Oak Brook, he's at this idiot's rehearsals." Bonnie nodded at Dwayne. "Wait. How do *you* know my husband?"

And at that moment Dwayne realized Bonnie had never met Coco, although she might have seen her photos if she'd looked at the company website. "Ah, Coco is in the show," Dwayne said. "All the actors have met Chaz."

"Chaz took the publicity photos of me," Coco said with a flaunt to her voice, leaning back against the bar.

Holy Jesus of the Pacific Coast whores!

"And what are you doing here?" Angela said. "Soliciting acting advice from my husband?"

Dwayne had been so busy watching Bonnie's green eyes glow yet greener with suspicion and jealousy, he hadn't noticed his own wife's hackles had gone up.

"Nah. I didn't even know Dwayne would be here. I'm staying in a room here tonight." She turned to Dwayne. "Could you have my drink order sent up to Room 207? I'm hoping I'm going to find what I'm looking for up there. I'm not going to wait all night." She turned and sauntered out of the room, the natural sway of her hips even more pronounced than usual. The two wives watched her all the way out of the room. Dwayne felt a draft of chilly air waft up from them.

"This hotel is a little pricey for an actress who's working in a low-budget show like yours, isn't it?" Angela asked.

"I'd think," Dwayne said. "Let me get your Brandy Alexander going and get these other people's drinks." He put brandy, crème de cacao, and ice cream in the blender and shot down to the other end of the bar, took some orders and served drinks as quickly as he could.

A pair of octogenarians requested Harvey Wallbangers. As he turned with the two collins glasses for their drinks in his hands, he saw Chaz cautiously poke his head out of the Men's Room. Just at that moment, Bonnie's head swiveled in his direction. What to do? He flipped one of the collins glasses off the tips of his finger and watched it twirl downward and smash loudly into pieces on the floor. All the nearby faces at the bar swung toward him, and Chaz disappeared back into the Men's Room like a tortoise head retreating into its shell.

"Oopsy," Dwayne said.

"Butterfingers," one of the old men quipped.

"Got to clean that up," Dwayne said, starting to head out to get a broom.

"Hey, make our drinks first! My friend is eighty-five with a bum ticker," the old guy said, cocking his thumb at his companion. "He ain't got much time left!"

Angela laughed. "Yeah, Dwayne, get these delightful codgers their drinks first."

The further codger leaned into the bar to get a better look. "Oh, aren't you the pretty one," he said.

"Get a load of the wild ginger hair on her friend," the first one said. "And look at those freckles! I'd bet you twenty-five bucks the rug matches the drapes."

Bonnie's mouth dropped open, and Angela laughed.

"I'd *give* you the twenty-five bucks if she'd let us look," the further one replied.

Bonnie choked, and Angela laughed the harder.

"Gentlemen..." Dwayne admonished them.

"Their next round is on us," the one with the supposed bad ticker said.

"Okay." Dwayne flipped another collins glass onto the bar to replace the broken one, slopped vodka and orange juice into the glasses, floated some Galliano atop, garnished them with maraschino cherries, and slid them in front of the old men. Then he headed for the Men's Room. Chaz was leaning back on the edge of the sink, looking terrified.

"Bonnie is out there!" he said.

"I thought you knew that!" Dwayne scolded. "You have to stay in here."

"What about Coco? I don't want them to meet." Chaz looked pale and sweaty.

"They already did. That's why you can't come out! Bonnie thinks you're in Oak Brook!"

"And Coco is out there? What if she says something?"

"Coco went up to Room 207. She wants her drink sent up there."

"She's going to wait for me?"

"Maybe she'll wait." Dwayne unlocked the mop closet and brought out a broom and dustpan. "Hide in this closet so you don't look a pervert hanging out in here. I'll come get you when they're gone."

Chaz stuck his head in the closet. "I don't like the smell."

"It's cleaning products. You can smell that or smell your lawyer wife skinning you alive in divorce court."

Chaz groaned, turned an empty bucket upside down in the closet, and sat on it. "Don't leave me in here all night."

"You'd deserve it if I did."

"I don't deserve this."

"You richly deserve it," Dwayne said. "You have no more sense now than when you had sex with Karen while she was still in high school."

"She begged me for it."

"She threw herself at Aleister, too, but he managed to turn her down."

"You're never going to forgive me for that, are you?"

"Do you deserve forgiveness for fucking your best friend's sixteen-year-old sister?"

"Karen was super-hot at sixteen."

Dwayne slammed the closet door on him, exited the Men's Room, swept up the broken glass, and hustled to catch up on his drink orders. The crowd picked up, so he was pretty busy. After two drinks, the wives took off. Dwayne felt himself slowly relax. He'd felt as nervous as if it were he who could be caught with Coco. He returned to the Men's Room to release Chaz from the closet. Chaz practically ran out of the cocktail lounge to see if Coco was still waiting for him.

Like a moron.

21

Sunday, January 4, 2004

"Sooner this sword shall plough thy bowels up," said Orlando (playing Aaron) as he struggled to hold a swaddled baby doll, thrust with his sword, and read from his script all at once. Dwayne felt like his head might explode. Everyone was supposed be off-book, lines memorized, so that they could move and work.

"Stay, murderous villains!" Aaron commanded Tamora's sons, struggling with the three objects in his hands. "He dies upon my scimitar's sharp point that touches this my first-born son and heir! What, what, ye white-limed walls! Ye alehouse painted signs!" He accidentally dropped the doll on its head, surprising bursts of laughter from his castmates. He cried in a high falsetto: "My baby!" He dropped his script and sword, swooped up the prop infant, and held it to his breast.

"Okay," Dwayne said, as the laughter subsided. "This is why we all need to be off-book. We can't move into the action with books in hand. It's impossible." He noticed Ingrid walking in to the back of the rehearsal room, drying her hair with a towel. Odd...

"With all due respect, Dwayne," Wallace said, standing up from a group of actors offstage, "I can never fully absorb the lines until I've got the blocking down. The line memory and the muscle memory work together." For some reason Joan was nodding along with him and giving Dwayne a disapproving look.

"We blocked the whole show before the holiday break so you could have the blocking in mind as you memorized your lines," Dwayne said.

"Sure, we swiftly blocked it," Wallace said, "but we didn't *work* it enough to get it into our bones." All the actors who'd been grabbing their scripts nodded sagely along with him.

"Another thing," Orlando said. "I'm not always sure what everything means. Then the lines are just strings of words, and that is so hard to learn."

"You can't learn it—and you can't properly deliver it—if you don't understand it," Dwayne agreed. "So you've got to reference your glossaries."

Orlando picked up his script and read: "*Ye white-limed walls! ye alehouse painted signs. Limed* means trapped with birdlime—like birds trapped with their feet glued to a branch with whatever birdlime is. How does that make sense?"

"If I may," Ingrid called from the back of the room, "traditional whitewash, like the type Tom Sawyer tricked his friends into using to paint his aunt's fence, was a suspension of lime in water. It's the old version of white paint. So white-limed walls would just be white-painted walls. It's a different thing from bird-lime."

"So he's just ridiculing them for being white?" Orlando said. "That makes sense. The next thing I say is: Coal-black is better than another hue."

"Fie, treacherous hue, that will betray with blushing the close enacts and counsels of the heart! Their blushing white faces reveal their embarrassment," Dwayne said. "Aaron's black face doesn't blush."

"Yes! And I'm very proud of my trickery," Orlando said.

"We are both delighted to be tricky," Coco said, sidling up to Orlando. She put her arms around his neck. "And we love to love who we love, no matter who is married to what," she said.

"Yes." Dwayne wanted to slide past her innuendo. This was the first rehearsal with Coco that Chaz had not attended. "But this scene also adds a human depth to Aaron," he said. "He protects his son when its own mother, Tamora," he said, gesturing to Coco, "has sent the baby to be killed, since its blackness reveals this is not the son of her white husband, the emperor. But Aaron falls in love with his son the moment he holds him."

"Yeah," Orlando said, smiling. "I like that!" He turned to face Coco. "'Tell the empress from me, I am of age to keep mine own, excuse it how she can.'" Coco gave a good-natured humpf and walked back off the stage. Orlando scanned down in his script and lifted the baby doll in his arms. "'Look how the black slave smiles upon the father, as who should say Old lad, I am thine own.' This really gives a lot of heart for someone who revels in his evil!"

"Yes!" Dwayne said, very pleased.

"But why are Tamora's older sons white?" He pointed at the two actors on stage. "I mean, they are just *white* white."

"Yeah," Dwayne admitted. "I guess we are presenting a world in which a white father produces white children and a black father produces black children, despite the color of the mother."

"Wow! That's crazy," Orlando said.

"I guess I just don't got no DNA of my own!" Coco called. Everyone laughed.

"Obviously, we are taking liberties," Dwayne said.

They didn't quite get to the end of the script by the end of the night as Dwayne had planned, but they were close.

Ingrid came up to Dwayne as the actors filed out. "I have a pretty thorough knowledge of Shakespearean language. I can help the actors gloss their lines, if you want."

"How do you have time? And why are you walking around with wet hair? It's twenty degrees outside."

"Hey, look at this!" Chaz charged into the rehearsal space, waving a vintage sword over his head.

Tom jumped out of his seat, took the sword from Chaz, and hefted it in his hand. "It's beautifully balanced." Tom did a series of masquerade thrusts and parries, leaping gracefully over chairs and among the actors who were still gathering their things and filing out of the room. Everyone smiled and applauded to see him move. He was really quite graceful. Swashbuckling, you might say. Dwayne hoped he'd get the other actors to look as good.

Tom brought it back to Dwayne and Chaz. "This is a gorgeous piece." He held out the handle for them to see. The hilt was wound with textured leather, and the guard and pommel were inlaid with Toledo silver. "It's a short sword. Not too heavy. This would be an excellent piece to be wielded by Queen Tamora."

"In fact," Chaz said. "I borrowed it from a friend as a prop for more publicity photos of Coco. But we have to be careful. It's worth $8,000, and my friend's insurance does not cover it outside of his home."

"That is gorgeous," Coco said. She plucked the sword from Tom's hand and took it through a few standard fight choreography moves. She stopped and faced them with a huge smile. "This is like it's made for my hand. I've never held a weapon that felt so perfectly balanced."

"Let me see." Tom took the weapon back from her and ran the palm of his hand down its edge and tested its point. "The edge and tip are rounded like a weapon made for stage combat. We could actually use this for Tamora's scenes if you wanted."

"We don't have the insurance to cover an $8,000 weapon," Dwayne said. "And it'd probably make the rest of the weaponry look bad by comparison."

"I'm getting us pretty good-looking stuff," Tom said. "And it'd make sense for Queen Tamora to have a prettier sword than the one carried by an old warhorse like Titus."

Coco plucked it back from Tom's hand. "Well, I love it." She danced across the rehearsal stage, slashing through hordes of imaginary Romans.

"She looks terrific with that in her hand," Chaz said.

Joan appeared suddenly beside them. "You think she looks terrific whatever," her voice creepily without emotion.

Chaz laughed uncomfortably. "Well, who doesn't?"

"Woo," Coco cried, swinging the sword and strutting back to them. "This is the shit."

"Well, then, I think you should use it," Chaz said.

"Really?" she said in delight.

"Really?" Dwayne said in alarm.

"Yeah?" Chaz said. "Why not? Just be careful. I have to return it to the owner just exactly like it is right now."

"We can't guarantee that," Dwayne said. "Isn't it likely to get nicked up?" he asked Tom.

"Her violence doesn't call for sword-to-sword contact," Tom said. "I do love the way it looks. I'd be more worried about sweat stains on the leather hilt, that sort of thing."

"It came with this protective carrier." Chaz took the sword from Coco and put it away like a violin going into its case.

"That's nice," Tom said.

"It's settled then," Chaz said triumphantly.

"Fucking right!" Coco gave Chaz a huge hug, making him look both pleased and embarrassed.

"I am not responsible for any $8,000 prop." Joan poked her finger toward Dwayne. "That's on you." She went back to the table and gathered up her things.

"Can I take this home and get used to it?" Coco asked Chaz.

"I don't think that's…" Dwayne started.

"Absolutely," Chaz said. "I'll give you a ride."

As they walked off together, Dwayne heard her saying: "Nah, I think I'll give *you* a ride." The two of them laughed. Dwayne felt a little sick—and annoyed at being overridden once again.

"Okay," Ingrid said. "That was…interesting. But what about the other thing? Do you want me to work with the actors on language? I'm aware that sometimes I plunge into other people's turf. It's my Viking predisposition."

Dwayne laughed. "You *do* have that tendency. But how do you have the time? You're doing a lot on this show already, and you're working on other shows, as well."

"All I do is theatre," Ingrid said. "I don't have a day job."

"Really? Do you have a trust fund?"

"I keep my expenses low. I live in my van, so I don't have rent. A lot of theatres have showers for actors who have body paint, so I shower at the theatres where I work. That's why my hair was wet. I know where to find unrestricted free parking. I know which grocery stores have the most free samples and when. I take away leftover food from theatre receptions. There's some bakeries with day-old bread really cheap. I've got a cot in my van, a composting toilet, a five gallon water tank, and a little butane stove, so I can always make a batch of ramen or something. And I've got space for my tools and clothing and stuff. The bigger theatres, like this one, have washers and driers that I use." She spread her arms and gave a 500-watt smile. "My van is my

Viking ship in which I conquer the Chicago theatre scene."

"Wow," Dwayne said. "That's amazing."

"You should have a cup of tea in my van some time," she offered. "It's an ordinary panel truck, but the way I use the interior space is genius. You'd like it."

"Sounds great," Dwayne said. He felt suddenly warm toward Ingrid. She was intrusive and presumptuous, but she was also adventurous and entrepreneurial. She didn't wait for money or permission. She plunged in and did the work. Of course, he would have preferred that she consult with him before she made decisions, but she was effective and talented. Maybe she was what he needed. A director could go nuts trying to control everything.

She slapped him on the shoulder, gave him a big smile, and headed out of the rehearsal space in long, aggressive strides. He walked back to the rehearsal table he shared with Joan, who'd gathered her things and was ready to lock up and go. Everyone else had gone.

"Those women are going to be the death of you," Joan predicted without sympathy.

22

Wednesday, January 7, 2004

I t didn't take long to get to the next crisis. In the meantime, everyone was happy. They worked on the violence and dance choreography, which looked great. Every aspect of the show was improving. That is, until they arrived at rehearsal on Wednesday. Dwayne noticed something weird right away. Half of the actors were smiling, the other half looked at him resentfully.

Demons in the halls of Paradise.

He sat down at the rehearsal table with Joan. "What's going on?" he asked, sotto voce.

"What did you think would happen?" She looked at him with the dull regard a satiated cobra would give a mouse. She flipped open her laptop and brought up the Psychedelic Dream Theatre website. There was a new ensemble page. About half the cast was listed with bios and headshots as ensemble members. The other half was not. That was the half giving him resentful stares right now.

"If you were going to do this while the show was in rehearsal, why wouldn't you list them all? You had to guess what the reaction would be."

"Fucking Ingrid," Dwayne said quietly. "I had no idea."

Be cool. Be cool.

"It's a weak leader who has no control," Joan said.

"Hey," Tom said pleasantly, sitting down on the other side of Dwayne. "I see you're looking at the new ensemble page. That's created a bit of a stir." He lowered his voice. "I wondered about the reasoning behind the selection. You've certainly got all the *prettiest* actors, but I wouldn't say necessarily all the *best* actors."

Dwayne scanned the column of photos again. Some of the actors shown were some of the slowest about getting their lines down, and slowest to show an understanding of their characters. But they were very good-looking. "So Chaz had his hand in this, too," Dwayne said. One of them shuffled up to the rehearsal table.

"Thanks for the invitation, Dwayne," she said. "I'm really looking forward to being a part of the company. And I promise to help out, like Ingrid asked." She winked at Dwayne and shuffled back to the contingent of happy actors.

Wallace stepped up to the table and shook back his leonine locks. He turned Joan's laptop to face him and Dwayne. "Well, this is shabby, Finnegan," he said, keeping his voice to an intimate volume. "You expect me to find time to put up posters while learning a role as vast as Titus and working my day job? If I helped build the set, I'd be a company member. But since I intend to dedicate all my time to developing this role to the best of my ability, I am left out. I call that shabby."

He turned and walked away.

"Well, that was awkward," Tom said.

"You should have seen that coming," Joan told Dwayne.

"How could I see it coming, when I had no idea this was happening?"

"It's your job to know," Joan said.

Dwayne groaned deeply. "What am I going to do?" he whispered. "Do I tell everyone I didn't know what Ingrid was up to?"

"And then what?" Tom said. "Eliminate the ensemble and make all those actors unhappy? Or put everyone in the ensemble whether they help with stuff or not?"

"What does it do to your authority as director," Joan said, looking at no one, "if the cast knows this production is totally out of your control?"

"*Jesus Christ of the rebellious virgins,*" Dwayne said.

"You are weird, Dwayne," Joan said.

Ingrid walked into the rehearsal room, grinning like the Cheshire Cat.

Okay, Dwayne said to himself. He got up from behind the director's table. "Listen up, everyone!" he called to the cast. He turned back and gave Ingrid a meaningful look. The smiling contingent to his left and the sulking contingent to his right all turned toward him. "I was looking forward to greeting the new members of the Psychedelic Dream Theatre at the top of this rehearsal," he said, noting the sulky actors get sulkier. "However, there was a misunderstanding. Totally my fault, of course. I asked Ingrid to invite you to the company and also to see who might have time to help with things like the marketing and construction tasks ahead of us. I did not make it clear that those two things were independent of one another," he improvised.

Ingrid made an angry face and started to speak, but Dwayne raised a finger and made a warning sound to stop her. He turned back to the cast.

"I've been delighted with the progress we've made over the past couple weeks. You are an incredible cast! If we can make a success of this show and carry this company forward, I want nothing more than to be able to continue to work with you all. So I truly apologize for the confusion. As soon as she is able, Ingrid will be putting *all* your photos on the ensemble page!" Dwayne looked back at Ingrid with a meaningfully raised eyebrow. He started clapping and shouting: *Welcome! Hurrah!* and soon the full cast was cheering along with him, and the formerly cheerful actors were embracing the formerly sulky members. Ingrid, however, looked *very* sulky.

"Of course, we still need your help with those tasks Ingrid discussed with you," he continued when the hubbub died down. "It's one of those realities of working on a shoestring. But allow me to embrace you, my fellow Psychedelic Dream ensemble members!" And he waded out into them, shaking hands and giving hugs.

"Well, I guess he showed you," Joan said to Ingrid, looking straight into the middle of her paint-stained sweatshirt. Ingrid turned and stalked out of the rehearsal room, abandoning whatever she'd come there to accomplish.

23

Thursday, January 8, 2004

"**S**he's the managing director. Why don't you let her manage?" Chaz challenged Dwayne.

Each time Chaz showed up at a rehearsal, Dwayne was less happy to see his old friend. Tom was choreographing Coco's fight scene today, and Chaz came to shoot a promotional video.

"Come with me." Dwayne led Chaz out of the rehearsal room and down the hall to where the battered washer and dryer stood in a filthy alcove near the fire escape. He didn't want any of the actors to overhear.

Chaz looked with disgust. Puffs of dirty drier lint were glued to the walls with paint spatters. The slop sink was decorated up the sides with globs of every color paint that had ever graced a set in the Chicago Repertory Arts Theater. Petrified paint brushes waited on the messy shelves for someone to finally throw them away.

"I never *asked* her to be managing director," Dwayne hissed. "I *don't want* her as managing director."

"Well, she's *acting* as managing director. And now you've undermined her. How can she expect the actors she recruited to fulfill their pledges to work if the others won't do the same? You should have consulted her."

"*She* should have consulted *me!*" Dwayne said emphatically. "This is *my* company."

"Is it?" Chaz said. "Aleister and I are financing it."

Dwayne stepped back in amazement. "*Dangling balls of the octogenarian Christ!* You financed the company for *me* to run it."

"Ingrid offered ensemble memberships to get free help hanging posters and building the set."

"Have you ever been to an actor's apartment?" Dwayne asked.

"Yours."

"When you visit pretty much any actor's apartment, lurking somewhere atop a bookshelf you can find stacks of posters they promised to hang but didn't. They may have stacks of publicity materials from every show they've ever been in. If you depend on actor volunteers, *maybe* a fifth of your posters will get hung up. Probably less." He looked up at a filthy shelf above the drier that held a variety of dusty bottles of cleaning products. Beneath the products was a stack of paper. He pulled one out of the bottom of the stack. It was a poster for a many-years-gone-by production of *The Seagull*. He held it up, and Chaz looked at it doubtfully.

"Ingrid says she always hangs posters for her shows," he said defensively.

"Ingrid lives in a van so that she can devote herself totally to the theatre life." He pointed at the battered washer and drier. "This is where she does her laundry." He led Chaz down the hallway to the actors' washrooms, which were in a miserable state of repair. Between them was a tiny shower stall. The insides of the shower stall walls were spattered with paint. A bucket of dirty rags sat on the stall floor. "This is where she showers. She collects food from fundraisers and opening night receptions. She cooks ramen on a butane stove in her truck. You cannot predict anyone else's behavior based on Ingrid. If you want posters hung, you have to pay somebody."

"How do you know the hired people are going to do it?" Chaz said, still on the defensive.

"You hire them at fifty cents a poster. To get paid they have to write down each address where they're hung, and take a digital photo as proof. Only then do you know you are getting what you paid for and your posters are not in a dumpster or under somebody's bed."

Chaz looked at him, begrudgingly impressed. "Huh. That's the sort of thing you'd expect a managing director to know."

"Yeah. It is." Dwayne looked at his watch. "I've got to get this rehearsal started."

When they got back to the rehearsal room, the actors were warming up on stage. The rehearsal weapons were laid out on the floor to the side. Tom and Coco stood in the center of the stage. Coco looked defiant, and Tom looked mystified.

"I want to work with the actual sword," Coco said with her arms crossed.

"What you want me to do?" Tom said, right hand on his cocked hip, arm akimbo. "I'm not the one who lost it."

"What's this?" Dwayne asked.

Tom and Coco looked at him for a long moment, then Tom turned slowly and gestured to Coco for her speak.

"I don't have the sword," she said.

"Wait," Chaz said. "Are you talking about the vintage sword I brought in?"

"Yes," she said. She stood looking at them, head held high. Dwayne waited, but she didn't say anything further.

"Where is it?" Dwayne said.

When it seemed clear she would not speak again, Tom said: "She left it on the Red Line."

"Fuck!" Chaz shouted. "Fuck! Fuck! Fuck! That's eight thousand dollars!"

"When did you leave it on the El?" Dwayne said.

"On the way here," Coco said. "The northbound Red Line train. It's probably up at Howard Street by now."

"Did you call the CTA?" Chaz said, panicked.

Coco looked at him like he'd insulted her. "No."

"That sword is worth $8,000," Chaz whined. "We have no insurance on it." He looked slightly green-faced.

"I didn't realize I'd left it until I got here and I saw all the rehearsal swords on the floor," Coco said, shifting uncomfortably from defiance to guilt. "I was drilling my lines on the El, and I kept doing that walking over from the Fullerton Station. I just didn't think about it. And then I saw those," she said, gesturing to the swords on the floor, "and I suddenly remembered."

"Jesus Christ!" Chaz shouted.

"We had no business using an $8,000 prop in an unsecured theatre," Joan said to Dwayne. "And then to allow her to take it home?" She snorted derisively.

As annoying as Joan was, she was also right. "I've got to run this rehearsal," Dwayne said to Chaz. "Why don't you go and run it down with the CTA?"

"Yes." Chaz grabbed his coat and ran toward the door.

"Call Ingrid," Dwayne called after him. "She's up north a lot. Maybe she can dash over to the Howard Street station." He turned to Coco. "Do you remember what car you were in?"

"I was in the very first car, all the way at the front."

"Okay," Chaz said.

"I'm coming with you," Coco said. She ran off the stage and grabbed her enormous fake fur coat.

"Wait a minute," Tom shouted. "I have a rehearsal sword."

"I cannot work in this atmosphere of accusation!" Coco cried.

"We need you here!" Dwayne shouted.

"I cannot!" Coco screamed. "I cannot!" She stormed out of the room ahead of Chaz.

Dwayne sighed. He turned to Tom. "Can we work around her, get everyone else's movement down and plug her in later?"

"Jesus!" Tom shouted and turned away. He took a deep breath. "Okay. Sorry." He held his hands out to the sides. "Yes, I suppose we can." He turned to the actors who remained. "Okay, grab your weapons." Then he turned back to Dwayne and Joan. He took another deep breath. "One diva at a time."

24

Sunday, January 11, 2004

"You're not going to like this," Tom said in a sing-song voice. "You'd better get over to the Playhouse right now." That was the entire message on Dwayne's voicemail. He tried calling Tom back, but it went immediately to his voicemail.

What the fuck?

Six inches of snow had fallen and the temperature was to drop to three below zero that night. Chaz had volunteered to give Dwayne a ride to rehearsal, and Dwayne called him to come early. They climbed out of Chaz's all-wheel-drive Subaru and shuffled through the snow toward the Chicago Repertory Arts Playhouse, steam curling from Dwayne's nostrils in the cold. He stopped for a moment, remembering his walks home from school on the cold afternoons of his childhood. His coats were never warm enough, and he would shiver helplessly. His mother worked as a cashier at Sears and insisted on buying coats on sale with her employee discount, and they weren't the coats that really kept you warm. Dwayne never believed they were poor, but they definitely lived at the modest end of Evanston in a small ranch house.

At least he could buy his own coats now and make sure they were adequate—even though he had a long way to go to match the earning power of either his father or mother. Other than the mortgage, they never were in debt like him.

He took in a deep breath and blew it out powerfully through his nostrils, watching the fog curl out like the horns of a wild boar. He followed Chaz into the lobby of the theatre. They smacked their hands together and brushed the snow from their shoulders.

"Oh, Dwight," Raymond Green called, coming out of the ramshackle box office. "A word, please." Green grinned at him uncomfortably and rubbed the top of his head with the palm of his hand, releasing a little snowfall of dandruff onto his shoulders and shirt front.

"Dwayne," Dwayne said.

"What's that?"

"Dwayne," he said again. "You called me Dwight. My name is Dwayne. Dwayne Finnegan."

"Right, right, right," Green said. "Absolutely. Dwayne. Sorry," he said, rubbing his head again, and then scratching it, releasing more dandruff. "It's about the additional rehearsal hours. I'm not sure how much your team has added, but I've got to charge you for that. Can you have your stage manager provide me a revised rehearsal schedule?"

"If you are adding expenses," Chaz said to Dwayne, "you have to let me know." Chaz was suddenly very money conscious. They had not found the $8,000 sword. They were offering a $750 reward. Chaz figured that was more than someone would be able to get from a pawn shop or fence, but so far they'd heard nothing. It had been missing four days. He'd turned suddenly cold toward Coco, and she looked resentful whenever he appeared.

"We haven't added any rehearsal hours," Dwayne said to Green.

"Your people have been up there for two hours already today," Green said. "And how am I to know how much other time you've added when I've not been here?"

"My people have been here for two hours?" Dwayne said. "Why?"

"That would be for me to ask you." Green chuckled.

"We can't afford more rehearsal rent," Chaz said.

"I haven't added any," Dwayne said irritably. "You're sure it's my people up there?" he asked Green.

"Joan is there," Green said. "She opened the space with her keys."

"Let me get back to you." Dwayne climbed the stairs, plunged around the corner and down the hall. Sure enough, his full cast was seated in a circle in the rehearsal room.

"Would it be premature to discuss season selection?" Peaches Brown said. "I love period costuming. Do you guys like period theatre?"

"You know me," Coco said. "I love a gorgeous costume. Old style, new style. I love them all." She looked up, saw Chaz at the door behind Dwayne, and her smile faded.

"Whatever we do," Ry Joodey said, sitting with his guitar hugged in his arms. "We should continue to do shows with music."

Dwayne stepped up to the edge of the circle. "What's happening here?"

"Ensemble meeting," Wallace said in his rumbling baritone. "We wanted to get organized."

"Organize what?" Dwayne said.

"How decisions are made, old man." Wallace stopped speaking abruptly and stood looking forward, transfixed. Everyone looked at him. No one spoke for a moment.

What in the sacred grand mal of John the Baptist?

"Since this is an ensemble company," Orlando said, blowing past Wallace's strange behavior, "the ensemble should make the decisions. We don't want an artistic-director-dominated company. We want a democracy of artists." He grinned, and Dwayne suddenly saw the ruthless evil of Aaron glinting through his eyes. Why wasn't he seeing that in rehearsal? Orlando seemed apologetic when he delivered his most evil lines.

"If this is an ensemble meeting," Dwayne said, "how was I not invited?"

"There's ensemble," Wallace said, shaking himself alert and sweeping his arms around to indicate everyone in the circle, "and then there is management," he said, waving his hand at Dwayne and Chaz. "You and Ingrid and the investors."

Dwayne felt a flurry of anger in his chest. Now everyone wanted to usurp his authority.

Melinda, the actor who played Titus' daughter, got out of her seat. "Obviously, the ensemble gets first pick of the roles, but when more than one ensemble member wants a role, how do we decide?"

"The director and the artistic director decide," Tom said.

Coco shouted, "Naw! None of that top-down bullshit. Maybe a secret ballot of the ensemble members?"

What the hell?

"I have another question," Melinda said. "Is Tom really ensemble? Should he even have a voice in this? I mean, isn't he more management, like Dwayne and Ingrid?"

"Peaches is ensemble," Orlando said, standing up. "She's a designer, not management. Tom is choreographer. Those are both artist positions. They should be both be ensemble."

Tom looked exceedingly touched. "That is so sweet," he said, laying a hand on Orlando's forearm. Orlando gave him a warm (and sexy?) smile back.

"Yes, I think we should have a voice," Peaches agreed.

"I think so, too," Wallace said, his voice rumbling. "When it comes to casting, I wouldn't want actor popularity to trump the best talent for the role."

"What, are we stupid?" Melinda said challengingly. Dwayne wished she'd show more of that spirit onstage. After looking tremendously emotional early in the rehearsal process, lately she looked more like an automaton, especially after her hands were chopped off and her tongue cut out. Those losses meant she needed to be more expressive with her face and body, not less.

Orlando barked a derisive laugh. "You don't think we would put the good of the show ahead of our likes and dislikes?"

"Seriously?" Wallace said, a wry smile curling up on his mouth. "You know and I know that actors will put emotion ahead of intellect twelve times out of ten." That led to a general outcry, and the meeting broke into a half dozen individual and small group arguments.

"Okay, okay, okay!" Dwayne boomed over the crowd. "We've got a show to rehearse! This will all be moot if *Titus* doesn't kick ass!" The group slowly gave him their attention. "If we don't attract an audience, *Titus* will be our first and our last show, and we won't be casting *anything* ever again." That settled them down. He looked at his watch. "We are scheduled to start in ten minutes. Let's get these chairs back in place. Please check your rehearsal props, and be ready."

"Just one other thing," Orlando said. "We had a big discussion about the marketing of this show, and I think Chaz needs to hear our thoughts."

"Actually," Chaz said, stepping into the circle. "I'm pretty sure I *don't.*"

"*Oh great,*" Melinda said. A shimmer of disapproving murmurs shuffled through the cast.

"I mean, I'm willing to discuss your ideas over a drink after rehearsal," he amended. "But rehearsal time is for rehearsal."

"Well, some of us are wondering why our marketing makes it seem like the whole show is about Coco," Melinda challenged.

"Right!" Orlando interjected. "I mean, I'm playing the part Bobby was going to play. This was his company, and there is no focus on me, at all." Again Dwayne wished he'd see more of this spirit when Orlando was on stage.

"You see? No intellect. Totally emotion," Wallace intoned in his deep baritone. "Your Aaron is not the central character. I am playing Titus Andronicus. Where is my image?"

"Did you say I have no intellect?" Orlando moved in chest to chest with Wallace. "Why is that, old man? Because I'm black? Or because I'm gay?"

"I'm discussing the merits of your argument," Wallace boomed. "You aren't talking what's best for the production. You just say: *What about me?* Like some whiny bitch."

"A whiny bitch?" Orlando whined. "So it *is* about me being gay."

"Why would I care about you being gay?" Wallace said. "I'm bisexual myself."

"You're bisexual. Right," Orlando scoffed. "Since when?"

"Since when?" Wallace said. "It's neither here nor there, but I think you are a gorgeous man, and I would suck your dick in an instant."

Cries of shock, laughs, delight, and derision flew up from the cast.

"All right," Dwayne insisted. "All right! Enough. Let's get ready to rehearse, please!" He started pulling chairs off the acting area.

"Wait!" Melinda shouted. "Why is there not one shot of the ensemble in the marketing materials?"

"We've got the full ensemble on the web page," Chaz countered.

"Sure. Our headshots," Orlando said. "Wallace's headshot is older than Melinda."

"Hey!" Wallace said angrily.

"Look, you are all hired for your talent *as actors*," Chaz said forcefully. "And your talent is exemplary. But I am the marketing guy. And my talent, too, is exemplary."

Jesus Christ of the narcissistic hucksters.

"One of the biggest corporations in the world pays me a lot of money for my marketing expertise," Chaz continued at his most condescending. "So: you don't need me to tell you about acting. And I don't need you to tell me about marketing."

"All right, let's…" Dwayne attempted.

"You know about marketing *hamburgers*," Wallace corrected. "We live and breathe theatre."

"Hamburgers?" Orlando said.

"*Rehearsal* is…" Dwayne started.

"He works for McDonalds, for the love of God," Wallace said. This brought cries of derision from the cast. "*We* know what fills theatre seats," Wallace concluded.

"I have an MBA from the Kellogg School at Northwestern University," Chaz insisted loudly. "I started my career at a PR firm with a wide variety of clients. McDonald's, one of the largest corporations in the world, hired me away because I am damned good. Is anyone else here making over a hundred grand a year?"

"Jesus," Melinda sputtered. "You want to compare the size of your dick, too?"

"Well," Coco drawled, "his ain't the *biggest* I've seen, but…"

"Okay…" Dwayne attempted.

"You all should just keep your noses where they belong," Chaz insisted. This brought huge shouts of derision.

"Right," Melinda said. "And meanwhile *Titus Andronicus* looks like the *Coco Nesbit Sex Show*."

"You said what?" Coco said. "You ain't nothing but a basic white ingénue. You can't throw a dead cat in this town without hitting a basic white ingénue."

Melinda's mouth dropped open. No one spoke for a moment, then her eyes filled with tears. She choked back a sob and ran out of the rehearsal room. A moment later Peaches ran after her.

Whatever was holding Melinda back in her performance, that kind of talk was not going to help.

"So I suppose I'm the bad guy," Coco muttered.

If she weren't an absolutely brilliant actor, Dwayne would have been tempted to throw her out.

Joan stood up and clapped her hands three times. "Set the chairs. Set your props. Eight minutes to start!"

"Thank you, eight," all the actors responded in the traditional response that let the stage manager know they'd all heard her.

Dwayne walked out of the rehearsal space to find and soothe his basic white ingénue.

25

Monday, January 12, 2004

"What the hell is this, Dwayne?" Angela flapped a bill in front of his face. He'd just sat down on the couch to go through a stack of mail that had gathered over the past few days. Angela flapped it so close that it actually hit his nose.

"Don't do that." He snatched the paper away from her and looked at it. "It's our car payment bill."

"But why is it twice the normal amount with a fifty dollar penalty on top of that?" She put both hands on her hips and stood dangerously close to him. He felt pressed into the back of the couch.

Dwayne looked at the bill more closely. "Oh, it is, isn't it?"

"Is that a mistake? Can you call them up and get the penalty expunged?"

Dwayne got up and slid by her, got the check book out of their shared office, and flipped through the register.

"Shit," he said. He was standing near the entry to the apartment.
Wouldn't it be great to just run out the door right now?

"What did you do, Dwayne?" she demanded.

"Well, now, don't get all mad. I remember now. When last month's bill came in, I couldn't pay it on the day it arrived. Your check was coming the week after, so I just had to wait. You know, the cash flow. And so I put the bill...somewhere. I don't remember where I put it. But I put it somewhere so I wouldn't forget it."

"And?" She looked increasingly impatient with every word he said.

He hated when she got mad at him.

"Well, I guess I put it in the wrong spot. Because I forgot."

"And now we have to pay double plus fifty dollars? Fifty dollars down the sewer because you put the bill in the wrong place? Fifty dollars. We could have gone out to dinner on fifty dollars. Nowhere fancy, but at least a plate of pasta and a glass of Chianti. You don't think I could use a plate of pasta and a glass of Chianti?"

"I know you could, Angela," Dwayne said miserably.

"But now I'm not going to get that plate of pasta and glass of Chianti, am I?"

"I could make you some…"

"I mean in a restaurant, Dwayne! A nice mom and pop Italian restaurant with a checked tablecloth and the teenage daughter taking our order. I'm not going to get that. Am I?" She grabbed a handful of envelopes off the couch. "And what else is in here? More surprises lurking? Do I have to take over paying the bills? On top of lesson plans. Teaching. Grading papers. All the stupid meetings."

"No, no, no, I can take care of the bills."

"Can you? Because this fifty dollars makes it seem like you can't!"

"Anybody can make a mistake," Dwayne said. "I'll call them. I'll see if I can get the penalty expressed."

"Expunged, Dwayne. Expunged. I don't know what the hell will happen if you ask to get the penalty expressed. Maybe then it'll be a *hundred* dollars."

"Expunged. That's what I meant."

She threw the mail back on the couch. "I have to go take a walk by the lake, Dwayne. I've got to count the waves until my blood pressure goes down."

"It's really cold out," Dwayne said.

"Yes, it's cold but I still have to go," she said at a very high volume. "I have to freeze my fucking ass off while I'm counting the waves, because of you." She put on her heavy coat from the coat tree by the door, pulled on her hat, and wrapped a heavy scarf around her neck. "Somebody ought to have you expunged," she said darkly and stormed out the door.

Dwayne sat on the couch feeling miserable. Since the holidays were passed and they'd returned to rehearsal, he lost his bartending gig. The hotel was not interested in having him bartend during the day so now they had less income again.

He needed to take action.

The next morning he begged at his temp agency. They reluctantly gave him another assignment.

As fate would have it, the new assignment was back with Ron Buster and Wrigley Neighbors Realty. Buster had just fired another temp. Everyone else at Dwayne's agency was out on assignment, and Buster needed someone immediately. He begrudgingly agreed to try Dwayne again.

Dwayne got off the Red Line at Addison at 8:25 a.m. He was so sleepy he turned right instead of left and as he crossed the street, he found himself approaching Wrigley Field.

Get it together!

He turned around and walked east back under the El tracks and past the little storefront of El Burrito Mexicano. He'd once eaten one of their enormous burritos sitting on the curb drunk on beer after a Cubs game. He remembered it being tasty.

He hurried forward through the cold. He was pleased with himself that he'd be showing up early to his first day back at Wrigley Neighbors Realty, but he was not happy about the twenty mile per hour winds blowing sharp crystals of snow and five degree temperatures into his face. He thought he'd dressed warmly enough. Under his big puffy jacket and scarf, he wore a heavy tweed suit that had been purchased at a resale shop by a costumer two years ago when he'd been playing a young Sigmund Freud. The company had no storage space for costumes, so they sold the suit to Dwayne at the end of the run for ten dollars. It fit him beautifully.

He wished he'd put on long underwear under the heavy wool slacks. The wind was blowing hard from the east off the lake, carrying all that frosty lake-effect snow. He had to lean firmly into it as he walked. By the end of the five blocks from the Red Line CTA station to Wrigley Neighbors Realty, snow was frozen to his eyebrows and his face was bright red and aching.

Sometimes he hated Chicago.

Dwayne pushed into the door of the office and pulled off his hat. He was fully awake now.

"Please!" Ron Buster said. "Be careful where you drop your

snow!"

What an irritating voice!

Dwayne looked around him, his eyes still dazzled by the white-out blizzard. Wrigley Neighbors Realty was a small office. Snow had flown off his hat onto the closest of the desks.

"Sorry, Mr. Buster," Dwayne said. He flashed the "bite-and-smile" grin that he'd learned in a commercial acting class. It was a tricky acting skill. One had to take a bite of the advertiser's product and immediately register a pleased smile of taste-bud appreciation. Having worked at it so rigorously, it was a genuine-looking smile he could conjure instantly no matter his real emotions.

Dwayne's obvious good looks did nothing for him with Buster. The two leading sellers in the office were very good-looking people, and they treated Buster like dirt. He hated attractive people.

"Put your things in the break room," he told Dwayne. "I'm setting you up in the supply room today. Not many showings in this weather, so the agents will be wanting the desks."

The supply room? Dwayne didn't remember a supply room.

He stamped the snow off his feet and hung up his damp coat and hat on the coat rack in the break room. This was a small, unattractive, windowless room with a round table and four chairs, a small refrigerator, a sink, a microwave, and a fourteen cup Salton Jumbo Java coffee maker. Dwayne was about to pour himself a cup when Buster popped into the room.

"Come on. You can come back to that. Let's get you set up."

Dwayne forced another smile. The clock on the wall read 8:40 a.m. He wouldn't start being paid until 9 a.m. His brain still felt stunned from the five-block walk through the blizzard, but he was determined to cooperate.

When Buster led him to the "supply room," Dwayne realized why he had not remembered it. *Room* was a gross exaggeration. It was a large closet with a printer, fax machine, shelves of office supplies, and a tiny table with mailing supplies. There was floor space for one person to stand. Two, if they were having stand-up sex. The table had been cleared, a laptop placed atop it, a stack of hand-written spreadsheets beside the laptop, and a rolling desk chair set before it.

"Sit please," Buster said.

Dwayne squeezed past him and sat in the chair. It was too low for comfortable typing on the laptop. If he raised his elbows too quickly, he'd bang them on the wall. Buster seemed satisfied. His short, curly salt and pepper hair was brushed straight up reminding Dwayne of a celluloid drill sergeant. He glared down at Dwayne through large black-framed glasses, a tuft of chest hair showing at the opening of his button-down shirt.

"It'll be cozy, but it does have the virtue of no phone to distract you." He gestured to the hand-written spreadsheets. "This is the same project you were on before, so I don't need to waste time explaining it. However, the last person working on this was screwing it up, so please correct any mistakes you find."

Dwayne felt claustrophobic. The hand-written spreadsheets were a mess with the handwriting of fifteen different real estate agents. The Wrigley Neighbors Realty logo bounced like a pong ball on the laptop before him.

"Okay," Dwayne said.

"You may be interrupted when agents need to use the photocopier or the fax. Obviously, you need to accommodate the agents."

"Of course."

"Don't screw up." Buster left Dwayne in his tiny cubby.

Hoping to make a good impression, Dwayne got his coffee and started work ten minutes early. However, since Buster didn't pass by the supply closet again until 9:30, Dwayne's effort to impress was wasted.

At 10:15 his cell phone rang. It was Wallace Proctor. Dwayne had a moment's hesitation, then hit the "decline call" button on his phone and set the ringer to vibrate.

At 10:30 he felt his phone vibrating in his pocket. Wallace Proctor again. At the previous night's rehearsal, when they'd worked the scene in which Titus discovers his daughter, Lavinia, has been raped, he began to sob uncontrollably. Once it was clear that the sobbing had gone beyond anything that would work for the scene and that Wallace wasn't stopping, Dwayne called for a ten minute break to sit down with the actor. He talked with him, but nothing Wallace said made any sense. He kept talking about "ancient sorrows" and the "dangers of hidden emotions" but everything was disjointed. He seemed to be talking mainly to himself. Dwayne gave him the rest of the night off, and they went on to another scene.

Dwayne looked out of the storage closet and saw that Buster was just a couple cubicles away, talking with one of the agents. Wallace's call would not possibly be quick. He hit the "decline call" button again. A few minutes later he called up his voice mail to listen to Wallace's a message.

"Dwayne, old man," Wallace said in his rumbling baritone. "Ah…" And then came the longest pause. Dwayne could hear him breathing into the phone. "I don't think I can do it," he said finally. "I really don't."

I don't think I can do it? Was he quitting the show? Wallace could be a pain in the ass, but he had shown some real brilliance. Dwayne felt confident he was going to be an excellent Titus. And he had no understudies. Replacing him would throw the production into chaos.

His phone stutter-buzzed. Wallace had left a second message.

"Listen," Wallace said. Again a long, long pause with Wallace's breathing unaccompanied by words. Dwayne glanced out at into the office space. Buster was still just a couple cubicles away. *For the love of the comatose Jesus!*

"Yeah," Wallace's message said. "I, ah, I, really. I really don't think I can do this. I wanted to tell you in person. But. I'm going down to Louisville this evening. I don't know when I'll be back. I hope you'll understand."

What in the living hell?

Dwayne's phone buzzed in his hand once again. It was Wallace. He answered immediately.

"Don't go to Louisville," he whispered into the phone. "Meet me at 5:30 tonight."

"What's that, Dwayne?" Wallace said sadly. "I can't hear you."

"I'll meet you at 5:30 at John Barleycorn," Dwayne whispered slightly louder. "I'll buy you dinner. We'll talk."

"I don't think talking will do it," Wallace droned. "These are ancient sorrows. *Titus* is the giant paddle. The bodies float to the surface."

The Fuck?

"Listen: Maybe *that's* what's making you brilliant, Wallace. You are going to be monumental. I can help you manage the sorrows."

"Sometimes you have to return to the scene of the crime," Wallace said. "The scab is torn. You can't just wipe it and go on."

"Meet me at 5:30," Dwayne said.

"First marriage. First child," Wallace sighed.

"Let's discuss it at dinner. I'll buy."

"One daughter," Wallace said. "But she's gone."

Holy Jesus in the tomb.

"I can't do it, Dwayne. I truly can't."

"Wallace. Listen. This is more than the show. Come and talk with me." Was Wallace's daughter was dead? He was playing Titus, whose daughter is raped and mutilated and then he kills her to put her out of her misery. An actor had to feel the emotions of his character, and if he was also dealing with something similar in real life, it could be disastrous emotionally. He needed Wallace to play Titus, but he didn't want to drive the man to suicide. Just two days ago, Spalding Gray, one of Dwayne's favorite performers, had drowned himself in New York. He wouldn't be able to stand it if Wallace did that.

If he knew what Wallace was going through, maybe he could help.

"Listen, Wallace," he said. "George Aleister, one of the investors in the show, is one of the leading psychiatrists on the North Shore. Let's get together. With his expertise and our understanding about how theatre interacts with life, maybe we can heal this ancient sorrow."

Aleister really was brilliant. Dwayne was sure he could get him to do some pro bono work here.

But Wallace wasn't saying anything.

"Wallace?" he said. "What do you think?"

Wallace sighed deeply. He made some sounds that almost sounded like words, but not quite.

"Wallace?" Dwayne said again. "I want to see you triumph over this."

More breathing. Nothing but breathing.

"What do you think?" Dwayne repeated.

"I know what I think," Buster said, standing right outside the supply closet, trapping Dwayne in the tiny space, his hands on his hips. "I think you've been on your cell phone the entire time I was talking to Judith about the Anderson property. I think instead of doing the work you are being paid to do, you are once again chatting on the phone on my time."

Buster stood with his head cocked to one side like a cocker spaniel, a fierce look on his face. A furious fury little dog.

Dwayne gazed at him, frozen, with the phone to his ear. He heard Wallace continue his pained breathing. Dwayne felt like a school child caught by the angry nun, a feeling that took him straight back to the second grade.

"Hang up the phone, Mr. Finnegan."

Dwayne put his hand over the phone.

"Just give me one second, Mr. Buster," Dwayne said. "My friend's in a deep emotional crisis. I just need to arrange to meet him after work."

"Collect your things, Finnegan," Buster said. "You will never return to Wrigley Neighbors Realty ever again."

26

Tuesday, January 13, 2004

"They're trying to drive your husband mad," Aleister said to Angela, as Dwayne let him into their apartment much later that night.

"Really?" Angela said. "That's not a long ride."

Dwayne cocked his head at her, but she didn't smile. It was, after all, very late. Was something changing in her feelings toward him? Could he possibly lose her? That would be the worst thing of all.

"Aleister was kind enough to give me a ride home through the blizzard after he helped me calm down Wallace," Dwayne said. "He even sat through rehearsal while Wallace did the scene he failed to do last night. I promised him a drink." The men struggled out of their winter coats and snowy boots.

"You know you are always welcome," Angela told Aleister. In the three years since Lisa died, Angela always encouraged Dwayne to bring Aleister around. She felt sorry for him. His undertone of sorrow never quite went away.

She gave a second look to Dwayne himself, however, did not feel quite so welcoming. What was going on?

Dwayne brought out a bottle of red and poured glasses for them all.

A Red Line train rumbled by on the track outside their front windows. The track was just on the other side of the street in front of the building, so they could see people's faces as they went by on the El. Once they'd seen Tom on the train, and they'd all waved at each other madly. He lived one stop north of them.

Dwayne handed the glasses around

"Maybe we should drink to Wallace," Aleister said.

"Drink to *you*," Dwayne insisted. "I don't know if I could have calmed him down alone."

"What's wrong with Wallace?" Angela asked. She sat on a couch and curled her legs under her. She looked very tired.

Aleister laughed.

"*Our Lady of Perpetual Crybabies*." Dwayne put his face into his hands. "I thought his daughter had died. On the phone he says: *She's gone*. So sorrowfully…"

"Wallace is an interesting case," Aleister said, leaning back into the easy chair with his wine glass. "Over dinner, he tells us: She's dead *to me*. Turns out they fought. They're not talking."

"And for this I lost my job!" Dwayne blurted.

"Wait a minute," Angela said. She uncurled her legs and sat up straight. "You got fired again?"

You fucking blabbermouth. He felt panic rolling up his insides.

"Really, Dwayne?" She set her wine glass down firmly on the cable spool coffee table in front of her. "Are we heading toward more late fees?"

"Late fees?" Aleister said.

Angela waved him off. "What did you do?" she asked Dwayne.

"Wallace kept calling me." Dwayne's voice sounded pathetic and whiny. "I wasn't going to answer, but then I listened to his voicemail. He was going to drive to Louisville. He was quitting the show. Without him *I have no show*."

"How does that make you lose you your job?" she said.

"I called him to meet me after work, but he just kept breathing on the phone."

"Everybody breathes, Dwayne," Angela said loudly, tapping her finger to her knee.

"He's breathing into the receiver not saying anything, and I'm trying to get him to agree to meet me, but suddenly the boss is standing there. And he fires me."

"You couldn't get off the phone?" she demanded.

"I thought Wallace was freaking out because his daughter died, and he's playing Titus Andronicus who mercy-kills his daughter. And I think because his real daughter has died, it's totally freaking him out.

I think he's going to kill himself, like Spalding Gray in the East River after he saw that horrible movie, *Big Fish*. I'm staying on the phone because I think my actor is in a psychological crisis!"

"*Big Fish*?" Aleister said.

"Don't get into it," Angela warned.

"Wallace was being overdramatic," Aleister explained. "He had a *fight* with his daughter, who is pointedly not dead."

"And you lost your job over that, Dwayne?!?!" She pushed herself back in the couch and let out a pressured sigh.

"Wallace has issues," Aleister interjected. "He told his daughter she was dead to him, and he doesn't know how to fix the damage. Apparently he's been a mostly absent father. They've got some heavy lifting to repair their relationship."

"And that should be Dwayne's problem?" She turned abruptly to Dwayne. "What did the temp agency say? Are they going to send you somewhere else?"

"I had to beg to get this assignment," Dwayne said. "I was afraid to call in."

"Goddamn it, Dwayne!"

"But I did! I did call in. Ellen got huffy with me and said the client was right. I'm not being paid to talk with my friends on the phone. I should have turned off my phone until my lunch break."

"Excellent point!"

"In which case Wallace might be in Louisville right now, and I could cancel my show."

"I doubt it. Drama queen," Angela said.

"Anyway, the agency is short of temps. They might give me another chance," Dwayne said hopefully.

"Did Ellen say that?"

"Well... Not exactly. But they'd just sent me back to Wrigley Realty, which had already fired me once."

"That's not something to be proud of, Dwayne. But thank god your precious Wallace got what he wanted!"

"He's a mess," Dwayne said.

"And it's Saint Dwayne to the rescue." She walked into the kitchen. Dwayne followed her a few steps and saw her dump her wine down the drain. That wasn't a good sign. He slinked back to his seat and she followed into the living room.

"I'm sorry you guys are struggling," Aleister said. "I wish the show budget allowed Dwayne to get paid, but I can't put any more money in."

"Wait. What?" Angela glared at Dwayne with eyes of fire. "You're producing and directing and babysitting these actors to the point that you can't earn any money anywhere else, and you're not getting paid?"

A deathly hush fell over the room.

"Oh," Aleister said, embarrassed. "This was something…not discussed?"

"I'm not getting paid *right now*," Dwayne explained quickly. He really *had* meant to bring this up with Angela, but he hadn't found the right moment. "We had to make some choices. So my stipend is *deferred* until after the ticket sales. Once we get our expenses covered, I get my money. Don't worry."

She stepped in front of Dwayne. "*After* expenses? What about this eight thousand dollar sword that Ms. Coco-Pants left on the train? Is that one of the expenses?"

"I, um," Dwayne stammered, looking up at her uncomfortably. "I'm not sure how that issue is going to be…resolved."

"And if this show goes bust, what happens then?"

"Well, if there's no money…"

"Then no money for Dwayne and Angela," she concluded.

"Well, I guess, that *could* be the case…"

Dwayne wished she wouldn't stand right over him. He felt she might swat him at any moment.

"Is anyone else's stipend deferred?"

Dwayne said nothing.

"So everyone else gets paid regardless. You are one fuck of a negotiator." She shook her head and walked to the end of the living room.

"The point is, I needed this show for Gregor Foxx to see," Dwayne said, slightly relieved that she'd moved away from him. "I've got to make this the best show I can, and this seemed the way to do it. If I get work at the Public Theater, I could have a career like Brad

Cunningham. We could make some real money."

"There you go!" Aleister said. "Dwayne's got his eye on the prize."

"Brad Cunningham," Angela scoffed. "The creep who tried to get into your pants when you were in high school?"

"Well, he didn't try to get in my pants until I was in college. But he was Tony-nominated last year."

"You are so full of shit. You can sleep on one of your many comfy couches! And maybe tomorrow I'll be talking to Bonnie." She disappeared into the bedroom, then threw his pillow and pajamas out onto the living room floor. She slammed the door behind her.

"Well, that could have gone better," Aleister said.

27

Wednesday, January 14, 2004

"All right then, and *plunge!*" Tom cried out, as the actors playing Titus's sons Lucius, Quintus, Martius, and Mutius, plunged with their swords at Queen Tamora's oldest son, Alarbus. Alarbus threw back his head and his arms in a simulacrum of intense pain. Four dancers behind him swayed wildly with their arms in the air, impersonating the flames of a sacrificial bonfire. A recording of Ry Joodey's solo from his song, 'Gravity's Edge', played underneath them. "Good! Good all the way around!" Tom shouted. "And continue!"

Tom's choreography was exactly what Dwayne wanted. He wished he could feel good about the fine work he was seeing, but he kept wondering if his wife were calling Bonnie. Bonnie's office was filled with Chicago's most cut-throat divorce lawyers.

He owned so little, he couldn't lose much in a divorce. Except the love of his life. And all of his happiness.

He looked over at Ry, the virtuoso guitarist who served as his music director. Rather than watching the choreography, Ry was chatting up Melinda, who was smiling and flipping her chestnut-colored hair back, and cocking her hip just so.

Ry flipped back his own rock-and-roll pompadour and grinned her a sexy grin. She appeared to enjoy it very much.

Holy Magdalene of the fornicating dolphins.

"And circle!" Tom said. The sons of Titus swept clockwise around Alarbus and the human bonfire, their swords extended inward as they moved in long dance strides. It looked great.

"Ry!" Dwayne called, loud enough for the musician to hear him but not so loud as to disturb Tom and the group on stage. The guitarist looked at him. Dwayne nodded toward the dancing actors to remind him he needed to be watching this. Ry glanced toward the dancers, smiled, nodded back at Dwayne, and went right back to chatting up Melinda, who leaned in toward him eagerly. Were they already fucking, or were they just flirting toward penetration?

At the beginning of the play, Titus returns triumphant from the war with the Goths. The Roman Gods demand a sacrifice. Tamora's eldest son Alarbus is to be hacked to death and burned on a bonfire. Hendrix-style music would begin under Tamora's begging for the life of her son, and right through the sacrificial dance scene.

Tom took the dancers through the stages of throwing Alarbus into the fire to be caught and enveloped by the flame people, their swords streaming with ribbons of red fabric indicating his blood.

"Great!" Dwayne called. "That was beautiful. Are we ready to take it with the live music?"

"We are!" Tom's face glowed with the exertion of working with the dancers and the pleasure of his choreography looking so good.

Ry, still chatting with Melinda, did not seem to notice.

"Ry?" Dwayne called.

Ry looked at him, oblivious.

"Time to play."

"Right," Ry said. He nodded at Melinda and shrugged, and shuffled over to the corner of the rehearsal space where his drummer and bass player were set up.

With the band, the rehearsal space was doubly overstuffed and cramped. The drummer complained that he had to set his toms too close to play comfortably. The actors waiting to go on had to stand in the corners. There was no room for chairs. The table at which Dwayne and Joan worked had to be taken down so there was room for the dancers to dance. Joan worked with her prompt book on her lap, looking explosively sullen.

Ingrid burst into the space and laid some papers in front of Dwayne. "Signatures," she said.

"What's this?"

"I'm setting up accounts at Home Depot and Sherwin-Williams. They require both our signatures. There'll be more."

Dwayne gave it a look and signed. She flew back out of the room.

"This is the solo section of Gravity's Edge, right?" Ry called to Tom.

"Right!" Tom said. "Start in low with Coco's line: A mother's tears in passion for her son. Slowly build through her and Titus's speeches, and then erupt with the dance and sacrifice."

"Sure thing," Ry said, though he appeared to have stopped paying attention after Tom said *Right!*

"All right, let's take it from page four with Tamora's line," Joan called out. "Stay, Roman brethren. And we move right into the music and dance."

Coco stepped into place with the rest of the actors. "Stay, Roman brethren," she declaimed. "Gracious conqueror, Victorious Titus, rue the tears I shed." She was interrupted by a series of unmusical twangs from Ry's guitar. She continued, uncertainly, "A mother's tears in passion for her son..." but then stopped as the twanging continued. She turned to Dwayne. "Is that what he's going to be playing?"

"Sorry, sorry," Ry said with a smile. "Got to be in tune. Gimme a moment to tune."

Coco looked at him in disbelief. "Now ain't that something you do before rehearsal?" she snapped. "You don't see me doing vocal exercises when it's time to deliver a line."

"One minute." Ry continued to tune, the smile still on his face.

"Instead of getting ready, you mercilessly flirting with some basic white ingénue."

"Hey!" Melinda snapped in her direction. "Quit calling me that!"

"All right, everyone, let's please settle," Dwayne said. "Ry, could you please tune before in the future?"

Ry grunted. Dwayne decided to take that as an affirmative. "Thank you. And, Coco, respect for castmates, please?"

Coco rolled her eyes and grunted. Dwayne decided to take that as an affirmative, as well. "Thank you." He looked at Melinda who looked only slightly mollified. He nodded at her and smiled, and she smiled back, pleased at least to be acknowledged. Dwayne turned back to the band. The drummer and bass player looked ready. "May we continue? Ry?"

Ry cocked his head one way and then another. Dwayne decided to take that also as an affirmative. "Thank you. Let's begin again with Tamora's line."

"Stay, Roman brethren," Coco said, sounding more annoyed than desperate. "Gracious conqueror, Victorious Titus, rue the tears I shed."

Ry brought in his first note, very low, and began to build under Coco's lines. It sounded great. Just right. Ry continued to build as Coco's line climaxed with: "Sweet mercy is nobility's true badge: Thrice noble Titus, spare my first-born son!"

The guitar burst into full sound as the sons of Titus began the sacrificial dance and Wallace (as Titus) said: "To sacrifice your son is marked, and die he must. Away with him! and make a fire straight; and with your swords, upon a pile of wood, hew his limbs till they be clean consumed."

The fire people entered from the back, swirling and burning to the wildness of Ry's guitar, the drums rolling beneath him, and the bass keeping time. Titus' sons danced with the swords and plunged toward Alarbus in his pain. They pulled back and began to circle, but then faltered as Ry pulled one note excessively long, his eyes closed, his face expressing a kind of rock and roll ecstasy. The dancers tried to extend their strides, but as each had a different idea how to flex with the music, their unity was disheveled. They hesitated, waiting for the beat on which to grab Alarbus, but Ry was off on another musical thought, eyes closed to what was happening on stage. Three of the four sons grabbed Alarbus, looking more confused than fierce, and carried him up to the flame people. The fourth son had stopped and looked at Tom in hopeless confusion.

"Okay," Tom called. "Let's stop a moment." Ry played two more notes, oblivious, eyes closed. Tom moved up right in front of him and called: "Okay, stop, please!" Ry opened his eyes and stopped playing. He smiled his insouciant smile. "What's up?"

"You're playing the solo differently," Tom said.

"Yeah?"

"It needs to be exactly the same every time for the dancers," Tom said. "Their movements are choreographed to specific beats of the music."

"I've never played that solo the same way twice. That's what makes a solo cool." He glanced over at Melinda and winked. She smiled back at him.

"That might make it cool for a regular gig," Tom agreed, "but with dancers you've got to do it the same way every time. The same way as the recording."

"Are you kidding?" Ry said. "I wouldn't even remember how I did it in the recording."

Tom turned and looked at Dwayne for help.

"You're going to need to sit down with the recording and memorize that performance so you can replicate it," Dwayne said.

Ry snorted a derisive laugh. "That ain't rock and roll."

"Maybe not," Dwayne said. "But that's what the dancers require to do their jobs."

"Look," Ry said, gesturing to his drummer and bass player, "Lenny and Josh and I all listen to each other as we play, and we flex with it, and improvise together. It's all about listening and playing in the moment. Why can't the dancers do that?"

"They can't do that," Tom interjected, "because they have to look like a unit, dancing together. The sons of Titus all have to grab Alarbus at the same moment. They have to present him into the fire at the same moment. They have to hack his limbs one after another *on the beats*. If the beats aren't clear for them and for Alarbus, it's a safety issue with their swords. They could accidentally hit him. They could *hurt* him."

Ry looked back at Tom in continuing disbelief.

"I don't know, man," Ry said. "This is not what I imagined I'd be doing. At all."

Tom turned to Dwayne with a hopeless expression. Dwayne brought him over to Ry for a quiet confab. "Are all the numbers as tightly choreographed like this?" he asked Tom.

"Just this and the rape of Lavinia," Tom said.

Dwayne turned to Ry. "Just like these dancers, Melinda's physical safety is going to depend on that section being on the money." He hoped Ry would not want the object of his current flirtation to be hurt. "So we really need exactly consistent performances on both those. There will be room for you to breathe on the other numbers. But the dancers need you to be totally consistent for those two parts of the show." He looked Ry in the eye. "You can do that, right?"

Ry grunted noncommittally.

"Let's try the band playing in unison with the recording now. You three will have to memorize those two performances. Okay?" He looked at each of the musicians. They nodded reluctantly.

Dwayne clapped his hands. "Okay, everyone, we're going to take it again from Coco's line. Joan will start the recording of the music, and the band will play along. Let's try it!"

They ran the scene with everyone looking a little uncomfortable, but the pieces fit together and the dancers were able to make their moves in unison. At the end of the scene, Ry Joodey looked disgusted.

Sometimes a director had to make performers uncomfortable. If it pushed them to a great performance, they'd be grateful. Or not grateful. Either way was okay with Dwayne. He wasn't feeling happy, either, at the moment. He just needed the show to work.

28

Monday, January 19, 2004

Dwayne watched the climactic banquet of blood with rising excitement. Titus (Wallace) invites the Roman emperor and queen Tamora (Coco) to dinner. A meat pie is carried in with great ceremony. As everyone eats, Titus surprises them by killing his daughter Lavinia (Melinda) to end the shame of her rape and disfigurement. When the emperor demands the rapists be brought before him, Titus reveals that the sons of Tamora were the rapists and that they have been baked into the meat pie that Tamora is now eating. After she registers the horror of eating her children, he kills her. Then the emperor kills Titus. And Titus's remaining son kills the emperor.

The whole scene was played to the shimmer and cry of guitar, bass, and drums, the flashing of sword and splash of blood. It was truly spectacular. Titus's brother Marcus Andronicus moved in for the final speech, bodies lying all around him, red ribbons of blood everywhere.

"Okay, let's stop," Dwayne called. "We're going to run the violence again." He walked over to the band. "Guys, it's sounding really good, but remember to bring down the volume before the lines so we don't miss the first words." Ry seemed to be rubbing a smudge out of the neck of his guitar rather than listening. "Is that going to be difficult, Ry?"

"Naw. It's cool." The guitarist didn't look at him.

"Good." Dwayne wanted to grab him by the throat and throttle him. "And let's make sure to keep the tempo up."

"We know the tempo."

"It has to be played faster," Dwayne said.

"We know the tempo," Ry said again.

"Good." Dwayne pushed down his frustration. "Good!" He turned back to the cast and announced loudly: "Let's start again at the entrance of Titus and Lavinia into the banquet scene."

The actors took their positions, and Wallace stepped forward. "Welcome, my gracious lord; welcome, dread queen."

"WHERE IS HE, DWAYNE?!?!" A woman's shriek instantly stopped the action on stage. Chaz's wife, Bonnie, stood at the door of the rehearsal room, hands on hips, the curls of her red hair blazing as though lit by an internal electrical charge of fury. She looked like a supercharged apparition of the sixteenth-century Irish pirate, Grace O'Malley.

The rehearsal room stopped silent.

"Are you looking for Chaz?" Dwayne said, trying not to sound as timid as he felt.

"Who the hell else would I be looking for, Dwayne?"

"He's not here. Maybe he's at a McDonald's meeting?"

"Amazing he can take a break from fucking her!" Bonnie shouted, pointing straight at Coco.

"The what?" Coco said.

"Don't deny it, you steaming slut!" Bonnie pulled out 8x10 photos of Chaz and Coco athletically fucking on a hotel bed. She slammed them down onto Joan and Dwayne's rehearsal table.

"And there it is," Joan said in her entirely flat register, looking at the photos. Some of the cast edged forward to see and gasp and stifle giggles.

"And you, Dwayne!" she screamed. "Pimping out your actress to my husband. Is that why he put our money into this farce? So he could have his pick of your whores?"

"Hey!" Coco shouted.

"Shut the fuck up!" Bonnie blasted at her, her face pale and horrible, her cheerful freckles flattened to near invisibility by her rage. Coco backed off.

"Tell that son of a bitch he's got divorce papers coming!" Bonnie looked over at Coco. "And you, you fucking disgusting slut, you can have him."

She grabbed her photos and stormed out of the rehearsal room.

For a long moment no one said anything.

"I am not sitting still for this!" Coco stalked off the stage. She grabbed her bag and winter coat and dashed toward the door.

"Wait a minute," Dwayne shouted. He felt such a swirl of emotions: Guilt that he had not done more to stop Chaz. They'd been friends for decades. He'd stood up in their wedding. He was so sorry he'd brought him into this.

He looked for Coco in the hall, but she had already flown down the stairs and was gone. He felt useless and stupid. He could do nothing for Chaz and Bonnie now, but he still had to direct this show. And what about his own marriage? Was Angela as annoyed as he thought she was?

What a fucking mess!

He got back to the rehearsal table and suddenly Ingrid was next to him with a form. "Don't want to interrupt," she whispered. "Just a quick signature." She stuck a pen in his hand and indicated a line at the bottom of the form. He signed, assuming it was another account she needed for set materials. She had him sign two more forms, and she rushed back out of the rehearsal room.

"All right, everyone, let's take fifteen and regroup," he finally managed to say.

"No. No. No," Melinda insisted. "We are not sweeping this under the rug with a fifteen-minute break. You cannot create a hostile work environment and then pretend it doesn't exist." She looked around at the dumbfounded actors around her, and some of them perked up and began nodding with her.

"Hostile work environment?" Dwayne said.

"I don't come here to be called a whore."

"Obviously, Bonnie is very upset. There is no reason for *you* to take that personally. She's angry with Chaz and Coco...and me."

"Are we whores for you to pimp out?" Melinda insisted, looking as though she were on the edge of tears. "That's what she said. That's sexual harassment." A number of the other actors grunted voices of agreement.

"Well," Dwayne said, off-balance. Why was Melinda taking this so personally? "It's insulting, certainly, but I don't know how you could call it sexual harassment."

"You don't think it's sexual harassment when the producer of a show is taking advantage of one of the actors?" Melinda asked.

Dwayne blinked twice. "You think Coco is being taken advantage of?"

Could any of them possibly imagine that Coco was not the one calling the shots?

"There's an inherent imbalance of power," Wallace intoned in his most solemn baritone, agreeing with Melinda. "You have the producer, holding the purse strings of the production, controlling the marketing images, the very livelihood of the actors..."

"Well, now..." Dwayne started. No one's livelihood was dependent on *this* production. At what he was paying, they'd starve to death.

"And on the other hand you have the actor, always dependent for work on the producers, on the *money men*, to have an opportunity to ply our art," Wallace said with unusual bitterness in his voice. Both he and Melinda were taking this very personally. "When the overlord seeks sex with the supplicant, the situation is rife for abuse."

"Yes!" Melinda agreed, looking very upset. "Sexual harassment!"

"Come on now," Dwayne said. "You all know Coco. You've seen Chaz. I mean, it's obvious she has him wrapped around her finger."

"You deny the obvious power dynamic?" Wallace said disgustedly.

"There's some dynamic power, all right," Dwayne said. "And she's the one wielding it."

"That is painfully naïve, Dwayne," Wallace said.

"You don't think she's the one with the power?" Dwayne asked.

"Her sexuality is her only tool to stand toe-to-toe with the money man!" Wallace said. "That's the only currency she can wield."

Suddenly Joan was climbing up onto top of the rehearsal table, a prop staff in her hand. She began pounding it into the top of the table and chanting: "No exploitation!"

Joan!?!?

After a moment of confusion, all the actors took up the chant with her: "No exploitation!" they cried over and over, louder and louder. "No exploitation! No exploitation!"

Dwayne sat down in his chair at the director's table and buried his face in his hands.

29

By the time things calmed down, there was only a half hour of rehearsal time left, and everyone's energy was hopelessly scattered. Coco was gone. Melinda's face was wet with tears. Dwayne dismissed the actors for the night and took the long, cold El ride home. Snow blew by the windows of the train as he looked out into the lonesome night. At this hour there were only a few people in the car. An old lady in ragged clothes mumbled and shuffled through the multiple plastic bags at her feet. A middle-aged woman in a fur cap and fur trimmed parka read a copy of *Lies and the Lying Liars Who Tell Them* with a wry look on her face. At the far end of the car, a young man sat with a guitar resting in his lap. Dwayne sincerely hoped he would not start playing. He wanted calm. Would things be calm at home? Would Angela still be mad at him? She didn't typically hold a grudge for long. And what about tomorrow's rehearsal? Only eleven days remained until opening, and they had so much to accomplish. He'd hoped to perfect and set the climax tonight, but that hadn't happened. His stomach turned over with nerves.

This was nothing like the shows he'd done with Bobby. When Bobby was in charge, you never saw him sweat. Everyone adored Bobby. Nobody screamed *No exploitation!* at him.

This was Dwayne's production, but he had a managing director calling the shots; he had ensemble members taking votes; he had a stage manager who scheduled "ensemble meetings" without telling him, and tonight she stood up on the table and led the cast in: *No exploitation!*

St. Sebastian and the thousand penetrating swords.

What would Bobby do?

He imagined it for a moment.

Bobby would lean back, grin, nod his head, and say: *Right on.* And suddenly he would be at the forefront of the crisis. He would speak from the cast's deepest desires, and yet the new direction he set would fulfill Bobby's own needs. And once again everyone would love him and want to sleep with him or be his best friend.

How did he do that?

Dwayne was talented and smart and good-looking. Bobby was all that, but more good-looking, and also had a charisma well beyond Dwayne's.

Dwayne sighed deeply. He exited the train at the Loyola stop and walked down Albion Avenue through the blowing, stinging snow to his apartment building. He came up the steps to their door on the second floor. Angela opened it when his key was only halfway in the lock.

"We have company." She stepped back looking both quizzical and annoyed, and he saw Chaz and Aleister sitting in an easy chair and love seat at the curve of their living room. Chaz looked sadly deflated, and Aleister looked supportive but disappointed.

"Sorry about the invaders," Dwayne whispered to her. "Bonnie wants a divorce. Does he know?"

"Ingrid called him and told him."

"Ingrid? She was gone before Bonnie arrived."

"She told him Bonnie brought lurid photographs of him and Coco, shouted about divorce, and that the cast revolted over sexual exploitation."

"That woman always seems to know everything," Dwayne said in bewilderment.

"Chaz called Aleister and asked him to meet *here*." Angela stepped back and looked toward them with her eyes in slits. "Apparently our apartment is their apartment."

"Sorry about that. Things should calm down." Dwayne shook the snow off his coat, hooked it on the coat tree by the door.

"Yeah? Like when?"

"I wish I knew." Dwayne looked at her helplessly and went over to sit by his friends. Angela followed him in.

"In the end, this is your own fault," Aleister told Chaz.

"I know," Chaz said, looking at the floor.

"And I really can't sympathize." Aleister leaned back in the love seat. "You have a beautiful, accomplished wife. She's smart and fiery and dynamic. You can't have believed she would accept you fooling around."

"I didn't think she'd find out."

Angela snorted a bitter laugh. "You men. You think you're so tricky, but when you're guilty, it's so obvious."

"Did she see me that night when Dwayne was bartending at the Whitehall?"

Angela looked accusingly at Dwayne. "You didn't tell me he was there," she said coldly.

Dwayne cringed inside. "I was hoping this fling would end without damage."

"Did she know I was there?" Chaz repeated.

"She didn't see you," Dwayne said. "But Coco walked up, looking for you, ordered a drink, and pointedly said she'd be waiting in her hotel room. She looked Bonnie up and down like Bonnie was the competition."

"Christ," Chaz said.

"Bonnie would text me sometimes late at night," Angela said, "to see if Dwayne was home, because you told her you were staying late at rehearsals and production meetings. If Dwayne was home, I told the truth. So she knew you were lying."

"Fuck," Chaz said.

"What did you think was going to happen?" Aleister said.

"I figured Coco would get tired of me, and things would go back to normal."

"So you aren't in love with Coco," Angela said.

"No. I thought this would be a short wild ride, and I'd be happy to go home."

"You are so stupid," Angela said.

"Why did you think you had the kind of marriage where this would be okay?" Aleister said.

Chaz had no answer.

Angela poked Dwayne. "Don't you think it either, mister!"

"I would never," Dwayne said. "Never."

"Just shut up," Angela said.

Chas looked at Angela like a beaten puppy. "Do you think she'd forgive me?"

Angela cocked her head in disbelief. "She hired a private detective to get photos. She's already signed with a divorce lawyer. What do you think?"

"Yeah, but she *is* a divorce lawyer," Dwayne said. "She works in an office full of divorce lawyers."

"Do you think she'd take me back?" Chaz asked.

"She's got that wild Irish temper," Angela said. "They say Italian women can be sharp." She looked pointedly at Dwayne. "And they can." She turned back to Chaz. "But these Irish women like Bonnie? I mean, take a clue! Her hair looks like flames!"

Chaz nodded his head sadly. "I've been a complete idiot. It's like when I was a kid and I found the Valentine candy my dad bought for my mom. I ate the whole thing and threw up."

"I think this is a little worse than that," Angela said.

"I just meant, like, even while I was eating that candy, I knew it wouldn't end well. But they were so delicious, and no one was around to stop me, so I kept stuffing them in my mouth."

"A greedy little boy," Angela said. "And now you threw away an excellent marriage for a few rolls in the hay."

"Do you all hate me now?"

"I could understand better if you'd actually fallen in love, but you betrayed Bonnie for a fling," Aleister said. "And Bonnie is spectacular. Bonnie was so sweet to me when Lisa was killed. You betrayed her for a cheap thrill."

"You created a lot of chaos," Dwayne added. "My cast is up in arms, too."

"Are you still going to be my friends?" Chaz said.

"I am putting my friendship with Bonnie first," Angela said. "So I don't know how that will work out."

"You've made my life harder," Dwayne said. "But I won't abandon you."

"Nor I," said Aleister. "But now my friendship with Bonnie will be awkward. I'm not happy about that."

"Why is the cast up in arms?" Angela asked.

"They are calling it sexual harassment."

"They've got a point," Aleister said.

"Who says they are being harassed?" Angela asked.

"No one is saying *they* are being harassed," Dwayne said. "They are just calling it that." He looked at Chaz. "Correct me if I'm wrong, but it looked to me like Coco was the instigator."

"Totally," Chaz agreed.

"It's never okay for a producer to seek sex with an actress," Aleister said. "The balance of power is skewed toward the producer."

"What power?" Chaz said. "Everyone knows I'm not a real theatrical producer."

"Aren't you?" Aleister said. "You are producing this show. You are in control of the marketing. The marketing looks like this is a show about Coco."

Chaz squirmed. "I used her image because she's sexy, and desirable."

"Melinda is a very pretty young woman playing Lavinia," Aleister said. "Orlando Gunn is a striking young man. Wallace Proctor is handsome and distinguished—and he's playing the title role! Women buy more theatre tickets than men."

"There's an old advertising truism: you use a sexy woman because men want to have her and women want to be her," Chaz said.

"A truism cooked up by advertising *men*," Angela said. "You are totally in the wrong here, Chaz. All the way around."

"Unwittingly or not, you created a sexually hostile environment," Aleister said. "It gives the appearance that an actor traded sex for marketing exposure." He turned to Dwayne. "You *do* owe an apology to the cast and to Coco," he said.

"Wallace said the same thing," Dwayne said. "It never occurred to me…"

"You had no idea what your marketing looks like?" Angela asked him sharply, "and no idea that those two were fucking?"

"Well…" Dwayne said.

"You had a lot of other things to think about, so maybe you

didn't put it together," Aleister said. "But that doesn't change what happened."

A sudden sharp knock on the door startled Dwayne. He opened it, and Coco pushed him to one side. She walked up to Chaz and stood before him, her feet wide spread and her hands on her hips.

"I thought I'd find you here."

Chaz looked up at her, hopeless and speechless. Angela looked at her as though the Devil herself had arrived, but Coco did not glance at Angela.

"I guess I owe you an apology," Dwayne said.

Coco cocked her head at him. "What?"

"For the atmosphere of...sexual exploitation," he said uncertainly.

"The *what*?" she said incredulously.

"That a member of the producing staff would...solicit...sex...in return for marketing exposure," he said, yet less certainly.

"Are you talking about me and Chaz?" she said in disbelief.

"Well...yes."

"Sexual exploitation," she scoffed. She laughed a deep, throaty laugh of derision. "I am in control of what my body does and nobody exploits me!" She turned back to Chaz. "How long you going to be here?"

"I...I don't know," he said.

"Well, I ain't sitting around here. And frankly, I could use a little...attention to calm my nerves. At my place." She turned back to Dwayne, knocking snow off her shoulders onto the floor. "I'm not sure I'll be at rehearsal tomorrow."

"Coco..."

"I might need some time after being subjected to his wife!" she insisted. "If that woman shows up again, I'm out the door before she opens her mouth. But otherwise we need to be full speed ahead. My face is all over town on this show. It gotta be good." She walked back to the door and opened it. She looked back at Chaz. "My place," she said pointedly, walked out the door, and shut it behind her.

Chaz looked profoundly embarrassed.

"You go to her place," Angela warned, "I never want to see your face again."

30

Tuesday, January 20, 2004

Dwayne arrived with snow caked around the ankles of his pants, shivering and wondering what fresh hell awaited him. He pounded his feet to remove the snow. Why weren't the sidewalks shoveled? The entire sidewalk from the Fullerton El station to the Chicago Repertory Arts Playhouse ran in front of stores and DePaul University property. These weren't the sidewalks of little old ladies who couldn't get out of bed.

As soon as he got inside the lobby, stamping snow off his boots and ankles, Raymond Green stepped up, holding out an invoice.

"Tell Joan when she makes a change to your rehearsal schedule, I need forty-eight hours advance notice," Green said. "I'm happy for the extra income, but what if I'd rented that room to someone else?" He wiped his hand over the top of his head and flakes of dandruff fell down on the invoice like sand across the desert.

"They're up there early again?"

Green chuckled grimly. "It amazes me how little you know about what goes on in your own production." He stuffed the invoice for extra rehearsal time into Dwayne's cold, weather-reddened hand.

"Hey," Dwayne said. "I looked into upstairs mainstage yesterday. The set from the last show is still up. When is it going to be out of there?"

"Don't you worry about a thing, pretty mama," Green sang to the tune of an old Stevie Wonder song and walked off.

Green was so weird.

Dwayne looked at the invoice. This ad hoc meeting of his cast was no doubt precipitated by Bonnie's invasion of last night's rehearsal. That put it clearly into the category of Chaz's fault. *No need for me to feel bad about that*, Dwayne murmured to himself. He folded up the invoice and stuffed it into his back pocket.

He walked into the rehearsal room upstairs to find the cast sitting in a large oval, Joan perched grimly powerful in her seat at the top of the oval. Melinda stalked the center of the oval, addressing her castmates.

"We can't have it," Melinda said. "We can't let this be the way our company does business." The other actors nodded in righteous anger. True to her word, Coco was not in attendance.

Dwayne felt a momentary flutter of impotence. But then he thought: *What would Bobby do?* He would sweep in and make the situation his own. Maybe Dwayne couldn't *be* Bobby, but he could *play* Bobby. Right now. Without preparation or rehearsal.

"Right on," Dwayne said, sweeping his snow flecked coat from his shoulders and tossing it and his hat to a chair at the side of the room. "Right on, Melinda. I hear you." She looked at him in confusion. He grabbed another chair and flipped it into place at a gap in the oval and relaxed into it, his legs crossed at the ankles before him, leaning back into the chair. "And we can't wait for the end of this production. We need to make the change *right now*."

"Yeah," Melinda said, looking wildly surprised, but also pleased. "That's what we were saying."

"Absolutely." Dwayne leaned suddenly into the circle. "I mean, what is it when the money men are in control of the art?" He extended his arms to them all, his brethren. "We *artists* have to be in control of the art. Not the money men."

"That's right," Wallace intoned deeply.

"You go all around this city. You see our posters everywhere. Our ads are about to start running." He stood up into the center of the oval, and Melinda sat down, deeply curious to what he'd say.

What would Bobby do?

I'll show you what Bobby would do!

"Obviously, I'm not going to name any names," Dwayne said, "but what if you had a production where Actor A is having sex with Producer B and all the publicity featured Actor A all over town? That publicity boosts Actor A's career. Isn't that an insult to the integrity of

176 ◆ Richard Engling

Actor A? And isn't that also an affront to every actor who isn't having sex with Producer B? Everyone loses. We can't have that."

"We can't!" Melinda said.

"Producer B needs to make amends. And he needs to make it now." The Dwayne part of him felt nervous saying this, but he was playing Bobby, and his Bobby was driving this boat.

"Realistically," Joan said in her weirdly passionless voice, "is there budget to rework the marketing at this point?"

"That's not my concern," Dwayne said, totally ignoring his own feelings. Practical Dwayne could see no way to afford to redo any of the marketing. But Bobby wouldn't concern himself with that. "Ingrid is the managing director," he said in a sudden inspiration that filled him with an inner glee. "That's her job. *My* job," he said, making eye contact one after the other with every actor in the room, "is to make sure all of you look brilliant in this show. I want this to be one of the peak artistic experiences of your life."

"That's right," Orlando Gunn said. Wallace nodded along with him, and they smiled.

"I insist on an atmosphere that allows every one of you to flourish. And together we will create a kick-ass show that we will be proud of every single night!"

"All right, Dwayne!" Melinda said.

"Joan has heard your remarks," Dwayne said, in another moment of inspiration. "I propose we have Joan take our concerns to Ingrid. It will be Ingrid's job to work them out with Chaz and deal with the budget and marketing. *The rest of us* will turn our total attention to making *Titus Andronicus* the most dynamic, fascinating, impressive show we can possibly make. The play's the thing! Today is the twentieth. We open on the thirtieth. And you are all going to be brilliant in a show no one will ever forget!"

"Hear! Hear!" Wallace shouted. He stood up, applauding, and the rest of the cast followed. Dwayne applauded with them and went around the group, hugging them and slapping hands.

He loved this!

"Let's take ten and then be ready to rehearse this mother-fucker!" he shouted.

They all cheered. "Thank you, ten!" they all shouted.

Life was heaven!

This was what he loved!

31

Wednesday, January 21, 2004

Not even the sting of frozen sleet whipped into his face on twenty-five mile per hour winds could dampen Dwayne's mood after rehearsal the next night. He pushed past the Loyola students and walked up Sheridan past the bar and the head shop and turned left on Albion toward home from the El Station. He smiled all the way down the cold block past the two-flats and three-flats to his building.

Doing what Bobby would do had been a stroke of genius the night before. He wrapped up the pre-rehearsal ensemble meeting with his cast fully behind him. They'd had a great rehearsal, even with Joan, in her other-worldly emotionless voice, filling in the lines for the missing Coco.

Tonight, Coco had returned to the fold, avoiding any inessential conversations with Dwayne or her castmates, but doing a credible job as the ruthless Queen Tamora.

The show looked good, though he was still worried about Wallace, Melinda, and Orlando. Wallace could be noble, heartbroken, enraged, and ultimately vengeful as Titus Andronicus. But sometimes he stopped and stood staring into the light grid overhead. Titus was gone and Wallace was there, looking like a defeated old man. Thankfully, those moments passed quickly. But what was up with him?

Melinda started the show regal and elegant as his daughter, Lavinia, but after the rape scene, she lost all emotion and disappeared into herself. Early on, he'd seen her be brilliantly emotional, but now, nothing.

Orlando had a delightfully disturbing blend of sex appeal and evil as Aaron the Moor, but when he got to his most evil moments, he turned apologetic.

Happily, Coco was manipulative, desirable, amoral, and ruthless as Queen Tamora. On stage she was brilliant. Even better, Tom's choreography took the show into another realm. The violence that moved to the rhythms of Ry's guitar really put the show over the top. However, sometimes Ry still followed his guitar into time-altering variations and the changes put the dancers into confusion.

There were nine days until opening. Nine days until Gregor Foxx would witness his work, and Dwayne might be selected for the *Emerging Directors Program* at the Public Theater in New York City! He could taste it! All the way home he'd felt elated. Even the slashing sleet and the frozen wind could not dim his enthusiasm.

He loved directing. He loved preparing for the production, having a concept for what he wanted it to be, and then seeing what the designers and actors brought to it, and how the concept evolved and grew. Sometimes a quiet word in an actor's ear in the midst of rehearsing could help them open up something astonishing.

He pulled open the heavy door of his apartment building and stomped into the lobby, knocking the snow off his boots. He took off his hat and shook it, but the sleet was frozen to it. He took off his gloves and used the fingernails of his bright-red hands to scrape away the frozen sleet from his eyebrows.

It was way too fucking cold in this city.

He climbed the stairs to his apartment and discovered Chaz and Aleister sitting in his living room. How was Angela taking the presence of these intruders again? He really didn't need any help from them in annoying his wife.

"You aren't in a position where you can make any demands," Aleister was saying to him.

"Hey, boys," Dwayne said, surprised to see them there.

"Hi," Aleister said. Chaz just nodded, looking like he'd been pummeled for an extended period of time.

"I'm wet," Dwayne said. "Give me a minute to hang up these things." He grabbed a couple hangers out of the closet, went into the bathroom, and hung up his semi-frozen winter coat. The ankles of his jeans were solid with a tube of frozen sleet around them. He took off the pants and hung them on the shower curtain bar. His legs were bright pink. He was heading toward the bedroom for a dry pair of pants when he heard Angela sigh in the office they'd set up in the second bedroom. He went in and closed the door behind him.

"Hi."

She looked him up and down. "Nice gams," she said. "Your legs look rosy."

She didn't seem angry at him. That was good. "Yeah. What are the boys doing here?"

"Between the divorce papers and your play, Chaz is reeling. Aleister is trying to keep him off the ledge. I have papers to grade for tomorrow. I have too little sympathy for Chaz's stupidity to be supportive, so I'm in here."

"Okay. I'll leave you to it." He gave her a kiss. She accepted it! Great happiness! "Sorry about the intrusions."

"Maybe next time they could meet wherever Chaz is staying," she suggested.

"Absolutely! Yes," Dwayne agreed.

"And put on some pants."

"You think?" He gave her a deadpan look, but she just waved him away. He returned to the bedroom feeling relieved, finished clothing himself, and went out into the living room. Chaz was collapsed back into a threadbare easy chair under the first of the windows that gave onto the street scene outside. A CTA train rumbled by on the El tracks across the street, barely visible through the swirling snow.

"You have got to keep that crazy woman away from me, Dwayne," Chaz whined toward the ceiling. He'd heard Dwayne enter the room, but he hadn't turned his head to look at him.

"Ingrid showed up at McDonald's this afternoon," Aleister said.

Ingrid had not, of course, consulted with Dwayne about her plans.

Chaz sat up abruptly. "She shows up at my office with a new marketing plan this afternoon. She wants to schedule a new photo shoot with various cast members. New advertising insertions. New posters to lay out, print, and distribute. New online advertising. She wants me to spend an additional twelve thousand dollars!"

Aleister laughed grimly. "Okay, just to be clear, I will not put up any more money."

"I can't either. Especially now," Chaz said. "I came home last night, and my key doesn't work in the lock. Bonnie opens the door, shoves divorce papers in my hand, and slams the door in my face. She'd changed the locks on the condo. Our bank accounts are frozen. I can't even get my clothes. I had to stay in a hotel and buy new clothes to go to work. Thank god my credit card still works. My friend Bernie calls. He wants eight grand for his missing sword. Then Ingrid shows up right before I go into a meeting. She's insisting we have to do all this new marketing work, without any *marketing* justification, by the way. This is driven totally by actor resentments. I promise to see her in the evening to discuss. I'm late to my meeting with a reporter from the *Tribune* to unveil a new initiative. I get there and the VP of PR is waiting with the reporter, looking annoyed me with me for being late. So I apologize, and I bring out my presentation. I thought Ingrid had left, but she follows me into the meeting and starts talking, right in front of everybody, about how the marketing is necessary to alleviate the toxic work environment created by the sexual harassment. And so the Tribune reporter assumes there's a toxic work problem at *McDonald's*, and my boss is livid, and I'm explaining, no, there is no such thing, and Ingrid is standing there saying, *Yes, yes, it's real, and you have to spend the dollars to make it go away.* I'm making McDonald's look bad in front of a reporter from the biggest paper in the Midwest. Exactly the opposite of why they pay the salary that made it possible to invest in your show!"

"Jesus," Dwayne said.

"You have got to keep her away from McDonald's," Chaz insisted.

"I'll talk to her, but she never consults me about what she's doing."

"She said the whole idea came from you! She said your orders were to work up a new marketing plan that would alleviate the toxic environment that my sexual harassment had created. She said those were *your* orders."

"We didn't discuss a plan or going to MacDonald's," Dwayne said, feeling suddenly very guilty.

"So I lied to Ingrid to get her off my back," Chaz said. "I told her I'd get right on it with the marketing program she'd outlined, and she left, and then I had to do a ridiculous tap dance with the *Trib* reporter and my boss."

"What did you tell them?" Dwayne said.

"I told them I was providing pro bono marketing help to a new theatre company in the city. I told them the director was sleeping with the lead actress and featuring her in the marketing, and the other cast members got jealous. The managing director wanted me to run interference to keep the production from imploding."

"So you said *I* was doing what *you've* been doing," Dwayne said.

"I didn't mention your name!" Chaz protested. "You want me to lose my job on top of everything else?"

"I don't want you to lose your job…"

"Besides," Chaz interrupted, "if the *Tribune* wrote about backstage shenanigans at *Titus Andronicus*, it'd probably boost ticket sales."

"If the *Tribune* writes that *I'm* having sex with an actress…" Dwayne could not complete the thought.

"They say there's no such thing as bad publicity," Aleister offered.

"Tell that to my wife," Dwayne said.

"Do you think Bonnie might forgive me?" Chaz said. "You saw her when she came to the rehearsal. What did you think?"

Chaz looked pitiful. Dwayne wanted to give him hope, but it wouldn't be a favor to lie. "She looked really upset. She slapped those photos on the table in front of everyone and said she was getting divorce papers. She called my cast a bunch of whores."

"And now she's changed the locks on your condo and frozen your assets," Aleister said. "Maybe she's spent her fury. It's possible. After you suffer a while, she might be willing to reconsider."

"I thought I was hot shit, but I was a moron." Chaz closed his eyes and leaned back limply in the easy chair.

The three friends sat quietly for a time.

Chaz sat up and looked pleadingly at Dwayne. "Do you mind if I sleep on your couch tonight? I don't want to go to a hotel."

Dwayne imagined Angela's expression upon finding Chaz on the couch in the morning as she got ready to go to work. "Angela likes her privacy in the morning," he said.

"I really feel like I'm standing on the ledge here," Chaz said. "And frankly I'm in no condition to drive." Dwayne noticed an empty pint whiskey bottle lying on the floor beside him.

Chaz looked so defeated. So miserable. And it really was partially Dwayne's fault, *doing what Bobby would do*. Could he really turn him out into the blizzard on a night like this?

"All right," he said.

The next morning it was freezing outside.

It was also a bit chilly around the breakfast table.

32

Saturday, January 24, 2004

Ry's guitar wailed through the solo, keeping time as Queen Tamora's sons, Chiron and Demetrius, stage-raped Lavinia in suggestive violent choreography. Then they cut out her tongue and cut off her hands to prevent her from communicating who attacked her. At the moment of cutting off her hands, they secretly slipped bloody prosthetic stumps over her hands that had battery-operated fans to blow red ribbons into the air, suggesting flowing blood. The scene was gorgeous and horrifying and beautiful. But Melinda still looked like an automaton. What had happened to her emotions? And Orlando looked apologetic again about the depth of Aaron's evil. How was Dwayne going to get Orlando to do what Bobby would have done so brilliantly? It was maddening.

This was the final run-through in the rehearsal room. The actors would have Sunday off while the staff would load-in the set. Tech week would start Monday.

After the run-through, he gave the actors notes on their performances, and looked at his watch. He had twenty minutes left.

"Okay, everybody, I want to take the post-rape scene. If you aren't in the post-rape scene, you can go home. Have a relaxing Sunday, and we'll see you on Monday for tech!" A few of them groaned in anticipation. "Everyone else, take five. Melinda, could I talk with you?"

"Thank you, five," they called.

She approached him looking confrontational. "Don't I get a break?" she said, tossing her dark hair back.

"I gave the rest a break so I could talk with you privately," he said. She looked suddenly shocked and nearly tearful. Her face was so mobile and emotional now, but where was that in her performance?

"Let's go over here." He led her to the back of the rehearsal space as the other actors were milling out, going home, or taking a break. He pulled two chairs together into the corner, sat down with her, and spoke quietly so no one else would hear. "It's an odd thing. The more convincing the action becomes in the rape scene, the less emotion I see in your performance for the rest of the show."

She sat up defensively. "Well, how *am* I supposed to play a character who has her hands and tongue cut off?" she said with tears suddenly welling up in her eyes.

"You play her like she's a real person," Dwayne said gently.

"Oh, right, that's helpful," Melinda said, attempting to tamp down her emotion with sarcasm.

How to lead the way? Dwayne leaned in toward her.

"Let's look at who she is: She's one of the Andronici. Her father is Rome's greatest General. She comes from a family of warriors. She wouldn't collapse into devastation like most of us. Right?"

"That's why I am playing her as stoic."

Stoic, Dwayne thought. "Yeah, that's a good choice," he said. *Now, how to lead her to a better choice?*

"Stoicism makes total sense. But she's still suffering inside, isn't she? The better experience *for the audience* is to see that suffering." Dwayne liked this approach. She was paying him rapt attention. "They need to see her move through the story as a damaged human being. Not a weak one. She asked for death rather than rape and dishonor. They raped her anyway, and then cut out her tongue and cut off her hands. She is disgraced and in horrible pain. She has the strength to be stoic—and she is stoic just to keep living—but the audience needs to see the truth of her physical and her inner suffering. You see?"

"I think so," she said uncertainly.

"If you let her feelings show through, she can be the audience's touch-stone. While her father flails through the action, she lives the emotion. She is the audience's guide on how to receive the violence. Her performance gives them the emotional arc of the story. She's fantastically important."

"Wow," Melinda said. "I hadn't thought of it that way."

"Absolutely. Who else can they trust? Titus is so crazy driven by what he believes to be his duty, he kills his own son. The audience can't identify with him. The emperor is manipulated by evil Tamora. Aaron is straight out evil. Only Lavinia is consistently noble and sympathetic. When Titus finally kills her, all is lost. The story spins into the final deaths and ultimate tragedy."

"Huh," she said.

"So if you are withdrawn into the horror of what has happened to you, where can the audience find an emotional center? The play feels too chaotic. You have to be there for them. The audience depends on you."

"That's really interesting," she said. "I'd been feeling almost like a weird walking prop after my hands were chopped off—like I was just there for the visual effect."

"Right," Dwayne said. "That's what too much stoicism can do. But instead you can become the emotional heart of the audience. You witness and react, even though you cannot speak."

"Thanks, Dwayne." She grabbed his hand and squeezed it.

"Go take a quick break before we get started again."

"Thanks!" She smiled and ran off.

Holy Jesus of the performative breakthroughs. His logic had been perfect. It made her central to the audience experience. What actor could resist that?

However, when they ran the scene again, she was only marginally better. He was so disappointed. He'd felt certain she would be transformed.

After rehearsal, as the rest of the actors were leaving, Ingrid plunged into the room. "Have you been in our performance space today?" she demanded of Dwayne.

"No."

"The set from the last show is *still up*. What the fuck?" she said angrily. "We load in tomorrow morning. That set is supposed to be down, the floor repainted to black, the lights down and sitting in the seats, the cables wrapped and ready to use. None of that has been done!"

He followed her into the upstairs mainstage. It was just as she had said. There was no way they'd be able to load in their set in the morning. It was maddening.

"Goddamn it!" Dwayne said. "Have you talked to Raymond Green?"

"He was here when I got here. I said, *What the fuck, Green?* And he's rubbing his hand on the top of his head, making a snow-storm of dandruff everywhere, and he says: *Don't worry, it'll be down when you need it.* And I tell him: *We need it right now! Our load in starts at midnight.* Then he gets a phone call, and while he's talking I go back in to look at the space, and when I come out he's gone. I've been calling him, but he's not answering my calls."

"Shit."

"So unless he's planning to bring in a crew between now and eight a.m., that shit is going to be in our way."

"What do you want me to do?"

"You promised to help with load in tomorrow at 9 a.m. Just do that," she said. "Leave the rest to me."

"Okay." He felt both relieved and worried. Ingrid was a hard worker *and* a loose cannon. He probably didn't really *want* to know what she was going to do.

◆ ◆ ◆

He tossed and turned all that night. He kept making lists of things to be done in his head. And then trying to fall asleep.

He replayed his conversation with Melinda. He thought he'd been brilliant, but apparently not. He wished he had Aleister's skills with psychology. Maybe then he could have broken through with her.

Angela sat up in bed suddenly. "Hey, Dwayne," she said in exasperation. "Stop thinking so loud! You keep waking me up!"

33

Sunday, January 25, 2004

Dwayne was fifteen minutes early walking into the Chicago Repertory Arts Playhouse the next morning, stamping the snow off his boots. It was Sunday morning, he'd slept poorly, and it was fucking cold out. He was worried about all the crap Green had left on their stage.

For a place that normally bustled with activity, the lobby had an otherworldly quiet. The outdoor sounds were muffled by a layer of fresh snow from overnight. Inside, the building sounded deserted. The quiet made him nervous.

He climbed the stairs. The door to their performance space was wide open. The work lights were on, but no one seemed to be about. He walked in quietly, feeling an uncomfortable anticipatory fear. Where was Ingrid? Was she running late? They'd planned to meet at nine to solidify plans, and the rest of the crew was to arrive at nine-thirty.

Apparently, Green's crew had worked on striking the set overnight, but they had not finished. They'd carefully disassembled flats, platforms and door and window units and stacked the pieces along the back wall and atop the audience seating. The middle of the stage was filled with rubble. The sight of it filled Dwayne with a sudden rage. They had enough work to do without Green's shit in the way!

He stepped forward to examine the crap on the floor. There was splintered wood, the remains of mocked-up cabinetry, fake potted plants, and a big pile of painted canvas. He pulled back some of the canvass and jumped back in horror. There was a dead body! Blood streamed down its side. He shrieked.

The body sat up groggily and looked at him.

"Jesus, Dwayne, you scream like a little girl," Ingrid complained. She rubbed sleep from her eyes, got up out of the pile of torn canvas, picked it up and stuffed it into a garbage can. There'd been a couple of couch cushions underneath her.

"I thought you were dead." Dwayne's heart pumped wildly. "You're covered with blood!"

Ingrid touched the color down the side of her shirt and jeans. "It's paint," she corrected. "From the set of *The Best Little Whorehouse in Texas* two seasons ago. I fell off a ladder with a bucket of red paint. I was working without enough sleep. As usual."

"What were you doing on the floor?"

"Sleeping. I knew that fucking Green wouldn't strike this set on time. I've been working on it all night long. Since we've got extra marketing expenses coming, I salvaged all the lumber and useful pieces from this set that I could. I cancelled most of our wood order to save money."

"But this isn't our lumber."

"It is now," Ingrid said flatly. "As of midnight, this was our space. It was supposed to be clear. So now all this is ours."

"And then you slept here?"

"I guess I got an hour or two," she said, still groggy. "Even with my Arctic Wind sleeping bag, I sometimes get cold in my van in this weather. Better to sleep up here."

"We've still got all this rubble in our way."

"Yeah," Ingrid said. "I'm going to go pick up our reduced lumber order and a box of coffee and donuts. Since the lumber order is down to minimal wood plus paint and supplies, I cancelled our truck rental. I can get it in the van myself." She pulled on her boots and began putting on her coat, hat and gloves. "When the rest of the crew shows up, take all this stuff from the center of the stage and put it in Green's dumpsters in the alley. Then look over the wood I salvaged and make sure all the nails and screws are removed. Then get the dressing rooms cleaned out, and help Peaches load in the costumes. Green left the dressing rooms a mess, too. Peaches can decide what looks useful. Dump what's worth saving in the rehearsal room. We won't need that space anymore. And throw out the rest. I should be back by the time you finish all that, and we can put up the set and focus the lights."

"Will we be ready for tech by tomorrow?"

Ingrid looked at her watch. "We've got thirty-one hours before five p.m. tomorrow. Don't worry your pretty little head." She pulled her hood up, wrapped her scarf around, and plunged out the door without another word.

Between nine-thirty and a quarter to ten, Peaches, Aleister, Chaz, and two of the actors staggered in out of the cold. Aleister and Chaz had decided to come in and help with construction rather than pay for a crew. Everyone was dismayed to find the pile of rubble in the center of the stage, but once they discovered they could maneuver the dumpsters under the fire escape and drop the trash in from the second floor fire escape landing, they were much more cheerful. It was fun! Especially when there was something glass they could drop and see explode in the bottom of an empty dumpster. By ten-thirty they'd disposed of all the trash and swept the stage. Ingrid returned, and they hauled up the cans of paint, supplies, and lumber from her van. By eleven they'd cleared the dressing rooms and hung the *Titus* costumes on the racks, helping Peaches organize them by actor. At eleven-thirty, everything was in place to begin construction, and they stopped for coffee and donuts before Ingrid set them to their tasks.

That was when Green entered the space with his two man crew. "What the fuck!" he shouted.

Ingrid stepped forward directly in front of him, her legs planted solidly and wide, like a Viking warrior woman. "What the fuck, what, Green?" she said aggressively.

"Where the fuck is my set?"

"As of midnight, this was my space," she said. "Your set is gone, and you'll be getting a bill from me for the cost of striking it."

"I'm paying these guys to help me strike it," he said, gesturing to his two-man crew. "I planned to reuse a lot of that stuff."

"Too late."

"This is bullshit!" Green shouted. "I have until twelve a.m. to strike that set."

Ingrid looked at her watch. "Yeah. Twelve a.m. was eleven and a half hours ago."

"No, no," Green said. "Twelve a.m. is noon. It's part of the morning. Midnight is twelve p.m."

"Sorry," Ingrid said. "Other way around."

"Midnight! Night!" Green shouted. "P fucking M. Night! Are you stupid?"

"Uh, midnight is twelve a.m., Green," one of his workers said. "You just have to remember, twelve oh one is definitely a.m., so twelve midnight goes with twelve oh one a.m."

"Shut the fuck up!" Green said. "You think you're the fucking brain trust?"

"Let me put it another way for you, Green," Ingrid said, as though addressing a mentally deficient toddler. "Today begins tech week. Our contract states we have twenty-four-hour access to our performance space all the way through tech week. If your set wasn't out of our way until noon, that'd be only twelve hours today. That would be in violation of our contract. So get the fuck out of here. We have work to do."

"You're getting a bill for the cost of my set!" Green shouted. He looked at Dwayne. "I'll add that to what you owe me for extra rehearsal time."

"I didn't authorize any extra rehearsal time," Dwayne insisted.

"Yeah?" Green said. "Well, theatre is a collaborative art. And you are responsible for what your collaborators do."

Ingrid put her face right to Green's, nose to bulbous nose. She was just as tall as he, and she was in much better physical condition. "We're not paying anything additional," she said in a deep and threatening voice. "You are in breach of contract. You'll be getting *my* bill for striking your stupid set."

Green backed off. "Yeah?" he said, attempting to sound threatening, continuing to back toward the door. "Yeah? Well, if you don't pay, see if you can run your show without any electricity." He rushed out the door and banged it behind him, his two-man crew following at a sauntering pace.

Ingrid looked after them, then turned toward her team, put her hands on her hips, tossed her blond hair back and laughed heartily, like a Viking who'd just dunked an enemy's head under the icy waters of the Baltic Sea.

"He wouldn't fucking dare," she exclaimed.

34

Monday, January 26, 2004

When Melinda arrived the next night, she immediately ran across the set, up the two platforms, and grabbed Ry's guitar from its stand. She put the strap around her shoulder and swung her arm around as though playing the guitar like a windmill. "People try to put us down," she sang at the top of her lungs.

"Talking 'bout my generation," Wallace croaked back.

"Hey, Pete Townshend," Ry drawled to her as he came back into the space with stands and microphones.

"*Who?*" she said, eyebrows raised high.

"Very funny." He climbed to the band platform, gave her a sexy wink, and set up his mics.

Orlando circled the playing area addressing each of the three sections of audience. "Now I'm talking to you," he boomed to the seats at stage left, "and now I'm talking to you," he declaimed to stage center, "and now I'm talking to you," he whispered stage right.

Tom romped onto the scene, a sword in each hand and Errol Flynned his way onto the first platform, killed a few imaginary opponents, and jumped off the side.

The actors loved having the set to walk on. For the first time they were working on the full size of their performance space, and it felt very large and airy. They had doorways and stairs and platforms. The wood, having been salvaged from previous sets, looked like a weird patchwork of colors with a surprising amount of pastel. Ingrid would paint it, but for now, even as oddly piecemeal as it looked, the actors loved it.

This night's rehearsal was not for them, however. They were

there for the benefit of the tech crew. The crew had one night to get all the technical aspects of the show in place. Props had already been worked out in rehearsals and all sounds were coming from the actors and the band, so light cues were the main concern. The company would skip through the script to work each of the cues, jumping over the dialogue and action in between. It was a tedious process, as light levels had to be adjusted for each cue.

After looking like a conquering Viking at load-in, Ingrid looked like a Scandinavian zombie today. The team had helped her build the set, taking breaks for pizza. They worked well into the night, then she sent them home. She re-hung and focused the lights on her own. Since Green's team had not taken down the lights and the cables, her job was complicated. For a while, she tried to see if she could simply adjust the hanging lights to work for her light plot, but that proved too frustrating. She took all the lights down before hanging them again where she needed them. She was up most of the night and a good portion of the day. When Joan arrived at 5:30 p.m., she found Ingrid sleeping on two couch cushions in the middle of the stage floor, using her winter coat and a paint-spattered drop cloth as blankets.

Ingrid's grogginess slowed the process of the cue-to-cue, as she found herself repeatedly confused by her own notes. Coco slowed the process, as well. Rather than watching for when she was needed, she immersed herself in a copy of *Savoy* magazine and had to be called to the stage for her every cue.

But the real trouble came in the rape scene. Since the scene included multiple light cues, special props, and choreography aligned with live music, they played the scene in full, with Ingrid and Dwayne shouting over the action about exactly when lighting changes needed to take place. They restarted repeatedly.

"Let's take it again, from the lift!" Dwayne shouted. "Can we take that moment so only Lavinia is lit, very hot, when they get her to the top of the lift?"

"As long as they lift her in the exact same spot every performance," Ingrid called back. "It's not like we've got a follow spot up here."

"Understood!" Dwayne yelled. "Bring all the other lights down simultaneously with the Lavinia lights going up, so it looks like the lights are sweeping in on her. And, Ry, really bend that long note when Lavinia is at the top of the lift, please!"

"Got it," Ry drawled back, and hit and bent the note again on his guitar.

"Good!" Dwayne shouted. "Chiron and Demetrius, make sure you center yourselves exactly in front of the center platform before you lift Lavinia."

"Got it," they answered.

Dwayne walked over to Melinda. "This is just tech, so the focus isn't on the acting," he said to her, "but I want to give you a note to remember."

Melinda nodded, with a deer-in-the-headlights look.

"Lavinia has already begged for death instead of rape. This is the moment. When they lift you into the air, we need to see the moment of rape on Lavinia's face, as though they are doing it to you in that moment. Then they bring you down, and your face is obscured, and the action is more suggested. So at the top of the lift you have to show the horror of the rape on your face fully. Okay?"

Melinda nodded, seemingly unable to speak.

"Good." Dwayne raised his voice for everyone to hear. "Let's take it! And continue into the rape choreography and the cutting off of the hands choreography until I stop you."

"Light cue forty-five," Ingrid called. The lights shifted to covering the full center of the stage. The actors took their positions, Ry pulled into a guitar note followed by the bass and drums. "Forty-six," Ingrid called. The lights began a gradual shift from amber to red. Chiron and Demetrius moved in on either side of Lavinia as she attempted to batter them back. They each grabbed an ankle with their outside hand and put their inside hands under her butt cheeks and lifted her into the air as though their hands were the seat of a chair. They extended their lifting arms all the way over their heads, so she was carried high into the air, with their hands holding her ankles extended fully in front of them, facing the audience. It was like some sickening parody of a cheerleader lift, for Lavinia's legs were spread wide, her arms thrashing in fruitless battle, and her spine arched in an ecstasy of pain, while the men wore faces of ruthless lust and violation. White light grew more and more dazzlingly brilliant, focused solely on her face and body in this horrifying posture of rape. The pain and panic blossomed on her face and her body attempted to shrivel in on itself in protection as Ry bent the note on his guitar loudly and viciously. Lavinia cried out loud in pain and outrage and despair as she attempted to keep them out, flailing her arms to protect her most sacred vulnerability until she threatened to make the men lose their grip on her, high at the apex of their reach as she screamed. Then she bent forward, collapsing her torso to her thighs as they brought her legs back together and brought her down to the ground to stretch her out spread-eagled on the floor. They took turns covering her body with their own.

But something was wrong. Melinda would not allow them to extend her body again. The character, Lavinia, was gone and the actress, Melinda, remained, crying and screaming and balling her body into a fetal knot. The actors playing Chiron and Demetrius pulled at her for a moment, but then realized she wasn't acting and stepped back away, looking out at Dwayne like two confused and frightened adolescents. Melinda remained curled tightly on herself, sobbing as though she'd actually been raped.

"Hold! Joan, let's take ten," Dwayne said.

"Take ten, everyone," Joan called. Some of the actors slinked out of the space, deeply disturbed by what they'd seen. Dwayne gestured to the others to give him a moment, and he went to sit down on the stage floor next to Melinda, still collapsed and weeping.

"I'm sorry, I'm sorry," she apologized through her tears. "I know we have so much to do."

"No, no. This is a tough moment." He waited beside her, shoulder to shoulder, as her sobs wound down. He offered his hand, and she took it, and then leaned against him. Dwayne felt relieved that she showed this amount of trust.

"This makes me...think of something." She looked up at him, her eyes thoroughly blood-shot with tears. "It's been getting in my way."

"Yeah, I wondered. It's a really tough moment."

"I can get through it," she said. "I just need to get hold of myself."

"We're going to skip past this for tonight," Dwayne said gently. "We'll come back to tech it tomorrow night before dress." He felt his own body tense as he said it. Continuing tech on dress rehearsal night was not a great idea, but he had to take care of his actor. "You can relax. Mark your way through it. Just be Melinda, say your lines and be in the right place so Ingrid can adjust the lights. And let's talk at the end of the night, okay?" She nodded. "We can start early and talk about whatever adjustments we need to make so this is doable for you tomorrow. Okay?"

She smiled through the wounded look on her face. "Okay."

"Good." He patted her hand gently. "I'm in this with you."

"Thanks, Dwayne." She brushed a tear from her cheek. They both stood. She hesitated and moment and then gave him a hug.

"We're all in this with you," he whispered in her ear.

"Okay," she said. He watched her walk unsteadily toward the exit. Orlando intercepted her and put his arm around her shoulders, and she looked grateful.

Whatever the scene was triggering in Melinda, Dwayne knew he was over his head. He called Aleister and asked him to come in at the end of rehearsal. He had to find a way to make this scene work without traumatizing his actor, but it still needed to shock and dismay the audience. The actors working with Tom's choreography and Ry's music created a scene of incredible intensity. Dwayne didn't want to lose it. But he didn't want Melinda to suffer, either.

The rest of the cue-to-cue continued in its sometimes frustrating and tedious way, but they got though the evening. He noticed that Aleister had arrived and was watching the action from the back of the audience. He walked over to his old friend. "Did you bring it?"

"Yes," Aleister said reluctantly. He handed over a copy of an article about his psychiatric practice that had appeared in the Health and Beauty section of the *Chicago Tribune*. Dwayne knew Aleister found his photo and some of the text, though very complimentary, somehow embarrassing.

"She doesn't know you," Dwayne said. "It's a matter of establishing trust."

"Right," Aleister said. "Otherwise what would be the point of dragging your old friend out into an eight degree blizzard in the middle of winter?"

"Exactly." Dwayne walked down to where Melinda was sitting, slumped and miserable in the front row of the audience. She watched Ingrid climb up and down the ladder, strapping cables neatly to the overhead grid. He sat down next to her.

"My oldest friend, Aleister, is something of a star psychiatrist," he said to her. "He also put up money for the show. You saw him at the first day read-through." He handed her the *Tribune* article with the headline: North Shore Psychiatrist Soothes Trauma. Beneath was a photo of Dr. George Aleister looking almost absurdly grave and sincere.

"Yeah, I remember him," Melinda said. She began to scan the article.

"I asked him to join us as we discuss the scene. Is that okay?"

Melinda read a few paragraphs. "Okay."

Dwayne led them into the dressing room where they could have some privacy, introduced them, and gave Aleister a description of what had happened in rehearsal. Melinda looked uncomfortable, hearing it described.

"You're probably thinking: *Oh, she was raped and now she's remembering it, and that's why she's acting this way,*" she said with a challenge in her voice. She looked at Aleister and then at herself in the makeup mirror and then down at her lap.

"That's one possibility," Aleister said gently.

"Then what do you think is wrong with me?" she demanded. She looked challengingly at Aleister again, and then at herself in the mirror, and back at Aleister.

Dwayne regretted for a moment his choice of the dressing room as a place to talk. The mirror was always a distraction for an actor. But a dressing room was also a familiar place. At low rent performance spaces like the Playhouse, the dressing room also served as green room where they'd wait for their entrances. They spent so much time in dressing rooms, getting ready for the performance, it was a home base to their life on the stage.

"I wouldn't assume there's anything wrong with you," Aleister said. "You were enacting something horrible, and you had a reaction."

"I had a reaction that stopped the whole rehearsal," she complained.

"Right," Aleister agreed.

"I can't be stopping the show," she said, sounding angry at herself.

"Why don't we talk about what you experienced at that moment?" he said.

She shot him a look from under her dark brows, leaned back in her chair, and then forward. She shook her head, clearly uncomfortable. "It's not like something happened to me like what happens to Lavinia." She pushed her hair behind her ears and held it there as she looked up at Aleister and said, "If that's what you were thinking."

"Whatever your feelings and experiences, they are yours," he said simply.

"Right. My feelings. Versus his feelings. My experience versus his experience. Nobody would agree it was rape. Not even my best friend." She shook her head. "I had to just put it behind me. Because it was just a weird misunderstanding. There's no reason it should be doing this to me now," she insisted.

Dwayne felt the urge to ask what happened, but he forced himself to keep quiet. Just sit and look sympathetic. Let Aleister do the talking.

"Would you like to tell me what happened to you?" he said.

"It's not like it was rape." She laughed bitterly. "This was my boyfriend. We'd been sleeping together for almost a year." She put her hands on her knees and clutched them tightly. "I actually *loved* this guy. So when he wanted to do some role playing, I thought, *why not?* He was excited because I was an acting student. He was in accounting, and theatre was a whole different world to him."

Melinda looked up at Aleister plaintively, as if wondering if he could understand that. He nodded, and she nodded back and pushed her dark hair back behind her ears again.

"He was a graduate student, so he was older and had his own

apartment. No roommates. I was just a sophomore. He seemed really sophisticated to me. Not boring like you'd think an accountant would be. He knew about wines and good food and he had a car and could afford to take me to restaurants. He was very good-looking."

"Sounds nice," Aleister said.

"It was. One of my girlfriends had just lost her boyfriend—he was an actor who decided to come out of the closet. That would never happen to me with Dave. He was totally heterosexual. When he wanted to do some role playing, I thought: *why not?* Role playing was my thing on stage. Why not try it in bed? And he was excited. He thought it would be *so awesome*," she said bitterly.

She squinted at the bare light bulbs surrounding the makeup mirrors and then looked at Dwayne. "Could we turn some of those off?" she asked meekly. "It's so bright."

"Sure." Dwayne got up and took a wad of tissues to protect his fingertips and unscrewed every other bulb. The light became much more gentle. Melinda took a deep breath. Her face looked pale, framed by her dark brunette hair. Her lips trembled as she attempted to speak, and stopped. She shook her head. "I feel stupid," she said in a tiny voice. "This happened so long ago."

"Some things never let go," Aleister said.

She took a deep breath and nodded. "Yeah. SO HE WANTED TO TRY BONDAGE." She spoke loudly, having forced herself to say the words. "Sorry." She sucked in a breath and made herself speak in a normal volume. "He wanted to try bondage. But I felt really nervous as he was tying my wrists and ankles, and attaching the ropes to the bed. He'd found this soft rope somewhere, and he made sure they weren't hurting me. But he thought, apparently, that my nervousness was role playing. And when he started role playing, the things he said were really shocking to me. I told him to cut it out. He thought that also was part of the role playing. He stripped off my clothes, and I told him to stop it, that I didn't like it, and it excited him even more. When he took off his clothes, he was really hard, and I screamed for him to stop, but it excited him even more. I pulled and shifted, and tried to get away from him, but the ropes were tied in a way I couldn't escape. And when he stuck his dick in me he had the most explosive orgasm he'd ever had with me, despite—or maybe because—I was shouting, pleading, begging him to stop. And then I was crying, and he was like: *oh man that was amazing,* but when I didn't stop crying, he was like: *what's wrong? What's wrong? What's wrong?* And I said *I wanted you to stop.* And he looked really shocked, and he said: *Why didn't you say 'pillow talk?'* And I'm like *what the fuck?* See, because when he was tying me up, he said: *the safe word is 'pillow talk.'* I was so nervous, I didn't know what he was talking about, and I didn't ask him because I was nervous, and it just passed me by. I didn't know what a *safe word* was. I didn't know that if I had said *pillow talk,* he would have immediately stopped. So my boyfriend fucked me thinking we were having a good time, while I felt like he was raping me."

"And so he was," Aleister said.

"No, he thought we were…doing this thing."

"It makes no difference what he thought," Aleister said. "You experienced rape. You begged him to stop. That was rape. Whatever *he* thought was happening, he raped you. And now doing this scene in *Titus Andronicus* is bringing back that experience that was never properly acknowledged or forgiven. Did he make amends to you?"

"He apologized like crazy for a while. But then he got angry about the safe word. If I didn't understand, why didn't I ask him what he meant? Like it was my fault for ruining his fun because I hadn't paid attention. But I didn't know anything about bondage. I'd never heard of a *safe word.*" Her pain and frustration came back to her so vividly, she started crying.

"That's his fault for not making sure you understood," Aleister said.

"Why couldn't he see that I was in a real panic?" she said between sobs. "Why would he go ahead and fuck me anyway?"

"Maybe he didn't want to see," Aleister said.

"Bethany, my own best girlfriend, told me you can't be raped by your boyfriend. She said that's not rape."

"She was wrong," Aleister said. "Most rape victims are raped by someone they know. Not by a stranger."

"I never talked to him after that. He started leaving angry phone messages because I wouldn't call him back. He finally gave up. And I stopped being friends with Bethany. But then I was so lonely because I'd had this horrible thing happen, and I lost my boyfriend and my best friend, all at once. I had no one to talk to. For a while I swore off men altogether. I even tried to date women, because, I figured *they* wouldn't rape me. But my heart wasn't really in it. And then was I horrible sometimes. It's like I'd blame a girl because I couldn't love her. I think I've been really mean with Peaches. Our costumer? We started seeing each other a while back, before this show. She didn't deserve that. I could tell she really liked me."

"Once you're feeling stronger, you can make amends, too," Aleister suggested.

"Yeah," she said quietly. "But even after all this time, I still feel so alone. I never told anyone in my family. I didn't want to risk that they'd all be like Bethany and treat me like I was stupid."

"I'm so sorry that happened to you," Aleister said. "But I'm glad you have someone to talk to now."

"But do I?" she said, looking both hurt and suspicious. "I mean, you're talking to me because I had a meltdown on stage."

"I'm going to make time for a few sessions for us to talk," Aleister said. "I have an office in Winnetka and another in the Loop."

"I don't have health insurance. Or much money, frankly."

"This will be pro bono. You don't have to pay a thing."

"Oh." She sat up straighter and wiped a tear from under her eye. "Thank you."

"But right now you need something so you can feel safe *here*," Aleister said. He considered it for a moment. "Now that you know what a safe word is, you should have one for the show."

"How would that work?" Dwayne said.

"Let say Melinda is in the scene, and she gets overwhelmed. She needs to get out. So she says something that everyone will recognize as not part of the show."

"Everyone except the audience," Dwayne added. He thought about it for a moment.

"I don't want to make the show weird," Melinda said.

"No, Aleister has an excellent point," Dwayne said. "You can't do your job if you don't feel safe." He held up a finger and thought another moment. "You know, despite all the hate in this show, no one ever says *I hate you*. But if Lavinia said *I hate you* in the midst of that scene, it would seem in character." He stood up. "That's it. If you start to panic in the midst of that choreography, you just shout out, or mutter, or cry: *I hate you*. And whatever move they are in, they will set you on your feet, and you can turn and step upstage. You face away from the audience, and they will continue on with the choreography as if you were still there. When you are ready, you turn and rejoin them. We'll practice it that way so everyone knows what to do."

"Nice," Aleister said. He turned to Melinda. "But do you like it? That's what matters. Does that sound safe enough?"

She looked at them both and tried to smile, but then burst into tears. She got up and hugged Dwayne. "Thank you."

35

Tuesday, January 27, 2004

Dwayne, Tom, and Joan got in early with Melinda and the actors playing Chiron and Demetrius. They tried the rape scene with Melinda calling out the safe words at two different points. They were able to shift gears, move Melinda upstage facing away from the audience with her arms stretched out as though nailed to a cross, and go on with the choreography as though she were still there receiving the brunt of their violence. Melinda had the presence of mind to twitch her body as though she were receiving their brutalizations. It actually looked quite effective.

"That is amazing," Tom whispered to Dwayne. "I hated it when you said we had to prepare this. But I love how this works." He grabbed Dwayne's arm. "I want to rework this choreography right now and make this change permanent."

"No," Dwayne said quietly. "If you rework it like this, you've taken away her safe words and her power over the scene, and we've lost the point of doing this."

"But this looks so good!" Tom whined.

"No," Dwayne insisted quietly. "Your original choreography looks fantastic and disturbing. You don't get to change it the night of dress rehearsal."

"But you do," Tom said resentfully.

"Yes. *I* do. Because it's for my actor's safety. And you can suck it up."

"Humph," Tom groused. He dropped himself into one of the front seats of the audience.

Ry and the band came in to run the full tech for the rape scene before dress rehearsal began. It looked good, and although she was not playing the scene at full emotion, Melinda appeared comfortable.

Joan stood up, checked her watch, and announced: "It's seven thirty-five. We have an eight o'clock curtain, everyone. Make sure you've signed in. Get into your opening costume and make sure your props are set." She turned to Dwayne. "I'm going to make sure the rest are all arrived and getting ready."

Dwayne nodded. He took a deep breath. He really wanted this dress rehearsal to go well. It was just days until Gregor Foxx would be here for opening night.

Joan walked off to the dressing rooms as Coco stormed on in costume. She stopped center stage and spread her arms.

"What is this supposed to be?" she demanded. She picked up the skirt of her soiled and torn dress. "It's hideous!"

"It looks like your Act One Scene One costume," Dwayne said calmly.

Peaches, looking exasperated and exhausted, came in from backstage.

Coco pointed at her as though she were the enemy of humanity. "That's what she says! But look at it! I look like I've been dragged through the mud!"

"Well, you have been captured and brought to Rome as a captive, and your eldest son gets his arms chopped off and his entrails thrown into the sacrificial fire," Dwayne reminded her. "So maybe you *shouldn't* be beautiful in this scene. Peaches has you in gorgeous stuff for the rest of the show. You are the hottest queen Rome has ever seen."

"Yes, Peaches, yes." She took the costumer's wrists and shook them in momentary gratitude. "I especially love my Act Two entrance. It's a knock-out. But this! This! Why does my *first entrance* have to be like this?"

"Because you've just been brought to Rome as a captive?" Peaches said uncertainly. "I mean, everyone saw the design drawings at the first rehearsal. This is not different than the drawing."

"This costume makes sense for this scene," Dwayne told Coco.

"Yeah? If I look like this, why would Saturninus choose *me* as his Queen over Lavinia Andronicus? Why would he say: 'Therefore, lovely

Tamora, queen of Goths, that like the stately Phoebe amongst her nymphs dost overshine the gallantest dames of Rome'… if I am dressed in this dirty bag of a dress? Lavinia Andronicus looks all *white-girl-pretty* in her gorgeous Roman ingénue garb. How do I *overshine the gallantest dames of Rome* like this?"

Dwayne looked at Peaches. He hated to admit it, but Coco had a point.

Peaches cocked her head to the side. It looked like she was hit with sudden doubts, as well.

"Look," Coco said. "If I have to be in rags, let's at least make them sexy rags." She grabbed a fistful of the fabric and pulled it tight to her body. "Let's tailor this in tight to show off my figure and put in a few strategic tears to expose some advantageous flesh."

"We could do that," Peaches agreed. "That would still fit the design concept."

"Yeah!" Coco said. "Let's make this dirty frock so hot Saturninus springs wood."

"Dwayne?" Peaches said.

"If you like it, I like it," he said.

"I guess we could try that," Peaches said.

"All right!" Coco said in triumph. "Let's get to it!" She clapped a hand over the costumer's shoulder and the two women exited upstage.

A moment later, Peaches came running back out to Dwayne.

"Listen, I heard you did a really nice thing for Melinda, and I wanted to thank you." She reached out a hand and squeezed Dwayne's arm. She looked really jumpy to be saying this to him.

"Yeah, um…" Dwayne wasn't sure what to say. He felt like everything Melinda had said was told in confidence.

"Yeah, don't worry. She told me all about her boyfriend, the bondage king. I think she could tell me because I'm an even bigger mess than her." She laughed in a sad way and shook her head. "I mean, when I get into a manic phase, all I want are dicks. I go man-crazy. Just fuck, fuck, fuck. And then I feel awful afterwards, but I can't do those drugs. They just make me dull as a brick. But a long-term relationship with a man? Forget it." She stopped and her eyes widened. "Why am I telling you all this?" She looked up into the lights overhead. She shook her head hard again, took a deep breath and looked Dwayne in the eye. "And then, of course, she dumped me. But what did I expect? I mean, obviously, she was slumming. I mean, look at her. So *pretty*. Those eyes. And that mouth. I mean, everything about her. And look at me." She waved her fingers around her face and hair. "A weird-looking multi-colored nerd."

"Don't sell yourself short," Dwayne said. "Any girl would be lucky to have you."

"Yeah, hmmm…" she said doubtfully. "Anyway, I don't think Melinda is destined to be with a girl. I was what you might call a stop-gap measure. Ha, ha!" She looked up musingly at the lights again and then back at Dwayne. "But thanks so much for taking her seriously. You did good, Dwayne." She tapped him on the arm in some sort of parody of manly congratulations, made a supremely uncomfortable face, and hurried backstage to rework Coco's costume.

Dwayne felt suddenly endeared to Peaches. "Any girl *would* be lucky to have you," he said under his breath.

Shortly before 8 p.m. about half dozen friends of the company, including Chaz, Aleister, and Angela, filed in to provide a small, friendly audience for the dress rehearsal. With the audience in place, Ry played a short, show-offy solo as the band performed their final sound check and tuning.

The dress started nearly on time, with Ingrid needing a short delay to switch out a lighting instrument that quit working, cursing the name of Raymond Green for his inventory of ancient, beaten, and jury-rigged equipment.

The show started well. Titus Andronicus returned to Rome triumphant over the Goths. They sacrificed Tamora's oldest son. Tamora, though in rags, now looked incredibly hot, with slashes in her skin-tight garb exposing hints of side boob, bottom boob, thigh and buttock. Dwayne wondered if her appearance was too distracting. However, Coco played her scenes brilliantly, pleading broken-heartedly for her son and then seducing the new emperor away from chaste young Lavinia Andronicus.

But then it turned weird. Toward the end of Act One, Tamora made peace between Titus and her new husband, the emperor, who said: "Rise, Titus, rise; my empress hath prevailed."

Titus rose to his feet and replied: "I thank your majesty." But then he looked out into the audience and began to weep. Since he'd always played this as a happy moment, it took Coco aback, but she continued: "Titus, I am a Roman now adopted happily, and must advise the emperor for his good. This day all quarrels die, Andronicus; and let it be my honour, good my lord, that I have reconciled your friends and you."

Titus continued to weep, quietly, as the scene continued, and pulled himself together just in time to invite the emperor to go hunting the next day.

Dwayne had been glancing at his audience, who did, indeed, seem confused by Titus's weeping, as did his fellow actors on stage. What was this weirdness?

Much later, when they reached the rape scene, however, Dwayne blessed Aleister and the preparations they'd made with Melinda. The scene was deeply affecting. She played it beautifully and bravely without resorting to the safe word, and her subsequent scenes with her tongue and hands cut off were eloquent. Lavinia's every emotion shown forth from Melinda's eyes and body. She was brilliant.

At the intermission break, the other actors surrounded her backstage and gave her a round of applause. Her eyes filled with tears and she shared deep hugs with her closest castmates. Dwayne felt great relief. Then he noticed Peaches standing in the corner looking pleased but sadly abandoned. She quietly left the room.

Well, there was nothing he could do about that. He circulated backstage to congratulate the actors on their work so far and encourage them onward.

When he reached Wallace, he hesitated. "So you had a new moment tonight."

"Ha!" Wallace barked. "The weeping, you mean. Yes, that was new." He shook his head. "A stray thought," he said reflectively. He turned his attention back suddenly on Dwayne. "How did it look? Did it work?"

"Not really. The audience seemed confused."

"Hmm. Well…" Wallace laughed as though blissfully

confounded by an inexplicable universe. "One never knows."

"Any developments with your daughter?" Dwayne asked.

"Actually, I did call her. We had a pretty good conversation. A little rocky. But we're talking."

In the second half, the cast got jammed up on some of the fight work. They needed to stop, and go back, and run through the choreography twice to make sure they had it right. The run took forty minutes longer than it should have.

Dwayne sat alone in the seats after rehearsal, fighting down a burst of internal panic. If the actors could do it all without stopping, without losing anything, they'd be okay, he told himself. They could actually be brilliant.

If only.

Holy Jesus, savior of stumbling humanity and lost causes, bless this show.

36

Wednesday, January 28, 2004

The stairs going up to the second floor of the Chicago Repertory Arts Playhouse the next night were slathered in slush. The snow that had come down two days ago was now a black slurry in the streets and crusted into dirty piles on the parkways. The air outside was slightly warmer, so the snow everywhere was a soft mess. And everyone was tracking it into the building. Dwayne stamped his boots as he climbed the stairs, trying to get the rest of the slush off.

As he reached the top, Joan stuck her head out the audience door like a prairie dog popping out of its burrow. "You need to see something. This way." Joan led him into the upstairs lobby and around to the stairway leading up to the light booth. "At first I thought there was a snake with me in the booth." She stopped halfway up the stairs and turned back toward him. "Well, I didn't really think it was a snake, but that's what it sounded like. I kept hearing it all the way through dress last night." She led him the rest of the way up the stairs and ducked back into the right hand corner of the booth. "Here, sit down." She gestured to the ancient desk chair at the controls table. The table faced an open window above the center section of the audience, looking down at the stage over the heads of the audience. Atop the table sat a sound mixer, a battered light control board missing two of its dimmers, and a weird jury-rigged wooden box of household light switches with a million wires coming out of it. That was something Green had promised to remove. Dwayne was sorry to see it still there.

"Now listen," Joan said. She sat down gently in a rust-flecked metal folding chair behind him.

Dwayne listened. Mainly he could hear a half dozen of the actors on stage milling about, doing stretches and vocal exercises. To an outsider they would have sounded ridiculous, trilling through their vocal ranges from the highest note to the lowest, clucking through their consonants, some reciting tongue-twisters. When one went to an orchestral concert, seeing the musicians tune up was part of the experience. Dwayne couldn't imagine wanting an audience to see this.

"Focus your ears on the sound *in here*."

"Okay." Dwayne closed his eyes and sat very still, ignoring Melinda's voice from below repeating: "Ha! Ha! Ha!" with air forced from the diaphragm.

Then he heard it: *Hiss. Sput. Sput. Hiss. Click.*

"Where is that?" He got up and pushed away the rolling desk chair and crouched down on his heels to look under the table.

Hiss. Sput. Hiss. Click. Sput.

It sounded like it was coming from under the control table. He reached forward and discovered that what he thought was the wall was really just a thin sheet of plywood leaning in place.

"Wait till you see what's behind that."

Dwayne slid the plywood aside to reveal a morass of wire and cable twisted and flowing down from the back side of the control table in a tangle and then coming up again in strands to go out the top of the booth to the lighting grid over the audience and the playing space. Most alarming, some of the wiring came to cut bare ends lacking caps or insulation. Sparks flew from some of them.

Hiss. Sput. Hiss. Sput. Click.

"*Saint Eligius of the holy ozone*," Dwayne said.

"Saint What?"

"Sorry. Sometimes I forget I'm saying these things aloud. Saint Eligius. He's the patron of electrical engineers."

"I'm not going to ask why you know that," Joan said. "What I want to know is: Why would you, as a producer, put us in a shit hole like this?"

"Green promised he was going to have everything ready for us."

"Everyone knows Green's promises are worth crap. So why would you book us into this shit hole? And why did you force us to rehearse in a space that was too small?"

"That was Ingrid," Dwayne said. "She told me she was finding rehearsal space to our specifications."

"The buck stops with you," Joan said. "Have you noticed how the actors still huddle in the center of the stage? It's because *that's* the size they are used to."

"I'll give them a note to spread out."

"It's in their muscle memory!" Joan said. "And now what about this?" She gestured to the arcing bare wires.

"Did I see a box with caps and electrical tape up there?" He pointed at a shelf next to the entrance.

"You're going to reach your hands into *that*?" She stood up and fetched the little box of electrical supplies. She handed it down to him. "It's your funeral."

"Open the door to let in light so I can see down here."

She pushed open the door to the stairway going down to the upstairs lobby. A few patrons were milling down below. Joan didn't like them to be able to see up into the booth, but the open door did light up the area under the control table.

The box she'd handed Dwayne had three kinds of tape, a pair of scissors designed for kindergarten children, and a good pile of wire nuts and caps, all of them previously used. What it did not include was a pair of insulating rubber gloves, which would have been handy when he reached in to grab a wire.

The human nervous system is essentially a wiring grid for carrying electrical impulses of an infinitesimally low voltage. Imagine how such an efficient system would transmit current of a higher voltage when the back of Dwayne's hand accidentally brushed against a live, unprotected wire. The electricity surged eagerly into the back of Dwayne's hand.

"*Fucking, fuck!*" Dwayne's core muscles contracted, and his body curled in on itself like an armadillo. He lost his balance and rolled backwards in a tight ball. Joan screamed as he turned a reverse somersault through the open doorway and down the stairs.

"*Fuck! Fuck! Fuck!*" he screamed as he tumbled backwards out of control and rolled uncontrolled downward, feeling the stair edges pummel him as he rolled, over and over, hitting his back, his buttocks, the back of his head, his shoulders, somersaulting backwards all the way down to the bottom of the stairs and crashing into the calves of an elderly patron, knocking her down like a bowling pin, and surprising from her a bloodcurdling shriek as she flopped face first into a well-worn sofa, breaking her fall.

"*Ow fuuuuuck,*" Dwayne wheezed.

Had he broken any bones?

Had he killed anyone? He wasn't sure whom or what he'd hit.

He was afraid to move. If he'd broken his neck or a vertebra in his back and he made a wrong move, he could be paralyzed for life.

He was going to lie still. Just lie still for a moment. Take an inventory of his pains.

His right arm was twitchy. The back of his hand felt burnt. His muscles ached like they'd suffered mother of all cramps.

All the way up his back from his buttocks to the back of his head, he felt horizontal stripes of pain where he'd hit the stair edges. His knees and ankles had taken some hits, too, somehow. Tomorrow he'd be decorated with bruises. But had he broken anything?

He heard the disturbed chatter of the elderly couple behind him, and then Joan, shrieking and coming down the stairs, and noticed suddenly he was surrounded by half of the cast, who'd heard his screams through the control booth window and had found their way to him.

He opened his eyes to see them surging toward him, shouting and exclaiming and wanting to know what had happened. An old lady lay face down on the sofa above him with her dentures on the cushion three feet in front of her head. Joan was chattering nonsensically from above on the stairs, and suddenly Orlando was shouting: "Help me get him up!"

Dwayne attempted to cry: *No!* But his tongue was still quivering. Somewhere in the background Wallace shouted: "No!" but no one heard him either. As Dwayne attempted to scream, *No! No! No! For the Love of God, no!* Orlando and another young man grabbed Dwayne by the upper arms in some misguided sense of emergency and pulled him abruptly to his feet.

As they lifted him up fast with all their might, Dwayne's neck snapped back and bounced forward painfully.

He was on his feet.

People were shouting.

Was he all right?

He was on his feet, being held upright by the two young actors. Orlando held him by the arm and put a hand on his chest. "Are you okay?"

Was he now paralyzed? Would he never walk again because of the misplaced urgency of two young men who'd spent their college years learning to emote for a crowd rather than anything remotely useful?

Dwayne bent his head forward gingerly.

And then back.

He could move his head.

He lifted his right foot. And then his left.

He lifted his right hand and wiggled his fingers. His right hand had long, skinny electrical burn on the back.

He was sore all over, but apparently he was not paralyzed.

"I think so," he said at last.

"He's all right!" Orlando shouted to the cast. They all cheered.

Their enthusiasm, at least, was heartening.

The elderly patron had recovered her dentures and wanted Dwayne's contact information for her attorney. Dwayne asked Joan to give her what she wanted, as he felt an immediate need to lie down.

"Come with me, old man," Wallace said to him, taking his arm from the youngsters.

Joan turned toward the actors. "Everyone return to your preparations!" she shouted. "Curtain at eight p.m." Then she turned back to the elderly couple.

Wallace led Dwayne through the dispersing actors, some of whom patted him sympathetically as they went back to their routines.

"There's no show in the studio right now. You can lie down in their dressing room," Wallace told him. "I thought those boys were going to break your neck."

"I was afraid of that, too."

Unlike the mainstage, which had two roomy dressing rooms, the studio theatre had only one long narrow dressing room for the use of its entire cast. It also housed a large dimmer relay unit and two long costume racks. Wallace led him in.

"Hmm. No couch in here." Wallace opened the entrance door to the back of the stage. True to the modus operandi of Raymond Green, it had not been cleared of furniture from its previous show. Upstage right against the wall sat a vintage chaise lounge with tattered red brocade upholstery. "Just the thing." Wallace led him to it, and Dwayne sat.

"You might want this." Wallace pulled a pill case from his pocket and offered Dwayne a white oblong pill. "Vicodin. If you want it."

"You carry Vicodin?" Dwayne asked.

"*When you get to be my age, you start to get a pain for every bad thought you've ever had,*" Wallace quoted, using a pronounced Chicago accent. "That's my favorite line from *NYPD Blue*. Sipowicz to Bobby Simone. The most Roman Catholic line ever pronounced on TV."

Wallace gave him the pill and fetched him a bottle of water. Dwayne considered the many sharp pains he felt up and down his body and took the pill.

"Just rest. Nap if you can. I'll fetch you before curtain." He took off to get ready for the show.

It was very quiet, lying on the chaise lounge on the stage of the studio. Dwayne lay there, recounting the errors of his ways. After a while he began to feel the pleasant intoxication of the Vicodin. His pain began to subside, and he fell asleep.

When he awoke, he didn't know where he was, but the drug-subdued ache of the impact points on his back, neck, and buttocks reminded him. He sat up gingerly on the lounge and staggered to the entry door of upstairs mainstage.

The show was already in progress! What kind of organization started its first preview without fetching the director? Wallace, apparently, had forgotten, faced with readying himself to play the title role. But what about Joan? Why hadn't she sought him out? Had she assumed he was in the audience? Or was she deliberately ignoring him?

He didn't want to disturb the actors or audience by entering the house now, so he went back to the upstairs lobby and climbed the stairs to join Joan in the light booth. She gave him a disapproving look as he set up the folding chair and sat down in the right half of the booth.

How much of the show had he missed? Titus Andronicus and Tamora were on stage with her sons and Aaron. Ry's guitar was wailing and Titus's sons were performing the ritual sacrifice of Tamora's eldest son. Okay, they were still in the first scene.

Titus's son Lucius completed the killing and Alarbus was cast into a "fire" of dancers and lights.

"See, lord and father, how we have performed our Roman rites: Alarbus' limbs are lopped, and his entrails feed the sacrificing fire, whose smoke, like incense, doth perfume the sky," he said.

"Why, foolish Lucius, dost thou not perceive that Rome is but a wilderness of tigers?" Titus said, looking sad instead of triumphant.

Dwayne felt suddenly confused. So did the other actors on stage. Coco put her hand on her hip and cocked her head to one side, looking decidedly more modern than the Queen of the Goths.

"*Fuck!*" Joan breathed under her breath beside Dwayne, flipping through the pages of her prompt script.

"Tigers must prey, and Rome affords no prey but me and mine," Titus continued. "How happy art thou, then, from these devourers to be banished!"

Joan leaned over and whispered to Dwayne: "He's jumped past the election, the weddings, the rape and murders, and his sons' executions!"

"But who comes with our brother Marcus here?" Titus said, completing his speech. Lavinia walked uncertainly on stage, on time for her entrance. And then suddenly, hearing his name, Marcus lurched onstage behind her.

"Lavinia can set them right," Joan whispered. But as the actress opened her mouth to begin the speech that should have happened at this moment in the play, Marcus responded to the cue from Titus and jumped into his lines from much later in the play.

"Titus, prepare thy aged eyes to weep; or, if not so, thy noble heart to break," he said mournfully. "I bring consuming sorrow to thine age."

Lavinia looked both mystified by and pissed off at Marcus. At the point of the speech he'd given, she would have already suffered rape and had her hands cut off and her tongue cut out. She looked from Marcus to Titus and then down at her hands, which she promptly hid behind her back. The action was so nonsensical that Joan actually laughed.

Saint Philomena and the premature ejaculators.

Continuing like this, the show would be a twenty-minute one act play in which Titus enacted a series of wild revenges for no apparent reason.

"Hold the action on stage," Dwayne called loudly through the window of the booth. The actors on stage and the audience in the seats looked startled to hear this voice from above. The actors' shock turned quickly to relief.

"Sorry, ladies and gentlemen," Dwayne announced to the audience, "but things crop up sometimes at previews. We had a technical difficulty. We are going to restart at the end of the sacrifice of Alarbus with…" He paused to look down on Joan's prompt book. "Lucius's line: Alarbus' limbs are lopped, and his entrails feed the sacrificing fire, whose smoke, like incense, doth perfume the sky. Followed by Titus's line: Let it be so; and let Andronicus make this his latest farewell to their souls… Reset please."

Dwayne saw the light bulb go off in Wallace's head as he realized where he'd gone wrong. The actors got into position, and Dwayne called: "Action."

After that, Wallace was masterful. Rather than his fuckup throwing him off balance for the rest of the show, he seemed refreshed and refocused in a whole new way. His performance was one Dwayne would have been proud for Gregor Foxx to see.

But how would he be opening night? Would Dwayne be flying to New York? Or would his $2,000 fly to New York without him?

Orlando, however, did not fare so well. He still seemed embarrassed in Aaron's most evil lines. Those were the lines that gave Bobby his reason for wanting to do the show in the first place. Orlando was casting them off like unwanted children. They had one more preview and then it would be opening night. Dwayne had to do

218 • Richard Engling

something.

He circulated through the dressing rooms after the show, giving his notes to the actors individually. When he came into the men's dressing room, Wallace looked up at him and started laughing.

"Interesting edit," Dwayne said to him. "That would have been an incredibly concise version of the show."

"Blah, blah, blah, rape, kill," Wallace rumbled in his deepest baritone. "We didn't really need all that other stuff."

"Nice recovery. Your Titus was brilliant tonight. Keep it."

"Sometimes you need a mulligan to find the sweet stroke," Wallace said.

Dwayne looked at him quizzically.

"A mulligan," Wallace repeated. "A do-over."

"Of course," Dwayne said.

"You ever play golf?" Wallace said. "Hit the links?"

"Not since I was fifteen."

"Splendid way to ruin a good walk."

Orlando was at the very far end of the makeup table. Dwayne went and sat beside him. Orlando looked at him, then lay his face down on the table and kept it there.

"How did your show feel tonight?" Dwayne said.

"How did it look?" Orlando said into the table surface.

How to say this? Dwayne wondered. The director was the eyes for the actor. It was his job to tell them how they looked, what they communicated. It was always best to tell the truth. Not the brutal truth, of course, but the generous, helpful truth. "I saw an actor who looked embarrassed by some of his lines."

Orlando sat up abruptly. "I love Shakespeare. Mostly. I love research. I find it hugely useful. But so many critics think Aaron is an expression of Shakespeare's racism. It pisses me off. I don't want to be Shakespeare's mouthpiece to say: Niggers is evil."

"No," Dwayne agreed. He took a deep breath. How to help? "Look, whatever Shakespeare believed or intended doesn't matter. We can interpret his lines any way we want."

"But now that I understand his intent, it's pushing out all other thoughts. How do I deliver a line like: 'My fleece of woolly hair that now uncurls even as an adder when she doth unroll to do some fatal execution?' Black hair is equal to a poisonous snake? That's what I'm saying. And look how I describe my own son: 'Here is the babe, as loathsome as a toad.' My son is loathsome as a toad, because he's black! No other reason. And black people are evil: 'Often have I digged up dead men from their graves, and set them upright at their dear friends' doors.' Wow! He's *so* evil. And he's evil for no other reason than he's black."

Dwayne was out of his depth again. He couldn't call Aleister. A white psychiatrist was even more useless than a white director.

What would Bobby do?

Whatever Bobby would do, Bobby was black, and Dwayne wasn't.

"Well, Bobby had a different interpretation," Dwayne said.

"But he left town," Orlando pointed out. "And here I am."

"But he didn't change his mind about Aaron."

What would Bobby do? Let's find out.

Dwayne pulled out his cell phone and hit Bobby's number. Bobby answered, and Dwayne felt maybe his luck had changed. He put the call on speaker. "Bobby, this is Dwayne. I'm here with Orlando who is having trouble because Aaron is such a racist invention."

Bobby laughed. "Well, Orlando is absolutely right."

Judas Priest and the misplaced phone call. "How's that?" Dwayne said, his spine straightening with the intimations of panic.

"Aaron is even worse for blacks than Shylock is for Jews," Bobby said.

"See?" Orlando said. He shook his head in disgust.

"Then why did you want to play him?" Dwayne's voice rose an octave.

"Because you can turn that around and play Aaron as the avenging Blackamoor," Bobby said. "He wants to destroy all these racist whites. Fuck them over, make them bleed. He revels in it. He despises their racism, and he's going to make them suffer every indignity he can imagine."

"Huh," Orlando said slowly. "I guess that could work... But did you know Dwayne has a black woman playing Queen Tamora? The two most evil people in the show are both black." He looked at Dwayne. "Sorry, Dwayne, but I just don't get that. Tamora is the Queen of the Goths. Goths are super violent *white* people from Germany. They are like the Nazis of the Roman times. But in our production, she's played by Coco. What's up with that?"

"Shit, man, that wasn't *Dwayne's* idea," Bobby said. "I offered Coco that part. She's a fierce actor, great with Shakespeare, and super hot. She's as hot as me!" he laughed again. "Why would Aaron be propping up some proto-Nazi white woman? If my evil is going to be against white racists, then the woman I serve has got to be black!"

"Well, yeah, I guess that tracks." Orlando looked at Dwayne. "You think I should jump into Bobby's interpretation?"

"It makes sense to me." Dwayne watched Orlando mulling it over. "I could have cast Tamora with a white actor after Bobby left, but I didn't," Dwayne continued. "I wanted an emotional reality in that casting. The Goths were foreign to the Romans. Making Tamora black increases her otherness. It increases her contrast to Lavinia. It increases her solidarity with Aaron. And she's a strong object of lust for Saturninus."

"He's got that jungle fever!" Bobby laughed. "And rightly so. You guys good? Because I gotta go. I'm meeting Sarah."

"Sarah?" Dwayne said.

"Sarah Michelle Geller," he said quietly. "I think we might get a little *thang* going on."

"You are meeting Buffy the Vampire Slayer?" Dwayne said.

"We're doing a horror movie. We just starting shooting. You good, Orlando?"

"Yeah. Thanks. You gave me something, Brother." He smiled at Dwayne. Finally, Orlando looked more assured.

"Yeah," Bobby said. "Whenever you aren't sure how to deliver a line, just think: *Fuck whitey!*"

"Yeah." Orlando laughed. He looked straight into Dwayne's eye and said, "*Fuck whitey.*" His venomous expression gave Dwayne a chill.

And that was a good thing.

37

Thursday, January 29, 2004

Dwayne leaned toward the window of the light booth with pleasure. Down on stage Orlando urged Tamora's sons to stop fighting each other over Lavinia and instead to rape her. In the past, he'd treated them like partners, but now he treated them as despised white-boy stooges, pretending to be their friend when he faced them and turning away to show his true face to the audience. Dwayne loved it. And since this was their final preview performance, it was right on time.

Melinda, however, was backsliding into the robotic quality. She and Aleister would have their first counseling session tomorrow, the afternoon of opening night. Dwayne hoped that would turn things around.

Coco mesmerized. Her physical beauty was a huge asset, but the liveliness of her eyes and face was even more magnetic. Whether she was pleading for her son, seducing an emperor, or plotting revenge, her emotions drew all eyes. Despite what a pain in the ass she could be, Dwayne felt blessed to have her.

But most revelatory was Wallace Proctor. He totally embodied the triumphant general who saved Rome. He began cocksure of his righteousness. He could have claimed the crown himself but he put it on the head of the late emperor's eldest son. When one of his own sons stood against the new emperor, he killed the youth himself. But then the emperor turned against him, his daughter was raped, and two of his other sons condemned to death. Wallace's descent into despair was heartbreaking. He seemed to lose his mind in his grief. He begged for relief, but no one was there.

"O reverend tribunes! Unbind my sons, reverse the doom of

death," he said, kneeling on the empty stage, tears running down his cheek.

"Noble father, you lament in vain," his son Lucius replied. "The tribunes hear you not; no man is near."

"Why, tis no matter if they did hear," he said, a deep despair washing over him. "They would not pity me, yet plead I must."

Wallace stopped and stared down at the ground before him. As the moment dragged on, Dwayne lost the feeling of being enthralled in the moment and suddenly feared Wallace had forgotten his next line. Wallace gazed past the other actor on stage out at the audience, scanning each of the sections surrounding the three sides of the thrust stage. He gazed up into the lights, looking nothing like Titus Andronicus, but totally like an old actor looking around at the run-down theatre in which he worked. He broke down into the deepest tears, bending forward and sobbing with abandon, tears running down his face and dripping off his nose.

"My noble lord," the actor playing his son said in confusion.

Wallace shook his head and covered his face in his right hand, sobbing long and hard. He drew his hand away, and shook the tears and snot off of it onto the stage. He took a deep gasp of breath, attempting to get control of himself. He shouted aloud: "Ha!" toward the ceiling, wiped the wet off his face with both hands, and then brew his nose loudly into his fingers. Dwayne heard sounds of disgust rise from the audience. Wallace wiped the snot off his hands onto the floor of the stage, then wiped his hands together, trying to dry them so as not to soil his costume. He took a deep breath, and gestured, finally, to the rocks on the floor, weeping openly, his words incomprehensible.

The actor playing Lucius looked increasingly confused. "My gracious Lord," he said again, knowing not what to say, but hoping against hope to return the scene into action, as Wallace's sobbing lightened into gentler weeping.

The audience stirred in their seats, looking at one another and whispering. Should Dwayne stop the scene? This was the final preview. Tomorrow was opening. He didn't want to interrupt, but Wallace looked totally lost.

Wallace moaned. He looked at his scene partner standing with a sword in hand. "But wherefore standest thou with thy weapon drawn?" he said.

"To rescue my two brothers from their death," Lucius said, the relief painfully evident on his face, "for which attempt the judges have pronounced my everlasting doom of banishment."

"O happy man! they have befriended thee," Wallace said, pulling himself back fully into Titus. "Foolish Lucius, dost thou not perceive that Rome is but a wilderness of tigers? Tigers must prey, and Rome affords no prey but me and mine: how happy art thou, then, from these devourers to be banished!"

"What the hell was that?" Joan whispered.

"I don't know," Dwayne replied. "But I hope he doesn't do it again."

The rest of the show went reasonably well, but every once in a while Wallace looked around as though he were lost before snapping back into his role. He never got back to achieving the depth he'd attained the night before.

After the show, Dwayne hurried around giving his notes to the actors. To Wallace he said: "Can we talk?"

The old man sighed, and his shoulders slumped. He hadn't yet started to get out of costume, sitting frozen at the makeup table in a reverie. "Only over whiskey."

When they'd finished their various post-show duties, the two men went up the street to the John Barleycorn Memorial Pub. Wallace headed straight to the bar and settled onto a stool. He took a deep breath of the beer-scented air and sighed deeply. He looked more at home here than he had all night on stage. Dwayne sat beside him.

"Act three, scene one," Wallace said, his face still deeply melancholy.

"Yes," Dwayne agreed. That was the moment when Wallace's performance had gone to hell.

The bartender approached.

"Barry," Wallace greeted him.

"Wallace," the bartender said back.

"Bushmills neat," Wallace said. "A double."

Barry nodded and looked at Dwayne. "The same," Dwayne said.

"Act three, scene one," Wallace repeated. "It's really the fulcrum point of Titus' life." Wallace gazed at the bottles on the shelves behind the bar against the mirrors. Deep-brown, carved woodwork surrounded the shelves. Classical music played gently in the background of the clatter of conversation around the room. Wallace took a deep breath, gave Dwayne a quick glance, and went back to staring at the bottles. "He's dedicated his whole life to Rome," Wallace continued. "He's led his army, *including his twenty-three sons,* into battle. Most of them have been killed in action, and yet he has no regrets. They've died in service. And now, despite the purity of his devotion to Rome, the city has betrayed him. Repudiated him. Disrespected. Two sons wrongly put to death. He's about to discover his daughter has been raped and mutilated. And then he's tricked into cutting off his own hand."

Barry the bartender set the whiskeys in front of the men and headed off to serve another patron.

"It's the moment in which he despairs and changes. He turns from service to revenge."

"And last night you did all that so brilliantly."

"And you want to know what happened tonight."

"Yes," Dwayne agreed.

"Do you know how old I am?"

Dwayne felt taken aback by the question. "Fifty something?" he guessed.

"Fifty-five. I am fifty-five years old. I have already lived three years more than Shakespeare, but what impact have I made on culture? If I died tomorrow, my life would not make a ripple. I'll be totally forgotten by the time you're my age."

"I don't know that that's true," Dwayne protested.

"On stage tonight, with Titus's doom looming before me, I saw my life reflected. Some of the lights overhead were kitchen spotlights in fixtures made of juice cans. And clip lights with gels taped to them. The floor shows gaps between the planking. Backstage you can see arrow shapes in the wood left from when the theatre was a bowling alley. I've spent a life on ill-equipped stages."

"Some great shows have graced that stage."

"Sure," Wallace said dismissively. "But I'm talking about the grand procession of the life of Wallace Proctor, theatre artist. At fifty-five years of age, I'm still taking roles that don't pay enough to cover my carfare to the theatre."

Dwayne winced.

"I'm not blaming *you*. I'm talking about my life." Wallace raised his eyebrows increasing the deep folds of the wrinkles in his forehead. He turned on his barstool and leaned in toward Dwayne. "Some years back I did a one-man show I co-wrote with a friend. I thought I was finally taking my career into my own hands. I wasn't waiting for someone else. I wasn't auditioning, hat-in-hand, mother-may-I. I was making something happen as playwright and actor and producer. Finally." Wallace took a deep sip of his whiskey and chuckled ruefully. "I had so much of my heart riding on that show. I worked for five years on the script, going back and forth with my writing partner. We did readings. We got notes from invited audiences. We revised and perfected. Finally we felt ready. He would direct. I would act. We each raised half the money, most of it coming from our own pockets. We rented a venue. We hired a PR man. To save money, we rehearsed at my friend's apartment." He leaned in toward Dwayne and lowered his voice to an intense whisper. "But a strange thing happened. I was always confident working on other people's scripts, classics or contemporary." He leaned back and raised his voice. "I commanded the stage. I had presence for miles. But as we rehearsed our own piece, I felt more and more like a fake."

"The imposter syndrome," Dwayne said.

"What actor hasn't experienced it?" Wallace sat up straight and suddenly seemed a half foot taller. "I hadn't!" he exclaimed. "And now it hit me like five thousand pounds of shit. When my partner saw me floundering, he made everything worse. He was worried about *his money*."

Wallace closed his eyes and sighed. He picked up his drink, swirled the brown liquid, and took a deep sip. He swirled it again and drained it, then caught Barry the bartender's eye, and pointed into his glass for another.

"The show bombed. My partner blamed me. The cunt. I was

humiliated. I'd depleted my savings. We still hate one another." He shook his head. "What a mistake to let him direct. After that, I quit theatre for five years, but when I heard about your audition, I thought maybe it was time to get back on the horse. Even though your stipend is a joke, if I could triumph in a role like *Titus*, I'd take a step towards redemption. But I didn't anticipate what playing Titus would mean: His long slide into disrespect and betrayal feels too much like my own."

"And that hit you in act three, scene one," Dwayne said.

"Right in front of our final preview audience."

"So, that's good," Dwayne said. "You got that over with."

"I never recovered for the rest of the night."

"That's not totally true," Dwayne said. "You had moments afterwards that were right on. And other moments where you backslid. But now you've experienced that, and you are done with it."

"It's my life, boyo," Wallace protested. "How can I be done with it?"

"I mean you are done being *surprised* by it," Dwayne said. "You were taken unawares once. You can't be surprised again."

Wallace grunted noncommittally.

"Look," Dwayne said. "You were brilliant last night. What you discovered onstage tonight can help you go even deeper. You just need to use it and stay in control of it, and stay in Titus. Wallace has to wait until after the show if he needs to mourn his life. While you are on stage, you are Titus. You know how to do that. You are a veteran Chicago actor. This is the perfect role at the perfect time of your life. I'm not telling you anything you don't already know."

Wallace grunted again. Barry brought him his second whiskey, and he took a thoughtful sip.

"I *am* a veteran Chicago actor," Wallace agreed. "And that does mean something."

"Hell yes it does." Dwayne leaned in toward him. "You've got the chops," he said with quiet intensity. "You've got the talent. You've got the experience. You have castmates who understand what *ensemble* means. And you have a tremendous instrument: you are physically and vocally commanding. You are a handsome, expressive man with a beautiful baritone voice."

"That's all true," Wallace said, quietly nodding. Dwayne loved how he said it with neither false modesty nor puffed-up ego.

Dwayne got an idea. There was a chance it could backfire, but the man needed something. Dwayne decided to risk it.

"I am going to tell you something that almost no one in the company knows," he said. "For some, it would make them too nervous. But you are thirsting for a breakthrough. I believe this will spur you forward."

That captured Wallace's attention. "What?"

"You have to promise me that you will keep this confidential. I don't want the other actors to get self-conscious."

"Of course."

"Gregor Foxx is coming to see *Titus Andronicus*," Dwayne said proudly.

"Gregor Foxx, the artistic director of the Public Theater?" Wallace said doubtfully.

"Yes," Dwayne said.

"Get the fuck out of here," Wallace said.

"He is."

"No fucking chance. The Public Theater in New York City?"

Was Wallace looking nervous? If Wallace went into a fit of nerves, that would be the worst irony.

"He'll be there tomorrow night for opening," Dwayne said.

"Why? Why the fuck would Gregor Foxx come to the Chicago Repertory Arts Playhouse? No venue has ever more richly deserved its acronym."

"I'm up for a slot in the Emerging Directors' Program at the Public, and *Titus* is my audition."

"Really?" Wallace said, deeply impressed.

"Yes," Dwayne said.

Wallace sat up straighter and smiled. "Well, I wouldn't mind having Gregor Foxx see my title role performance in Shakespeare's *Titus Andronicus*."

"I didn't think you would," Dwayne said.

Wallace raised his glass of whiskey until Dwayne raised his, and they clinked them together. Wallace smiled broadly, his chest expanded, and he looked suddenly three inches taller. "Well then," he said cheerfully, "I guess we had better not fuck it up."

Dwayne grinned. "I guess we had better not."

38

Friday, January 30, 2004

D wayne spent hours vacuuming and mopping his theatre space and the public bathrooms. That should have been the job of Raymond Green and his staff, but at this point Dwayne knew better than to expect anything from Green. He even swept and tidied the ground floor and second-floor lobby areas. He wanted the place to look great for his opening and for Gregor Foxx. And, frankly, he needed to occupy himself. It helped keep his prevailing nervousness from advancing to screaming panic.

He wished Angela were here. She knew so many ways to calm him. Some of those ways included sex, which, of course, was not an option at the moment.

When the box office manager arrived, Dwayne gave him the extensive comp list for the night. He had eight critics coming and seven representatives of the Jeff Awards committee. (The Jeffs were Chicago's version of the Tony Awards). Plus, eighty of the company's closest friends and acquaintances were receiving free tickets. Dwayne was packing the house with friendly faces. That was standard practice in theatres all over town. Of the one hundred twenty seats in Dwayne's theatre tonight, only eighteen of them would be occupied by holders of prepaid tickets. He needed good reviews and a "Jeff Awards recommendation" to generate demand among the ticket-paying public.

Dwayne set up a greeting table at the door of his theatre from which he would hand out press kits to the critics and greet the Jeff Awards people and his audience in general. He was especially looking forward to meeting Gregor Foxx, whom he'd never met in person. He was hoping against hope that all his actors' performances would come together tonight. Wallace and Melinda had been weak in the final preview. Orlando, finally, had played Aaron well, but he'd been shit the night before. Coco, thank God, had been consistently good. If only they could all come together and be great at once!

Dwayne was collating the insert sheets for his press kits when he heard a painfully familiar sound coming up the stairs from the lobby below: one of his actors sobbing.

He set down the papers and turned to see Melinda on the arm of Aleister, sobbing and leaning on him as she walked.

"Is the stage floor clean?" Aleister asked him.

"Yeah," Dwayne said, mystified. "I wet-mopped it myself."

"Go ahead," Aleister told Melinda.

The young woman, eyes puffy and red from crying, walked into the performance space without looking at Dwayne. She lay face down in the center of the stage with her arms spread and her palms down on the floor, and she began to moan. She moaned and began to sob again. Aleister closed the theatre doors to give her privacy.

"Good. That's good," he said to himself. He turned to Dwayne. "How's it going?"

"That's good?" Dwayne wondered how an actor being exhausted from weeping could be good.

"Yeah. We made a lot of progress this afternoon. We talked for nearly two hours. I can't tell you anything she said, of course, but she did a lot of crying. A lot of suppressed grief. Then she had this idea to let her emotions out into the stage floor. So that's what she's doing."

"And that's going to have her ready for tonight?"

"What?" Aleister said.

"Tonight. Opening night," Dwayne said. "This exercise is going to have her ready to perform tonight?"

"Oh!" Aleister said, truly surprised. "I don't know. I'm helping her deal with her trauma. I have no idea how that'll affect her performance."

"You don't?"

"No. How would I know that?"

From inside the theatre the sounds of her sobbing grew louder.

"I thought that was why you two were meeting the afternoon of opening night," Dwayne said, his nerves rising precipitously. "So you could help her be ready to perform tonight."

"No!" Aleister shook his head as though that had been the furthest thing from his mind. "I offered her this afternoon because I had the time open. I'm a psychiatrist. Not a theatre coach."

"But you are also one of the producers of this show," Dwayne protested. "I assumed you had one eye on helping her be a better performer, so this could be a better show, and so you wouldn't lose your investment."

"Jesus, Dwayne," Aleister said, clearly insulted. "What do you think I am? A race track veterinarian, juicing a horse to compete?"

"Well, I'm not suggesting that," Dwayne said annoyedly. "But I did assume that if your therapy might risk wiping her out, you would have scheduled it some time other than opening night."

"Well, I'm a little more concerned about the health of a young woman's psyche than I am about one performance of this play."

Inside Melinda shrieked as though in horrible pain and slapped her hand repeatedly on the floor.

"*Jesus Christ of the tortured harpies,*" Dwayne said. "Her face was a mess. Her cheeks were puffy and swollen." He looked at his watch. "Five-thirty." Another shriek broke from within the space. "Is she going to have anything left to bring on stage?"

"You'd know better than I," Aleister said, looking very put-upon. "I'll have a word, and then I'll get out of your hair. I'm sure you have preparations." He ducked into the theatre space. A few minutes later he came back out. It was blessedly quiet inside.

"What did you tell her?" Dwayne said.

Aleister hesitated a moment. "I guess it's nothing confidential. I just suggested she not give herself a hoarse voice before the show. She smiled and thanked me and sat up on the floor."

"Thank you," Dwayne said wearily.

"Sure. Break your legs."

"Yours, too," Dwayne said darkly.

Aleister walked off to meet Chaz and Angela for dinner before the show.

Lord save me from the well-intentioned.

Dwayne's phone rang and he answered it.

"This is Gregor Foxx."

"Hey, Mr. Foxx," Dwayne said. "Great to hear from you. I'm really looking forward to meeting you tonight."

"Yeah, that's why I'm calling," he said. "I had something come up. I meant to call you earlier. Stoppard's in town, and tonight is the only time he's got available. He's got a new script, so naturally we are interested."

"Of course," Dwayne said. Tom Stoppard. No one was going to put Dwayne Finnegan ahead of internationally famous genius playwright, Tom Stoppard.

"Look," Foxx said. "Put me down for two tickets Saturday night of your third weekend. I think that's going to work for me. Good?"

"Absolutely," Dwayne said, working his hardest to keep the disappointment out of his voice. He'd rounded up eighty people to paper the house for Gregor Foxx and make him believe he was watching a great, popular, well-attended production. Would Dwayne be able to round up a great house again in week three? Of course, one hoped by then they'd be selling most of the seats.

"How's the show looking?" Foxx said.

"Great!" Dwayne's voice sounded incredibly false to himself. One of his lead actors had just been sobbing on the floor, a second hated his role because it was racist, and a third felt the play rubbed the failure of his life in his face. What could possibly be better?

"Great," Foxx said. "I'm really looking forward to it. See you in week three." And he rang off.

Jesus, Mary, Rosencrantz, and Guildenstern! Dwayne felt the urge to smash his cell phone to the ground.

He took a deep breath. Maybe this was a good thing. This would allow his cast to settle into the roles and grow and find themselves in their parts. A performance in week three was always better than opening night. This should be good.

But Dwayne was so geared up to receive Gregor Foxx tonight! It felt like a tremendous let down.

He would get over it. It was better this way.

He had to keep telling himself that.

Joan came up the stairs and stopped in front of him, her backpack on her back, snow on the shoulders of her coat, her face rosy from the cold but still as emotionless as usual. She stood before him for a long moment, saying nothing, and he wondered what insanity might come out of her mouth.

"Opening night," she said at last.

"Yes, it is," Dwayne agreed.

She nodded. "Away we go." She turned and walked into the upstairs lobby and up the stairs to the light booth.

"Away we go," Dwayne agreed. His stomach felt so agitated, he thought he might throw up.

Ingrid came in carrying some weird-looking rectangular metal box with a top surface full of large glass knobs. "Wait until you see this!" she said excitedly. She led him up to the front of the stage and used a cordless drill to anchor the metal box into the floor.

"What is that thing?" Dwayne said, alarmed at her screwing something so large into the stage floor.

"LED footlight," Ingrid said excitedly. "These are mostly used for rock shows because the color quality is so weird. No good for a realistic show, but I thought it might look amazing on our fight scenes with the guitar in the background and all! I was able to trade a favor!"

She jogged backstage and came back with a light cable, handed one end up to Joan to plug into an open dimmer, and ran the cable down under the audience seats to where she'd screwed the footlight into the floor, and plugged it in.

"Joan, please take out the house lights, bring up cue fourteen and the new dimmer," she called up to the booth.

"Okay," Joan said in a long-suffering voice. She had her own long list of things to do before the curtain.

The lights shifted into what they had set for one of the fight scenes, augmented by a sickly orange light from the floor.

"Now watch."

The floor light began cycling through a variety of garish colors. Ingrid moved around the stage, pretending like she were the actors moving through the fight choreography.

"That's hideous." Joan called down from the booth.

"It really adds an uncanny element," Ingrid said. "I love it!"

"Yeah, well, it's interesting," Dwayne said diplomatically. "But it puts a big clunky box on stage that the actors aren't used to working around. Plus you're shooting weird lights at them during their choreography."

"We can bring them out to try it before the house opens!" Ingrid said. "Easy!"

"No," Dwayne said. "It's a safety issue. I'm not adding anything they could trip on."

"Nobody steps that close to the audience," Ingrid complained. "You don't know what I promised for borrowing that."

"Sorry. No surprises for the actors on opening night."

"They'll adjust!"

"No," Dwayne insisted. "They are going start their pre-show warm-ups soon, so please remove that right away."

"Goddamn it, Dwayne! This would be amazing!"

Dwayne walked over and put a hand on her muscular shoulder. "The lights you designed already look amazing. Tom's violence choreography, the actors, the band: It's all amazing. We've got to trust what we've got, Ingrid. Jamming in one more thing at the last minute is asking for trouble. But thanks for always trying to make it better. I appreciate that."

"You really think it would throw them off?"

"I absolutely do."

"All right," she said regretfully. "But it could have been awesome."

"It's ugly," Joan called from the booth.

"Violence is ugly!" Ingrid yelled back at her.

"We are here to support the actors," Dwayne said to them both.

"Theatre would be so much better without actors," Ingrid muttered. She unscrewed the light box from the floor and pulled up the cable from under the seats. An ancient soda can rolled out into the aisle, dislodged by Ingrid's whipping of the cable. Dwayne had swept the audience rows, but there were places under the seats he could not reach, harboring God knows what trash from decades past.

Joan bustled through the space, checking the locations of props, making sure everything was in place. The actors arrived, did warm ups, and got into costume and makeup. Some looked withdrawn. Others happily chattered and gossiped. Melinda had spent time bathing her face in cold water which had brought her puffy eyes back nearly to normal. Dwayne offered encouraging words, answered last minute questions, and helped wherever he could.

Ten minutes before the house was due to open to the audience, he called all the performers onstage. They gathered in a circle, their arms around each others' shoulders.

"Tom, what do you have to say?" Dwayne said.

Tom looked around the circle, towering over most of them. "Listening is everything," he said. "Dancers, combatants, listen to the music. You know your moves, harmonize your moves with the rhythm of the music. Musicians, listen to the dancers. Watch their moves and play in harmony with them. When you all lock in, it's incredible!" He looked at each of them again and nodded to Dwayne.

"Just a couple words from me before we start," Dwayne said. "I have seen every single one of you be brilliant. Never yet *all on the same night*." Some of them chuckled at this. "But you've all been there, so I know you *all* can do it. So tonight, *have fun*. Keep up the pace. Listen to one another. Pick up your cues. Be alive in the moment. Okay, everyone put your right hand into the center. And on the count of three, we throw up our hands and shout: *Be brilliant!*"

They all put their hands into the center, hands atop one another in solidarity, and they counted out together, bouncing their hands with each count: *One, two, three, Be Brilliant!*

Everyone cheered and hugged.

"Break a thousand legs!" Dwayne called. They all dispersed happily (or nervously) to make their final preparations.

Tom took both of Dwayne's hands in his and looked him happily in the eyes. "Break a leg, my friend."

"None of this could have worked without you," Dwayne replied. They shared a deep hug, and then Dwayne stationed himself outside the entrance. When the house opened, he handed out press kits to the critics and greeted the audience as they entered.

At fifteen minutes before curtain, with the house half full, he heard a man shout for help from inside the theatre. He ran in to see an elderly woman, one of the members of the Jeff Awards committee, lying on her back in the second row, her husband standing over her, pulling things out of her purse madly.

"What's happened?" Dwayne said.

"Her heart's stopped," the old man said frantically, looking up only a moment from going through her purse. "I can't find the remote!" People all around the theatre were standing by their seats to see what was happening.

Where the old woman was lying there was little room around her. Dwayne knelt awkwardly beside her, inserting himself between her and the seats. He opened her blouse at the top to push her pearls aside, got into position, and started giving compressions to her heart. With one hand on her chest in his awkward position, he lost balance a little and caught himself with the other hand on the floor well under the seat. His hand fell on a little collection of detritus including something long, thin, and metal that Ingrid's maneuvers with the lighting cable had dislodged from its hiding place.

Instantly a surge of 120 volts flowed into his hand, traveled up his arm, through his chest, and down his other arm into the old woman's chest. The rapid contraction of his muscles knocked him backwards into the little aisle as the current surged into the old woman's chest and shocked her heart.

"Woo, whoops!" the old woman said, sitting up suddenly. She took a deep breath. "How *do* you *do*," she said to herself. "That was something." Her elderly husband helped her to her feet.

"Did you find my remote?" she said.

"Just now," he said, tears of panic in his eyes. "I thought I was going to lose you."

Dwayne sat up in the aisle, his arms and chest twitching in pain, amazed at what he was seeing.

"Thank you, young man," the woman said to him. "I've never experienced anyone with a heart compression technique like that!"

"I'm sure you haven't," Dwayne said dumbly.

"Let me see that remote," she said to her husband.

Dwayne took some deep breaths, recovering from the intense

electrical shock. The old woman performed some kind of adjustment on the round white remote and held it to her chest.

"Okay," she said to her husband. "That'll be good. Could you get me a glass of water? I'm suddenly very thirsty." She sat back down in her chair.

Dwayne struggled to his feet. "I'll call you an ambulance," he said.

"Oh, that won't be necessary," she told him. "This has happened before."

"Am I mistaken?" Dwayne said. "Didn't your heart just stop?"

"Yes," she said. "I'm scheduled to get a new pacemaker on Monday. It's stopped a couple times lately. But we restart it with the remote."

"Shouldn't you go to the hospital now?" Dwayne said in amazement. "After your heart just stopped?"

"It didn't stop for long," she said. "I don't want to miss the show."

"There is a lot of violence in this show," Dwayne warned.

"Yes, I know," the old woman said with pleasurable anticipation. "That should keep the old ticker tocking."

Dwayne felt as though he should debate the woman's decision to stay, but he felt so disoriented from getting yet another electrical shock to his system that he just turned and moved away. A contingent of the nearby audience broke into applause for his remarkable act of restarting the old woman's heart.

God the Father, God the Son, and the lightning blasts of the Holy Spirit, he muttered. Ingrid appeared from nowhere with electric tape to insulate the latest unprotected wire he'd discovered. Dwayne staggered back to his station outside the entrance to the house.

When Angela entered with Chaz and Aleister, she gave him a long look. "You're pale as a ghost," she said. "Opening-night nerves?"

"Human defibrillator," he replied. "Taking shocks, saving lives."

"Huh," she said. She looked a little tipsy from her pre-show dinner with the boys. Dwayne spotted another of the critics entering and gave him a press kit. "Well, I'm sure there's a story there," she said. "But I'll leave you to your duties."

Still feeling disoriented and experiencing cramp pains across his chest and arms, Dwayne opted to watch the show in the booth with Joan again rather than in his seat with his friends.

The show went well. The actors come out with a few surprising lines. Some of the choreography got oddly redone because the tempo of Ry's guitar solo turned maddeningly slow. But overall the show was a rousing success. The audience loved it.

Everyone in the cast had some great moments. Dwayne was simultaneously overjoyed for them and gnashing his teeth that Gregor Foxx was not there to see it, especially when the crowd gave a standing ovation at the end.

Dwayne climbed down the stairs from the booth to eavesdrop on the audience as they exited. The old woman from the Jeff Committee was one of the first out of the theatre.

"Thank you again for restarting my heart," she said. "I was told you are the director of the show."

"That's right," Dwayne admitted.

"Congratulations," she gushed. She signaled him to lean down so she could whisper in his ear. "I don't know what the others will do, but I don't mind telling you I am going to recommend the show for best ensemble, best direction, and best incidental music," she said.

"Thank you!" Dwayne said. "And next time your heart stops, you let me know."

The old lady laughed and poked him in the chest with her index finger. "You'll be the first one I call." Her husband smiled at him and said *Thanks* as the two continued out toward the elevator.

Ingrid swept in from the tables she'd set up with snacks and drinks for the opening night reception. She stuffed a glass and a bottle of sparkling wine into his hands.

"Hurrah!" she said.

39

Tuesday, February 3, 2004

"Dwayne, you'd better come in here!" Angela called. She was watching television in the living room. Dwayne was washing the dinner dishes in the kitchen. He was feeling pretty good. Saturday morning, the day after opening, he'd received the call that the show was officially Jeff-Recommended. Saturday and Sunday's shows went well, and two more critics attended. Yesterday was his first Monday night off in weeks, and the first review had appeared in an online theatre blog. It was a rave.

Now that the show was open and the madness of tech and opening was done, he was looking forward to spending some time with his wife again. "Be right there," he called back to her. He finished washing a wine glass and dried his hands as he strode to the living room. "What's up?"

Angela was curled up on one of the couches, already in her pajamas, watching the ten o'clock news. She pointed at the television, which sat on a couch across the room. It was a small, boxy TV that sat atop a bookshelf when they were not using it. Outside the dark window, the CTA train rumbled by on the elevated tracks.

Tom Skilling, the weatherman, was saying: "...which, again, will give us dangerous temperatures in the twenty-five to thirty below zero range by Thursday night. Temperatures will remain dangerously low through the weekend, rising no higher than five below zero by midday Saturday. And now sports..." Angela pointed the remote at the TV and shut it off.

"The polar vortex is coming," she said loudly as the last cars of the El train passed.

"The what?" Dwayne sat down in one of the easy chairs, rocking slightly to one side due to an oddity of its ancient springs.

"The polar vortex. Apparently there's this giant swirling cyclone of incredibly cold air that twirls around the North Pole constantly. That's where it's supposed to stay, but something meteorological is pushing it out of its spot, and the whole thing is going to come swirling down over us. We are going to have North Pole weather on Thursday. Twenty-five to thirty below zero."

"The polar what?" He tossed the towel onto one of the chairs under the windows.

"Vortex," Angela repeated. She sat up. "The polar vortex. Listen to me, Dwayne. It's like this giant spinning toupee of cold air that sits on top of the earth's head, at the North Pole. But now the toupee is slipping, and the edge of it is going to slip over us, and we're going to be freezing our asses under that frigid cold fake hair."

"That's what the weather guy said?"

"Tom Skilling. He didn't call it a toupee, but that's what it looked like on the radar thing. And then he made some joke about Janet Jackson's wardrobe malfunction from the Super Bowl. I don't get why everyone is upset with Janet Jackson when it was Justin Timberlake who opened the peek-a-boo thing to show her titty. Why aren't they mad at him?" Angela picked up her snifter of brandy off the plank-atop-two-milk-crates coffee table in front of her and leaned back into the sofa.

"Seriously? Twenty-five to thirty below? Thursday?"

"That's what he said."

"We've got a performance that night," he said. "We can't have a polar vortex."

"I don't think anyone will come to *Titus Andronicus* if it's thirty below."

"We're Jeff Recommended," Dwayne whined.

"Even still."

"We might have to cancel." He shook his head. "Bobby runs to balmy California, and we're here in the fucking polar vortex. And you know what?" he said in further outrage, "the last time I talked to him, he was having a thing with Sarah Michelle Geller!"

"Buffy the Vampire Slayer?"

"Yeah. Apparently they are shooting some film together."

"That boy…" Angela shook her head and chuckled and stopped. "Wait a minute. Isn't she married to Freddie Prinze Jr.?"

"Who knows? All I know is he gets sunshine and starlets, and I get the Arctic Toupee."

"You can't have actors come out when it's thirty below. Most of them don't even own cars. They'll get frostbite walking from the CTA."

"Maybe the toupee will stay up on top of the head where it belongs…"

"Maybe," Angela said. "But if this predication still stands tomorrow, you have to give everyone at least twenty-four hours' notice."

"Yeah," Dwayne said sadly.

◆ ◆ ◆

On the six o'clock news Wednesday, the prediction remained the same. Dwayne phoned everyone personally to cancel the Thursday night show.

On Friday the temperature rose to five below zero. A review also appeared in the Friday *Tribune*, and it was a rave, using words like *exciting*, *sexy*, and *kinetic*. The *Trib* reviewer loved the choreography and the Hendrix-like band, and they found Wallace Proctor's Titus *tragic and moving*. Coco was *a revelation* and *someone we want to see more…much more*. The show was *highly recommended*. Dwayne was beside himself with joy. Sadly, they didn't mentioned his direction, but you couldn't quibble with a rave in the *Tribune*, the biggest and most influential paper in town.

The *Sun-Times* review also appeared, but, oddly, nearly the entire review was taken up with an explanation of why it made no sense for Tamora to be played by Coco Nesbit, a black actor. The reviewer had not read the play herself, but she recounted her companion's argument that casting Tamora across the race line was a mistake. The director could not have understood the play if he thought the Queen of the Goths could be a black woman. It was astounding how many words she spent presenting this argument and how few on her experience of the show. The only lines from which Dwayne could quote were at the very end, when she said: "Despite all that, I found the production enjoyable. The combination of music and action was exciting."

"Enjoyable! Exciting!" –*Chicago Sun-Times*, Dwayne jotted down to use in his publicity.

Despite the Jeff Recommendation and the rave in the *Trib*, the actors outnumbered the audience Friday night.

Saturday, when the temperature rose to zero, was a little better.

At the Sunday matinee, with a temperature of a balmy five degrees, a full thirty-five people came to the show. All in all, expenses were much, much higher than income for the first two weekends. He wanted at least enough sales to repay his friends' investment.

Dwayne looked so crestfallen when he returned from the Sunday matinee, Angela decided he needed a surprise to perk him up.

40

Saturday, February 14, 2004

T he temperatures still hovered below zero the third week of the
run. Additional good reviews helped the audiences grow a
little, but they were still not what they might have been.

Saturday morning, Angela woke Dwayne with a cup of coffee and
a croissant in bed.

"Well, this is nice," he said, sitting up and adjusting the pillow
behind his back. He pushed his tousled hair out of his face. "You look
nice."

Angela clearly had not just woken up. Her curly black hair was
brushed, face made up in subtle shades, and she was wearing much
more attractive sleeping garb than she'd worn to bed the night before.
Dwayne noticed a single rose in a stem vase on the little table beside
the bed. He took a sip of the coffee and a bite of the croissant. It was
the delicious chocolate-filled kind that he loved.

"Wow, this is really nice. Is there some occasion?"

"Happy Valentine's Day, silly." She snuggled up next to him in
the bed and gave him a long, generous kiss. Dwayne's wife was a sexy
woman.

"Valentine's Day!" he said, a little embarrassed. "I completely
forgot it's Valentine's Day!"

"I figured. Don't sweat it. You've had a lot going on. So I wanted
to give you a surprise," she said seductively.

"Valentine's Day sex?" He liked that idea.

"Yes," she said, drawing out the word with a smile. "But another
surprise, a bigger surprise than that."

"I don't think there could be a nicer surprise," Dwayne said,
echoing her smile back to her and adjusting his pajama pants.

"Maybe not nicer, but much more surprising. I got us an eight o'clock table for dinner tonight at Crocodile."

"Tonight? Crocodile?" Dwayne said dumbly.

Eating at Crocodile had been a dream of Dwayne's. A dream he did not believe would ever come true. "How did you get a table at Crocodile?"

"I know! People make reservations for Crocodile, like, fourteen months in advance," she said happily. "But I wanted to do something really special for you. You've worked so hard, and there have been so many frustrations, and sometimes we've even fought a little. I wanted to make reservations for us for a nice dinner, and just on a whim, I called Crocodile, never thinking I could actually get a table. We've never felt like we could afford to eat there anyway. But I called and the host had just gotten off the phone with someone who cancelled. And apparently he couldn't be bothered to call anyone on his waiting list. And *voilà*! We are in!"

She looked so radiantly happy and proud, it broke Dwayne's heart.

"I can't go," he said meekly.

"What do you mean you can't go?" Her face crumbled into disbelief.

"Tonight is the night Gregor Foxx is coming to the show. I promised to meet him there. Tonight is my audition for the Public. I can't not be there."

"Are you shitting me? You are going to stand me up for Valentine's dinner at Crocodile? I had to pay in advance. I spent $250 on that dinner."

"After he sees the show, we have to talk. The show's my audition and the conversation's my interview. That's how he'll decide whether I'm in."

"Goddamn it, Dwayne!" she said. She got out of the bed and stood hands on hips in her fancy lingerie with an expression of extreme disgust. He'd never seen anyone look simultaneously so sexy and pissed off.

"They can get someone else to take our spot, right? I mean, the demand must be unbelievable for Valentine's Day."

"Sure," Angela said. "They can get someone else. But that doesn't mean I get my money back. That's the deal. It's nonrefundable. Those people who cancelled before we got the table? They don't get their money back. Our table is already being paid for twice."

"That's not right," Dwayne objected.

"It's fucking Crocodile!" Angela said. "They are booked fourteen months in advance! They have two Michelin stars. They can do whatever the fuck they want."

Dwayne set the rest of the croissant back on the plate, feeling suddenly no longer entitled to it. "I wish you had told me before you reserved..."

"I wanted to surprise you!" she shouted. "Why didn't you tell me Gregor Fucking Foxx was coming Valentine's night?"

"I told you he was coming the Saturday of the third week of the run. Which is tonight. I totally missed that it was Valentine's Day."

"This is the third week? I thought this was... Never mind! How could you forget Valentine's Day? I mean, even as a theatre producer. Don't theatres typically do a Valentine's Day promotion?"

"*Titus Andronicus* does not make for a romantic evening out..."

"Oh, Dwayne!" She got up and started changing into jeans and a flannel shirt.

"Does this mean Valentine's Day sex is out?"

"With you? Yes! Maybe I'll have Valentine's Day sex with whoever I can find to go to Crocodile with me. Because I am not throwing away two hundred fifty dollars to go smile at Gregor Fucking Foxx with you while someone else eats my Michelin-starred dinner! And maybe you should find somewhere else to sleep tonight! Like with your stupid buddy, Chaz!"

♦ ♦ ♦

By seven-forty that evening Gregor Foxx had not yet appeared. Dwayne waited at the box office, greeting the theatre goers. There were many who were happy to see him. He'd given away sixty tickets to make sure there was a good house. People loved getting free tickets to a show getting the kind of raves *Titus Andronicus* was getting, even

246 ◆ RICHARD ENGLING

if it was freezing outside.

But Dwayne was so nervous! His nerves went straight to his intestines. He'd taken two shits at home, another when he arrived at the theater, and now he could feel the tension in his guts again. He didn't want to miss greeting Gregor Foxx, but he really had to go again. If he didn't go now, he might risk shitting his pants in front of the man who could catapult his career forward.

Dwayne slid into the men's room stall on the main floor. There wasn't, frankly, a lot left. But that did not diminish his nervous peristalsis. His guts ached as he excreted watery turds the diameter of earth worms. Sweat broke out on his brow. It went on and on, the clenching in his guts. He blotted his brow with toilet paper. He was in the can for a full ten minutes, unable to relax the squeezing of his large intestine. When he finally got out, he went straight to the box office. Ingrid was standing next to it, a disgruntled expression on her face.

"How many comps did you release for tonight?" she said.

"About sixty."

She cocked her head back in disbelief. "Are we not trying to make money on this show?"

"That's not the objective tonight."

"People are coming in here claiming free tickets who are not even on this list," she said.

"I might have missed some. I told Nikki to let in anyone who said I'd promised them a ticket," Dwayne said, cocking his thumb at the box office manager.

"Anyone could walk in and say that," Ingrid said.

"How would anyone know to say that?" Dwayne's intestines still hurt, and he was feeling irritable.

"Some of them aren't even giving your name. We had one woman who said someone else put her on the list. Nikki asked me if that was all right, and I sent her packing."

"What? Who?" But before she could answer, Dwayne's phone began to ring. He looked at the face of it. The caller ID said *Gregor Foxx*. He held up a finger to Ingrid and answered the phone, stepping away from the box office to a quieter corner of the lobby.

"Hello, Mr. Foxx."

"What the hell, Dwayne?" Foxx said. "Laurie Anderson just called to tell me you turned her away at the door."

"What?" Dwayne said.

"I'm not going to be able to make it during your run, after all. Laurie is in Chicago, and I asked her to go in my stead. I trust her opinion. But you turned her away at the door."

"*The* Laurie Anderson?" Dwayne said. "*Home of the Brave*? *Strange Angels* Laurie Anderson?"

"Yes, *the* Laurie Anderson," Foxx said.

"I...I was in the men's room," Dwayne sputtered. "I love Laurie Anderson."

"Yeah, well, somebody was very rude with Laurie, and now there's nobody to see your show."

"Wait!" Dwayne said into the phone. He ran out in front of the theatre, nearly slipping on a patch of ice. "Laurie!" he screamed, great plumes of fog exploding from his mouth. "Laurie Anderson! Come back! Come back, Laurie Anderson!" He looked around, starting to shiver. People looked back at him quizzically. None of them were Laurie Anderson, the performance artist he'd loved since he was a teenager in the eighties He had some of her LPs on vinyl. He'd gone to see her in concert. He adored Laurie Anderson.

He could have been discussing *Titus Andronicus* tonight over drinks with Laurie Anderson?

Why the fuck had Ingrid turned away Laurie Anderson?

He put the phone back to his ear. "Mr. Foxx? I tried to see if I could find her on the street, but I don't see her anywhere. Could you call her? I'll hold the show as long as it takes for her to get back here. I'm so sorry that happened."

His teeth were starting to chatter. He'd run out into the subzero weather without his coat. He hurried back into the lobby.

"She's already moved on," Foxx said. "She had friends she wanted to meet tonight. I had to beg her to see your show. As annoyed as your people made her, she was happy she'll be able to meet her friends after all. I'd never to be able to get her to come back now."

"Could you give me her number to call her?" Dwayne begged.

"No," Foxx said flatly. "You aren't calling her, and I'm not calling her."

"And you won't be able to get here next week or the week after?"

"I'm afraid that's it, Dwayne."

"What if we shot a video, and I got it to you?"

There was a long pause. "Being a great director is not all about artistic expression," he said at last. "It's also about creating a responsive organization. Not the sort of organization that would turn away Laurie Anderson when she's standing in for Gregor Foxx. Sorry to say, Dwayne, I already know everything I need to know."

Dwayne felt his heart sink so quickly, he felt he might collapse to the lobby floor.

"We're getting great reviews," he said weakly.

"I hope you have a fine run," Foxx said in a dismissive voice. He hung up.

Dwayne looked at his phone in disbelief.

So that was it.

No Gregor Foxx.

No Laurie Anderson.

No Emerging Directors program at the Public Theater in New York City.

Chaz and Aleister would almost certainly lose money on the show.

Angela was having a $250 dinner with their friend Bonnie who was divorcing their friend Chaz because of this show. And Dwayne was missing his chance to eat at Crocodile and have wonderful post-Crocodile Valentine's sex with his beautiful wife.

He didn't even know where he could sleep tonight.

And for what?

No Gregor Foxx.

No Laurie Anderson.

If Ingrid hadn't been there to interfere, if he hadn't been in the men's room, Laurie Anderson would be sitting in the theatre right now. He would be sitting next to her. Laurie Anderson!

It was heartbreaking. His whole body clenched with frustration, and he sobbed in regret.

He got hold of himself enough to look at his watch. Five after eight. Joan would be holding the house for him. Angela would be tasting her first *amuse bouche*. He dragged himself up the stairs and told Joan to start the show, then went backstage, grabbed his coat, and walked over to the John Barleycorn Memorial Pub to order his first of several double whiskeys. Much later that night, he quietly crept into his apartment to sleep on one of the sofas. If she murdered him in his sleep, so be it.

41

Friday, February 27, 2004

Week four saw the return of the polar vortex. Dwayne bought flowers for Angela, but they froze on the way back from the store and wilted almost immediately. She wasn't warming up to him yet either. She'd eaten the Valentine's meal at Crocodile with Bonnie, who annoyed the hell out of her by complaining about Chaz nearly the entire time. Nor, despite the big bucks she made, did she offer to reimburse Angela for her half of the meal.

Temperatures dropped into the teens below zero, and ticket sales dropped nearly as low. No one wanted to risk frostbite to see one of Shakespeare's least popular plays, even if the reviews had been sensational. Thursday night's show was cancelled again. The rest of the weekend warmed up a little, rising almost as high as zero. Audiences remained sparse.

Meanwhile, Dwayne was cooking Angela her favorite meals every night. After several days of groveling, he finally graduated from sleeping on his choice of vintage sofa back to their marital bed. He began planning an extended bicycle trip for the two of them in the summer, something she loved to do with him. If he couldn't take her to Italy, he had to have something. He gathered maps and itineraries and books from the library. He charted a course with camping stops at Illinois Beach State, Kettle Moraine State Park in Wisconsin, and over to Lake Geneva. She was favorably impressed.

The fifth and final weekend rose into the middle twenties above zero. It felt like heat wave. They finally started to get the houses the show deserved. Audiences were enthusiastic.

Chaz and Aleister watched the Friday night show with Dwayne

and afterwards went for a drink at John Barleycorn.

"Wow," Aleister said, sitting down at a stool at the shining dark wood bar. "That was a performance! You really did it, Dwayne. And the audience was right with you the whole way. Really wonderful theatre."

"It does make a difference, having a good house," Dwayne said. "And the cast has grown in their roles throughout the run. Ry finally learned to watch the actors while he played his guitar solos to keep his tempo. Thank god."

"Yes," Chaz said slowly, looking down at his shoes. "It was a good show."

Aleister and Dwayne noted his grim face as he waved for the bartender, but they didn't comment. Chaz ordered them a round of whiskeys.

"You must be proud," Aleister said to Dwayne.

"I am proud of the show. I'm especially proud of the actors. Thank you for your help with Melinda. Not just for the show. I think you made a real difference in her life. But I'm disappointed about the Emerging Directors' Program. I wouldn't have begged the investment from the two of you." He took a deep breath. He hated to tell them, but better to get it over. "And now, I'm afraid to say, your investment is lost."

"You had a great house tonight," Aleister said. "Didn't that bring in some money?"

"Yeah. But we had two disastrous polar vortex weekends. After paying the rent for last weekend, Ingrid said most the money was gone. She thinks the good houses this weekend will allow us to pay the actors and designers and the final weekend's rent, but nothing beyond that."

It was all bad news: He'd lost his friends' money. There wouldn't be enough to pay his own stipend. And he would not be working at the Public Theater at any point in the foreseeable future.

"Well, everything's turning up roses, isn't it?" Chaz said.

"No change of heart from Bonnie?" Aleister asked.

"When your wife who works with the most cut-throat divorce attorneys in Chicago wants a divorce, you can bet you'll be getting screwed." Chaz raised his glass. "Gentlemen, I'd like to toast my epic stupidity." At that moment, Coco pushed through the doorway into the bar on the arm of Wallace Proctor, laughing long and loud. Wallace smiled, looking inordinately pleased with himself. Coco noticed the trio at the bar and stopped.

"You are *hilarious!*" she said loudly to Wallace, turning heads. She took his face in her hands and kissed him long and deeply on the mouth.

Chaz set his glass back down. "The hell? She can't be fucking that old man!" He looked at Dwayne. "Please, say it ain't so."

With this cast it seemed anything was possible. "I...I don't know," Dwayne said.

"Jesus." Chaz watched the two of them move to a large table along the wall. Coco slinked along with her arm through Wallace's, and Wallace strolled like the cock of the walk.

"Fuck," Chaz said. "Look at him. He's old enough to be her father."

"What she's doing is really not your business, is it?" Aleister said kindly but firmly.

Chaz looked away. "No. You're right. By the way, did you know she found the sword?"

"The $8,000 vintage sword she left on the El?" Dwayne said.

"Yeah," Chaz said. "She didn't leave it on the El. She just forgot to take it with her to the theatre that day. It was sitting in her closet the entire time. She finally noticed it there. And guess what else?"

"What?" Aleister said.

"She wanted the $750 reward I'd offered! Can you believe that shit?"

"I hope you didn't give her $750," Dwayne said, unable to keep from laughing.

"Of course not. I got the sword from her and gave it back to Bernie, who is still annoyed even though he got his sword back. I fucked up an excellent marriage with a beautiful woman for that crazy...actress."

"Did you ask Bonnie if she'd go to couple's counseling with you?" Aleister asked.

"She won't talk to me at all," Chaz said. "I leave messages. I've written her letters and put them under the door. I can't even get into our place. The only communication is through her lawyers." He looked at Dwayne. "I'd been looking forward to getting my investment back to help pay divorce expenses."

"I am so sorry." Dwayne gave a deep sigh.

"Greetings, Dwayne." Suddenly Wallace was standing next to him. A number of the other actors from the show were at the long table on the wall with Coco, laughing and talking and hugging. Dwayne noticed Tom and Orlando looking very chummy, foreheads almost touching, talking intimately and smiling deeply. Were those two an item now? Wallace handed him a sheet of paper with a list of titles on it. "The company members have put together a list of shows they'd be interested in doing in the future."

Dwayne looked at the list. There were about two dozen plays listed, both classics and new, and after each of the titles were listed suggested castings: Wallace as King Lear. Melinda as Nora in *A Doll's House*, Orlando as Hamlet, etc.

"Huh," Dwayne said.

"We know, traditionally, it's the job of the artistic director to select the season, but this being an ensemble company, we really think you should select from a list of our choosing. That seems fair, don't you think?"

"I hadn't really thought past this show," Dwayne said.

"Well, think it over, old man." Wallace clapped him on the shoulder. His face went suddenly sober and he lowered his voice to a near whisper. "Say, what about Gregor Foxx? What was his reaction?"

"He didn't make it again," Dwayne said sadly. "And now he's not going to."

Wallace squinted his eyes. "Did you make up that whole thing about Gregor Foxx just to help me back on the horse?"

"No." Dwayne felt his throat constrict as he remembered how close he'd come to watching the show with Laurie Anderson.

"Well, if you did, it was a good gambit. Thanks for the help!" He slapped Dwayne on the shoulder, then he turned thoughtful. "Frankly, in my experience, we never get to the Public Theater, as

254 ◆ RICHARD ENGLING

much as we want to." He breathed in a few more thoughtful aspirations, then clapped Dwayne on the shoulder once more, nodded at Chaz and Aleister, and went back to his group at the big table along the wall.

"Future seasons?" Aleister said. "How are you planning future seasons?"

"I'm not," Dwayne said. "Unless there's suddenly a way to produce theatre with no money whatsoever."

42

Sunday, March 1, 2004

T he final performance was so good, it made Dwayne's soul hurt. He and Angela sat in what might have been the worst seats in the house, but even from there it looked great.

The attention he'd given the staging made it visually stunning from every angle. The pace of the show rattled along with a brisk, tragic inevitability. The actors gave performances that made his heart swell with pride. Everything he'd tried to bring out in them was there, and so much more that they'd discovered on their own. They were brilliant. Tom's choreography was a revelation. Ry and the band's music drove and deepened the action, and the performers and musicians were totally in sync. It was everything he could have hoped for. The temperature had risen all the way to thirty-two degrees, and hibernating Chicago theatre fans climbed out of their burrows for this last chance to see *Titus Andronicus*. The house was full and responsive.

It just broke his heart. It was so perfect, at last. And now it had to close.

At the end of the performance, when the audience rose in a standing ovation, it choked a series of sobs out of him. He was happy, proud, and miserable, all at once. Angela smiled at him, then saw the tear rolling down his cheek. "Aw," she said, wiping it away with her thumb. "It really was good, Dwayne. You should be pleased."

He nodded, too overwhelmed to speak.

They went out into the upstairs lobby, and Dwayne received the well wishes of many in the crowd. Aleister and Chaz had come to the final show, as well, but they sat in some of the better seats.

"Okay, boyos," Angela said to them. "Don't think you're having a drink with Dwayne tonight. God knows how long he'll be dealing with strike." She gave him a kiss on the cheek. "I'll see you at home. Don't wake me when you come in." She put her arm through Aleister's. "And you, doctor, may buy me a martini."

"Done," Aleister agreed. "Great show, Dwayne. Certainly the most personally expensive show I've ever attended. But great performance."

"It was good," Chaz managed to say. He looked much too conflicted to choke out another word.

"Easy come, easy go," Angela said. "Let's get out of here before the *actors* come out." They all knew whom she wanted to avoid, and they headed down the stairs.

Dwayne heaved a heavy sigh as the rest of his audience flowed down and out into the slushy night. The show was finally so good. He wished he had the ability to extend the run so more people could attend. It broke his heart to see it end.

He walked back into the theatre. Ingrid was already disassembling the set. She had a stack of modular flats and set pieces leaned against the wall.

"Are we junking all this?" he asked her.

"Absolutely not!" Ingrid said. "I'm taking this to the Flat Iron Building in Wicker Park for a show I'm designing over there."

"Great. Nice to see it getting recycled." He picked up a cordless electric drill to begin removing screws.

"Right. That's how I put together the seed money to launch us as a not-for-profit." She looked suddenly excited. "Did I tell you? Our 501(C)(3) came through yesterday!"

"What's that?" Dwayne said.

"Yeah! I never thought it would get approved so quickly."

Dwayne set the drill back on the bench full of tools. "What are you talking about?"

"I knew we'd need to do some serious fundraising after this show. Your friends aren't going to pump in any more money. We needed to be a nonprofit federal 501(C)(3) corporation. That way donations are tax deductible, and we're eligible to apply for government and corporate grants." She raised her arms. "And I did it! Ta da!" She did a little spin.

"This company?" Dwayne tried hard to understand. "You got a 501(C)(3) for the Psychedelic Dream Theatre? How? The company was never incorporated."

"Of course it's incorporated!" She gave Dwayne a little shove as though he were being silly. "That was the first thing. I had to incorporate as an NFP in Illinois. Then I could apply for a federal 501(C)(3)."

"So the company is you?"

"Not just me!" she laughed.

Some of the actors started to come back from greeting their friends in the lobby to help with strike. They looked around at the set and chatted, in no hurry to get to work.

"You have to have a minimum of three board members to incorporate an NFP in Illinois. So it was you and me and Joan."

"You and me and Joan?!" Dwayne said. "How am I on the board of a nonprofit theatre company?"

"You signed the papers," Ingrid said, tossing back her short blond hair.

"I never saw any incorporation papers!"

"Well, it didn't seem like you read them, or even looked at them much, but you signed them. The 501(C)(3) application, too. You signed both."

"I never signed anything like that!"

"Well, you did. One of the actors was having some kind of meltdown when I brought them in. I didn't want to distract you. So I just set them down in front of you, and you signed them. But surely you knew. I mean, why would we have invited people to be part of an ensemble if there was only going to be one show?"

"That wasn't my idea! You started the ensemble thing."

"But then you invited everyone!" Ingrid whispered back. "Why would you do that if you weren't thinking of the future?"

"I was thinking of this show!" Dwayne whispered angrily. "The actors you didn't invite were resentful! I was keeping harmony for *this show!*"

"Well, that's why I didn't want to bother explaining all the ins and outs of NFPs. I didn't want to distract you. It's complicated stuff.

But now we've got it, and we've got an ensemble, and we've got seed money."

"How do we have seed money?" Dwayne asked in outrage. "My friends lost twelve thousand dollars. There wasn't enough money to repay them or pay me my stipend."

Ingrid gestured to the set. "Through the miracle of recycling. The for-profit incarnation of the Psychedelic Dream Theatre Company had a budget for the set, which it paid to me, and I supplied the set. But rather than purchase the lumber, paint, and everything, I scavenged as much as I could, a lot of it from the show Green failed to strike. Then I created a new checking account for the Psychedelic Dream Theatre NFP and personally donated that money to the new company. There was also a budget for hanging posters. I hung the posters myself and donated that money, as well. And I'm charging the company at the Flat Iron Building for this lumber I scavenged and putting that money in our account. I've been building cash without begging from anyone!"

Dwayne looked at her in disbelief. "So my friends lost every cent they invested, but the company lives on with their cash?"

She put her hands on her hips. "You make it sound like I'm stealing, when I'm giving money out of my own pocket! Everyone approved those budgets. They got the set they paid for. The posters were hung. I hung even more than I was paid for. If we hadn't had the polar vortexes, they would've got their investment back."

"My friends gave that money in good faith!" Dwayne said.

"They gave money to fund this show in the expectation that it would earn money. It didn't. I received money for services I provided. It was my money, and I donated it. Now the money belongs to a federal not-for-profit corporation."

"We have to give it back to them!" Dwayne insisted.

"If I pulled that money out now and gave that to them, you and I and Joan could go to jail."

"*Screaming Jesus and money-changers!*"

"You say the weirdest things, Dwayne."

"So I'm a board member of this new company?"

"You are a board member and the artistic director," she said.

"And what are you?"

"I'm the board chair, executive director, and treasurer."

"Of course! And Joan?"

"Board member and secretary."

"Anybody else? Chaz? Aleister? The cast members?"

"We three are the board and staff. Our Articles of Incorporation state that we have an ensemble, but it doesn't delineate what their duties or powers might be."

By now most of the cast was milling about the space, chattering amongst themselves, but also glancing occasionally at Ingrid with expectation.

Wallace approached them. "Not to interrupt your confab, but we have some drinking to do. So if you want help with the strike, best to get us started. Yes?" He gave them a forced, impatient smile.

"Of course!" Ingrid reached into her backpack, pulled out a stack of envelopes, and shoved them into Dwayne's hand. "You can pay everyone their stipends."

"Except me," Dwayne said.

"Except you," she agreed. "And me. In honor of our partnership, I also donated my stipend. This is going to be great!"

She scurried about organizing strike teams and giving them tasks.

Despite the disturbing revelation, it did Dwayne good to walk around handing out pay envelopes. It gave him a chance to thank everyone individually and acknowledge the work they'd done and the things they'd achieved. They'd made a wonderful production. No one could deny that. They could all be proud.

He found Joan up in the light booth, typing away on a laptop. He presented her with the pay envelope. "Thank you," he said.

"Right," she said brusquely. She gestured at her computer screen. "I find it best to write up the post-mortem ASAP."

"Post-mortem?" Dwayne said.

"On this production. If you don't learn from your mistakes, you never improve."

"Well, we have plenty to learn from," he said.

"Agreed." She returned to her keyboard.

"I have a question," Dwayne said. She turned and looked in his general direction. "I've had this sense through the rehearsal process, and even through the run, that you hate me. Is that true?"

Joan seemed to have no emotional reaction to that whatsoever. She sat for a moment, presumably mulling it over. "I do find your existence…troubling." She thought for a moment more, then seemingly satisfied with that reply, went back to her computer.

Wow.

"Could I ask why?"

She turned back to him, her eyes slightly wider. "I'd think you know why," she insisted. "Before any rehearsal process begins, I memorize the ground plan. I can sense in my body the full size of the set and the actors moving on it. This allows my blocking notes to be exact. But when a rehearsal space is not as large as the ground plan, the disparity causes me physical pain. My head hurt in every single rehearsal. It was agony when the actors approached the edge of the room and could not continue to the edge of the set design as my body understood it. That was your fault."

"You sense size in your body?" He cocked his head to one side and took a step back in the doorway of the light booth. The back of his heel hit the doorway threshold at top of the stairs. He grabbed the doorjamb to keep from tumbling backwards down the stairs. Tumbling down these stairs once was more than enough for a lifetime.

Joan looked in his direction and sighed deeply. "I have extremely acute proprioception and visual depth perception combined with a photographic memory, especially for set designs," she said impatiently. "And when that sense of designed space is thwarted, it gives me physical pain. That was your fault."

"I've never heard of anything like that," Dwayne said. He wondered if that was some special autistic ability.

"There are more things in heaven and earth than you have heard of, Horatio."

"Your brain thinks in terms of space?"

"Space and objects moving in space," she said. "See where my show case is on the floor?" She pointed at the case she brought to every rehearsal and performance. It had drawers with first aid supplies, gaff tape, and anything else a stage manager might need. "The corner of my case is five feet four inches or one point six meters from your toe."

"Really?" Dwayne said. He was tempted to measure it.

"Don't move," she said. She got two tape measures out of her case and measured the distance from his toe to the corner of the case. Five feet four inches on the imperial tape measure and one point six meters on the metric.

"That's amazing," Dwayne said. He'd seen the *X-Men* movie. He could imagine Joan among the magical mutants attending the Xavier School for Gifted Youngsters.

"When you try to rehearse a 575 square foot staging in a 448 square foot rehearsal space," she said, "it hurts my head. We will never do that again as long as I'm a board member."

"So you knew about Ingrid's plan to create a nonprofit?" Dwayne said.

"Of course," she said. "I signed the papers."

"I didn't realize."

"You signed papers without reading them?" Her voice dripped with disapproval.

Dwayne sensed himself falling even further in her estimation. "I thought she was giving me papers to open accounts for buying set materials," he said.

Her expression of disbelief and reproach only deepened.

He handed over her stipend check. "Thanks so much for all your work," he said, feeling hopelessly lame.

She grunted and snatched the envelope away from him.

He climbed down the stairs. How odd his relationship with these two women. He'd only hired Ingrid to design and build the set, but she made herself executive director and chairman of the board of the company. These women were the hurricane and he the leaf in the wind.

The teams finished deconstructing the set and loading the useful parts into a rental trailer attached to Ingrid's van. They stacked lights in the theatre seats and coiled the cables on the floor. They folded costumes and loaded them into Peaches' car. They dealt with the props and swept everything clean. Ingrid locked up the space, and Dwayne followed her out into the night. Ingrid and Joan drove off to deliver the set pieces to Ingrid's next show. He and Peaches walked down to John Barleycorn, where the actors were already accelerated by liquor into love and congratulations and hilarious reminiscing. Every awful thing that had happened was now being transformed into comical legend.

"Before we go in, Dwayne, I'd like to thank you for not calling me out on the thing with Joan and Ingrid," Peaches said. She clutched his shoulders in a highly dramatic fashion, then dropped them and turned decisively to continue toward the bar.

"The what?"

"You know, because of Coco and all." She looked somehow both embarrassed and pleased with herself. She had an unusual, peppy bounce to her step.

"I don't know what you mean," Dwayne said. They hesitated in front of the pub doors.

"You don't?" Peaches seemed absolutely delighted.

"No."

"Really?" She smiled super brightly.

"No. I really don't have the slightest idea what you're talking about," Dwayne said.

"Okay!" Peaches giggled, pulled open the pub doors and plunged inside without another word.

There were so many things Dwayne did not understand—and apparently never would. But watching Peaches bound into the presence of the actors and begin hugging them wildly, he suspected Peaches was moving into one of the manic phases she had told him about. Would she go man-crazy?

Dwayne's entrance brought a loud cheer from the actors, which was gratifying. But then, as he circulated among them, almost every actor he talked with wanted to know what he was planning for the coming season. They assumed he'd pick something from the list Wallace had given him. Would company members have to audition, or would he simply assign them roles? Some of them started campaigning immediately for the roles they wanted to play. A few even had fundraising ideas.

He didn't know how to respond to any of this. He'd been certain that the Psychedelic Dream Theatre would vanish with *Titus*

Andronicus, but now it lived on as a Federal nonprofit. And he was on the board! It made him profoundly uncomfortable.

He looked around the room. Wallace and Peaches were canoodling in a corner. Well, someone would be getting laid, no doubt. Not that it was any of his business. And why not? Wallace was still a handsome man. His face was weathered, but not wrinkled with age. Still. They seemed like an odd couple. And once Peaches was past her manic phase, if that's what was happening, Wallace would be left behind.

Enjoy it while it lasts, old man.

When Coco had been hanging on Wallace's arm, was that just calculated to annoy Chaz? Or had they been an item and Peaches had somehow stolen Wallace away from Coco? Is that what Peaches had been talking about on the way in? But no. That wouldn't have involved Joan and Ingrid. Would it?

Who knew?

He looked around. Coco was laughing with her hands on Ry's and Melinda's shoulders like they were all the dearest of friends.

The cast in general was having an uproarious time. They deserved it.

Tom left Orlando's side and came to give Dwayne a huge hug. Tom's hugs always felt a little strange. Because of his height, one's face was pressed into his breastbone.

"Look, Dwayne, I know you must feel sad about the Public Theater," Tom said. "How could you not? But here's something: I've made my ruling on the $2,000. According to the wager, Foxx had to see the show and not like it for the money to go to Brad. Since he never saw the show, the money goes back to you. And if Brad doesn't like it, he can go fuck himself."

"Thank you, Tom." He felt sincerely grateful and gave his tall friend another hug, then looked him in the eye. "Your choreography was half the show. You've been a wonderful creative partner."

Tom reared back, and his face twisted up. "Oh, now, stop, Dwayne. You're going to make me cry." He gave Dwayne a huge kiss on the cheek. "Thanks so much. I really loved it." He scurried off to rejoin Orlando and the other actors.

Thank Jesus (and Tom) he'd still be able to surprise his wife with a trip to Italy. That would beat the hell out of the biking trip he'd planned to Wisconsin. Maybe they could rent bicycles and tour the Sicilian villages of her ancestors.

This had not been a total disaster. His people had put on a kick-ass show. They were drinking, happy, hugging one another. Some of them had formed friendships that might last the rest of their lives. But he felt suddenly on the outside of it all. There was always an intimacy among cast members that did not extend to the director. He was management. They were equals. Should he slip out of the pub and let them party on?

What would Bobby do?

Dwayne stuffed his hands into his pockets and felt some paper crumple beneath the fingertips of his right hand. He pulled out a twenty and a five and a nickel and a quarter. He stepped up to the bar.

Here's what Bobby would do:

"Hey, Barry," he said as the bartender approached. "What are the chances I could buy a round of shots for my cast and crew with twenty dollars?"

"That's all you got?" Barry asked.

"Plus five dollars and thirty cents for a tip," Dwayne said. He laid it on the bar. Barry looked at it.

"How big's your group?"

"I've got twenty-six."

"This is closing night?"

"Yeah."

"I'll give you twenty-six shots of rail whiskey or rail tequila," Barry said.

"Whiskey. You're a saint, Barry. I will pray to St. Amand for you."

"Who's that?" He set up shot glasses on a large tray.

"Patron saint of bartenders."

Barry laughed. "You just happen to know the patron saint of bartenders?"

"I know the patron saint of pretty much everything. We spent the whole of fourth grade on the lives of the saints. Plus some arithmetic and diagramming sentences. For some reason, all those saints stuck with me."

"Okay," Barry said. "Who's the patron saint of prostitutes?"

"St. Vitalis of Gaza. Prostitutes and day laborers."

Barry began sloshing whiskey into the twenty-six shot glasses. "St. Vitalis! Ha! Patron saint of barbers, too. Am I right?"

"Nope. That's St. Martin de Porres." Dwayne nodded his thanks and carried the tray over to the tables the company had pushed together. "A round of shots on me—and Barry," he said, gesturing back toward him. "Don't forget to tip your bartender!"

Hurrah! they all shouted and waved to Barry. Barry smiled and waved back.

Dwayne raised his shot glass as the others picked theirs up from the tray. "It's been an honor to lead you all," he said, his voice raised so they all could hear. Some of them had arms around each other. Melinda was sitting on Ry's lap, looking happy. Peaches was leaning into Wallace and sneaking a finger between the buttons of his shirt. He was leaning against the wall, looking very pleased with himself.

"We had a dream of a production that we realized beyond my wildest dreams. You brought forth performances and created the spectacle and the sound in a way that made the whole much vaster than the sum of its parts. Some of you had to surmount serious difficulties. But you all pushed through, and I am proud and grateful. I only wish the fucking polar vortex had stayed at the fucking North Pole, because you deserved to be seen by the multitudes. Nevertheless, you did yourselves proud!" Dwayne raised his glass above his head. "*Titus Andronicus!*" he shouted.

"*Titus Andronicus!*" they all shouted, and drank back their shots.

That's what Bobby would do, Dwayne thought.

They all cheered and many of them hugged Dwayne, and said thanks, and remembered moments with him. Wallace noticed Dwayne's hands were empty and brought him a pint of Guinness. And later someone else bought him one, and later yet someone else. And someone bought another round of whiskeys. And then Dwayne was looking at his watch and feeling the compression of alcohol on his skull. It was one forty-five. That was enough, he decided. Not only

266 ◆ Richard Engling

was he drunk, the booze was starting to make him feel sad again. He slipped out of the bar. He wasn't many steps down the sidewalk when Melinda caught up with him.

"You are *ghosting* on us?" she said, holding on to his arm.

"What's that?"

"Disappearing without a word? Like a ghost?"

He smiled sadly, and pulled his collar up around his neck. It was cold. "I guess I am."

"It's always sad to end a show," she said. "We'll all be mourning tomorrow. Can I convince you to come back and celebrate a little more? Buy you a drink?"

He looked down at the sidewalk and felt the stir of mixed feelings and the beginnings of vertigo. "No, I don't think so. But thanks."

"Before you go, I want to thank you personally." She put her hands on his shoulders. "You saw I was struggling, and you were so nice. I've never had a director treat me so kindly. Bringing in Aleister to help me. That was so huge and generous. Not just for me as an actor, but for me as a person." Her voice began to shake a little with emotion. Dwayne started to feel choked up, too. "I was carrying a huge weight. It was getting in the way of my life. You two helped me see how to start getting around it."

She hugged him tightly. "Thank you." She gave him a big kiss on the cheek. "Don't be sad! Wallace told me you missed out on something big. Whatever that was, I'm sorry. But for me, this could not have been better." She smiled at him and her eyes glistened. She was so pretty, and so grateful. It touched him deeply.

Dwayne smiled. "I'm really proud of you," he said. "You showed a lot of heart."

She hugged him again and ran back inside the bar, shivering.

He stood in the cold for a moment on the sidewalk. He was tempted to go back in and let her buy him that drink. But what more was there to say? She had given him the best moment of the night. Let that be the topper.

He turned and headed to the CTA.

◆ ◆ ◆

Angela was coming out of the bathroom in her pajamas when he came in the door.

"I wasn't expecting to find you awake this late." He hung his coat on the hat tree by the door.

She stepped into the living room and sat on the arm of one of the sofas. "We were out longer than I expected," she said. "We stopped at Cunneen's for a drink. Chaz was super quiet, and then suddenly he had *everything* to say. He relived his entire marriage. It wasn't one of those nights where you could politely excuse yourself."

"I guess not," Dwayne said. He flopped onto the sofa across from her.

"I feel bad for him," she said. "I didn't before. Letting himself be led around by the dick. But he's so sad. He's remembering everything he loves about Bonnie. He must have spent twenty minutes just on the quality of her hair."

"She does have amazing hair," Dwayne agreed.

"But he'll never get her back."

"You never know."

"Yeah? You didn't share a meal with her on Valentine's Day. She is done. And how about you? You have fun with the actors?"

"It was nice. It's always sad when it's over. And it looks like I'll never work at the Public." He sank deeper into the couch cushions.

"Truth be told, Dwayne, I wasn't all that excited about you directing in New York while I'm at home alone." She moved over to his couch and snuggled up to him as a train went by on the El tracks outside their window.

"I hate missing the opportunity, and the money," he said. "I hate not being able to pay off our debts."

"You directed a kick-ass show. Shakespeare or not, that was a dumb-ass script, and you made it amazing."

"And now Chaz and Aleister are going to find out that some of their money was shuffled into another account right under my nose. I don't know how they're going to feel about that."

"How's that?"

"Ingrid built the set with salvaged lumber, and kept the money budgeted for buying wood. She put that money in an account and incorporated Psychedelic Dream Theatre as a new not-for-profit company. And I'm listed on the Board and as the artistic director."

Angela sat up straighter. "How could she do that without your consent?"

Dwayne looked embarrassed. "She would bring me papers to sign? Contracts for the performance space and rehearsal space, and then for opening accounts to buy materials and paint, stuff like that. She slipped incorporation papers in without telling me what they were."

"And you couldn't be bothered to look?"

"Sometimes she'd slip in when there was chaos in the room…"

"*Jesus Christ and the sleepwalking nincompoops!*"

"Well…that's a bit harsh, isn't it?" Dwayne said.

Angela groaned. She shook her head. She looked at her husband for a long moment. "And now what?"

"I honestly don't know. I guess I'll have to figure out how to get my name off the incorporation papers."

"Well, that's just great." Angela sat thinking it over for a moment. Then she started to laugh. "But you got to hand it to her. She gets things done. Living in a van through the worst Chicago winter on record to keep her expenses low? That woman has balls!" She laughed some more. "Bathing in that scummy backstage? I couldn't believe when you showed me that shower stall! She's hilarious."

"She's a loose cannon," Dwayne said.

"Give her credit, Dwayne. She waits for nobody's permission. She incorporated a company and put money in its checking account from cash she saved by scrounging materials. She just might be the engine you need to move you where you want to go."

"Are you serious? She nearly made me lose my mind."

"Well, you had expectations. Maybe if you went in knowing she was going to do her thing and you were going to do your thing, you'd be happier."

"Really?"

"You always wanted to work in an ensemble. Now you have

one."

"But these people are all nuts."

"Are they really any crazier than the other people you've worked with? I always liked Bobby and Tom. But they're both bonkers."

"So you think I should give this company a try?"

"It's not like you're going to the Public Theater any time soon."

"Ouch."

"I didn't intend that in a mean way." She wrapped her arms around him. "You know what, Dwayne? Let's go to bed. Let's clear our minds with some nice friendly sex and get some sleep. Tomorrow is another day."

The End

About the Author

Richard Engling is an actor, director, playwright, novelist and musician. His books have been published by Penguin/Putnam, Headline House UK, and Polarity Ensemble Books. He played drums with the jazz quartet Midnight Blue for several years. He was co-founder and Artistic Director of Polarity Ensemble Theatre.

His books include *Body Mortgage, Visions of Anna,* and *Antigone and Macbeth: Adaptations for a War-Torn Time.* His plays include *Ghost Watch* and *Anna in the Afterlife.*

Richard holds a Masters of Arts in Creative Writing from Indiana University and majored in Theatre as an undergraduate at Northern Illinois University. He lives in Evanston, Illinois, with his wife Gail.

Find more information about Richard's events and upcoming work at www.richardengling.com.

Now that you have read *Give My Regards to Nowhere* , please leave a review at your online retailer and/or your favorite social media. We depend on you to spread the word!

VISIONS OF ANNA

by Richard Engling

"PASSIONATE, POIGNANT" —Elizabeth Cunningham

"Matthew Harken's urgent questions about his friend Anna's suicide and his own critical illness compel him to risk a perilous, spiritual quest. His heartrending, heart-opening journey through the interwoven worlds of memory, dream, and shamanic magic lead him not only to visions of Anna but to visions of grace. A passionate, poignant novel."
—Elizabeth Cunningham, author of *The Maeve Chronicles*.

"...a strong authorial voice, motivated characters, and a plot that propels the book... The novel's most transcendent moments occur in Matthew's flashbacks to the time he spent in Paris with Anna. Both young emerging writers subsisting on meager meals in less than modest living situations, Matthew and Anna immerse themselves in the Parisian literary scene. In recalling these memories, Matthew squires readers through a vision of The City of Light so charmed and romantic even he questions whether it truly was as magical as he believed it to be. Engling displays an enviable gift for dialogue and a painter's eye for clear detail."
—Jarrett Neal, *New City* (Chicago)

BODY MORTGAGE

by Richard Engling

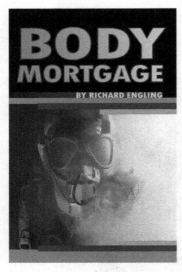

"Fast paced future thriller."
—SCIENCE FICTION AND
FANTASY REVIEWS

"This is a neat SF detective story in
the Mike Hammer / Philip Marlowe
/ Bladerunner mold...an engaging
and well-constructed thriller, very
enjoyable."
— BRUMM GROUP NEWS

A gritty thriller in a nightmare
America where human parts are
worth more than the whole.

The big market in Chicago used to be livestock. But now it's human
body parts. People can mortgage their own bodies to organ transplant
companies, but it's a gristly end when they can't pay up.

Gregory Blake is a private investigator in this savage city. His first
mistake is to take on a client whose body is marked for foreclosure.
His second is to try to find out why the most powerful forces in town
are in such a hurry to repossess. Blake thinks he knows all there is to
know about the underworld. But never did he expect to be lost in the
corporate corridors of perverse power—in the hell that future America
has become...

Originally published by Penguin Books USA and Headline UK.

Available wherever books are sold.
www.polarityensemblebooks.com

9 780977 661077